Katie,

Thank you for being the perfect model for our "Coming Back From COVID" video.

Ten Years Later

Enjoy the read!

LISA MARIE LATINO

www.lisamarielatino.com

10 9 8 7 6 5 4 3 2 1

ISBN: 099735240X
ISBN: 09780997352405
Library of Congress Control Number: 2016909786
Long Shot Publishing, Fairfield, New Jersey

Book design by Damonza

PROLOGUE

The clicking of her black high heels echoed throughout the quiet hallway as they expertly navigated toward her final destination. She opened the office door, and entered the cheery waiting room, lit up by the beaming sun outside.

She gave her name to the student receptionist, an awkward-looking teenage girl with big glasses and bad acne. She nervously sat in one of the stiff chairs in the waiting room. She was fidgety, folding and unfolding her hands as she looked around the room, marveling at how nothing had changed. She felt the girl's eyes staring at her but pretended not to notice. As the seconds went on, the clock on the wall ticked louder, and she started scratching her right arm with panic.

"Carla?" the receptionist asked politely.

She snapped out of her daydream. "Y-yes?" she stammered, promptly stopping her scratching.

"Mrs. Wright will see you now," she responded. "It's the-"

"First door on the right, I know," she said, rising from her chair.

She took a deep breath, collected her purse, smoothed out her black pencil skirt and started walking down the hall.

"Good luck!" the teenager called out to her merrily.

Carla nodded over her shoulder and slowed her pace as she approached the office door. She knocked.

"Come in!" a sweet voice called out.

Carla slowly turned the knob and was greeted by a familiar smiling face.

"Carla, how ARE you?!" the blonde woman exclaimed, extending her arms. "It is so good to see you. It feels like yesterday!"

"Hi, Mrs. Wright," Carla replied, taken aback by the older woman's enthusiasm, and warily threw one arm around her.

Mrs. Wright broke the embrace, took a step back, and gave her a look-over. "You were always one of my favorite students, and you are still as beautiful as ever. Turn around, let me see your backside."

Confused, Carla let out a tense laugh and did a quick rotation. "Ta-da," she sang weakly, facing the palms of her hands up and raising her arms, mock presenting herself.

Mrs. Wright's bright smile was replaced by a look of sheer disappointment, and it made Carla promptly put her arms back down.

"Huh," Mrs. Wright huffed, folding her arms. "Have a seat."

"Oh, okay," Carla said uncomfortably, quickly sitting down in one of the black leather chairs.

Mrs. Wright walked to the file cabinet, pulled out of a folder, and settled down in her oversized desk chair. "So Carla," she began, leaning in front of Carla's face. "Let's see how far you've come since senior year, shall we?

Carla nodded nervously.

Mrs. Wright opened the file folder and started reading. "Your last name is still D'Agostino, so I take it you never married or you did but got divorced."

"Nope, never married," she said, shaking her head.

"That's a shame," she said sympathetically, marking an "X" in her file. "Many of your former classmates have been married for years, or on their way to becoming so. Do you at least have a boyfriend?

"No boyfriend," Carla answered quietly.

Mrs. Wright furrowed her brow, making another mark on her sheet. She then had a thought, looked up and smiled. "Are you at least in a casual relationship?" She winked, her ice blue eyes twinkling devilishly.

"I haven't been with a guy in over two years," Carla deadpanned.

"Are you serious?!" Mrs. Wright exclaimed, clearly startled. "Honey, you are in the prime of your life, you should be getting laid all the time!"

"Not me," Carla said through gritted teeth.

"Well, do you have kids? Sometimes the sex goes away after you have a child."

"Clearly no kids," Carla retorted. "Unless by Immaculate Conception."

Mrs. Wright hurriedly turned the page in her file folder. "Okay, let's get off the topic of relationships. Let's talk about career. You wanted to be a sportscaster. Are you doing that now?"

"Not exactly," Carla said, "although I do work full time for the country's top sports radio station, W-S-P-S. I'm a show producer."

"Lovely!" Mrs. Wright exclaimed. "What does a show producer do?"

"I get stats, player injury updates, take listener calls, or get coffee if the host needs it, that sort of thing."

She scrunched her nose. "You get coffee?"

"Well, no," Carla continued. "It's actually more like tea or water. That's better for keeping your vocal chords hydrated."

Mrs. Wright's eyes widened. "You did graduate college, right?"

"Of course, I did! I graduated cum laude from New Jersey University in four years, just like my mother wanted," Carla said proudly.

"And you're getting coff—excuse me, TEA—for a living?"

"It's only one of my many responsibilities," she said defensively.

"Uh huh. So in the midst of running around getting beverages, you don't fraternize with your fellow co-workers or even guest athletes?"

"I do," Carla said slowly. "I have a lot of friends all over sports."

"And you still aren't getting laid?"

"I thought we were off that subject," Carla said sweetly.

Mrs. Wright frowned.

"However," Carla quickly said, "I am the producer for the stations top-rated show. The next natural step is for me to get my own sports talk show, just as I always wanted!"

Mrs. Wright perked up. "That's great! I'm sure you'll be on air before you know it, given you have no, um, PERSONAL distractions," she said pointedly, raising an eyebrow. "Having a job like that will make the rent easier to pay, and it will probably score you a lot of dates."

"Rent?" Carla asked innocently.

"Yes, like on an apartment," Mrs. Wright explained as if she were speaking to a child. "Unless... Do you own a home? Do you have a mortgage?"

"I have neither," Carla answered slowly. "I still live with my parents."

"YOU DO?! At your age?!" Mrs. Wright shrieked in horror.

Carla shrugged. "Radio doesn't pay all that well."

Mrs. Wright shook her head furiously. "Maybe it's time you think about a career change."

Carla frowned. "Mrs. Wright, you seem very upset with most of my answers."

Mrs. Wright took a deep breath to compose herself. "No, I'm not, it's just that..." she trailed off.

"It's just what?"

"You were such a vibrant student. I expected much more out of you at this point in your life. Your peers are light years ahead of you, and frankly, I'm concerned."

Mrs. Wright's words hung in the air as the two sat in silence.

"…And your ass has gotten even bigger, to boot," Mrs. Wright whispered.

Carla stood up, blinking back tears.

"Well…I've traveled to Europe! I may not be getting laid now, but I have had sex since I graduated; I wasn't doing THAT ten years ago! I may not have the most glamorous job, but I have my foot in the door! And I may not be married or have kids or whatever like everybody else but hey, my time will come! Isn't that something to hang my hat on?"

"NO!" Mrs. Wright exclaimed, slamming her hands on the desk and jumping up inches away from Carla. "You need to grow up. You aren't a little girl anymore. Yet you are still the same person you were ten years ago… twenty years ago…SINCE BIRTH! How are you going to change this course? You are going nowhere in life, fast!"

Carla gulped.

"Get out of my office! And don't you come back until you've made something of yourself!"

"But…but…" Carla stammered.

"OUT!" Mrs. Wright demanded, pushing Carla towards the door, and giving her a final heave-ho into the hallway. Carla turned back towards the door, just in time to see Mrs. Wright give one last scowl before slamming it shut.

"She's right, you know," a familiar voice creepily whispered. Carla spun towards the voice and noticed a group of zombies, led by Carla's mother, slowly closing in on her…

"AHHHHHHHHHHHHHHHHHHHHHHHHHHHHH-HHH!" I screamed, shooting up from bed. I panted as I looked around the dark room, touching my sweat-soaked face, chest, and arms.

"It was a dream, it was only a dream," I breathed, feeling relief washing over my body. I reached over to my left and turned on the lamp sitting on the white ceramic nightstand. The soft glow lit up the pink walls of my bedroom. I climbed out of bed and stood in front of the mirror, studying my face.

"More like a nightmare," I muttered to my reflection. I turned back to the nightstand and fixed my gaze on a brown piece of paper staring menacingly back at me. I swiftly grabbed it and plopped back down on my bed.

This will be the source of many nightmares to come, I thought as I read the gold foil script writing for the umpteenth time since it came in the mail earlier:

Save the Date!
June 24, 2017
Honey Creek High School
Class of 2007's
Ten Year Reunion!
(More Details to Follow)

I flung the pre-invitation across the room like a Frisbee. I fluffed my pillow in aggravation, turned the light off, and tried to go to sleep. Key word: tried. But as in many aspects of my life, I was unsuccessful.

What else is new?

1

My days off are precious to me, so it's really unfortunate that my unstable psyche got in the way of much-needed shut-eye. The birds chirping outside my window signaled that I should just give up and get ready for brunch with my friends at eleven.

I turned on the hot shower and tried to relax in its warmth, but instead, when I closed my eyes all I could do was play back my dream. It was too (unfortunately) on-the-money for it not to be real. (Except for the zombies; what was that about?)

After my shower, I wrapped myself in my favorite white terry cloth bathrobe and plopped down in front of my computer to write. One of the promises I made to myself after high school (and actually kept) was to keep a journal of my misadventures so I could look back years later and laugh at what a fool I was (and turn it into an Emmy Award-winning television soap opera series one day). Lately, though, my writing has been anything but award-winning. Since the end of my last relationship (*two years ago!*) with someone I thought was The One, my journal has been reduced to quarter-life crisis rants that only seem to worsen my mental condition and self-esteem.

Quick synopsis: The One was a guy I met the summer I graduated college, at a bar. (I should have known then; you NEVER meet The One at a bar!) We went on to have a solid, three-year relationship. About three months before Armageddon broke loose, he had locked himself up in his room to study for his Series 7 exam. Being the supportive, caring, understanding, saint-like person that I am, I gave him his space (well that, and because the faster he made money, the faster we'd get married, I reasoned. I had a deadline to be married by the time I was 25, and the clock was ticking!) So you could only imagine my despair when one day, I logged onto *Facebook* and noticed that The One's profile contained some very puzzling information. Seeing he was online, I instant messaged him:

> *Carla D'Agostino: Hey!! Gotta couple questions for ya....Care to explain why "Mark Falcone has listed his current city as Encino, California???? Surely that little detail didn't come up in our phone conversation last week.*
>
> *Mark Falcone: Uh yeah...Carla, I have something to tell you...*

Turns out, he met a girl on an online dating service, LoveAtFirstSite.com, fell head-over-heels in love with her via Skype, and moved out there. He didn't have the decency to break up with me in person, or on the phone, or even in a well-thought-out text, while still living in the Eastern Time Zone. I had to stumble upon our relationship's demise on my own, on a public social networking site. What a guy.

After our breakup, he fell off the face of the earth. He immediately deleted his Facebook profile and changed his phone number and e-mail address. His family and friends shunned me, and I have no clue of his whereabouts. (Not that I investigated; my best friends Andrea & Katie did. My Italian pride would not allow me to be that pathetic girl who tracks the guy down and begs him to come back, at least in this case anyway.)

You would think after being dealt a blow like that, the gods would look down on me, have mercy on my soul, and shower me with all the best that life has to offer (and in the same breath, rock the earth so hard that California finally did fall into the ocean).

You would think...

Two years later, I'm still stuck. Hell, 27 years later, I'm still stuck. I live in the same house I was born in, hang out with the same friends I've had since diapers, and deal with the same old heartbreak.

I typed out the play-by-play of my dream, and followed it up with everything I would have said to Mrs. Wright, had she not kicked me out of her office:

> *I didn't have these dreams for myself, Mrs. Wright. Don't think for a second that this is what I wanted out of life. I know I am capable of doing so much more than*

> *I am. I have no idea why I haven't moved to the next level. What do I DO to change this dead-end path, once and for all?*

The only answer I had was a mimosa, STAT! How many more hours?

■ ■ ■

"UGHHHH!" I moaned while lying back in bed. (No, I didn't meet a guy at brunch, so get your mind out of the gutter.) The zipper of my size 6 Capri jeans wouldn't go up over my ever-expanding pouch, so I lay in bed and sucked my stomach into my spine, hoping that would do the trick. "Come on, let's go; let's go," I pleaded softly to the zipper. This was the *last* thing I needed after being attacked by my subconscious. Ever so slightly, the zipper inched up, and in one big burst of strength, I pushed it all the way up.

"YES!" I exclaimed in a Marv Albert-type celebration, pumping my fist in the air. I hadn't been able to get those jeans on all spring! However, as I jumped in front of the mirror, my enthusiasm was immediately replaced by horror—the tightness of the jeans forced the fat around my waist to pour out. To quote the great Stewie Griffin from *Family Guy*: "Putting a pretty shirt over your muffin top does NOT make you a cupcake."

"Shitttttt," I whined, immediately unzipping the denim. I had to lie back down on the bed *again* to get the jeans down my body, and once they were finally off, I flung them across the room, landing on top of the wretched save-the-date.

I don't get it, I thought as I feverishly went through my closets for the 30th time that morning. I'd always been curvy, but when I hit 27, my hips just ballooned out. I didn't change my diet habits (I alternated between eating clean on the weekdays and completely pigging out on the weekends) or my workout schedule (because I didn't have one), so why did my body morph from "dangerous curves ahead" to pleasantly plump? Weren't these changes supposed to happen at menopause, or at least after childbirth?

"Your body knows you are never going to have kids so it's giving up from now!"

Mrs. Wright's Satanic voice boomed in my head.

I sighed as I pulled out the flowy white sundress that I've probably worn 50 times since the weather started getting nice because it's one of my few items that still fit. I paired my outfit with some cute beige wedges and silver hoop earrings. I hairsprayed my dark brown wavy mane while giving myself one last look-over, and headed out of the safe comforts of my bedroom and into the lion's den.

It was pretty much a guarantee that whenever I came in contact with my mother, it always ended up in a fight. For living in the same house, we didn't come face-to-face all that often, since our schedules were totally different. But when we *were* home at the same time during waking hours, I tried to avoid her at all cost, especially on self-pity days, but what was I supposed to do when I couldn't, parachute out of my second story window and make a run for it?

Luckily, I saw that she was on the phone while wiping down the kitchen counter. I threw a wave as I walked swiftly past her.

"I'll call you back. Carla just got downstairs," my mom said hurriedly.

I picked up my pace. "Mom, I'm leaving, there's no need-" But it was too late, the phone was already back in its cradle. Checkmate.

"Sit down, I need to talk to you," my mom said excitedly.

"Mom," I whined. "I don't have time. I'm supposed to be meeting everyone in twenty minutes!"

"SIT!" she ordered, motioning towards the espresso-colored countertop bar stools.

I rolled my eyes and sighed. No use in fighting. "You have five minutes," I said, glancing at my cell phone, "starting now."

"Guess where Jimmy and Daddy are?"

I shrugged my shoulders. "I don't know. I'm not psychic."

My mother ignored my sarcasm with a bright smile. "Diamond shopping!" she squealed.

I was confused. "Why would Dad bring Jimmy to go buy you a diamond? Like Jimmy cares."

She shook her head. "It's not for me; it's for Gwen. Jimmy went to Gwen's parents' house last night and asked for their permission to propose! Jimmy's proposing! My son is getting married!"

My face froze in horror as Mom lunged forward and wrapped me in a big hug, rocking me back and forth. "My son is getting married! My son is getting MARRIED!"

I didn't hug back. If I moved an inch, my nausea would have bubbled up to the surface and across the sparkly clean, rustic kitchen tile. *My baby brother was getting engaged... BEFORE ME!* I fake-politely broke my mother's embrace. "Don't say he's getting married; you may jinx it," I half-joked. "She has to say 'yes' first."

"Carla!" My mother exclaimed in horror. I was bracing for her to yell at me, but she swung her arms around me again. "The answer won't be *no*! The answer will be yes! YES YES YES!"

Of *course,* she wasn't going to say no. Why should Jimmy D'Agostino, Jr. have to face *any* adversity in his charmed life? Unlike mine, my brother's course had been charted out at birth. It was common knowledge around these parts that when Jimmy graduated high school, half of D'Agostino Construction would be his. If I had known I'd be heir to a successful business, I would have only spent my time working out, partying and chasing the opposite sex too, instead of worrying about petty things such as grades *and where* I fit into life's master plan. Everything always came easily for Jimmy; work (see above); sports (he was an all-state football, track and baseball player); looks (he was classically handsome); and love (he met his future bride, southern belle Gwendolyn Carrington, his freshman year of high school after she moved up here with her family from Texas, and has been an amazingly doting boyfriend to her ever since). Granted, he's not always the sharpest tool in the shed, but he basically has me beat in every category, including getting engaged at age 24, my expired engagement benchmark.

Meanwhile, since I was the oldest (and a girl) my parents were much harder on me, and I bore the brunt of their old-school Italian mentality. I had a midnight curfew until I was 20; anything below a B was unacceptable, and I wasn't allowed to move out before marriage (among other things they didn't want me doing before marriage). They were New Age in the sense that they pushed me to establish a career, but the fact that my chosen profession was sports broadcasting was baffling to James and Nancy D'Agostino…

"You want to work in sports?!" Mom shrieked as she started crying and babbling nonsense to herself.

"Yea, I do!" I said defiantly.

"A sportscaster?! No girls do that! Do something practical with your life. Become a nurse or a teacher!" Dad barked.

"Hey, it's your fault, you introduced me to sports!" I shot back.

"Why do you want to work in sports?" My mother continued. "Are you a lesbian? Only butch girls like sports as much as you do."

"MOM!" I screamed in horror, partly due to her close-mindedness, and partly due to my prudish mother saying the word lesbian. "What is this, 1920? Women can do whatever they want!"

"No, they can't!" My dad argued.

"YES, THEY CAN!" I yelled.

"So you ARE a lesbian?"

"NO!" I shrieked.

"I don't believe this," my father sighed.

"I thought this sports thing was a phase," my mother added dramatically.

Long story short, I went off to college (as a commuter, I wasn't allowed to live in a dorm) and compromised with them, double majoring in broadcasting and business. If an on-air career didn't work out, I could at least fall back on working at D'Agostino Construction (which was as appetizing as a trip to the gynecologist). Luckily, I proved them wrong and landed a job at WSPS Sports Radio 950 AM right after graduation...but as a producer, light-years from where I wanted to be.

But more on that later. Let's get back to the latest blow to my ego. My mother, in her blacked-out excitement, finally started to regain consciousness and picked up on my quietness. "What's wrong?" she asked wearily, pulling away from me. "You don't seem happy. I thought you liked Gwen."

"No, what do you mean? I LOVE Gwen!" I exclaimed. That was no lie, I loved her like the little sister I never had (her perfect size two, however...)

"So what is it?" My mom pressed.

I sighed. I could take this a few ways. I could tell her about my dream; I could admit my extreme jealousy over the engagement. I could tell her about the jeans debacle. I could tell her about the save-the-date OR I could just do what I normally did and plead the fifth.

"Nothing, it's just...*shocking*, that's all. I can't believe my little brother is out buying a diamond and proposing. Wow!" I said, half-heartedly.

My mom narrowed her eyes at me. "That's not it," she pressed.

I swiftly got up from my chair. "You never believe me when I talk. Why?" I snapped.

"I'm a mother, and I know these things. I can tell when my kids are lying and when they tell the truth!" she snapped back, meeting me at eye level.

I had to give her something to shut her up. Otherwise, I could see this fight escalating and cutting into my brunch (and subsequent bitch session). Besides, I *was* genuinely happy for Jimmy and Gwen and didn't want to spoil the mood for everyone.

"It's really nothing....I got the save-the-date for my ten-year high school reunion yesterday, and it had me a little bummed out. But I'm fine now," I lied.

"I told you something was bothering you," she boasted.

I pursed my lips. "Congratulations, you got me *yet again*."

"What about the event has you bothered?"

This woman is always on a mission! "Nothing really, it's just that ten years have flown by in a flash!" I exclaimed, faking nostalgia. "It's crazy that we are all adults now! I was reminiscing about the good old days, when we were little kids running around the neighborhood, and got a little sad that those memories are from so long ago." I crossed my arms and gave my mother a wistful look, hoping my little act did the trick.

"Uh huh," she said, eying me up and down accusingly. "Some people are a little more adult than others."

"Anyway," I continued, ignoring her. "When is Jimmy planning on proposing?"

"Oh, it's the cutest idea!" she beamed, snapping back into her euphoric state. "He's going to set up a romantic picnic on the 50-yard-line of the high school football field, and he's going to pop the question then. It's where they first met-"

"-during the football pep rally, when he was the star junior varsity quarterback, and she was the captain of the junior varsity cheerleading squad, I know," I finished dryly, my heart sinking to my feet.

"Isn't it such an adorable idea?" Mom cooed.

"It is. It's perfect," I swallowed. "But let me go, I don't want to be late."

"Where are you going again?"

"Brunch with the Jade Meadow Drive crew."

"Where?"

"On the moon, Mom," I laughed. "We've been doing brunch one Sunday a month for the past three years at the same spot. Nothing's changed." (Including her need to know my coordinates at all times.)

"Okay, have fun. Tell everyone I said hello. Don't drink and stay away from carbs since we're having pasta for dinner," she said, leaning over to kiss me on my forehead.

"Are you trying to imply something?" I snapped. My mother was a health nut and always trying to impose her views on me.

"No, I just want you to keep healthy. I couldn't help but notice that you've been living in that dress," she said with her eyebrow arched, pointing her index finger accusingly up and down. "I must have washed it twice a week since April. What are you hiding under there?"

"I'm sorry, did I forget to tell you I was pregnant?" I mocked.

"GOD FORBID!" she said dramatically, giving me a death stare.

Yes, God forbid I have sex and procreate. "I like how you knew I was joking. You are getting better at the pick-up," I said, grabbing my purse. "Text me when the diamond has landed!"

2

I got to Downtown, the hippest brunch spot around, precisely at eleven o'clock. I sat at our usual table, on the second floor by a window overlooking the center of town, and waited for my three best childhood friends, with whom I'd grown up with on Jade Meadow Drive. Instead of looking forward to seeing them, though, my green-eyed thoughts were churning around in my head. I rested my chin on my clasped hands and gazed outside, thinking about the latest turn of events and came to one general conclusion: This blows.

I studied my reflection in the window. *Blossoming hips and borderline size 8 notwithstanding, I guess I'm not that bad,* I reasoned. I have long, thick brown hair, intense, hazel eyes and an olive-skinned complexion. On the inside, I have a heart of gold (a quality that hasn't shown itself to you yet, but you'll see) and a sharp, quick mind. I'm fun, passionate, and will kill for those I love. Oh, and I can tell you what the New York Giants did versus the Dallas Cowboys in 1993 while sipping on a glass of wine and rocking out a designer dress with stilettos. How many girls do you know who can blend the best of both worlds so seamlessly?

But on the other hand, nothing has been easy for me. I feel that I'm never enough, and the older I get, the more this realization manifests itself through all facets of my life. In high school, I didn't fit into any stereotypical category. I was never the "prettiest" or the "smartest" or the "coolest"—I was never at the top of anything (or anyone; I was probably the only virgin in our graduating class). I did all of the announcing for our school's events and games, and I wrote sports for our school newspaper, The Bear Cave. Despite my eager-to-please attitude, I was always an afterthought. Even then, I was always the bridesmaid, never the bride.

"Hiii!" A familiar female voice said, breaking me out of my trance.

I broke into the first genuine smile of the day and rose to embrace Katie Lansford. I was hoping she would be the first one to arrive, and my wish was granted (for once).

"I'm so happy to see you--even more than usual," I said.

"What, you don't see me enough?" Katie quipped as she settled into her seat across from me.

Like yours truly, Katie hadn't been able to forge her own path outside of Jade Meadow Drive. Unlike yours truly, she couldn't have cared less. She was happily single, worked as a pastry chef and lived with her parents (no siblings). Katie was a Honey Crest townie through and through, and I would not be surprised if she ran it one day.

I studied her as she earnestly picked up the menu. Katie was a beautiful Irish girl--red-blonde hair, piercing green eyes, white porcelain doll skin. While I sat there and fretted about being in-between single digit sizes, Katie had always been a bigger girl, and was a proud size 14. She was teased growing up (her nickname in middle school was "Katie Cake"), but her infectious personality won the critics over, and by high school she was easily one of the most popular girls in school. She was class president and was even voted Mama Bear at our senior year homecoming.

Katie's positivity was her most endearing quality. While everyone else (read: me) stressed out endlessly about their problems, Katie laughed her way through life's curveballs. She was not a clown, but it took a lot for her to lose her toothy grin (the beer she almost constantly had in her hand didn't hurt either). Don't mistake her kindness for weakness; if you crossed her, you were better off dead. She was always on my case for being "a pushover" and urged me to be more resolute like her. However, I was not lucky enough to have people naturally gravitate towards my aura the way she was; I had to bend over backward to gain the respect of my friends, co-workers and lovers (I hadn't had to do much bending lately for the aforementioned third group.)

"What are you having?" she asked without looking up.

"I don't know," I replied glumly. "Probably just scrambled egg whites and a water."

Katie looked up with a sour look on her face. "What the hell kind of meal is that?"

"I can't fit into any of my clothes," I moaned. "I have to go on a diet."

"You people and your diets," she said, rolling her eyes. "It's ridiculous. If you want a Belgian waffle, go ahead and have the damn Belgian waffle *with* extra whipped cream! Who cares?"

"She does," I said, pointing to a dark figure making its way to us.

"Hi, guys!" Andrea Deveroux chirped, dropping the five bulging shopping bags to the floor. She leaned in to give us each a kiss on the cheek. "What are we having?"

"I'm having a meal, and Carla apparently is going to sit here and suck on a lemon for brunch," Katie joked.

"Ha-ha. I'm sure Andrea will want exactly what I'm having."

"No lemons for me," Andrea said, clearly not picking up on the joke. "I'm in the mood for some pancakes and bacon!"

Katie and I looked at our friend, shocked. Andrea lived at the gym and hardly ever cheated on her strict diet.

Of all the Jade Hollow Drive alumni, Andrea was clearly the breadwinner. Her goal in life was to marry rich and never have to work a day in her life. Well, mission accomplished. She married neurosurgeon Richard Deveroux, 20 years her senior in a lavish, 300-person wedding extravaganza two years before.

They lived in the ritzy Honey Crest Falls section of town, in a giant mansion that she didn't have to worry about cleaning (thanks to her live-in maid, Dottie). Andrea spent her days working out, shopping, doing lunch with the other high society wives, and... well, I was not entirely sure what else.

I was as close to Andrea as I was to Katie, but just in a different way. I'd go over the Lansford's when I wanted to watch movies and eat comfort food after a shitty day. I'd go over the Rocha's when I wanted to drink underage without judgment or needed to get ready for the clubs so my parents couldn't criticize my risqué outfits. Andrea's parents were off-the-plane Brazilian and very free-spirited. If I had brought home an old man to marry, my father would have had my head, no matter how much was in his bank account. But the Rocha's were very happy with their union and celebrated their daughter's "achievement." Ah, nothing like reaching the full potential of the American Dream!

If I wasn't practically family with Andrea, I'd probably hate her. She had a tall, model's body, brown-black eyes, and a flawless cocoa complexion that's graced the pages of *Seventeen*. But Andrea could also be a fiery bitch. In high school, when she wasn't busy dating her newest flavor of the week, she was putting her latest frenemy in place. *We* knew that her bark was bigger than her bite, but it wouldn't have shocked me in the least if there had been an Andrea Rocha dartboard floating around somewhere. The stunning five karat diamond that now adorned her finger, coupled with a closet full of couture fashion and her husband's infinite bank account, just added fuel to her *Mean Girls* persona.

Knowing all this, Katie and I were baffled that Andrea was willing to subject her perfect body to fatty meats and complex carbohydrates like us normal folk.

"Are you feeling okay?" I asked.

"I'm fine, why?" Andrea said innocently.

"Oh, it's nothing," Katie said, catching my eye. "We just thought pancakes and bacon fell into your "poison foods" category."

"Can't a girl live a little?" Andrea asked defensively. "And you, Katie, of all people, should not be questioning my choices."

"Hey, guys!" A male's voice interrupted.

The three of us looked up, startled.

"Dante Ezra, on time for brunch? I thought I'd never see the day!" I exclaimed.

"Dante's on time AND Andrea's ordering real food! Okay, where are my friends and where did you hide them?" Katie laughed.

"Very funny girls," Dante said, swinging the wooden chair diagonal to me around so he could rest his arms on its back. He grabbed a menu. "What are we having?"

I shook my head and laughed, which I constantly found myself doing whenever I was in Dante's company.

Dante rounded out our little neighborhood group, and if he hadn't been like a brother to me, I would probably have fallen victim to his charm at one time or another. Dante was my go-to friend when I wanted to head over to Prudential Center to catch a New Jersey Devils game, or randomly book a weekend to Baltimore to see the New York Yankees and Orioles play. In return, I would always help him with his songwriting when he was stuck on a particular lyric. In high school, generally the jocks and choir geeks didn't mix, but Dante was the exception. He was the state's top football star, and he balanced that by singing lead in our school's nationally-recognized chorus. He even started his own rock band, "Dante's Inferno" that enjoyed some local success. Dante's number of conquests may have made Wilt Chamberlain take pause, but even if he had not been super talented, he would have had no problems with the opposite sex. With his jet black hair and piercing blue eyes, he was nothing short of drop-dead gorgeous.

Unfortunately, post-Honey Crest High, things hadn't been so easy for him. A fractured vertebrae ended his football career during his junior year of college, and when he lost his scholarship, he dropped out of school. Ever since, he's been trying to break into the music business while working various side jobs to pay for the studio apartment he rented in town. I knew the past few years had taken a toll on his psyche, but his pride didn't allow him to admit his pain.

"I'm not very hungry," I lied.

"Stop! It's Sunday, you can start your stupid diet tomorrow," Katie reasoned.

"It's that kind of mentality that got me into this predicament in the first place," I retorted.

"Where is this waitress?" Andrea asked impatiently, clicking together her French manicured nails. "I'm starving!"

"And I'm hung-over," Dante yawned.

A few seconds later, a marginally attractive, dirty blonde waitress appeared to take our order. I saw Dante's eyes light up, his hangover a distant memory.

"Here we go…" I muttered.

"Welcome to Downtown. My name is Stacy!"

"My name is Dante," he said with a wink.

The rest of us groaned.

"Let the poor girl do her job," I pleaded.

"No, it's fine," Stacy said, waving Katie off. She started giggling nervously while staring deep into our friend's eyes. Dante had a big smile on his face, his eyes glazed over with lust.

Andrea cleared her throat loudly and picked up her menu. "I'll give you my order first," she proclaimed, breaking their love connection. Stacy hurriedly grabbed her pen out of her apron and focused her attention on her other customers. Dante continued to stare at her with his bedroom eyes.

"I'll have the panca- no, wait a minute," Andrea said, getting distracted by something else on the menu. I smirked. How did I know she was going to wuss out and order something healthy?

"...I'll have the stuffed French toast with bananas and strawberries, bacon on the side," Andrea said with delight. "With a tea, please. Decaffeinated."

My jaw almost hit the table.

"I'll have the same thing," Katie added with a huge grin. "With a Stella."

"Nothing looks as appetizing on the menu as what's *off* the menu," Dante said to Stacy with a smoldering look. Stacy started playing with her hair and looked as if she was about to lose her composure again. "But for now, I'll have a Bloody Mary, three scrambled eggs, white toast and sausage."

I sighed. "I guess that leaves me."

"Do the right thing, D'Agostino," Katie warned, as if the balance of the world hung with my brunch order. Andrea stayed silent, probably because she had noticed my weight gain and agreed that I needed to do something about it.

Screw it. I thought. *It's been a rough morning.* "I'll have a Frittata with spinach, feta cheese and sundried tomatoes, rye toast and home fries. And a mimosa."

Katie smugly crossed her arms in victory. Dante waved to Stacy as she nervously collected all of the menus and walked away.

"So what's new?" Andrea asked cheerfully.

"Too much of the same old," I retorted.

"Did you guys get this?" Katie said, reaching into her purse. She pulled out a brown piece of folded paper and placed it in the center of the table. I instantly knew what it was.

"That fucking save-the-date! Get it away from me!" I threatened.

"I got it yesterday. You did such a cute job with them, Katie," Andrea gushed. Since Katie was class president back in the day, it had been her job to plan this little shindig.

"Thanks!" Katie beamed.

"What is this? I didn't get it," Dante said, picking it up. He started reading, "Save the date..."

"Read it to yourself, please!" I begged.

"...June 24th, 2017..." Dante continued louder, smiling.

"No!" I moaned, burying my face in my hands.

"...Honey Creek High School class of 2007's ten-year reunion. More details to come. Holy shit, it's been ten years already?" he asked, flinging the invitation back on the table.

"Don't remind me," I begged.

"So what are the other details, Katie?" Andrea asked sweetly. I glared at Andrea. Why was she in such a syrupy mood? Did her husband *not* need Viagra last night?

"Well," Katie said, inching up to her seat, clearly excited, "I want to recreate our senior prom!"

I groaned.

Katie continued, ignoring me. "So it's going to be at our school gym, and I'm treating the night as if it's literally prom 2007 again. Only music from that time will play. I'm also going to do a "now and then" slideshow, and we're going to have an awards ceremony, like 'Most Changed in Appearance?' and 'Most Likely to Retire by Age 50?' and of course, Reunion King and Queen. Things like that."

Andrea and Dante nodded their heads in approval.

"I should get the guys of Dante's Inferno back together for the night," Dante eagerly suggested.

"That would be AMAZING!" Katie gasped.

I had to slam on the breaks of this runaway train. "Oh come on; give me a break!"

"What's wrong?" Andrea asked.

"Well, the whole idea of a ten-year reunion is stupid enough, but to make people come in prom dresses? Superlative awards? Haven't we *matured* a little bit in ten years? High school was painful and embarrassing then, let alone now."

"You don't *have* to go," Andrea said coolly.

"Thanks for that, Andrea," I replied sarcastically. "I forgot that the Constitution allowed for freedom of choice."

"She's right," Katie said shortly. "If you are going to be negative about it, don't come."

An awkward silence fell among the table, broken only by Stacy, who had arrived with our drinks.

"Thank God," I muttered, chugging down my mimosa as soon as she put it down in front of me. "Another one, please," I ordered.

Dante, who was transfixed on our waitress the second she reappeared, snapped back to real life once she left. "Carla, you have to come to our reunion," he said. "It wouldn't be the same without you."

"How so?" I asked.

Dante fell silent. "I don't know, it just…wouldn't."

"Yea, my point exactly," I replied.

"Well, I for one can't wait to show up in my old prom dress," Andrea proclaimed.

"Good for you!" I replied wryly.

"But...," Andrea trailed off, ignoring me. "Before I can even think about my outfit, I have to tell you guys something." She reached into her purse, pulled out a shiny black and white paper, and proudly held it up. "I'm pregnant!" she squealed, waving around the ultrasound image.

We all looked at her, wide-eyed, and all the frostiness from a few moments before had melted away. "Oh my God!" I exclaimed, reaching over to hug her.

Katie ran to the other side of the table and hugged both of us. "You are going to be a mommy?!" she shrieked.

Dante, obviously overwhelmed by the surge of estrogen, watched the three of us embrace and smiled. "Congratulations, Andrea!" he said warmly.

After a few more moments of hugs and happy tears, Stacy brought our food, and we sat back in our seats. "When are you due?" Katie asked.

"The babies are due in December, so that gives me six months to get back into shape before the reunion," Andrea said confidently, taking a big bite out of her French toast. "I'm going to be the hottest MILF there!"

"Wait, did you say 'babies'?" I asked.

She nodded her head "yes," and she swallowed. "Twins!"

Katie and I put our forks down to rise up, and this time, Dante joined us. We shared more hugs and tears.

"Well," I said as we settled back into our chairs. "I know the first wedding the Deveroux twins will be in."

"Whose?" The girls asked.

"Jimmy's proposing to Gwen. He and my father are out diamond shopping as we speak," I answered.

"JIMMY'S GETTING…wait," Andrea said, stopping herself.

"I guess this explains your pissy mood," Dante added.

"A little bit," I said, taking a big sip out of my glass for effect.

"Try to be happy for him," Katie said. "I know how you get with your age hang-ups. At the end of the day, it doesn't matter that he's younger than you and getting married first. Your time will come."

"Your time will come." One of the most hated single-girl sympathy phrases, second only to, *"Everything happens for a reason."*

"Thanks," I muttered, not wanting to combat Katie's words. I had already said enough.

The rest of breakfast breezed by. My early-afternoon buzz stabilized my mood, and for a while I forgot about my problems. We traded stories, witty remarks, and laughs. Andrea showed us the contents of her shopping bags, and for once, none of the designer frocks were for her. Dante, of course, got Stacy's number.

Two hours later, we bid each other goodbye.

"We'll see you soon!" Andrea exclaimed, rubbing her belly as she walked to her white BMW.

"Bye girls," Dante waved as he walked to his apartment.

It was just Katie and I left outside the restaurant. Before I walked to my car, there was something I wanted to say. "Katie, look, I want to apologize for how I reacted towards the reunion. It all honestly sounds great."

"No need to apologize," Katie said. "I know you didn't mean to hurt me; you just hate the idea of the reunion in general."

"You have no idea," I whined.

"You think I like it?" Katie asked.

I looked at her quizzically. Katie never cared about the future, she took everything one day at a time.

"I HATE the idea of getting old; I want to be a kid forever. But the difference is that I don't let these things consume me like you do."

"I just feel like such a *loser*," I moaned, ignoring her poignant mini-speech. "I'm going to show up at that reunion basically the same person I was ten years ago, and I'm going to be surrounded by successful executives and homeowners and married people and *mothers*!" I sat down on the black bench next to us and hung my head.

Katie was a step behind me. "You are not the same person you were ten years ago. You are *better*! You have a great job…"

I narrowed my eyes at her.

"Okay, you have a job," she continued. "You've traveled; you've learned a lot. Not everyone we went to college with has their shit figured out. Look at Dante!"

I laughed. "Comparing me to Dante is not a way to make me feel better. Can you believe he wants to get Dante's Inferno together for the reunion?"

"It might be good for him, though," Katie reasoned.

"I guess," I shrugged.

"Well, look at the bright side," Katie said. "I sent out those save-the-dates a year in advance so everyone would have enough notice. Consider yourself on the clock."

"What do you mean?" I asked.

"Instead of wasting time complaining about everything under the sun, get off your back and do something about it! You have always been your own worst enemy."

I let the words hang in the warm summer air. There was no use in arguing—she was right.

"Okay, well, I got to go," Katie said, rising up. "I'm going to get some beers and watch some movies. Come over for burgers later if you want; Mom and I are barbecuing." We hugged, and I watched her walk away to her car.

Get off your back and do something about it, her words repeated in my mind. "Get off my back," I muttered to myself. All of a sudden, a light bulb went off. I raced to my car. I had a lot of work to do, and less than 365 days to do it.

3

I couldn't get home fast enough. I parked my car, ran passed my mother cooking Sunday dinner (while gabbing away on the phone to probably the fiftieth person about Jimmy's pending engagement) and zoomed upstairs. I locked the door behind me and lunged towards my laptop. I knew what I wanted, but I needed to put those thoughts in writing:

> Title: Project: Reunion
> I have a little less than a year to turn this embarrassing joke that is my life around into something to be proud of. I'm fed up with this bullshit. Jimmy's getting married, Andrea's having kids (TWINS), and I'm going nowhere…until now.

I closed my eyes, and visualized exactly how my reunion night would play out:

> I will walk through the Honey Crest High School gymnasium doors an amazing, accomplished woman. I will have a handsome, successful lawyer on my arm, who has just recently proposed with a two karat, platinum Tiffany Novo ring. I'll have a rock-hard, size 4 body. I'll have my own sports-talk show on WSPS. My 500+ former classmates will rush to congratulate me on all my achievements (and when I'm not looking, most will talk enviously behind my back). My fiancé, my best friends, and I will merrily drink and dance the night away. At the end of the night, my man and I will retire to our brand new waterfront condo overlooking the New York City skyline, and make passionate love until the sun comes up.

I printed my entry and re-read my words, my body tingling with excitement over the prospect of my sparkling, perfect life. Before I could reach the summit, however, I had to map out a path. In order to be the changed person I wanted to be, I needed to spur into action. I turned the paper over, grabbed a pen, and scribbled the following:

> *"Project: Reunion" to-do list:*

- *Re-join the gym.*
- *Wake up at five a.m. every day and work out for at least an hour.*

- *Go on a diet...and stick with it! (Except on Sundays. Hey, I need one day to be human!)*
- *Assert myself with my bosses. I'm a hard worker, but I need to show them my true talents.*
- *Find a guy...How the hell am I going to find a guy?*

I puckered my lips in thought, tapping the pen on the desk. Love is the one thing that has eluded me my whole life. It's never come easy, and of the very few times I thought I had it, it never felt right. I had no time to dwell on this, though. I did the math—if I was going to be engaged this time next year, I had to start a torrid love affair by September. At our old age, nine months is more than enough time to figure out if that person is The One or not (and in my ex's case, it apparently only took nine minutes). But how do I find him?

"CARLA!" My mom banged on my door. "JIMMY'S HOME WITH THE RING! COME DOWNSTAIRS!"

This ring I needed to see. I stuffed the paper in my desk and hurried downstairs.

■ ■ ■

There I was, face-to-face with my arch nemesis. I was physically bigger, but her presence towered over me. Her dazzling demeanor blinded her from the fact that I loathed her mere existence. I wanted nothing more than to crush her with my bare hands, but she could not be defeated, for she was made from some of the strongest material on Earth and thus, indestructible. She sat there, taunting me, with her prism of brilliant colors that were magnified by the sun's rays pouring through the kitchen window.

In other words, the centerpiece to our Sunday family dinner was Jimmy's three (!!!) karat round-cut solitaire diamond engagement ring for Gwen. At my mother's insistence, she ordered Jimmy to place the open box in the center of the table so she could bask in its beauty. In turn, it made my penne with homemade tomato sauce taste like sawdust. (That didn't stop me from eating it, mind you.)

"Look at the engagement ring my son bought!" she would exclaim every five minutes.

Finally, I had enough. "Okay, Mom, we get it!" I snapped.

"What, I can't be proud of him? He bought a very impressive piece of jewelry with his own money. Have YOU ever bought something that expensive?" she snapped back.

Before I could respond, Jimmy cut in. "Mom, Carla's right," he said, reaching over his plate to grab the box. "I'm getting engaged. We know. We don't need to stare at the ring."

"Well I want to," she insisted, grabbing the box out of her son's hand.

My father said nothing, more interested in his heaping pile of pasta.

My brother and I groaned, but my mother zoned in on me. "Why can't you be happy for your brother? You haven't had one nice thing to say about this whole thing," she said accusingly.

"I AM happy!" I lied. "But it's, like, looking at us while we eat! It's creepy!"

"Well when you have a son who is getting engaged, you can do whatever you want," she replied smugly. "If I want to look at my ring, I'm going to look at my ring!"

"YOUR ring?" I asked incredulously.

"Well you only have a week until I give it to Gwen, so enjoy your time with it now," Jimmy said. "I plan on proposing on the Fourth of July."

"MY SON!" My mother exclaimed, jumping out of her chair to hug him. "I'm so proud of my son!"

My father stopped eating long enough to catch my and Jimmy's annoyed expressions, and we all rolled our eyes. "Nancy, sit down," my father barked.

Mom pouted. "You guys are no fun."

"Anyway," I said, changing the subject. "Guess who's pregnant?"

My mother's expression changed from happiness to fear. "Who?" she shrilled.

I took a dramatic pause, taking pleasure in her distress. She was probably thinking that I was going to reveal that the little pregnancy joke I made earlier that morning was actually no joke at all. "Andrea!" I exclaimed. "With twins!"

"Cool!" Jimmy smiled brightly. Dad, still more interested in his pasta, nodded in approval.

"Oh, wow," Mom replied. I could tell the winds were taken out of her sails over "her" engagement.

"She's due in December. I can't wait to be an aunt!" I gushed.

"I can't believe she's having two babies with that old man," Mom said, shaking her head in disgust, completely ignoring me. If I had a penny for every time my mother took a dig at Andrea for her marital choice, I could literally BUY my dream life scenario. I may not have agreed with it either, but I'd come to terms with it. "Acceptance" was not in my mother's dictionary, however. Instead of fighting her, I just broke off a piece of Italian bread and concentrated on dipping it into my sauce.

"Jimmy, you will have cute little flower girls or ring bearers for the wedding," I said absentmindedly. No answer. I turned to Jimmy and saw him deep in thought. "Jimmy, did you hear what I said?"

"Yeah, I did," he replied. "But I'm trying to think of what I learned in school about babies."

"What do you mean?"

"You said the babies are coming in December. Would they be able to walk down the aisle by May of next year?"

"WHAT?" I shouted in horror. My brother wasn't the brightest bulb in the chandelier, but I was more horrified by the other part of that sentence.

"That's only..." he counted with his fingers. "Five months. I thought they needed more time to walk."

"The- they, do," I stammered. "But what's this May business?"

"I don't want a long engagement," my brother said casually. "I know Gwen doesn't either. Her favorite season is spring, so next May sounds good."

My mother forcefully put down her fork. "Jimmy, you're going to get married in less than a year?" She said disapprovingly. I smirked. I think it was the first time I saw Mom not agree with one of Jimmy's decisions since he surprised her with a barbed wire tattoo he had gotten around his bicep down at the shore during his senior prom weekend. In other words, this was not a normal occurrence.

"I guess. I have to talk to her first, obviously. Why?" Jimmy asked.

She rose from her chair. "I have a year to lose 20 pounds," she said dramatically. "This family is going on a diet." And with that, she picked up her plate and leaned over to take my father's.

"Hey!" Dad exclaimed. "I'm still eating!"

"You ate enough," Mom snipped, leaning over to take mine.

I didn't even protest when she took my dish away; I was too deep in depressing thought to care. Not only was Jimmy getting engaged before me, at my expired benchmark engagement age, but he was going to be getting married at age 25, my expired benchmark *marriage* age. The icing on the cake? This was all going down the month before the reunion. Swell. *"Carla, I heard your little brother got married!"* A random former classmate will say. *"When do YOU plan on getting married?"* Instead of answering, I'll start hysterically crying, ripping the bobby pins out of my prom up-do while trying my best to run out of the gym in a heavy tulle gown.

"I have to go," I said to no one, clutching my stomach. The men had already retreated to the couch. My mom started washing the dishes, with the ring box watching her from the kitchen counter.

I ran upstairs and made a beeline for my laptop. I was going to write my millionth missive about the horrific state of my life, but a *Facebook* notification caught my eye:

> Katie Lansford has invited you to like Honey Crest High School Class of 2007 Reunion.

The grinning default picture of a cartoon bear, our school's mascot, didn't do much to break my frown. *Geez Katie; the save-the-date's weren't torture enough?*

I clicked on the page and noticed that 56 mutual friends/former classmates had already joined. Not wanting to hurt Katie's feelings, I clicked "like" and became Unlucky 57.

Surely there are some people worse off than me, I reasoned. I went into my iTunes and located my "FML" playlist (FML= Fuck My Life) and hit the play button. The angst of Kelly Clarkson, my musical soul mate, poured out of the speakers. For the next hour, I clicked on each name, keeping a tally of their life's accomplishments.

The numbers of my informal survey were certainly not tipping in my favor: Out of 56 people, 30 were married. Eighteen of those couples were with child. Seven couples were already with multiple children. Another 14 people were engaged. Ten were in relationships. That left a measly *four* people who were either single or too ashamed to list themselves as single. Furthermore, about eighty percent of those people listed their "current city" as somewhere far, far away from their hometown of Honey Crest. I was the farthest thing from a mathematician, but I was sure that if you applied those figures to the entire graduating class of 532, the statistics would be even more staggering.

What would Mrs. Wright have to say about all this?

I closed my laptop shut, cutting Taylor off mid-song. I dejectedly buried myself underneath my covers and hid there for the rest of the night.

4

Day 1

Despite still being down in the dumps over my study, I dragged my ass out of bed precisely at five in the morning to get ready for the gym. Unfortunately, I was not the only person who was awake at that time.

"What are you doing up so early?" Mom chirped when I got downstairs, not looking up from studying her room sketches. (She works as an interior designer, the perfect complement to D'Agostino Construction. Dad and Jimmy build the homes, Mom decorates them. Have you figured out who the black sheep in the family is yet?)

"I'm going to the gym," I replied, grabbing a bottled water out of the fridge.

She put her papers down and swiped her glasses off her face. "That's great honey! This is the best time to go – when you have no distractions. You can get it out of the way, and enjoy the rest of your day."

"Yup," I agreed, grabbing my keys to cut the impending lecture short. "See you tonight."

"Bye, honey!"

I could barely keep my eyes open while navigating my white Mazda M3 to Fitness World. When I parked, I contemplated just sleeping in my car but someone tapping on my window startled me.

"Good morning, Sunshine!" Andrea exclaimed through the glass. I rolled my window down. "You were the last person I expected to be here. Welcome back!"

Andrea and I used to work out together, but then I just got too busy (read: uninterested). On the other hand, Andrea was there every morning, seven days a week, without fail. (I wouldn't have been surprised if she snuck in a quick elliptical session on her way to the hospital to give birth.) I wished I could give her my body to work out, but I guessed tapping into her dedication could be a distant second best. I opened the car door.

"Happy to be back," I lied, rubbing my tired eyes.

"I can tell," Andrea laughed as we started walking towards the entrance. "How long has it been?"

"Six months?" I guessed as we walked inside. "I'm really not sure."

"Hi Andrea," a dark-haired body builder greeted us. He leaned in to give Andrea a big hug and kiss on the cheek. "Who is this?"

"This is my best friend, Carla. Carla, this is Xander, he's my trainer. He's *Superman*!" Andrea gushed. "My ass never looked this good until we started working out together!"

Xander laughed. "Well thank you, but don't wreck my work by succumbing to pregnancy cravings! Are you following the diet I made for you?"

Andrea glanced at me. I could see the guilt wash over her face as she thought about the big brunch she indulged in the day before. "Yes," she gulped.

"Good! Pregnancy doesn't give women the excuse to turn into gluttonous pigs."

What did he know? That was the EXACT reason to get pregnant! Then I had another thought.

"Hey," I said, playfully pushing Andrea's shoulder. "You told your trainer you were pregnant before us?"

Andrea let out a nervous giggle. "Well, we had to alter my workouts. I told Xander before I even told my mom!"

I smirked at her logic. Then again, I'd probably tell Xander, the gas station attendant, my priest, and the homeless man living under the Verrazano Bridge that I was with child before breaking the news to my mother. It was only then I noticed Xander staring at me, deep in thought. (I'm using the term "deep" loosely here.)

"Can I help you?" I asked.

"No, let me help *you*!" Xander exclaimed. He turned to Andrea. "Let me train your friend. She's a pretty girl, but she's soft. I can whip her into shape in no time!"

I gasped at his rudeness.

"Wh-why would you want to do that?" Andrea stammered nervously.

"Yea, I don't think so," I shook my head vehemently, agreeing with Andrea. There was no way I wanted to spend any more additional time with this vain cyborg.

"Why not? What do you have to lose?" Xander asked, eying me up and down. "Besides 15 pounds?"

My eyes bulged out of their sockets.

"What? You are going to tell me that's not the truth?" Xander challenged, looking me dead in the eye.

What was I supposed to say? He was right; I had morphed into the Pillsbury Dough Boy's long-lost sister. But I couldn't go down without a fight. "Even if that was the truth, that's not the way to garner potential new clients," I said dramatically.

"Being nice is not going to help get rid of this," he said, grabbing a handful of fat around my midsection.

"Ow!" I exclaimed.

"Do you want a better body?" Xander challenged.

"Of course, I do!"

"Then let me help you!" he repeated.

I felt abused and mortified, but…Was that a glimmer of hope I was feeling? Maybe I needed an intense meathead like Xander to help turn my bloated, flabby physique into fighting form. I looked over at Andrea. She had her arms crossed over her chest, and she looked annoyed. "What do you think?" I asked her.

"Do whatever you want," she snipped.

"Well, if you're going to be angry about it, I won't train with him." Andrea always needed to be the center of attention, and knowing her, she probably couldn't handle her trainer sharing his focus.

"She'll be fine," Xander insisted. Andrea glared at him.

"I'll do it," I said, ignoring Andrea. I extended my hand out.

"This is gonna be *fun*," Xander said devilishly, shaking my hand.

For the next hour, as Andrea carefully watched from her treadmill, Xander put me through the wringer. After weighing me and taking my body fat percentage (*so* embarrassing), we did all sorts of cardio and weight training exercises. It was horrible, yet actually exhilarating.

Afterwards, Xander and I sat down and mapped out a fitness and diet plan. We would meet three days a week, and he expected me to do forty minutes of cardio on our off days. He also gave me a diet plan full of vegetables, protein and other unsavory items. Luckily, he agreed to Sunday being my rest/cheat day. "Just don't go overboard. You can undo all the good you did that week with just one bad meal," he warned.

"Do you have goals?" he asked as we walked out of his office.

"Of course, I do," I responded.

"What are they?"

Where do I begin? I thought as I started mentally running through my ten-year reunion scenario. "Well, I obviously want to lose weight, get my dream job, meet a great guy, get married-"

He put up his hand. "I don't want to hear what your goals are. But what I need you to do is to visualize them."

"I do visualize them. Every single day of my life," I sighed.

"No, actually visualize them. Print pictures, rip out pages from magazines, even draw them up, I don't care. Put together a vision board of what you want your dream life to be. Hang it by your bed, desk, wherever you spend most of your time. That way, you can see what you are working towards. Trust me," he said, looking towards the treadmills, where Andrea was still speed walking. "It works."

I watched him lovingly gaze at my best friend. Something was definitely going on there. Was Andrea on *his* "vision board?"

"Anyway, what was I saying," he said, shaking his head to snap out of his trance.

"You were explaining how a kindergarten arts and crafts project will somehow help me achieve my goals," I replied.

"Oh, right. Besides making the collage, there are two important things you need to remember."

"What's that?"

"One—you need to be patient. Don't expect everything to happen overnight. If you do, you will get frustrated and quit. Two—you need to be positive. Negative thoughts will stall your progress. 'Act as if'."

" 'Act as if' what ?"

"Act out your dream scenario, and the universe will give it to you."

I was a taken aback by Xander's philosophy; I had not taken this meathead for a Buddha. "How am I supposed to do that? Do I put on a white string bikini, convince myself that I'm Adriana

Lima, and then go to the beach? I'm in no shape for that; people will report a beached whale to the authorities!"

"This is what I mean," Xander snapped. "Your physical body isn't the only thing that needs to get in shape. You are your own worst enemy!"

Didn't I just hear that from somewhere? "I'm just being honest," I replied defensively.

He sighed. "Do you have an answer for everything?"

"You learn quick!"

"Andrea should have warned me about you."

■ ■ ■

The good will Xander had instilled in me flew out the window a couple hours later, as I walked through the doors of WSPS Sports Radio 950 AM.

It was when Buffalo Bills kicker Scott Norwood's would-be game-winning field goal sailed wide right in Super Bowl XXV that I became a sports junkie. My parents had a huge party for the big game, and instead of going with the mothers and the other kids downstairs to our massive playroom, I opted to stay with my father and the other men. I had just turned four years old just days before; I had no idea about football. But I got a kick out of my father and my uncles sweeping me up in their arms and throwing me up in the air whenever the New

York Giants did something well. I was in awe over how crazy the men were. They held their breaths with every single play, paced around, and constantly screamed. Even though I wasn't completely clear on the game, I was immediately hooked. My parents even allowed me to stay up until the end of the game. To this day, I haven't seen my father cry the way he did when the Giants won that year.

From that day forward, all my essays in school were based around sports; football, baseball, the Olympics, I was obsessed with it all. I immersed myself in the history of how the New York Knicks came to be, and fantasized about being alive during the 1950s majestic New York Yankees World Series era, and read countless athlete biographies. In essence, I became an even bigger fan than any male in my family. My girlfriends didn't get it, and most guys I met were intimidated that I knew more than they did, which obviously did wonders for my love life.

But tell me, what's better in life than a Game 7? (Okay, there are a couple things; shut up.) But nothing packs more of a dramatic, breathless punch than a do-or-die sports competition. And you know how much us girls love drama! It's better than any Lifetime movie.

When I wasn't reading or watching sports (or failing miserably at playing them), I was constantly listening to people talk about them. My father always had on WSPS, the country's number one 24-hour sports talk station, and I followed suit. I would get ready for school listening to Joe & JoJo in the morning; I would do my homework listening to Harry & the Leatherneck in the afternoon; and later in life, I would stumble home drunk and listen to Thomas Jay in the overnight. It was my ultimate dream to work there, and right after college, my dream came true.

New Jersey University has one of the top-ranked college radio stations in the country, and I had hosted a weekly sports talk show called *Girl in the Locker Room.* (My mother freaked at the title, but it definitely got me noticed!) My program director at 90.5 WNJU got in touch with Dan "The Man" Durkin, WSPS station manager, and scored me an interview.

Dan was quite the interesting character. His nickname was self-imposed, and his borderline-sickening obsession with celebrity offset his intimidation factor. His walls were crammed with countless photos of him posing with the rich and famous, and he had piles of rare memorabilia everywhere.

In the midst of showing off the crown jewels of his collections, Dan asked me what my intentions were in the business...

Self-doubt gripped my throat. "I want to be a sports talk host."

Dan flashed a sympathetic grin and ran a hand through his salt and pepper hair. "You are very talented and knowledgeable, but I can't put a 22-year-old female with no professional on-air experience on a show right off the bat. It just can't happen. Not on this station."

Of course not. Why would a major radio executive give a lowly college graduate the keys to her own show? And had I been truly gifted and talented, his experience and infinite wisdom would have ignored my young age.

I would never mutter the intention again.

Dan ended up offering me the weekly overnight producing shift. It was as if I won the lottery (despite the crappy hours and the barely-above-minimum-wage pay). But who said no to a job at WSPS? I understood that at this stage of the game, it was all about paying your dues. I could move to East Bumblefuck, Wisconsin to get my start, or begin my career at the best sports talk station in the world. I took the job right on the spot.

At first, it was cool –working in Manhattan, making great friends at the station, and of course meeting the athletes. I quickly ascended from producing the overnight show to the mid-morning show to the afternoon-drive show, where I had remained for the past two years. The hosts even put me on-air once in a while. That certainly made up for the still less-than-stellar pay.

But the novelty wore off as I kept getting passed over for THE job. It actually sickened me to think about how many on-air personalities I'd seen come and go. They were usually brought in from other markets, and then had meltdowns because they couldn't handle the heat of New York City, where even the sports pundits have critics who critique their criticisms. However, I'd been one of the station's constants; whatever they needed I was there to do — unpaid overtime, coming in on my days off to train the newbie producers, whatever. No matter how under-appreciated I felt, I always showed up to work with a smile. I knew I was good. I had thick skin for the business, yet I kept getting overlooked. Why? Unfortunately, I knew my boss' answer--"*You just aren't good enough.*"

"Morning, Laney," I cheerfully greeted the station's receptionist and my best friend at work, Elaine "Laney" Lester. Laney has been there for 20 years and was their unofficial mascot. She could totally write a best-seller based on WSPS with all the wacky things she'd seen and heard.

"Morning Carla," she responded back, imitating my sing-song tone. Laney was off her rocker and came up with the zaniest things possible. She had this infectious, cackling laugh that could be heard all through the office. She was a tiny brunette but loomed much larger than her 4'11" frame.

She noticed me slowly walking towards her desk. "Why are you walking funny?" She asked. "Wild night last night?"

"I wish!" I awkwardly chuckle through my abdominal pain. "I went back to the gym this morning and got a trainer who completely kicked my ass."

"Oh yeah? What's his name? Bruce the Bodybuilder?"

I smirked. "No."

"Zeus?"

I laughed. "I don't know what's worse, that or his actual name--Xander."

"Xander to the rescue! Zapping vast amounts of fat in a single bound!" Laney said in a booming Superman-narrator-like voice, extending her arm to "zap" me, and then letting out her signature cackle. "Not that you have vast amounts of fat, of course."

"Oh, but I do." I grimaced, thinking back to the number I tipped the scale at.

She rolled her eyes. "You're really crazy for going to the gym so early and spending money on a trainer. You don't need to. Go on, have a hamburger. Or a burrito."

"Not anytime soon. But I'll see you later," I said, heading towards the newsroom.

"Wait, before you go, I have some gossip, *hee-hee-hee*," she cackled mischievously.

"Ooo, you know I love that," I replied, rubbing my hands together earnestly. "What do you have for me?"

"I heard that Dan wants a female presence on the station and that he is actively searching for someone," Laney whispered.

I frowned. "Why is he looking outside the station when I'm right here?"

"Well I know that; you know that, but does HE know that?" Laney asked.

"What do you mean? Of course, he knows. He knew what I wanted from Day One."

"Uh yeah, but Carla, have you mentioned anything to him since Day One? It's like day a million-and-one by now."

I bit my lip. "No."

"So maybe he thinks that you are happy being a little eager-beaver producer. Cut a new demo tape. Give it to him," she insisted.

"Yeah, but he hears me go on-air with Tommy sometimes. If he thought I had legitimate talent, wouldn't he reach out on his own?"

"Dan is in his own world; you know that. You need to be direct with these people. Do the tape!"

"I will," I said defiantly.

"Good, now go. And skip the sweets that are in the newsroom, or else Xander will give you a spanking!" Laney laughed.

■ ■ ■

Before I could even give thought to my demo tape, I had a show to produce. I was on my computer in the control room typing out notes when my host, Thomas Jay, approached me.

"Who do we have on the show today, Dags?" Tommy asked in his endearing New York accent, calling me by his nickname for me. Tommy is my best guy friend at the station, but also my sort-of boss. I produced his show in the overnight, and we've been a team ever since.

"We have David Wright in his usual spot at 5:05, we have author Tim Hicks at 3:05 to talk about his new Scandalous Tiger Woods book, and we have Tom Coughlin coming in-studio in the 2 p.m. hour to talk about his charity," I said, handing him a rundown of today's show.

"The Coughlin spot is nice. Good job," Tommy said.

"Thanks!" I smiled, going back to typing out my notes. It was too bad Tommy was married and old enough to be my father, because if he had been single and my age, I would have totally dated him (and if my name was Andrea, I probably would have been doing so already). He was just so nice, and we had a great connection. My single status infuriated him more than it did me: *"Boys your age don't know what a good woman is. If I were thirty years younger, watch out baby!"*

"So C-D, did you hear Dan wants to give me a partner?"

I shot right up, stopped typing and swirled my chair around to give him my undivided attention. "No, I didn't," I said, genuinely surprised. How the hell had Laney not caught wind of THAT one? The afternoon-drive time slot on WSPS was the equivalent to playing center field for the New York Yankees; the opportunity didn't go to just anybody. That slot scored the biggest ratings in all of New York.

"I hear he wants to give me a female," Tommy replied.

I gasped. Again, how did Laney miss this important piece to the story? "They wouldn't pair you with someone from within?"

"I guess not..." His voice trailed off.

"How do you feel about that?"

"I don't know, the closest thing to a female co-host I've had has been with you. Maybe I should put your name into the mix."

"Really?" I said, touching my heart.

"Sure. Why not? I'll talk to Dan for you."

My imagination started running wild. How could Dan possibly say no to hiring me for this position? Tommy and I had great chemistry. Our listeners knew we'd been a team for years, I had more than proven myself AND he was willing to go to bat for me. All these facts, along with a killer demo tape, surely would get me my dream job.

A few minutes later, we were on the air. I was smiling the entire time. What a day this had been for Project Reunion. I got a trainer, a diet plan, and a very tangible job prospect. The pieces were starting to fall into place already!

During our first commercial break, I whipped out my iPhone. This demo tape had to be cut tonight, and there was only one person I wanted to record it with.

5

As I drove through Honey Crest to meet up with Dante later that night, I thought about the soft spot I held for the town. (Don't get me wrong, the second I am able to afford moving out I'd be long gone, but as far as hometowns go, Honey Crest was legit.) Honey Crest was an upper-middle-class New Jersey suburb, located about an hour outside of New York City. It had a population of 8,000 but the feel of a town much smaller. You couldn't go to the bathroom without someone knowing. My favorite part of Honey Crest was its quaint center that had lots of cool shops and unique restaurants. My most beloved spot was the Kettle Black Café, because of its laid-back atmosphere, sinful desserts and amazing discounts (Katie was their pastry chef). Dante's apartment happened to sit directly upstairs from my sugar haven.

As I stepped out of the car, I caught a whiff of the newly baked goodies coming out of Katie's kitchen. I closed my eyes for a second and imagined stuffing my face with a piece of Katie's white chocolate raspberry cake. Immediately my stomach started to rumble; all I'd had to eat that day were egg whites, salad and grilled chicken. It was going to take every ounce of willpower I had (which wasn't much) to not walk in there and binge myself into a sugar coma. I walked past the display window, frowning at the sweets I had to, unfortunately, give up, and ran up the narrow staircase to Dante's place. I knocked lightly on the door. Nothing. I waited a few seconds and knocked again, harder. Still nothing, but did I hear the faint sounds of someone… moaning?

I banged on the door violently. "Dante, are you all right?" A few seconds ticked by.

"Just a second Carla; everything's fine!" He finally answered.

I sighed. I was tired, hungry and irritable. I wanted to get this over with.

The door flung open. "Hi!" A shirtless Dante exclaimed, a little too happily.

"Why the hell are you so cheer- ohhhh." My answer appeared in the form of a disheveled Stacy, our waitress from yesterday, sheepishly exiting Dante's apartment.

"Carla, you remember Stacy, right?" Dante grimaced, trying to make the best out of the uncomfortable situation.

"Yes, I do," I replied with a tight smile.

"Nice seeing you again," Stacy said, her face flushed with embarrassment.

I walked in the doorway past her and sat in a folding chair in front of the makeshift audio studio Dante used for song recording. I folded my hands impatiently as he bid his latest conquest farewell.

"Bye, I had a really good time!" I heard her say excitedly. I rolled my eyes. It was not like I cared about what Dante did, but it was yet another reminder about what I was *not* doing.

"Have a good night," Dante waved as he pushed the door closed. "Sorry about that," he chuckled nervously.

"No need to apologize— or lie. Next time, though, could you *not* double book your friends and fuck buddies?"

"She came over at three, and we lost track of time," Dante quickly explained.

"It's 7:30!"

"Well, you know how it is..."

"No, I don't," I bitterly replied. "Let's just get this taping over with. I have to do my cardio in the morning before work and gotta go to bed."

■ ■ ■

The awkward run-in with Stacy was quickly forgotten about, and we put together a beautiful tape. I sounded crystal clear, I hit on all my points, and had a great rapport with my "co-host."

"I'll have you as a guest on my show!" I joked as he walked me to my car.

"Oh yeah? As what, a former high school star-turned-nothing?" Dante replied.

I was shocked by his response. It was not like Dante to admit any kind of anguish. "You're not a nothing," I insisted.

"Well, I'm not a something either."

His words tugged at my heart. "You and me both."

"Don't sell yourself short, Carla. You are well on your way to a cool-ass job. But me? I've got nothing going on."

"Well, speaking of demos, are you still sending yours out to record labels?"

"It's an impossible process," he complained. "I have all these meetings where I'm promised the world and nothing ever comes of it."

"So what are you going to do?"

"I don't know," he said, his piercing eyes filled with worry.

"I don't get it. You have the voice of an angel, and you're an incredible performer. How could these record execs not see that?" I ranted.

"I guess for the same reasons why, five years later, your boss still won't give you a shot on air, yet you run circles around every single host they have on now," Dante reasoned.

"So in other words, the entertainment industry is run by a bunch of morons?"

"Exactly."

I drew Dante in for a hug, and he held on tighter than usual. "We'll find our way," I whispered, half-believing my words.

"I hope so."

■ ■ ■

The next day, without hesitation, I marched into Dan's office and handed him the CD.

"What's this?" he asked.

"It's my demo tape," I proclaimed.

If he had a semblance of interest, he didn't show it. "Okay, I'll take a listen and offer my advice."

I frowned. *Offer my advice?* "Okay, thanks," I replied hastily and made a beeline out of there.

■ ■ ■

"Why didn't you tell him the tape was for the job and not for him to critique?" Katie demanded later that night as we sat in the Kettle Black way after closing.

"Because he STILL obviously doesn't see me as anything but a producer," I said in between bites of her seven-layer fudge cake. It was only Day 2, and my boss' comment had spiraled me out of control and off my diet.

"Well, it's your own fault," Katie snapped. "Not only is he in the dark about your wanting the job with Tommy, but now your boss thinks you are sending your resume out to other stations!"

I slammed my fork down. "Shit, I didn't even think of that! I'm a disaster," I said, burying my head in my hands.

"You are not a disaster," Katie said, rubbing her hand on my back for support. "You're just not assertive enough."

"Yes, I am!"

"Don't get defensive with me," Katie responded. "Look at today!"

I groaned. "I know," I said, putting my head back down.

"How badly do you want the job?" Katie asked.

"You don't know the answer to that?" I responded, jolting my head up.

"No, I obviously don't, because anyone who wants a job as badly as you *apparently* want this one would have said something to set the record straight," Katie reasoned.

"So, in other words, get my ass in his office tomorrow?" I asked meekly.

"Uh, YEAH," Katie said sarcastically.

"I think I'm going to need another piece of cake," I said, handing her my empty plate.

Katie smirked, and dutifully cut us each a slice.

■ ■ ■

The next day, sick to my stomach with nerves, I tiptoed back into Dan's office. "Hi Dan," I stammered, not nearly as confidently as I had the day before.

"Hi, Carla. What's up?" he asked pleasantly.

"I just need to talk to you about something real fast," I replied.

"Yes?"

"Well," I began. "The tape I gave to you yesterday wasn't for you to critique. Not that I wouldn't want your advice, I mean, you're 'The Man,' " I quickly gushed.

"Okay..." Dan replied slowly.

"And I'm not looking for other jobs, I'm very happy here at W-S-P-S."

"Okay..." Dan replied even slower.

"So what I'm trying to say is, the purpose of the tape was to be under consideration for *The Thomas Jay Show* co-host position."

"Okay," Dan simply replied.

"Okay," I repeated.

We stared at each other in uneasy silence.

"And?" I blurted out without thinking.

Dan smiled. "I'm still mulling over what to do, and a decision will be announced soon."

"Oh, well, that's great!" I smiled brightly. "I'm glad that we are on the same page. Thank you!"

Well, he hadn't flat-out told me no. Could it be that he was juggling the producer lineup so I could seamlessly assume the co-host's position? Probably not, but as Xander said, "act as if."

I confidently walked out of Dan's office "as if" the job was in the bag.

■ ■ ■

"You made me go in there for nothing!" I accusingly said to Katie later that night, as we again sat at the Kettle Black after closing. Instead of cake, though, I was snacking on celery sticks.

Now that my psyche was stabilized, the reunion renovation was back on the wagon.

"Well, how was I supposed to know?" she said. "You came in like a raging lunatic last night, and I just offered my advice. And at least you know the truth now."

"How? He was looking at me as if I rode the short bus into work!"

"Well, for someone who has the gift of gab, I thought you picked a bad time to finally shut up," Katie joked.

"Ha-ha." I rose from my chair. "Well, it's past my bedtime, and I have a gym date with Xander tomorrow."

Katie disapprovingly shook her head as she walked me to the door. "Yea, I'll be up earlier than usual too, I have a doctor's appointment," Katie quipped.

"What for?"

"Just a routine checkup," Katie shrugged. "I still can't believe you are working out with Andrea's trainer," she added.

"I actually can't believe it either," I agreed. "And Andrea was definitely not happy when I agreed to let him train me."

"That's Andrea, though. She's probably scared you're going to wind up with a better body than hers, pregnancy notwithstanding."

"True..." I trailed off. I sensed something weird with Andrea and Xander's relationship since Day One, but I didn't want to start drama predicated on a gut feeling.

"Hey," Katie said, peering out the window. "Isn't that the girl who waited on us from Downtown?

I saw Stacy skipping away from the building, in the same tousled state as a couple days before.

"Yea," I sighed as we watched her throw her head back in post-orgasmic glee. "I saw her on Monday when I went by Dante's to cut the demo. That's his new plaything."

"Eh, whatever. She'll be gone in a week," Katie laughed.

6

Day 8

I spent my day off on the Fourth of July helping my mother get ready for our big Independence Day barbecue-cum-surprise engagement party extravaganza. My mom had invited about 60 people, so there was a lot to be done. No one but our immediate family (and my best friends) knew what our party guests would ultimately be celebrating later this evening.

Mom was going all out, as she normally did for events. Clusters of red, white, and blue star helium balloons flew lazily above each peak in our wrought iron fence. Under a pitched white tent were rows of tables decorated in American flag tablecloths, and each table was topped with a red, white, and blue rose center-piece. Floating in our key-shaped, in-ground pool were patriotic-themed lily pads, with not-yet-lit candles placed in their centers. She had two full-service bars set up on our property and hired a catering service to take care of the cooking, bartending, and clean-up. We were even having a DJ! Most *weddings* weren't even this nice. Luckily, the weather cooperated, for it was a picturesque summer day.

After we had finished decorating, Mom handed me a last-minute grocery list about a mile long. Chuckling to myself over how over-the-top she was making this evening, I walked to my car. But something stopped me— the sight of Jimmy sitting in his running car, holding the ring box over the top of the steering wheel while puffing on a cigarette, a nervousness Mother Superior had no clue about. *Uh-oh.* Problems in paradise?

I opened the front passenger door. He was in such a deep trance, he didn't even flinch.

"You know I hate smoking," I choked as I climbed into the black Range Rover.

"Sorry," he mumbled, flicking the cancer stick out the window.

"What's wrong, Junior?" I asked while opening the window.

"I'm nervous about tonight," he said, clearly shaken.

"Why? It's only the single-most important question you'll ever ask in your lifetime," I joked.

"How do I ask?" he said, ignoring me.

I was stumped. Very rarely was I rendered speechless, but positive matters of the heart had a funny way of doing that to me, probably because I didn't have much experience in that field. (If you needed someone to deliver a 10-hour presentation on "The Art of the Heartbreak" however, I was your girl.) "I have no idea," I answered. "I have never asked someone to marry me before."

Jimmy took a deep breath, and I noticed a drop of sweat falling down his face.

I reached over and affectionately wiped it away. "Look, I don't think this is something you can plan," I reasoned. "You will find your words once you look into your future wife's eyes. Just go with the moment." I was shocked at the tender words falling out of my mouth.

He turned to look at me, the tension from seconds ago melting away. "I like that," Jimmy nodded.

"Me too," I smiled. But now it was my turn to stare into space. *Will a guy ever be freaking out to his sister about proposing to me?*

"Thanks, Car," Jimmy said, reaching over to hug me, thus snapping me out of my self-destructive thoughts.

"Anytime."

"Wait," Jimmy said, breaking our embrace, the anxiousness back in his voice. "Do you think she's going to say yes?"

"Okay, now you're being ridiculous. Of course, she's going to say yes!" I exclaimed. "And if she says no--which she's not going to do--then she's a fool. I mean, look at that rock, come on!"

■ ■ ■

I know this may come as somewhat of a shock, but Gwen said yes.

At around 10 p.m., Jimmy texted my mom the news, and she immediately rushed over to me and my friends, who were sitting around our fire pit bordering between buzzed and drunk.

"Guys!" she hissed. "Gwen said yes! They are on their way here now to tell everybody. Carla, get the video camera!" She then darted away.

Andrea, Katie, and I shook our heads in unison and laughed.

"Your mom doesn't seem excited," Dante smiled, putting his arm around Stacy. For Dante to bring a girl to a family function was *huge*. Apparently, she wasn't going anywhere, anytime soon.

"Not at all," I laughed, rising from my seat.

A few minutes later, Jimmy and Gwen appeared by the DJ booth. Gwen's eye makeup was smudged, and Jimmy's eyes looked bloodshot, but their wide grins said how over-the-moon happy they were. They didn't even notice I was standing nearby, holding the camcorder.

The music was lowered, and Jimmy got on the microphone. "Can I have everyone's attention please?" Jimmy is not one for public speaking, so the shock of seeing him on a mic made the partygoers stop dead in their tracks. "Gwen and I have an announcement!"

Jimmy waited a few moments for everyone to stampede over to the booth. They both smiled at each other. "We're engaged!" they triumphantly said in unison.

Everyone started clapping and screaming. I recorded my Grandma Teresa nearly having a heart attack, she was crying so hard. "I cannot-a believe my grand-a-son is engaged! I'm going to be alive to see one of my grand-a-kids get-a married!" she exclaimed in her Italian accent. (Grandma Teresa happens to be Mom's mom; the apple doesn't fall too far from the tree.) Speaking of, my mother was crying as if it was the first time she was hearing the news. My father beamed proudly. Everyone was drooling over the ring. It was one big love fest.

I decided I had enough footage (and enough in general) and shut the camera off. I walked back by my friends, who very smartly hung away from the riot.

"The cops are going to drive by and think there's a huge fight going on," Katie joked as I sat down next to her.

"I know, I didn't think an engagement would elicit such loud emotion," I replied while pouring another glass of wine.

"Well, that's because you've never been engaged before," Andrea replied half-jokingly.

I narrowed my eyes at her. "I don't remember you screaming your head off when Richard proposed to you."

"However, I do remember you screaming all the way to the bank," Dante joked.

"Why would she go to the bank after getting engaged?" Stacy asked. We all ignored her.

"You guys are just jealous, so I'm not even dignifying your jokes with a response," Andrea huffed.

"Well, speaking of Richard, where is he tonight?" Katie asked seriously.

"You know he doesn't do parties," Andrea said dismissively.

"What do you mean, you guys are at a function almost every night of the week," Katie snickered.

"Well, *these* kinds of parties," Andrea clarified.

"Hey, what's wrong with this party?" I asked defensively.

"Yeah! Besides, he would have fit in great!" Dante added. "There are people here tonight that are his age. You know, Grandma Teresa, Grandpa Michael..."

"Ha-ha-ha, cute," Andrea said sarcastically.

"She's married to an eighty-year-old?" Stacy whispered to Dante.

Just as Dante was going to explain, Jimmy and Gwen appeared.

"Hi, Sis!" Gwen exclaimed in her Southern drawl.

"Hi, Sis!" I greeted warmly, jumping up and hugging her. "Welcome to the family!"

"Let me see the ring!" Andrea cooed, grabbing Gwen's ring finger with her right hand. I rolled my eyes as I watched Andrea make a quick comparison of diamonds. She nodded in approval. Unbelievable.

"So how did Jimmy propose?" Katie asked.

"Oh, it was so romantic," Gwen said, breaking our embrace, and stared lovingly at my brother. "He had a picnic set up on the high school football field 50-yard line, and as the fireworks started, he got down on one knee and asked me to marry him."

"I was originally going to ask her way before the fireworks started, but the moment didn't feel right until then," Jimmy added, looking at me. I smiled.

"That's so cute, Junior!" Katie exclaimed.

"Thank you," Jimmy beamed.

"Baby, let's go to my house and show the ring to my parents before it gets too late," Gwen cooed, grabbing my brother's hand.

"Go ahead, make the rounds!" I exclaimed. "Have fun!"

"Bye, guys!" Gwen exclaimed.

They started walking away, but then Jimmy turned around to me. "Thanks again for your advice, Car," he said and followed his new fiancé.

"You gave proposal advice?" Katie asked incredulously as I sat back down.

"I wouldn't say that," I replied. "He was freaking out this afternoon about how and when to propose, and I guess I calmed him down."

"So what did you say?" Dante inquired.

I looked across the flames shooting up from the fire pit. "I told him to go with the moment, and that when he looked at his future wife, he'll know exactly what to do."

He lightly nodded, locking eyes with me.

"Simple, yet sweet advice," Katie quipped, breaking my and Dante's moment.

"You know me, I'm just a regular Cupid," I joked, my heart-beat returning back to normal.

"Well, let's do shots to celebrate!" Stacy, a girl I'd known for five minutes and wouldn't know my brother or Gwen if they punched her in the face, suggested. But the night was all about love, not about being catty…

"To the bar!"

■ ■ ■

Much later that night, long after everyone had gone home, I sat in my room, nursing the last of the bartender's stash of special merlot. I stared at the collage hanging over my desk, the one that Xander insisted I make. I had to admit, it was a fun exercise (definitely a better time than the torturous hell he's been putting me through). It made my dream life come into focus more clearly than it ever had before. The header of my collage read: "Life isn't about finding yourself. Life is about creating yourself." I carefully studied each image underneath--a female radio host behind the microphone; a picture of "Radio Row" at the Super Bowl; a female reporter interviewing Odell Beckham Jr.; the condo I wanted to buy on the water in Hoboken; a curvy-yet-toned brunette bikini model; the Eiffel Tower, where I want to be proposed to; a close-up of a sparkling Tiffany Novo engagement ring; a bank vault containing wads of money. I sighed happily. Although none of this was physically mine yet, I felt as though it could happen in the very near future.

However, my optimism disappeared when my eyes fell on the last two images: an exuberant couple smiling broadly, next to another couple kissing passionately on a white-sands beach.

In kindergarten, I had the biggest crush on Ryan McKabe. Since I didn't know how to verbalize those feelings (and couldn't spell), I drew him pictures of how he made me feel— pictures of rainbows and butterflies and hearts and smiley faces. But alas, a playground relationship was never formed. He got grossed out, ripped up my art, and ignored me the rest of the school year, thus setting the stage for many men to come.

I truly was one of those girls who had been "sweet 16 and never been kissed". My first kiss came months after my 16th birthday, in the backseat of Dustin Galanga's grandfather's Buick. We were close, and although I didn't find him very attractive, I fell for his insanely funny and sarcastic personality. We ended up dating for two and a half years, right up until college. But I was just going through the motions; I didn't have a deep connection with him. Our relationship ensured that I would have a date for our proms and someone to exchange birthday and Christmas presents with. We didn't even have sex, mainly because we both weren't ready. (My mother's constant "my wedding dress was white, and I expect yours to be too" guilt speeches surely didn't help on my end.)

Since we didn't have sex, I entered college as the lone virgin on my campus (and probably among many campuses across America). Needless to say, my scarlet "V" did not bode well for my dating life. I mean, you try telling a 20-year-old frat boy during a heated make-out session at 3:30 in the morning that you've never had sex before, and see how fast he runs. So it was not that I didn't have many opportunities to get it over with; it was that I figured that because I waited so long, I might as well hold out for someone special. So I left college the way I started--"Sweet 22 and never been sexed." They should have given me a special achievement award on graduation day.

And then, as discussed earlier, I met Mark right after getting my diploma. He ended up being my first true love, among other firsts. So much for special. Just because the virgin monkey was off my back, didn't mean I went the way of Dante and whored myself around once Mark and I broke up. The same values I had in college still held true. It had to be meaningful, and unfortunately, I hadn't met anyone worthy since.

I tapped my now-empty wine glass. You would think, working in New York City and meeting all kinds of people, I would have been bound to come across *somebody*. However, I had become convinced that if you didn't meet Mr. Right while in school, you were forever screwed. All the good ones were taken, gay or dead, and all that was left were the mental cases. A commitment-phobe wasn't whisking me away to Europe to get down on one knee; I was lucky to get a phone call after a first date. I honestly wouldn't have wished being single on my worst enemy.

The ringing of my cell phone interrupted my thoughts. Who would be calling me this late? I got up and grabbed it off its charger on my nightstand. Katie. "Is everything okay?" I answered, my stomach filled with dread.

She giggled. "Do you want to do speed dating?"

How did she know? I smiled to myself. "Are you still drunk?"

She giggled louder. "Yes."

"No, I don't want to do speed dating. Only losers do that."

"Aaaand what are we?" she slurred.

"True."

"Come on. Let's try it. Maybe we'll meet someone to buy us a rock like Jimmy bought Gwen."

"Hey, that's my line!" My friends were scaring me lately. Maybe the impending reunion had made them all step back and reevaluate their lives.

"I'm signing us up!" she announced.

I sighed. It was one in the morning; I wasn't about to argue. "Go for it," I conceded.

7

Day 16

That Friday after work (where I still hadn't heard any news on the hosting job), Katie met me in the city, and we went together to 747 Lounge in Downtown Manhattan. I quickly changed in my building's lobby bathroom, not wanting to get asked a million questions by my nosy male co-workers, who could be worse than teenage girls.

I was now down four pounds, and although my clothes still fit about the same, I felt so much better about myself. I had on a pink sundress with white high-heel sandals. Katie had on jeans and a flowy purple top.

"I'm so excited!" Katie shrieked as we waited in the fast-moving line.

"Why, this already sucks," I replied wryly, looking at some of the men who were also in line. They seemed to be another breed of human. We checked in with a pretty Asian girl, and she handed us a pen with an index card.

"Write your name and e-mail address on top, and then list the names of each guy you date, and then circle the ones you like," she explained in a snooty Manhattanite accent.

"Sounds easy enough," Katie replied.

"And please, make sure you write everyone's name. You don't want these guys feeling bad."

"Like they don't feel bad enough coming to speed dating?" I quipped. The girl glared at me. We walked into this beautiful white room that was flashing multicolored lights, blasting club music. Pieces of old-school airplanes adorned the walls (I'm assuming old 747s). The cocktail waitresses were dressed up like slutty flight attendants, and the bartenders were dressed like (gay) pilots. Only in New York.

Unfortunately, the rest of the scenery was unsatisfactory. The room was full of people I would *never* glance at had this been a normal situation. However, this was anything but normal. And not only was I forced to look at them, but I also had to "date" them.

We made a beeline for the bar. "This looks, um, interesting..." Katie trailed off.

"I'm ready to jump out of this plane when you are," I replied, taking a big sip out of my merlot.

Another pretty but snobby girl started ushering us girls into the VIP area. Our nightmare was about to begin.

"Welcome to New York Speed Dating!" A female voice boomed on the microphone. She went over the rules that I only half-listened to. I finished my wine and motioned for the cocktail waitress to get me another. Katie was already on beer number two.

The first guy who sat in front of me, Brad, wasn't that bad. He was Italian, and worked as a musician. He actually reminded me of a creepy, less charismatic version of Dante. "You have very nice ears," Brad remarked.

"Um...thank you?" I replied slowly, instinctively grabbing my earlobes.

"They are a nice shape, they fit your head very well. They stick out, but not too much. They are pretty flawless," he said, his eyes lit up with excitement.

Yikes.

Next up was Perez from Peru. Looked to be about 45, was a professor, and. . .why am I still talking about him?

"I can't do this," I whispered to Katie. We had 50 dates to go through. Two down, 48 to go.

Now batting was Zach, who seemed nice. We did our "date" at the bar, and he bought me a drink. Now we're talking!

As my buzz escalated, the dates were easier to handle. . .until I met Adnan.

Adnan menacingly stared at me with the Look of Death. He had a black backpack slung over his bony frame and placed another mysterious black bag on his lap. I wasn't sure if I should "date" him, or call the police. I introduced myself, and started to scribble his name.

"What are you doing?" Adnan barked.

"What does it look like I'm doing?"

"Don't write my name," he warned.

"Why? They told us to write everyone's name down," I said, confused.

"Don't write it," he warned, his black eyes glowing with rage.

"Okay..." I clicked the pen closed, and we sat there in uncomfortable silence until the buzzer went off.

Then there was Bradley, in all of his sweat-stained shirt glory. He plopped down in front of me and opened up with "I'm a nerd." What a powerful introduction!

"Why are you a nerd?" I asked, faking compassion.

"I don't know..." he trailed off, thinking of a reason. Then put up his finger. "Eureka! I am a nerd because I read the newspaper every day."

"That's not nerdy!" I genuinely exclaimed. "I read the newspaper all the time! I like it better than reading stories online."

"Really?" he said earnestly.

"Yup," I nodded.

"Wow," he laughed, clearly over-excited by the fact that he had something in common with a seemingly normal girl. But the "in common" stopped right there, because he then started talking about his job as a mechanical engineer, never ONCE asking me about my job (not that I would truthfully volunteer that information anyway). How selfish!

My next victim (or was it the other way around?), Nick, had a huge top hat on "to cover up my hair loss," he explained. He spent more time staring at the pilot bartenders than talking to me, so I think he was there to try and convince himself that he was straight. Mission not accomplished.

Boris was actually cute. He looked like a blond Clark Kent. However, he answered every question I asked by saying "I'm from Russia," in a very heavy accent. Superman, he was not.

Finally...FINALLY...it was over. I didn't even get through all the dates, there were so many people. (Speed dating seemed to be a lucrative business. Thirty bucks multiplied by 100 miserable souls equaled a ton of blood money.) I had spent two hours being totally fake; I was wiped out and in a horrible mood.

"Let's get the HELL out of here!" Katie groaned. Even the eternal optimist's spirit was shattered by speed dating.

I was going to just throw the index card away, but I decided to circle Zach's name. He seemed normal enough and who knows, maybe he could be The One. This would certainly be a funny story to tell our grandchildren. Katie ended up circling no names. I handed my card in, and we raced out of the bar. We were halfway down the street when I heard someone screaming my name at the top of his lungs.

"CAR-LAAAAAAAAAAAAAAAAAAAAAA!" A male cried out.

I couldn't make out the figure running towards us, but as it got closer, I realized it was Zach.

"Hi Zach," I said slowly.

"I looked...all over...for you. You ran...out of there...so fast," he panted, as he put his hands on his knees, trying to catch his breath. Katie and I just looked at each other, dumbstruck.

"Can I have your number?" he spit out.

Even though I had circled him as a match, there was no way I would want any more communication with the Speed Dating Midnight Screamer. "Uh, well, I circled your name on my card, so they'll be getting in touch with my information, so call me and we'll go out," I lied.

"Really!? Score!" He exclaimed, giving me two thumbs up. "Thanks, Carla!" Then he proceeded to run back to the bar, screaming into the night "I got a date, I got a daaaaaaaaaaate!"

"Got any other bright ideas?" I asked, my eyes fixated on Zach leaping in the air like a crazed gazelle in heat.

"Online dating?" Katie offered meekly.

■ ■ ■

We proceeded to go back to Katie's house and sign up for LoveAtFirstSite.com, the same dating service that aided Mark in his great escape. As much as it pained me to be on that website (and to sign up for online dating in general), I figured I'd earned some karma points with them since they most definitely owed me a boyfriend. Besides, what other options did I have at this point, the nunhood?

One thing was for certain. Anyone I met on here would be serious about getting into a long-term relationship because they put you through a thousand questions--compatibility survey-boot-camp--that took *hours* to complete. The faint of heart would not be able to sit through questions such as: "What flavor birthday cake do you prefer?" and "If you were a bird, what kind of bird would you be?" (So what, if we both put "chocolate fudge filling" and "flamingo" that meant we're destined to be together? Please.)

Once you completed the hours long endurance test, "Cupid" then "shot his arrow" at all your perfect matches, and a few at a time were delivered daily via a series of floating hearts that danced across your homepage. If you thought someone was cute, you "blew" them a kiss and started some sort of guided communication that eventually led to normal contact (that was, if you answered even *more* questions "correctly"). If you weren't feeling them, you "broke" their hearts and they were banished from your world forever. (Judging from the seven matches Cupid delivered immediately after I signed up, I was going to be breaking a lot of them.)

All this fun, for a three-month membership costing *only* 180 dollars! Honestly, the whole thing made me dizzy. What happened to the good old days of meeting someone through a friend of a friend, or at a club, or even at church? Hell, how about arranged marriages? Were speed dating and corny, gimmicky websites that cost half a week's worth of salary really what the single's society had resorted to?

8

Day 48

The fact that the only dates I had in the last month and a half were with the fifty freaks from speed dating tells you off the bat what I *didn't* do this summer. (LoveAtFirstSite.com FAIL!) The rest of my reunion resolutions didn't fare much better, no matter how many hours I stared at my vision board of dreams.

For starters, despite Xander's rigorous coaching, passionate pep talks and motivational morning text messages, I hit a plateau with my weight loss at the start of August - plateau as in gained five of the seven pounds I had lost. (In my defense, Xander didn't really explain that you aren't supposed to celebrate a torturous, hour-long jog on the beach by indulging in your favorite cookies 'n cream waffle ice cream dessert from the Point Pleasant boardwalk.) But how else was I supposed to get through the incessant talk of my brother's wedding, on top of everything else that *still* wasn't happening?

I knew I was disappointing Xander with my backward progress, and I actually felt guilty about letting down one of the only non-family member males that gave a shit about me. He was annoyingly relentless, but the condescending gorilla I met on Day One turned out to be a genuine sweetheart (whose silent crush on my best friend was growing by the minute...and seemingly, vice versa).

As for work, the days endlessly dragged on. I still had no word about my demo tape (not that I was expecting any), and Laney's rumor mill wasn't churning out any news on Tommy Jay's possible partner. On the outside, I was the same rah-rah Carla, but on the inside, I was screaming for mercy. In short, patience and positivity certainly weren't my virtues, and since I wasn't getting the instant results I needed, negativity took hold across the board.

And then, the Friday of Labor Day weekend happened. I was cleaning up the control room at work, fresh off another successful show, when I heard a man say, "Carla, can I talk to you in my office?"

I froze. I didn't need to turn around to know who that voice belonged to. "Sure Dan!" I chirped to my boss, Dan "The Man" Durkin. I grabbed my purse and followed him to his office.

Butterflies filled my stomach. I mean, it made perfect sense. Summer was over, and the NFL season started the next week. There was no better time than now to introduce Carla D'Agostino to the masses.

Then again....summer was over, and the NFL season was starting the next week. Was he cutting me to make way for new producer blood?

"Sit down." He motioned.

I took a deep breath, silently prayed he couldn't hear my pounding heartbeat, and smiled a little too sweetly.

"I listened to your tape," he began.

"Oh wow," I blurted out a little too quickly. "Thank you!"

"Who did you cut it with? His name wasn't on the label."

Definitely *not* the first question I was expecting. "Um, a friend of mine."

"What's his name?"

"Dante. Dante Ezra."

"What station does Dante work for?"

"Um, none."

"Really?" Dan said, surprised.

"Yea, he's a singer, but has absolutely *no experience* in this particular field," I carefully explained.

"Really?" Dan repeated, sounding even more surprised. "By any chance, do you have a number that I can reach him at?"

"Uh-huh," I muttered, taking a pen and scribbling it down on a Post-It from my purse. *What was going on?*

"Thanks, Carla," he said, sticking the yellow paper in the middle of his computer screen. "Now, as for the co-host's job with Tommy, we have finally come to a decision."

"Oh, great!" I said wearily. I knew what was coming next.

"We've decided to bring in Ruby Smith from K-F-S-S in Los Angeles."

My heart skipped a beat. I wasn't getting the job. I mean, I KNEW I wasn't based on the flow of conversation, but my fears were a reality. I blinked back tears. *Don't cry, don't let Dan see you cry.* "Oh, um, that's cool," I stuttered.

"We've been trying to get Ruby in here for years, but the timing was never right. Her station's been having issues lately, so she's been lobbying hard to come here. Her dream has always been to be on our airwaves, so here we are," Dan explained.

She's not the only one, I sadly thought. "When does she start?"

"We want her to start on Tuesday, right in time for the start of the NFL season."

"Great!" I feigned enthusiasm.

"Tommy is very excited to have her here too. She was his top choice. I think you three are going to make a great team," Dan remarked.

My face fell. *Tommy was behind all this?* "Go, team," I said through clenched teeth, slightly punching my fist in the air. Except that was not what I wanted to punch.

"Thanks, Carla, I know we can count on you to make Ruby's transition as smooth as possible," Dan replied.

"Thanks, Dan, I appreciate it," I lied. "Well, have a good weekend." I rose up and quickly bolted towards the door. I barreled down the hallway, and coming towards my direction was Tommy.

"Hey darling," he said.

"Ruby Smith was your first choice?" I snapped. "I thought you had my back. How could you?"

"Dags, please, let me explain...."

"I'm done with this conversation." And I was out the door.

■ ■ ■

It takes a lot for me to cry, so the fact that I spent my car ride home hysterically in tears speaks volumes. I felt betrayed, worthless, and angry. Judas, aka Tommy, called me three times, but I let it go to voicemail.

"He didn't even acknowledge me on my own tape?" I repeated in agony for the millionth time.

I wanted nothing more than to lock myself in my bedroom for the rest of the night, but my mother would probably call the fire department to break through my bedroom window once I ignored her millionth plea to "open up."

So where else could I go to cool down? Laney was on vacation so I couldn't call her to vent. I couldn't go by Andrea's; she was probably getting ready to go out to dinner at a swanky five-star restaurant with Richard. Katie was at work, and this was her busy time; I didn't want to bother her. Dante? Until I could find out why Dan gave me the third degree on him, I was staying as far away as possible.

So my only options left were to go to the gym for a much-needed cardio session, sit at a seedy local bar— alone— and drink, or drive my car off a cliff. But before I could make a U-Turn to the nearest mountaintop, my phone rang. Dante. My sixth sense kicked in and knew that Dan had already reached out for him. As much as I couldn't handle any more bad news, curiosity superseded my better judgment.

"Hey, I was just going to call you," I fibbed, trying to control the shakiness in my voice.

"I wish you had. It would have been nice to have gotten the heads up that your boss was going to call," Dante retorted, his voice booming all around me from my car's Bluetooth system.

"I've been on the phone since I left work," I lied again. "I didn't think he would call you on the Friday of Labor Day-"

"He wants me to interview on Tuesday for the overnight show host position," Dante interrupted.

"That's great!" I exclaimed, my heart in my mouth. "Dan worked in the music business before this. He has so many great connections, and he could be great asset-"

"Cut the crap, Carla," he interrupted again. "This dude needs an answer, and I wasn't going to do anything without talking to you first. I know this has to upset you."

"As a matter of fact, *Mr. Know it All*, it doesn't bother me at all," I coolly replied as I rubbed my aching chest with my free hand. Was this a heart attack?

"Oh, really?" He wasn't buying it.

"Not in the least. I have a full-time job with full benefits," I snipped. "What kind of friend would I be to get in the way of your finally making an honest living?"

He stayed silent for a minute. "Thanks, Carla, I appreciate it," he replied suspiciously.

I saw red. He was going on the damn interview! "Let me just ask you one question though. Is this something that you even want to do?" Surely my question had to be a dead give-away to my best friend that I did NOT approve of any of this.

"Well, I don't need to tell you how much I love sports, and I realize how this could open other doors for me. So why not?" Dante answered, obviously not taking the hint.

"Why not!" I repeated with a manic laugh as I strangled my steering wheel. Dante WANTED this job, the little backstabber! He and Tommy were going to be *great* friends. "What time does Dan want you to come in?"

"Ten o'clock in the morning."

"Awesome," I replied as I watched my knuckles turn white.

"Yeah..."

"Well, I'll talk to you later," I said, eager to hang up the phone. "Good luck."

"Wait!" Dante exclaimed. "Would you want to drive in together? Knowing me, I'll probably oversleep or something. Then I'll just take the train back after the interview."

Was he serious? "Of course," I sighed. The word "no" sometimes seemed to be the most elusive in my vast vocabulary.

"Great. Well, I'll talk to you Monday night. Stacy and I are staying at her aunt's shore house for the weekend. We leave tomorrow night."

"Have fun," I replied coolly, and we hung up.

By then I had arrived back in Honey Crest. I decided that, despite my lack of privacy, the only place I wanted to be was home. I pulled into my driveway and picked up my cell phone to turn it off for the night.

I dragged myself inside and faked a migraine to my inquisitive mother. When I walked into my bedroom, I was greeted by my once dazzling dream board taunting me. I promptly took it off the wall and slammed it face down on my desk. *You were a lot of help.*

I collapsed onto the bed, a fresh batch of warm tears streaming silently down my face. As I miserably lay there, I came to the sad realization that no matter how hard I worked, I didn't have a substantial future at WSPS or anywhere else in the business. At almost thirty years old, I have to start over from scratch. I'd be very ashamed at throwing up the white flag, but wasn't being an adult all about making tough choices and knowing when to walk away from something that wasn't working?

But where would I walk to?

9

Day 49

"Your boss doesn't have a clue!" Andrea exclaimed to me the next morning while walking out of Fitness World. I had just finished a killer kickboxing circuit training session with Xander (where I pretended to beat the crap out of a select choice of human beings), and Andrea was fresh out of a prenatal yoga class.

"He's not the only one," I puffed.

"You deal with too much drama," she laughed while rubbing her pregnant belly. "See, this is why I never wanted to work."

The worker bee in me wanted to defend my stance, but right then I totally saw her point. Maybe I too should marry rich and become a fellow trophy wife.

"Hey, Richard's at work. Do you want to come and see the babies' nurseries? The rooms are so adorable, it may make you feel better."

I stopped in my tracks. "You really think that's going to make me feel better?" We don't get invited to Andrea and Richard's too often, which is fine by me because their house is the epitome of everything I do not have in life: Love, money and success. (Okay, money and success.)

"No," Andrea laughed. "But I at least deserve points for trying."

"Sure, why not," I sighed. It's not like I had anything else better to do. I climbed into my little Mazda and followed her white BMW to the sprawling Deveroux compound. We walked into the mansion, as she was rattling off stats about cribs and diaper genies and things that we both already established I don't give a shit about, but I played along gamely.

"Want something to drink?" Andrea asked.

"Sure, I'll take a bottled water."

Before entering the kitchen, I studied the gigantic crystal chandelier hanging in her three-story foyer. I wondered how much that bougie light fixture cost? I probably couldn't even afford one of its light bulbs.

The unmistakable sound of a man groaning from upstairs broke my trance.

Worried, I rushed into the kitchen. "Andrea! Someone's upstairs! We have to call the police!"

"What?!" Andrea shrieked, dropping the open bottled water on the marble floor. There it was, the groaning again, much louder this time. She clutched her stomach and started breathing very heavily.

"Okay, stay calm for the sake of the babies," I urged her. "Sit down and call 9-1-1. I'll go upstairs and see what it is." I handed her the cordless phone that was sitting on the granite countertop, but she stopped me.

"I KNEW IT!" she screamed and stormed out of the kitchen.

"You knew what?" I asked frantically, following her through the foyer and up the sprawling staircase.

"I KNEW IT!" Andrea repeated

"Knew what? Andrea, you can't go up there, they could have a gun or a knife—"

"I KNEW IT!"

"YOU KNEW WHAT?!" I shrieked.

We stopped in front of the closed oak double doors that led to her bedroom. We heard the male screaming again coming from the other side. Now confident that this was not a burglary, I was going to hang back; after all, this was between husband and wife. But I was worried sick for her and twins' health, so I stood closely beside her. (Plus, my curiosity wasn't going to let me miss this show for the world.)

"RICHARD!" she screamed, and she threw the doors open. We both gasped at the sight before us. Butt-naked, in their California king bed, was her husband...with a short, stocky Spanish man who couldn't have been older than 25. Apparently, Richard's penchant for young blood spanned both sexes.

"Holy...shit, ," I breathed, my jaw dropping to the floor. I was too paralyzed to pick my hand up to cover my poor eyes.

"Andrea, I'm so sorry," Lover Boy apologized in a slight lisp.

"You know your husband's boyfriend?" I gasped.

"Andrea, I thought you were supposed to be at the gym," Richard howled, covering him and his lover with the navy Ralph Lauren comforter.

"And I thought you were supposed to be at work. AND STRAIGHT!" Andrea shot back. "I can't believe you. And with our landscaper, to boot?! You wanted to fire him last week!"

"Heyyyyy!" Lover Boy exclaimed.

She pulled the comforter off, and the men used their hands to cover their privates. "Come on Cupcakes, rise and shine." She rubbed her stomach, and before exiting the room, said defiantly: "You'll be hearing from my lawyer."

■ ■ ■

"Katie, can you save us a table? We have a major crisis on our hands," I explained cryptically into my iPhone. I glanced at Andrea, who sat next to me in silence.

"There are no tables here. Ever," Katie answered glumly.

"What do you mean? What's wrong?" I shrilled, not sure if I could take any more bad news this weekend.

"Kettle Black was shut down effective last night. The owners didn't pay their taxes. I'm out of a job. So what's going on with you?"

I gasped. "Well, Richard is gay, Andrea and I just caught him in bed with their landscaper. Meanwhile, W-S-P-S passed me over yet again for the co-host job, but they want to give Dante a show."

It was Katie's turn to be surprised. "Meet me at Downtown. We need beverages."

■ ■ ■

We sat at our usual table in silence. No words could justify how each of us was feeling.

"Hey, girls!" Stacy, Dante's girlfriend, greeted warmly. "What can I get you to drink?"

"Heineken."

"Merlot."

"Okay. Andrea?"

Andrea didn't say anything. I lightly touched her hand. "Hey, what do you want to drink?"

"Oh, um, water," she muttered.

"And keep it *allllll* coming," Katie added, making an air circle with her index finger. Stacy nodded and quickly walked away.

"Had I known she was working, I would have suggested we go somewhere else. I thought she'd be packing for her romantic Jersey Shore getaway," I muttered.

"Who would have thought that Dante would have his shit together more than all of us combined?" Katie quipped.

Andrea continued to say nothing.

"Well, not that this is a contest, but as crappy as I feel, at least I still have a job and don't have an outted significant other," I reasoned. "Besides, I can't bitch too loudly about my situation because his girlfriend is our waitress. Since Andrea is still shell-shocked, Katie, I give you the floor."

"The owners of Kettle Black were sent to jail by the IRS," she responded. "I spent all morning checking positions in bakeries and cafes in the area, but no one is hiring. I have no idea what to do."

"Jesus Christ," I muttered. Voluntarily quitting WSPS suddenly didn't seem like such a slam-dunk decision, when you looked at it from a monetary standpoint. (Making barely above minimum wage was better than nothing.)

"Will you guys help me look for lawyers?" Andrea suddenly asked.

"Of course!" Katie and I replied in unison.

"Will you guys help me move back into my parents' house?"

"Of course!"

"Thank you," Andrea sniffled, drying her eyes with a napkin.

"I know it must be hard," Katie said sympathetically. "You can't blame yourself!"

"Yes, I can." Andrea cried harder. "I figured he was up to something."

"How?"

"Because we barely had sex, all right?" Andrea stated bitterly as she threw down the tear-stained napkin on the table.

Katie gasped.

"Oh stop it, Katie. Don't act surprised," Andrea sneered.

There was no disbelief coming from me. I knew Andrea sold her soul when she married such an old man, but I always thought she was at least performing her wifely duties (while hopefully blindfolded, judging by what I'd just seen).

"So you knew he was a homosexual?" Katie grilled.

"No, I had no idea about him being gay," Andrea sighed. "When we first started dating, everything was great. But after we got engaged, our sex life fizzled out. I thought it was weird, but what was I going to do? I wasn't going to suffer the humiliation of a broken engagement..."

"And finding your husband in bed with another man *isn't* humiliating?" I blurted out.

"...So I stuck it out, thinking it would get better," Andrea continued, ignoring me. "But it's been next-to-nothing. We've basically been leading separate lives for the past two years."

"I didn't know I had company," I added.

"I said next-to-nothing, not completely nothing. Clearly," Andrea shot back, pointing at her pregnant belly.

I narrowed my eyes at her.

"So you had your suspicions, but you did nothing about it? Why wouldn't you just leave?" Katie probed.

Andrea looked at her as if she just sprouted a third head. "Yeah, like I would *ever* give up this lifestyle."

She definitely got points for honesty; at least she was a *self-aware* gold digger!

"Ok, fine, but why would you get pregnant with his babies?"

"Because that's what you *do* when you get married," Andrea exhaled. Then, her tone got hushed. "But there's more."

I knew it. Something didn't add up. The only thing Andrea enjoyed more than bottomless bank accounts, couture fashion, and being put on a pedestal was sex. Since she lost her virginity at thirteen (an event which, oddly enough, occurred in my basement; I'm surprised my house didn't combust into flames after such sin was committed!), Andrea has had an extremely salacious sexual appetite that many of her lovers found hard to keep up with. So you mean to tell me that she's been with this dude for years and never got it from him…or elsewhere? Impossible. Not only would I bet my life that she had been cheating throughout the duration of her marriage, I could personally guarantee who she has been currently cheating with.

I had enough of Katie's questioning. It was my turn to step in, shine the figurative interrogation light into her face, and crack this case once and for all.

Of course, before I could lay into her, Stacy appeared with our drinks. "You girls ready to order?"

"Yes!" Andrea bellowed, happy to be off the hook. She picked up a menu. "I'll have-"

"Come back in a little bit, Stacy," Katie interrupted.

She gave us a quizzical look. "Is everything okay? I mean, I *am* Dante's girlfriend now. I consider you girls friends, so if you need to talk, I'm here." Such off-base rhetoric would usually have triggered an eye-roll out of me, but my eyes were too busy cutting into Andrea, whose hands were visibly shaking while they held up the laminated menu.

"This is none of your business," Katie retorted.

I broke my stare to view Stacy's reaction. "Whoa. Okay," she said, her hands shooting up defensively. "Just call me over when you are ready."

"Katie, why did you tell her to leave?" Andrea whimpered as we watched Stacy jog away. "I'm *starving*!"

Katie and I simultaneously crossed our arms. Andrea turned back to us and studied our stern gazes.

"Ok fine," Andrea hissed, sitting back down. "But I don't want you guys to yell, criticize, or lecture me, especially YOU," she pointed at me.

"What makes you think I'm going to do any of those things?" I asked innocently.

"Just tell us," Katie demanded.

Andrea sighed. "Ok, when Richard and I stopped being intimate...I fell in love with someone else."

"What the hell, Andrea!" Katie scolded. "You're sitting here crying over your husband deceiving you, yet you are doing the same thing to him!"

"And you thought I was going to be the one to get on your case," I remarked.

"You're not listening, Katie. I said I fell in love with someone else, but nothing about sleeping with someone else," Andrea corrected. "This guy is too much of a gentleman to even kiss me while I'm in this delicate state."

"Is it Xander?" I finally asked.

Katie gasped. "The personal trainer you guys work out with?"

"How did you know?" Andrea panicked, not even bothering to deny it. "Did he tell you something?"

"He did not say a word, but considering you told him about your pregnancy before your own family, I'd say it was a tad obvious that you two were close."

"I really like him, you guys," Andrea genuinely smiled. "I have never connected with anyone like I did with Xander. But..."

"But..." Katie and I repeated in unison.

"How can I leave one of New Jersey's most prestigious, richest doctors...for a personal trainer at a gym?"

"If you truly love him, who cares how much money he makes?" Katie pointed out.

"The money thing matters, Katie. I'm sorry, but it's true. What do you guys want me to do, go from caviar to McDonald's? Alimony and child support will only cover so much."

I sympathetically looked at Katie's puzzled expression. Poor, delusional Katie. This is a girl who believes in equality for all, including the right to love freely among tax brackets.

"Sorry Andrea, but get your food stamps ready. It looks like the decision was already made for you," I quipped.

Andrea's pout signaled the end of the conversation, and the three of us silently studied our menus. As I debated between ordering a grilled chicken Caesar salad or a bacon burger with waffle fries, my mind went to Andrea's predicament. No matter what, she would be provided for— both in the form of a human ATM machine or in an actual relationship— so on some level, she was going to come out a winner.

I wouldn't describe Andrea's situation as a good thing, but some people really do have all the luck.

■ ■ ■

Two hours later, we helped Andrea pick up her essential items from the Deveroux estate. (It would take an entire fleet of U-Hauls to collect the rest.) Richard and the landscaper, thankfully, weren't upstairs enjoying round two.

After we had finished packing, we drove Andrea to her parents' house. We sat with her as she turned on the waterworks and tearfully broke (part of) the news to her family. Her mom and dad were upset, yet understanding. They hugged their little girl tightly and whispered softly in her ear. Despite the circumstances, the scene before me was kind of touching.

The whole time, I imagined this same conversation going down in my household. Dad would immediately threaten to kill my rogue husband. Meanwhile, my brother would sit there, laughing like a ten-year-old: *"Ha-ha-ha, Carla's husband is GAY!"* And of course, my mother would be offering sweet, comforting words such as: *"How blind could you have been to not know your husband was sleeping with other men?"* or *"Boy, you must have been a real beast to live with to make him go the other way!"* or *"Did you get an HIV test?"*

The Cleavers we D'Agostinos are not.

10

Day 52

"I can't believe you drive into the city every day. This traffic sucks," Dante remarked.

"*You* were the one who asked to ride in together. You could have taken the train if you wanted to," I shot back.

As laborious as Labor Day Weekend turned out to be, a huge part of me did not want it to end since I knew a wider scope of misery was awaiting me on the other side— the first post-news gym session with Xander, a painful car ride into New York with WSPS's future star, and a pre-show meeting with the woman who took my job and the guys who gave it to her. All this, before 9 a.m.

The morning's workout with Xander had not been easy, and I was not talking about drop sets; I wanted to cry for the man. Surely, falling in love with a morally conflicted married woman was *not* on his vision board. To keep myself from accidentally saying anything hostile to Dante, I thought back on my morning at the gym.

"Albert Einstein once said: 'In the middle of difficulty lies opportunity,'" Xander had proclaimed after listening to me vent.

"Wow," I'd gasped while on the floor struggling through mountain climbers, "you actually have these things memorized, huh? You're like a human meme generator."

"They are pearls of wisdom given to us by the greatest influencers on our society. I try to apply them in my everyday life."

To what? Get you through your weight lifting? *I'd thought mordantly. "Well I'll see your quote and raise you another," I'd told him, pushing myself off the mat. "Vince Lombardi: 'Winning isn't everything, it's the only thing.'"*

"And that kind of "all-or-nothing" mentality is the exact reason why you are in the quandary you are in. Life is not a contest."

I shrugged. "That mantra worked pretty well for Lombardi."

"So did this one: 'Perfection is not attainable, but if we chase perfection we can catch excellence.'"

"Eh, what do you know," I'd retorted, slinging my towel over my shoulder. "You don't even like football."

"No, I definitely appreciate it, it's just that the train is so much easier," I heard Dante say, interrupting my daydream.

"What are you talking about?" I barked.

"Driving in the city versus taking the train in," Dante replied slowly.

"Oh, right. Well, basing my life on someone else's schedule is not me; I don't need to tell you that. I like the freedom to come and go as I please. Besides, we have our own garage; we're right outside the Holland Tunnel, and they cover gas and tolls. I'd rather sit in traffic than next to someone who wasn't taught proper hygiene."

"I understand," Dante said quietly. He was clearly picking up on the animosity of my tone.

"Besides, you'll get your train experience when you leave the station, unless you plan on sticking around nine hours to wait for me to bring you home."

"No, that's okay." Dante gulped.

I surfed through my preset FM radio channels and settled on a classic rock station. I turned up the volume, in hopes of turning down Dante's attempts at more conversation. I was in no mood to entertain. Yeah, well, that didn't work so well.

"SO W-S-P-S, HUH? WHO WOULD HAVE THOUGHT WE'D BE WORKING TOGETHER? THAT'S SO COOL," Dante shouted over the blaring Metallica music.

"NAIL THE INTERVIEW FIRST, THEN WE CAN TALK ABOUT HOW 'COOL' IT IS," I yelled back.

More silence.

"WHAT DID YOU DO THIS WEEKEND?"

"The usual."

"WHAT DID YOU SAY?"

"THE USUAL!"

More silence. I noticed Dante mutter something to himself, and then watched him lean over and turn the volume knob down.

"Hey, this is *my* car! You don't get to control the music!" I protested.

"And these are *my* ear drums. You don't get to ruin them!"

Fine. I wasn't about to argue. Besides, he would need those *precious* ears to field calls while on the air.

More silence.

"So how are Andrea and Katie doing?" Dante asked. "I haven't talked to them in a while."

"I don't know. Call them, especially Andrea. She has some interesting news."

"Oh yeah? Like what?"

"Did I stutter? I said to call her. I'm not at liberty to say."

More silence.

"Stacy and I had an awesome time down at the shore. We could just lie there for hours and talk about anything. I think I'm starting to really fall in love with her," Dante gushed. My chest clenched at his words.

"And we're here!" I announced, jerking my car into the garage. I did a quick Sign of the Cross as I jumped out.

"Good morning Carla!" the garage attendant, Charles, greeted. "Is this your boyfriend?"

"Definitely not," I chuckled. "This is my friend, Dante."

"Nice to meet you, Dante," Charles said. "You have a good girl here."

"The best," Dante added, shaking his hand.

"See you later, Charles!" I waved.

"Have a good day, baby doll!"

We took the elevator up to the 30th floor without saying a word to each other. I was still processing what Dante had said before about Stacy; he had *never* talked about a girl like that. How had a barely attractive waitress with an IQ of a pebble made him change his playboy ways?

Dante's blue eyes lit up when the elevator doors opened to reveal the WSPS red logo on the wall. "This is so cool," he excitedly breathed.

"Get a hold of yourself," I ordered. "The studio hasn't been upgraded in fifty years; it's nothing to get crazy over."

Laney saw us and buzzed us in.

"Well, hello, young dearie!" Laney exclaimed.

"Hello, Laney!" I exclaimed, showing joyful emotion for the first time this morning. "This is my friend, Dante. He has an interview with Dan today. Dante, this is Laney, the longest-tenured person at the radio station. She knows *all*."

"Hi Laney," Dante said, extending his hand.

Laney started mock hyperventilating as she shook Dante's hand. "Carla, you are always complaining that you can never meet anybody, yet you hang out with people that look like *this*?"

I laughed. "Dante and I grew up together; we're like family."

"What's a little incest between friends?" Laney bellowed. "He's like an Italian Ken Doll! Hey, can I be your Barbie? I'm not tall and blonde, but you know, hee, hee, hee," she cackled.

Dante looked at me, clearly taken aback by Laney's over-the-top personality. I smirked. What, poor little Dante couldn't handle an audience? How was he going to be able to handle the lunatic New York Mets fans calling up to complain about the team being out of the pennant race in May? "Laney, I'll be right back, let me take Dante to Dan's office."

"Okay. But hurry back, Momma Hen has some eggs she'd like to hatch."

"Oh, I will!" I was salivating over what Laney had to tell me; she probably wanted to give her first take on WSPS's new hire, Ruby Smith.

"Laney's...interesting," Dante commented as we walked down the hall.

"She's the best," I corrected. "If it weren't for her, I'd really lose my mind in this place."

I knocked on Dan's door. He flung it open, and I saw Tommy sitting on the black couch with a striking blonde woman who I knew was Ruby, thanks to the Google stalking spree I'd partaken in after the Andrea drama subsided.

It must have taken Ruby three hours to get ready for work that day. For starters, her makeup looked professionally done. She wore a cream three-piece suit, with dusted gold pumps and accessories to match. Her short golden, pixie haircut fit her round face perfectly. Overall, her look was flawless. I self-consciously pulled at my New York Yankees baby doll tee as I gave a quick glare to Tommy, who slightly hung his head in shame.

"There she is!" Dan greeted warmly. He was obviously putting on an act for the new hire(s).

"Hi Dan," I replied sweetly, joining in the charade. "This is Dante Ezra."

"I know I'm mad early, but I took the ride in with Carla so I wouldn't get lost on the way to our interview," Dante added.

'Mad early?' I snickered. *Way to be professional, Dante.*

"It's all good!" Dan exclaimed. "I'm Dan 'The Man' Durkin. It's nice to meet you!"

"The pleasure's all mine," he replied, smiling broadly.

I wanted to throw my hands up and walk away; it was complete love at first site.

"I'll tell you what. Carla, come in the office so you can meet Tommy's new co-host. Dante, wait here and I'll be with you shortly. Cool man?"

I cringed at Dan's desperate attempt to be "hip." I've been around Dan long enough to know when he was trying to impress someone, and he was laying it on thick for Dante.

"Cool!" Dante exclaimed. In the corner of my eye, I watched him take a seat in the sterile waiting area.

I walked in and waited for Dan to introduce me. Ruby didn't even acknowledge that a new person had entered the room. She continued to stare into space, her hands neatly folded in her lap.

"Ruby, this is your producer, Carla D'Agostino."

Ruby snapped to attention. Like a lioness eyeing her prey, she looked me up and down, one eyebrow cocked up.

"It's so nice to meet you," I lied, extending my hand.

She continued to stare me down, not bothering to stand up to greet me and leaving my hand dangling in the air. When it became evident that she had no intention of returning the gesture, I slowly placed my right arm down at my side. What? They don't do handshakes in LA? Should I have air kissed her instead?

"Does she know what she's doing?" Ruby questioned in a rich, deep voice that was better quality in person than through my MacBook speakers, and admittedly much nicer than my raspy vocals. So *that* was why she got the job. Dan thought she orated like a pre-Bobby Brown Whitney Houston while I sounded like a poor man's version of Demi Moore.

But wait a minute; did she actually just question my producer abilities? Say what you want about my on-air skills (and evidently, there's not much to say), but I am confident that I am the *best* at what I get paid to actually do.

I opened my mouth to answer, but she put her hand up to stop me. "I believe the question was directed to Mr. Durkin," Ruby said sternly.

My eyes widened in shock. *Was this woman for real?* I looked at Tommy, who hung his head a little lower than before.

"Carla has been with the station for five years. She's a very solid producer," Dan explained.

Okay, so I was not "the best," I was just solid. Duly noted.

"That's reassuring because I've worked with some SHIT producers in my day," she declared. "I'm going to assume that, since this is the station's most important show, Karen knows what she's doing."

I pointedly cleared my throat. "It's Carla."

Ruby turned her attention to me. Judging by her facial expression, you would have thought I had just lit her closet full of

Louboutin's on fire. "I thought I told you I was addressing Mr. Durkin."

"I understand that," I replied slowly. "But you got my name wrong. I'm not Karen, I'm Carla."

Ruby rolled her eyes. "Whatever."

I shook my head in amazement. Thirty seconds into our initial meeting I could tell that this working relationship was going to be a disaster of epic proportions. I had prepared myself for a lot of different circumstances and emotions leading into today, but I had *not* seen this coming. As I mentioned earlier, this "solid producer" had done her homework on Ruby, and it went beyond studying her vast modeling portfolio. I read her glowing biography, listened to her hard-hitting interviews and watched fan-made tributes on YouTube, all while scarfing down my large cookies n' cream frozen yogurt (hey, it was better than ice cream!) and not feeling the *least* bit jealous. So while I had thought Google gave me everything on Ruby short of her social security number, it missed any mention of her deplorable personality. (I guess someone forgot to meta tag *Ruby Smith Major Bitch.*)

"Okay then, so I think we're all set," Dan said happily, clapping his hands together, pretending to be oblivious to the shit storm brewing in front of him. "Carla and Tommy, why don't you take Ruby and show her around the studio and newsroom, and you can chat about today's upcoming show." He opened the door to rush us out.

Ruby grabbed her briefcase, adjusted the cream blazer that fit over her very slender frame, and walked out ahead of us. Tommy and I raced to catch up with her, but someone pulled me back.

"Who is that woman, and who the hell does she think she is?" Dante whispered, his face full of concern. "I watched her walk out of the office and-"

"I can't talk about that now!" I hissed, cutting him off. "Let go of me!"

Dante released my arm, and I sprinted down the long hallway. "So Ruby, this is the newsroom," I heard Tommy say. I appeared next to him, nodding with a big, fake smile plastered across my face. We watched as she eyeballed the messy row of worn-out desks, beaten chairs, and archaic computers.

"This place is a pigsty. You would think one of most lucrative radio stations in the country could afford to have a nicer work environment," Ruby scoffed.

You would also think a person so beautiful on the outside would have a soul to match, I wanted to shoot back.

"Let me show you the studio real quick before the morning show goes back on air," Tommy said, without missing a beat. As she slithered into our run down studio, I shuddered at what her reaction was going to be. If she was turned off by our newsroom...

"WHAT THE HELL IS THAT SMELL?" Ruby exclaimed, running out of the small room as if it were on fire. Her face was contorted, as if in extreme pain, and she pinched her nose for added dramatic effect.

"You will get used to it," Tommy replied nervously.

"Vanilla candles will become your best friend," I joked.

"It smells like mothballs and death!" Ruby shrieked, waving the air in front of her face.

"You will get used to it," Tommy meekly repeated.

Ruby sighed. "I cannot believe I am in a studio in New York City. Los Angeles was top-of-the-line everything. I am *not* impressed."

I bit my lip to prevent me from saying: *"Then go back to Los Angeles!"*

"But did you see the view? It's stupendous; you see almost all of Manhattan!" Tommy exclaimed.

"How could I pay attention to such details? I couldn't breathe!" Ruby wailed.

"But the Empire State Building is, like, right in your face," Tommy weakly protested. "You're from California. That's supposed to impress you."

"Do you think I have time to think about *stupid* buildings while I'm putting on a daily five-hour performance?"

"Performance? This isn't Broadway. What are we going to do, tap dance through our program?" Tommy shot back.

As I watched the two hosts ping-pong back and forth, all I could think about was how to get Ruby to the top of the "stupid building" and push her off without getting caught. After a couple more minutes of further inspection, Ruby did a sharp pirouette in our direction. "Thomas and Karen, tell me; is today some sort of dress down day?"

I didn't even bother to correct her. "No, why?"

"So explain to me why you two are in jeans. Don't you know that is not proper work attire?"

"As long as you are not looking like a complete slob, casual attire is allowed, including jeans," Tommy responded defensively.

"You have to dress for the part. Jeans don't scream 'I'm successful', they say 'Mailing it in,'" she stated, smoothing out her cream skirt.

"Jeans also say 'I'm here to focus on my job and move around comfortably.' The newsroom is not a runway," I replied.

"Are you talking back to me, Karen? Do we have a problem?" Ruby snapped.

I looked her dead in the eye. "Nope." That was no lie; this situation had more going on than just "a" single problem.

"Good. Besides, I've worked as a model, and it's a good thing you don't pretend to be anything of the sort. Someone of your height and build would never make it in the fashion world."

My mouth dropped in horror as I watched her sashay away. I had made no mention of wanting to be "anything of the sort," yet she just basically called me short and fat!

"Don't listen to her. Look at Kim Kardashian. If she could make it, so could you," Tommy lightheartedly remarked.

■ ■ ■

Not only was she a spineless, vulgar wench in real life, but on the air, Ruby sucked. In the clips I had heard from LA, that wasn't the case. She was charming, bright and relatable. (She was also hosting by herself...gee, I wonder why.)

Her animosity towards the whole WSPS situation carried over to the show. She was rude to callers, had no chemistry with Tommy, and shared her disdain for her new home studio more than once. Another thing that was evident was that she had not done her homework on the New York sports scene. I couldn't even begin to count the times Tommy and I had to bail her out by feeding her player statistics and names. (Ironically, I got more airtime with Ruby there than ever before!) This fact was not lost on Ruby; every time I spoke, her head practically did a 360-degree rotation. Oh well!

In short, our first show was an utter disgrace. I wasn't sure how much more of this I could take, and judging by the listeners writing into the show via Twitter, they couldn't take much more either.

"In this business, it's not who you know, it's who you blow, hee-hee-hee," Laney cackled as she popped her head into the control room during a commercial break. "Start opening wide, Carla!"

After the show, I packed up my belongings as quickly as possible so I could run out without talking to anyone. However, the sight of Ruby standing menacingly in the control room doorway thwarted my plan.

"Uh, Karen, I have a very important question to ask."

"It's *Carla*, but yes?"

"When I was in Los Angeles my producer NEVER participated on-air with me."

How did I know this was coming? "Okay…"

"So my question is: Why did you feel compelled to intrude on the show this afternoon?"

I knew I had to choose my words carefully here. This ego maniac would fly through the roof if I told her the real reason, which was that I had to bail out her dumb ass in order to save the show. (Or that *other* real reason, which was that I should have been in her chair and she should have been in California getting a colonic.) "If you recall, Ruby, I never just freely cut in on you guys," I replied in the nicest way possible. "Tommy would ask me a question, and I would answer. What was I supposed to do?"

"Well, we are going to change that right now. Wait one second," she ordered, holding up her palm to me. She leaned out into the hallway. "Thomas, can you come into the control room please?"

I started to get dizzy from my rocketing blood pressure and leaned on the desk for support.

Tommy walked in, looking as tired as I've ever seen him. His usual jovial mood had taken a beating from today's brutal broadcast. "What's up, ladies?"

"There seems to have been a misunderstanding here," Ruby stated. "Our producer seems to be caught in between wanting to be on-air versus actually doing her job."

"What do you mean?" Tommy questioned.

Ruby threw her hand on her hip. "This show is not a trio; she is not to interject her thoughts, and you are not to invite her to do so."

"But I like doing that. She adds another dimension to the show," Tommy argued.

"She's a producer. She's to be out of sight, out of mind," Ruby shot back.

Tommy looked at me, startled.

"Do we all have an understanding?" Ruby asked.

"Of coursc, Ruby," I replied sweetly, bailing both of us out. Tommy's jaw dropped.

"That's good, Karen because I would hate to go to Dan with this matter," Ruby threatened. Tommy and I watched her march out.

After a few more moments, Tommy turned to me. "Carla, I'm really sorry about how all this went down."

I snickered. "Our advertisers and listeners are too. Marconi must be spinning in his grave."

"I'm not talking about today, I'm talking about this whole situation," Tommy replied quietly.

"What is there to be sorry about? You and Dan both got what you wanted."

"You're wrong, Carla. I didn't want Ruby. I made it very clear that if I was being forced into having a co-host after all these years doing the show solo, that I only wanted you. But Dan had his sights on Ruby, and thought you were too inexperienced to take on such a huge role."

"INEXPERIENCED?" I shouted, my eyes welling up with tears. How was *that* for confirmation that he listened to my portion of the demo? "I know you, this show, this station and this city like the back of my hand, yet he still thinks I'm clueless?!"

"Shhhh, compose yourself, I don't want anyone to hear you," Tommy whispered, hugging me tightly. I buried my face into his shoulder and took a few deep breaths to regain my composure.

"Why didn't you tell me about all this before?" I sobbed.

"I called you all weekend, you knucklehead," Tommy replied playfully, breaking our embrace. "Ask my wife, I was a wreck the entire weekend over this."

"This is just so hard," I sniffled.

Tommy grabbed both of my shoulders and looked me in the eye. "Look, Carla, you are so young. In this industry, it takes *years* to make it happen for most people. I'm in my fifties and reached a level of success only fairly recently. You have to be willing to tread water for a long, long time, and unfortunately, there is no promise that it will work out. Nothing good comes easy."

"That's reassuring," I deadpanned.

"You have to have faith that down the road, your hard work will pay off."

I let out a loud, exaggerated sigh. "I don't have time for down the road; my ten-year high school reunion is nine months away, and I need it to happen now!" I immediately felt ridiculous confiding to Tommy about my reunion insecurities. I was sure a 50-something man could care less about a girl's quarter-life crisis.

Tommy's boisterous laughter confirmed my assumption. "Are you serious? In today's world, you think anybody your age has achieved much of anything?"

"Without getting into the numbers of it, yes they have," I replied wryly.

"Relax, please?" Tommy pleaded. "You are more than fine. You have everything going for you, and you are going to sit there and worry about high school?"

I shrugged. I didn't want to extend the conversation any further by painstakingly explaining to Tommy how my life resembled a hamster wheel, and I was too tired to put up with any jokes or positive reinforcements.

"So...are we friends again?" Tommy asked.

"Friends," I smiled, and we hugged again. "For the record, what are your thoughts on Ruby?" I asked as we broke apart.

"The same as yours, and more," Tommy laughed.

"Fair enough. Let's get out of here." As we walked out of the control room, the singing of a very familiar male voice floated down the hallway. Tommy and I stopped in our tracks.

"Wow, is Stevie Wonder in the building?" Tommy quipped. "Who the heck is that?"

I had a pretty good idea. "Tommy, I'll see you tomorrow." I barreled down the hallway towards Dan's office. I noticed that the door was cracked open, and I peeked in. There was my best friend, eight hours after his scheduled interview, standing in the middle of the room singing The Beatles classic *Yesterday* while my boss, sitting on the edge of his couch, followed along on his acoustic guitar. Dan's face was filled with admiration as he watched Dante soulfully belt out the lyrics.

The day's events faded away as I was drawn into Dante's rendition. I had listened to him croon an infinite amount of times, but each performance captivated me as if I were hearing him for the first time, and I was not the only one. No matter what venue he was at— coffee shops, bars or catering halls— people of all ages dropped what they are doing to listen to him sing. Not a lot of performers could take hold of a room the way Dante did so effortlessly. He was such a huge talent and the world didn't know what it was missing.

I shook my head to break my thoughts. This was not the time to wax poetic on Dante's many gifts; I needed to get to the bottom of why he was still there.

On one hand, maybe the interview never happened. Dan and Dante could have simply agreed that sports talk radio wasn't his thing and bonded over their love for music. Dan might have asked Dante to stay so he could try him out before handing his demo over to his record executive friends. On the other hand, this could have been a celebratory jam-out session with WSPS's newest talent.

Which scenario do you think I was pulling for?

I waited until after the song was over to make my grand entrance. I pulled on the doorknob. "Hey, guys."

"Hi, Carla!" Dante exclaimed.

Dan smiled as laid the guitar on his lap.

"Dante, what are you still doing here? You've been here forever," I asked innocently.

"Dan and I got into this big music discussion and we kind of just got lost rocking out. He plays an amazing guitar."

"This kid could sing the pants off anything," Dan added. "He's unreal."

I crossed my arms over my chest. "I see. But onto more important matters...Dan, what did you think of the show?"

"Um, I caught a few minutes of it," he responded distractedly as he started to fiddle with the guitar strings. "It sounded great! Good job."

I was irate. He hadn't listened to a *second* of the train wreck! What kind of radio boss blew off his paying job to play music with a stranger all day instead of listening to the first of a brand new show, a show that he (foolishly) put together? Dan was a little bit left of center, but he was so anal about the WSPS brand. If he had actually worked instead of playing, he would have known that his sports empire was in serious jeopardy. But instead, he ditched work to play with his crush, much like a love-struck high school freshman girl who skips classes to go make out with the hot senior boy behind the football field bleachers.

"Well Dante, I'm getting out of here," I said through gritted teeth. "Do you want a ride, or are you guys having a slumber party?"

"I'll leave with you. Dan, thank you again for the opportunity, I can't wait to start on this weekend."

My right hand went instinctively over my heart. I thought I had just stopped breathing.

"The pleasure is all mine. Get me your demo so I can give it to my label friends."

"Of course! I'll bring some CDs with me on Saturday and leave them on your desk!"

"Sounds good, bro!" Dan and Dante pounded fists, and Dante motioned for me to follow him out. I didn't even bother to say goodbye to Dan.

"So what do you start on Saturday?" I immediately grilled Dante as we exited Dan's office.

Dante broke out into a huge grin. "Dan offered me the weekend overnight shows!"

The worst had happened. The same man who told me I had to "work my way up" and still dubs me as "inexperienced" after being with the station for five years had just offered Dante, a college dropout, an on-air job on the spot. "That's, um, great!" I lied.

"I'll be working Saturday and Sunday morning, two to six," Dante added.

"You're okay with giving up your weekends?" I asked innocently. Most people have been passed out for hours by the time 2 a.m. rolled around; for Dante, 2 a.m. was dinnertime.

"I have a steady girl now, I'm not into going out and causing trouble like I used to." He shrugged.

"That's right," I muttered.

"But the only reason I'm doing it is because the dude seems to like me, and as you said on Friday, I think he could help me with my music," Dante continued.

"I did say that," I exhaled. "Of course, he can help." We walked the rest of the way to the parking garage in silence. With each footstep, my animosity towards Dante grew to supersede what I felt for Dan or even Ruby. How could my best friend, who had been there every step of the way as I tried to break into this business, take this job without consulting with me first?

"I have a favor to ask of you," Dante asked as we buckled our seatbelts. "Will you come with me on Friday night to the studio? I know it's so late, but I'm actually kind of nervous about my first show."

Every fiber of my being wanted to say no. My ego had been battered and bruised enough; how would my psyche be able to handle having a front row seat to my best friend living out my dream? "Of course, I'll be there," I sighed. Our 27-year history wouldn't allow me to say otherwise.

■ ■ ■

"What do you mean your boss gave Dante a job?" Katie barked into the phone later that night.

"I don't know, Katie! I've been working my ass off for YEARS and because Dante is a pretty singer he gets on-air over me? How would Dante like it if I got a record deal over HIM?" I was feverishly pacing around my room, talking much louder than I normally would this late at night. However, I couldn't care less whether my mom, Andrea next door, or Dante's family down the street could hear me. My rage for the situation had grown worse after I got home and reflected on the full scope of the day's events.

"You know what kills me the most about this whole thing?" I continued. "Dante didn't have to *ASSERT* himself. He just got the job HANDED to him, *despite* not having EXPERIENCE! And, he didn't even have the decency to ASK ME if it was okay to take it, or my thoughts on the whole things PERIOD..."

"I'm just as shocked as you are," Katie interjected.

"...And can you believe he actually had the balls to ask me to come to the studio Friday because he was '*nervous*'? Like, what planet is he on?!"

"You said 'no', right?"

"No," I wailed, plopping down on my bed. "How can I let him go in there blind?"

"Carla, it's not your job to groom him. Dan's the boss. Let him schlep into the city and help his new guy work the graveyard shift. The station has done nothing but shit on you. Why do you keep trying to be its savior?"

"You're right," I replied defiantly. "I'm not going."

"Well now you have to go, you made the commitment."

"Not if I conveniently get a stomach bug that day," I said innocently.

Katie sighed.

"Katie, I want you to tell me the truth. Am I being over-dramatic about this whole thing?"

"You are over-dramatic over everything," Katie laughed. "Look, I can't take sides here. I love you both very much and want nothing more than for you guys to succeed, but I do see where you are coming from. Maybe you can use Dante to your advantage."

"How?"

"After he settles in, pitch the idea that you two do the show together. If Dan heard how well you two worked together on the tape, how could he turn that down?"

"Dan dubbed me *inexperienced*, remember? How could he let such a "rookie" get on the air with Sir Ezra?" I snapped. "Besides, don't you think that Dante should have brought that up in today's meeting? That's what a true friend would have done."

"At the end of the day, every man only looks out for himself; you know that."

"Don't I ever," I muttered bitterly.

"Well, if you want you can go into business with me," Katie laughed.

"What do you mean?"

"I'm buying the Kettle Black!" She squealed. "I talked to my parents, and they are lending me the money to re-open it!"

"What?!" I exclaimed, dizzy from the jarring change of subject.

"Well, I was thinking about it this weekend. Why should I waste my time sending out resumes when I have a golden opportunity right in front of my face? I was born for this!"

I couldn't agree more. Owning a business was a huge step, and it was hard to imagine anyone our age running one successfully, but if anyone in the world was equipped to handle the pressures, it was Katie. She'd managed Kettle Black as though it was hers anyway, and she had the perfect mix of passion, bossiness, and organization a good entrepreneur needed to prosper.

"I want to change the name too, but I'm not sure what to call it. Any ideas?"

"Katie Cake?" I joked, referencing her old middle school nickname.

"That's not a bad idea," she mused. "It's pretty damn catchy."

I chuckled. Only Katie would seriously consider naming her business after the mean moniker the bullies used to taunt her with back in middle school.

"Katie Cake, Katie Cake, baker's wo-man...get your cakes as fast as you can!" Katie giggled.

I groaned. "Stick to making the cakes and please leave the slogans to the professionals."

11

Day 56

"I don't understand why I have to waste my Friday night sitting here with you guys and Gwen's parents as you plan the wedding," I complained to my mother as I watched her set the dining room table.

"Because I said so," Mom weakly argued.

"But this has nothing to do with me!"

"This is going to be your new family too, Carla. We've only met the Carringtons a few times, but now we really have to get to know them. After Dad and I die, it's only going to be you and your brother. I have to make sure you two stay close."

"That's not going to happen for at least another 40 years… unfortunately!"

Dad sooooo owes me for this, I thought as I watched Mom inspect the wine glasses. He asked if I could keep Mom company so he could finish cooking and Jimmy could get ready in peace. (*"She's in rare form today,"* he warned.) It would probably be less frustrating babysitting a newborn chimpanzee.

Mom took a step back to inspect the table, rubbing her chin in thought. "I don't like these wine glasses," she decided. "I'm going to go in the basement and dig out the ones Grandma Teresa bought us for our 20th wedding anniversary."

I shook my head as I watched her hurry out of the dining room. I sat down on one of the padded dining room chairs and picked up one of the "faulty glasses". As I studied it in the light I wondered, *Will I ever be lucky enough to have 20th wedding anniversary gifts at my disposal?*

I wish I could say things have gotten better since that fateful Tuesday after Labor Day weekend. Unfortunately, I kept doing the "one step forward, two steps back" tango. For example, I made great headway at the gym, but then something set me off, and I slipped back into my old eating ways. Maybe I should have considered checking into a food addiction rehabilitation center and focused on just that facet of my reunion checklist; one goal achieved would be better than nothing. But how else could I deal with life's hardships, other than washing down a plate of greasy mozzarella sticks with a bottle of wine? If you come up with a better remedy, please let me know, I'm all ears.

The story of my love life has always read like a Greek tragedy, but lately, it's gotten even grimmer. I've been getting rejected before I even had a chance to be rejected! A month ago, on LoveAtFirstSite.com, I was actually matched up with a seemingly normal, handsome Italian guy from Brooklyn, who worked for a major public relations firm. What sold me, besides his looks and resume, were his creative writing skills, as evident in the following open-ended guided communication question:

> **Carla, 27, New Jersey: If Hollywood was to make a movie about your life, which movie star would play you and what would it be called?**
>
> **Luca, 30, Brooklyn: My movie would star James Marsden and Lea Michele, and break all kinds of box-office records. It would be called "Cupid's Arrow," the dating website that serves as the starting point to the movie's plot.**
>
> **Tired of finding love in all the wrong places, our hero (we'll call him "Lucas") decides to sign up for the country's number one online dating service, CupidsArrow.com. The young, handsome, successful (did I mention handsome?) man isn't on the site for more than a week when he meets this beautiful, equally successful Italian girl named "Cara." ;-)**

Cara and Lucas meet at this beautiful Italian restaurant on the Hudson River, and they immediately click; the conversation and merlot are flowing like water. However, the date is interrupted when she gets an urgent call to produce the American radio broadcast of the Japanese Baseball Championship Series, since the original producer gets deathly ill from some bad sushi, and must leave immediately. Cara rushes out of the restaurant, and Lucas is sad because he doesn't know when he'll see her again.

With "Already Gone" by Kelly Clarkson playing in the background, Lucas dejectedly wanders the streets of New York City until a brilliant idea hits him: he will fly to Japan to find Cara!

He takes a cab to JFK, plunks down $2,000 in cash for the plane ticket, and takes the next American Airlines flight out to Tokyo. He spends the entire 14-hour flight dreaming about having Cara in his arms again.

Lucas lands the next afternoon, and despite the language barrier, finds his way to the stadium and talks his way up to the press box. Cara's hazel eyes light up as she sees Rafael

> **standing at the doorway, and they embrace to Taylor Swift's "Wildest Dreams." The screen fades to black, and Cara and Lucas live happily ever after.**

In other words, Luca incorporated the few personal details I was willing to divulge on my profile to write an eloquent, thoughtful and sweet answer. This was a guy I hadn't even met yet, and he took the time to do that! To put it into perspective, I was with Mark Falcone for two years and, on the off chance he actually *remembered* to get me a card on special occasions, he never wrote anything extra. Like, not even an "I love you." He would sign the bottom with just plain old "Mark."

Needless to say, I was eager for "Lucas" and "Cara" to meet. Luca's overactive imagination was on par with my own, and I was giddy with anticipation of where it would take us…

The meeting never happened. After that message, he fell off the face of the World Wide Web. At first, I was concerned; leave it to me to find my soul mate and then have him get hit by a bus. But LoveAtFirstSite.com shows when people last log on, and he checked in almost daily. What was going on? Just yesterday, a month after our last digital meeting, I got this:

> **Luca, 30, Brooklyn: Hey Carla! I hope you've had a good month. I'm sorry that I've been MIA, but I was dealing with end-of-relationship drama. Now that it seems to be over with, I hope we can continue talking. You seem like a great girl, and I'd like to get to know you, maybe take you to that Italian**

restaurant on the Hudson. But if not, I understand. Sincerely, Luca

I zipped my mouse over to the "Close Connection" tab on the bottom and did just that. I didn't think I'd be logging back on anytime soon, if ever.

I could have picked every pathetic word of his apart, but why bother? It turned out that Luca and Mark had a lot in common after all. They were both using this website to help them escape their current situations. But instead of getting too down about Virtual Player Luca and what could have been, I thanked God for sparing me the inevitable heartbreak and wasted time.

I was trying to keep positive by telling myself that things could always be worse; for example, I could have a really stressful and unfulfilling job that I dreaded going to every day. Oh, wait a minute...

Ruby Smith was officially the vilest, most disgusting human being on the planet. While her grasp of New York sports had gotten markedly better, her attitude had not. Tommy and I had adopted an approach that my grandmother called *"fesso contento"* which in Italian meant "to play stupid and happy," even if you were angry or frustrated with the situation. Unfortunately, it looked as though we were going to have to play clowns for a long time. The ratings had actually gone up, thus proving Dan right in his hire. (Although I thought the ratings hike could mostly be contributed to the NFL season.)

Dan was also right about another new WSPS talent. The week leading into Dante's first show, he somehow coerced me into not only accompanying him to the studio for his debut but also helping him brush up on his sports knowledge. Each night, after I got home from work, we would pour over newspaper articles and online blogs while ESPN played in the background. When we weren't together, I would randomly dial his cell pretending to be a caller:

> *"Carla from New Jersey, you're on W-S-P-S."*
>
> *"Hi Dante, I'd like to talk to about the Mets. What are we going to do about Carlos Guzman? He's dragging this team down! We have to get rid of him!"*
>
> *"Well Carla, unfortunately, he's locked in until 2020 so he's not going anywhere. What the Mets need to do is drop Guzman in the lineup and take the pressure off him..."*

On the eve of his premiere, we did a mock show in front of Stacy.

> *"Yay!" She clapped like a hyper seal. "I have no clue what you guys are talking about, but you two sound so amazing together!"*
>
> *"Thanks!" we said in unison.*
>
> *"Carla, you should really do this for a living," Stacy continued.*
>
> *"She'll be on-air soon enough," Dante reassured her.*
>
> *I grew uneasy. "Well, I sort of do. I'm just behind the scenes."*

I was still twisted up over the fact that he got the job I'd been coveting since I was eight years old, but what kept me afloat was the show pitch I decided I was going to present to Dan after Dante settled in (if I ever grew the balls to do it). If anything, practicing with Dante fine-tuned our eventual show, I reasoned. And look, we already had our first fan in Stacy! (Who cares if she thought a field goal was when "they shoot the football into that tall basket thing. Two points!")

Before we knew it, the big night had arrived. Dante was a jittery mess our whole ride into the city.

"What if I screw up?" he asked for the hundredth time.

"It's 2'oclock in the morning. Three people are going to be listening. You are putting unnecessary pressure on yourself."

"What if I blank out on a name, or I give the wrong statistic?"

"Shake it off. Ruby does it once every five minutes, and she doesn't seem to catch any flack for it."

"True."

It was a good thing I was there for Dante's first show. The overnight producer was half-passed out among a sea of empty Chinese takeout food cartons; Dante would have been doomed. I helped him neatly lay out his notes, and gave him a quick tutorial on how to work the gadgets in the studio.

I sat down next to him and impulsively grabbed his hand. "Okay, before you go on the air, just remember to let it all flow. Don't depend on your notes too much. You know this shit; take command of it,"

He squeezed my hand tighter. "You're right, okay." He continued to hold onto me as he put his headphones on.

"We're coming on in ten seconds," the producer mouthed through the glass.

The color rushed out of Dante's face. "Don't leave me."

"I won't, I'm right here," I reassured him. I never saw Dante get so edgy before a presentation of any kind. I was picking up on his nervous energy.

The on-air light sparked on, and the producer signaled for him to go. Dante took a deep breath before speaking. I clenched my eyes shut.

"Good morning folks, I'm Dante Ezra, and you're listening to W-S-P-S New York, sports for the people, by the people..."

As he went into his introduction, he slowly let go of my hand. He was going to be okay.

It was a very bittersweet moment for me, for a variety of reasons. I was wistful, like a mother dropping off her child at school for the first time. I had imparted my wisdom to him, and all I could do was hope that my teachings would be able to guide him through. And while I was genuinely happy to see Dante slide into his new role as easily as he did, I felt hurt that I was never given this opportunity. What did Dante have that I didn't?

Dante only got better since his first show. I haven't gone back with him during his shift, but I've listened to each one. His delivery is smooth; he's charming and has a blast with callers. He's a true natural.

I started to realize what Dan saw in Dante and not in me. I couldn't dazzle the listeners the way he did. I never dazzled *anybody*. I simply didn't have that "x-factor" to be a media personality. Because of this realization, I had quietly decided against going to Dan with my idea that Dante and I co-host the weekend overnight shows together. Why tinker with radio gold?

The same doubts that briefly settled in over Labor Day weekend had now been confirmed. I never followed through with exploring different options, since my life was dominated by making sure Princess Ruby was comfortable in her new environment. Now, screw Ruby; I had to take a page out of Katie's tycoon handbook and worry about me. But where would I even begin?

"Aren't these so much better?" Mom interjected, holding a wine glass in front of my face that looked nearly identical from the one I was holding.

"I suppose," I sighed.

"They *are*," Mom corrected, swiftly swapping out the glasses. Once she finished, we both nodded in approval.

"The table looks nice," I commented.

You would have thought we were having dinner with the Pope. Our dining room looked like a showroom straight from the pages of *Better Homes & Gardens*. Mom brought out her finest linen and fanciest chinaware. She spent hours cleaning the entire house, even rooms that the Carrington family wouldn't step foot into. My parents spent all week prepping the menu of antipasto, with the finest Italian meats and cheeses (Course 1), penne a la pomodoro (Course 2), chicken marsala, spiraled ham, mashed potatoes and string beans (all Course 3), not to mention freshly picked figs and chestnuts from the garden and homemade tiramisu for dessert. (Do you see why I have food issues? What was this, our last meal before being sent to the electric chair?)

"I know I went a little overboard, but I wanted to show the Carrington's how I expect them to do things," Mom explained.

"What are you talking about?" I braced myself for her answer.

"Do you think these people know how to plan a New Jersey-style wedding? They are *Amedigans* from TEXAS! What do they know about anything?"

Really, did she know how stupid she sounded? "The Carringtons have money and are nice enough to pay for the wedding," I replied defensively, "Let them do what they want."

"Carla Catherine, I can't let strangers plan my son's wedding! I have to make sure it is suitable for our family. My son is not going to have a wedding in a horse barn on paper plates!"

"Mom, Texas isn't Mars. They supposedly do everything big down there. I'm sure they are going to meet your expectations."

"Let's hope." Mom looked extremely worried.

Ding Dong!

"They're here!" Mom gasped. She scatted out of the dining room. "Jimmy, get down here!"

I followed Mom into the foyer so I could be in place just in case I had to run interference for her making an ass out of herself. Jimmy appeared next to me, wringing his hands together tensely.

Mom swung open the door. On the other side was an older and heavier version of Gwen, a jolly man in a cowboy hat and matching boots, and my future sister-in-law.

"Howdy!" Mr. Carrington bellowed in a deep southern drawl, taking off his hat and revealing a full head of gray hair. He placed the hat over his chest and did a slight bow.

"It's so nice to see you again, Nancy. It's been far too long!" Mrs. Carrington purred in a matching accent. "I made you a pecan pie; it's a Texan specialty!"

"We also brought you some wine. We know how you Eye-talians love your wine!" Mr. Carrington laughed.

"Thank you very much; that's so nice of you!" Mom exclaimed. Gwen and Jimmy stood in the corner, anxiously watching the exchange. This was all very amusing.

My father appeared in the foyer, and the pleasantries repeated themselves.

The Carringtons then turned to me. "Carla, it's so nice to finally meet you! Gwen has said so many splendid things about you!" Mrs. Carrington exclaimed.

"Gwen told me you were pretty, but she didn't mention that you were drop-dead gorgeous! You are one beautiful Eye-talian girl!" Mr. Carrington added.

I blushed. "Thank you. You two have a great daughter."

"Come on, let me show you around!" Mom cut in.

"I thought you'd never ask. This house is beautiful!" Mr. Carrington exclaimed. He handed me the wine and followed my parents with the rest of the herd behind them.

Looking down at the bottle's Duckhorn 2012 label, I already decided I liked Jimmy's future in-laws. I proceeded to march right into the kitchen and pour myself a glass. In between sips, I heard the Carringtons praise each room ("This is so MARVELOUS Nancy! You have such an *outstandin'* eye!") If their over-the-top admiration was authentic, fine. But if not, I give Gwen props for impeccably coaching her parents in how to deal with Nancy D'Agostino. Either way, I knew Mom was lapping it up with a spoon.

Soon after, everyone came back downstairs and settled into the dining room. I strolled in, wine bottle in one hand and wine glass in another. "Thanks for the wine, it tastes great!"

"You opened it already?" Mom hissed.

"Yeah," I shrugged. "Long day."

"A glass of wine cures all stress!" Mrs. Carrington laughed.

"I'll toast to that!" I smiled, pouring her a glass.

We sat down and dug into the antipasto.

"You Eye-talians sure know how to eat! I don't even want to tell you how much weight I've gained since we moved to New Jersey," Mrs. Carrington sighed.

"Oh stop it, you look fine!" Mom gushed. She was firmly in full kiss-ass mode.

"Thank you, sweetie pie!" Mrs. Carrington laughed. "But I'm afraid this is the most I have ever weighed, even when I was pregnant. But I must say, I am very jealous of your shape. And that skin! Your face doesn't have a single line!"

"Oh stop it!" Mom gushed proudly, instinctively smoothing her hand over her cheek. If the Carringtons weren't already in her good graces by complimenting her decorating talents, they surely were now by flattering her near wrinkle-free appearance that she spent hours a day (annoyingly) maintaining. "I always tell my daughter, the best way to keep wrinkles away is to not to drink, stay out of the sun, and moisturize, moisturize, moisturize! She doesn't listen, though."

I rolled my eyes, which caught Mr. Carrington's attention. "Your daughter looks fine," he chuckled.

"What kind of cream do you use?" Mrs. Carrington asked.

I'd had enough. Before my mother could open her mouth to run down her beauty regime, I rose up and ran to the kitchen to get a glass of water. I stood there and timed out how long it would take Mom to fill Mrs. Carrington in on her practices. After I silently named the 10th step, I deemed it safe to walk back in.

"We have four daughters, you know," I heard Mrs. Carrington explain as I walked in, mercifully on a different subject now. "And we've hit the jackpot with all of our sons-in-law. I mean, they've met some great, wonderful men, including your son."

"All of your daughters are married?" Mom asked.

"All married. Gwen's the baby. She's actually getting married late in comparison to her sisters. They were all hitched by the time each turned 23!"

"If only we were so lucky," Mom sneered. "Carla's still single."

The table talk had gone from fairly annoying to brutal. I had to steer the conversation back to the lesser of the two evils. "Mom, weren't you in the middle of explaining to everyone how you keep your youthful look?"

"We're past that, dear," Mrs. Carrington responded, clearly not taking the hint. "How old are you, Carla?"

"Twenty-seven," I responded glumly.

"Well, you people in New Jersey seem to do everything late. In Texas, you'd be considered an old maid!" Mrs. Carrington roared, with my mom following suit. Jimmy gave me a sympathetic look, and I glared back at him.

"I don't understand how on earth a girl like you can still be single!" Mr. Carrington chimed in. "These men nowadays are *backward*!"

"I don't understand it either!" Mom added. "She was prettier than I was growing up, yet I had a different boyfriend every week while she barely goes on any dates! Boys should be breaking down our front door, I tell her that all the time!"

"No, you don't!" I snapped.

"Why are you single, Carla?" Mrs. Carrington asked.

I felt my face turn red with fury. How dare this woman who barely knows me ask the dreaded question that every chronically single person hates to hear (and honestly, if we knew the answer to the question, don't you think there wouldn't be a question to begin with?). However, being alone most of my life, I'd learned how to diffuse these types of uncomfortable situations with either self-deprecating humor or straight-up sarcasm. I decided to take the sarcastic route. "All the good ones are taken or gay, Mrs. Carrington. So at this point, I either have to try and turn a gay man straight or convince a straight man to get a divorce." My parents looked at me in horror, while the Carringtons burst out in boisterous laughter. At least someone appreciated my comedy.

"Doesn't it seem like everyone is gay nowadays?" Mr. Carrington said in between breaths. "Society has gone down the drain."

"Carla's friend's husband just came out of the closet!" Mom exclaimed. "Carla and her friend caught him in bed with their landscaper one day."

I shot my mother a death stare.

"I'll be damned..." Mr. Carrington burst out laughing.

"MOM!" I freaked. "That is top secret information; NO ONE is supposed to know that but family!"

"We're all family here, darlin'!" Mrs. Carrington whooped. "We won't tell a soul!"

After their laughter had settled down, I thought I had drawn the attention away from me, but the Carringtons weren't done yet. "Gwen tells me you have a great job at W-S-P-S. I love that station; even though they aren't too kind to my Cowboys!" Mr. Carrington proclaimed.

"Thank you," I smiled, feigning enthusiasm. "I produce the "The Tommy & Ruby Show" and have been at the station overall for five years." Just saying Ruby's name in passing made me nauseous.

"I love him, but I HATE her!" Mr. Carrington exclaimed. "She's awful!"

He was not the first person to utter that phrase, but every time I heard it, I got giddy as if it was the first time hearing it. "She's from L-A. She still has to get used to it," I said as diplomatically as possible.

"We agree with you; we don't like Ruby around here," my father added. "She beat Carla out for that job."

"Well, I'll be darned!" Mr. Carrington exclaimed, throwing his fork down. He turned to my father. "But you do know why, right?"

"Because my boss is an ass-clown?" I blurted out.

"Carla, no cursing at the table," Mom sternly ordered.

"It's because she's probably sleeping with the big boss," Mr. Carrington continued. "You hear about them lady sports-casters makin' the rounds all the time!"

Mrs. Carrington slapped her husband on the arm.

"He's right, though," Dad answered. "That's exactly what I told Carla when it happened." The two men laughed while the rest of the table simultaneously covered their eyes with their hands.

Sexist comments and annoying mothers aside, the rest of dinner was uneventful. The conversation thankfully switched to the whole purpose of the little shing-ding--the wedding, which would be taking place May 20th of the next year, as in a month before the reunion. The Carrington family had booked a restored castle in northern New Jersey, a location that my mother glowingly approved. Gwen showed me her choices for bridesmaid dresses, which were all very pretty and elegant. Best of all, Mom actually played nice while working out all the details. It turned out to be a good night after all, although I was sure the three glasses of wine (and two slices of Mrs. Carrington's succulent pecan pie) had something to do with it.

■ ■ ■

At around two in the morning, as the wine buzz carried me to off to sleep, I was woken up by my cell phone ringing. Annoyed, I leaped out of bed to see who it was. My aggravation switched to dread when I saw the name on the caller ID: *Dan Durkin Cell.*

"Hello?" I screeched, throwing my light on.

"Where is Dante?" Dan growled.

Whatever was left of my buzz quickly evaporated. "I have no idea. I was almost asleep when you called."

"Well, he's not at the station for his shift."

I started to panic. "I'm sure there's a logical explanation for this," I started to say.

"Carla, you better fix this; he's your friend!" Dan threatened.

"Well, he's YOUR employee!" I shot back, fully awake. How dare he throw the weight on me!

"What do we do if we can't find him?" Dan cried.

I racked my brain for an answer. Even though I wasn't being paid the big bucks to search for missing radio hosts and come up with solutions to programming problems, I felt a crushing pressure to come up with the right remedy for the situation.

All of a sudden, a light bulb went off in my head; the solution to ALL solutions. If I couldn't find Dante, I had a perfectly suitable substitute ready to go. I licked my lips in anticipation. "I can fill in for him," I sweetly suggested.

"You?!" Dan incredulously replied.

"Yeah, me," I assertively stated. "The listeners know me. You've heard my tapes, and I'm sure you've heard me banter on-air before with Tommy. I'm more than able to handle the hosting responsibilities tonight." I wasn't sure where this confidence was coming from. Hadn't I just thrown up the white flag on my radio career a mere few hours ago?

"I don't know...um, Carla...You have no experience," Dan stammered.

A pang of frustration hit my chest, but I wasn't backing down. "As of a month ago, neither did Dante," I pointed out.

"Yeah but..." Dan trailed off.

"But, what?" I challenged. "You don't have someone to host a show for you right now."

Dan remained silent, but I was not letting up. "How irresponsible is it that your host ditched work? If he doesn't take the job seriously enough to show up and perform, then you should consider hiring someone who does." I made a face at my words; I sounded more like Ruby than myself.

"Carla, no, just...You need to find Dante, and you need to find him now!"

Click.

I stared at my phone in bewilderment. He actually hung up on me! "Why is it my job to fix this, you're the ASSHOLE program director!" I growled into the disconnected phone. I felt my eyes well up with tears. Dan hadn't even given my suggestion a thought. He really had to think I was a talentless hack. What if I couldn't find Dante?

Dante...where the hell was Dante?

If I really wanted to leave the station, this was the perfect time to do it. Dan's bullying tone somehow convinced me into thinking that both Dante's and my job depended on my ability to locate him. If that was really the case, then I could easily crawl back into bed, give the figurative middle finger to Dan and the whole operation, and start my new life in the morning.

But what if Dante was in real trouble? I could never live with myself if something happened when I could have prevented it. I dialed his cell, but he didn't answer. I sprinted downstairs and went outside to look down the street. Maybe he spent the night at his parents' house? No, his 2006 metallic gray Jeep was absent from their driveway.

Dejected, I went back inside and phoned Katie. Maybe she was at the shop prepping for her impending grand opening, and saw him at one point enter or leave his apartment.

"HELLO?" she shouted into the phone. A mix of music and crowd noise blared in the background. Unless Katie was turning Kettle Black into a rock club, I figured she was at one of her favorite dive bars that I skeeve.

"Have you seen Dante?"

"WHAT?! SPEAK LOUDER, IT'S HARD TO HEAR YOU OVER THE MUSIC!"

"Have you seen Dante?!" I repeated.

"WHAT ABOUT DANTE?"

"Is he with you?"

"IS HE HERE? NO. DOESN'T HE HAVE TO WORK TONIGHT?"

"Yeah…" I trailed off.

"WHAT?"

"Never mind Katie, I'll talk to you tomorrow." I had no time to deal with her right then.

I felt bad waking up a seven-months-pregnant Andrea, but it was worth a try. No answer.

I didn't have Stacy's number, otherwise, I would have tried her. The only option I was left with was to check out his apartment.

I threw on a New Jersey University sweatshirt and stormed into my parents' room. "There's an emergency at work, I'll be right back."

"Okay. Be careful," Dad mumbled in his sleep. Mom, probably too worn out from her exciting evening, didn't flinch. (Thank God. Otherwise, I'd never find Dante due to being held captive for three days' worth of questioning.)

I rushed to my car and made a beeline to his place. As I ran towards the building, I could hear the familiar music of Alanis Morissette's *You Oughta Know* blasting from an open window upstairs. "Dante?" I asked aloud.

I dashed upstairs and down the narrow hallway. Dante's apartment door was wide open. I peeked in and saw my disheveled friend singing Alanis' song at the top of his lungs while holding a beer and throwing his clothes all over the place.

For a moment, my heart sank seeing my friend is such dire straits. But my sympathy was quickly replaced by anger. How irresponsible could you be to get sloppy drunk knowing you had to go to work? I had no time to launch into a lecture, because even though he was clearly in no shape to host a four-hour sports-talk show, I had to somehow get him to the station.

"DANTE!" I screamed. He was in such a tizzy he didn't even realize I was standing there.

"DANTE!" I repeated. He still didn't notice me. I picked up a sneaker from the floor and threw it at his back.

"Ow," he softly whimpered. He unsteadily turned around.

"What do you want?" he slurred through bloodshot eyes, shaking his beer bottle at me.

I leaped towards the stereo and lowered the volume. "I'm here to take you to work. Let's go; you're late for your shift."

"YOU go do the show! I don't wanna!"

Gladly, but I'm not allowed, I glumly thought. "Dante, your career rides on this. Dan will fire you, and then you can kiss ANY kind of career goodbye. Please, just get in the car."

"Stacy dumped me," he howled. "I don't care about my life. I want to DIE!" He squatted down to sit in a chair that wasn't there.

"Dante!" I flinched as I watched him fall hard on the wood floor. He had no reaction to bruising himself; he just took a big sip of his beer and curled up in a ball, hysterically laughing.

I slid my arms underneath his armpits and tried to prop him up. "I know you're drunk, but please, I need to get you to the station."

He took another sip of his beer. "Whatever, man."

After I got him steady on his feet, I went to collect the binder that I knew he kept his show notes in. When I turned back around, I saw him stumble towards the door and trip over the sneaker I had thrown at him earlier, his beer bottle shattering on impact. "Ouch," he muttered, his right cheek planted firmly on the floor.

"Jesus Christ!" I gasped. I inspected his face to make sure he wasn't bleeding, but he didn't have a scratch on him. I grabbed his left arm and again helped him up, avoiding the shattered glass. "Hold on tight to me," I ordered, draping his arm around my shoulders. We walked slowly out of his apartment, down the stairs, and into my car. He was nearly passed out as I buckled his seatbelt. What a disaster.

I flew down Route 1&9 towards the Holland Tunnel. Judging by the cars I left in my dust, I must have been going over 90 miles an hour. How I didn't get pulled over was a miracle.

"WEEEEEEEEEEEEEEE! Go faster!" Dante squealed, suddenly alive. "I feel like I'm on a roller coaster!"

"A roller coaster ride to hell," I replied. But at least he was showing signs of life; I had to keep him talking. "So what happened with Stacy?"

"Oh, you mean the BITCH?!"

"That's the one!" I snickered, not taking my eyes off the road.

"She couldn't handle me being on the air and working on weekends. She's a very jealous, immature, bad, evil girl. But I love her."

A chill ran up my spine as he spoke those last words. The only time I'd heard Dante utter that phrase was in song.

"Soooo what do I do?" he slurred. "I've never been dumped before."

I chuckled. "Well, everyone's different. But every approach generally contains crying, massive amounts of alcohol, and listening to the saddest songs ever recorded. So congratulations, you've already mastered the basic art of the heartbreak."

"You've spent half your life doing *that*? That's a horrible time."

"Thanks for that," I replied sarcastically. "But I would watch your mouth, Ezra. Remember who came to your rescue tonight."

No response.

"Dante?" I looked over and saw him clenching his stomach, his face twisted in pain.

"Pull over," Dante moaned.

"Um, can you wait five minutes? I'm almost in New York." Indeed, I was about to speed through the EZ Pass lane to enter the tunnel.

"Pull over," Dante repeated. I noticed he was dripping sweat, and could tell he was about to throw up all over my car.

"Un-FUCKING-believable," I screamed, accelerating into a gas station.

"Don't do that!" Dante grunted. "You're driving is making me sick."

I jerked to a complete stop, making Dante moan even louder. "Lose your lunch and let's go!" I ordered.

Dante swung the door open, and without stepping out of my car, promptly vomited all over the pavement. My hands immediately covered my nose, but the putrid smell still managed to seep into my nostrils. "You couldn't even get out of the car? You better not be getting any of that inside!" I threatened.

A couple minutes later, he was done. "Sorry," he sighed, wiping his lips with the back of his hand. "I feel so much better now."

"I'm so happy for you," I replied, trying to dig up some gum and hand cream in my purse while clasping my nose tighter. "Now *I'm* going to be sick."

I pulled up to the station at 2:45a.m., 45 minutes after Dante was supposed to be on the air. I kicked him out of the car.

"Just say you had food poisoning and that you were so sick you couldn't answer your phone," I instructed.

"You're not coming upstairs with me?"

"Are you kidding me? No!"

"But girls NEVER decline the opportunity to go upstairs with me!" Dante proclaimed, awkwardly raising his eyebrows up and down.

"Get out!" I growled.

His face fell. "Thanks for the ride," he mumbled, and exited my car.

On my drive home, I flipped on the radio to WSPS. I was scared for what I might hear, but it would serve both Dan and Dante right for being so irresponsible in their respective roles.

As it turned out, Dante sounded as if nothing was wrong. You would never have known that minutes before, he was a drunken mess, rocking out to Lilith Fair tunes and yakking all over an Exxon station. I promptly shut off the radio.

Starting the next morning, I would be sending my resume to every station in the country. I'd had enough.

12

Day 99

I was the first to arrive the morning of Katie's grand opening. WSPS would be broadcasting live from her shop later in the day, and I had to make sure the engineer had properly set everything up. But I would have been there early regardless; I was her unofficial head of marketing, plus Katie had shrouded the renovations in secrecy and forbade anyone to see anything but the finished product. I was *dying* of curiosity.

While I'm still WSPS's bitch, I had made good on my vow and had spent the past two weeks e-mailing and snail-mailing my resume and demo tape—the same one I cut with Dante—to nearly fifty radio station program directors around the country (contacts I never would have gotten had Laney not broken into Dan's Rolodex). One of the programmers I contacted was Ruby Smith's former Los Angeles boss; I knew it was a long shot, but getting a job there would have been the sweetest of poetic justices!

I was going to cut a new tape, but I decided the old one was too good to let it go to waste. While I knew I ran the risk of (again) having these people inquire about Dante instead of me, I wasn't sweating it. I doubted Dante would leave the bright lights of the number one market in the world to challenge me for a morning drive sportscaster position in Green Bay, Wisconsin (regardless of his being a huge Aaron Rodgers fan) or for a weekday evening host job in LaSalle-Peru, Illinois.

I hadn't heard from Dante since I had to swoop in and save his professional life two Fridays before. You would think I'd at least get a "thank you," but it's me we're talking about here. (In my past life, I was probably a garbage receptacle.) After a few phone calls and text messages went unanswered, I decided to leave him alone. I figured he was probably wallowing in his misery over Stacy, and I certainly knew what it felt like to cut myself off from the world after a bad breakup. However, Katie had mentioned to me that she booked him to sing for the grand opening. Why he would take her calls and not mine remained a mystery.

While we're on the topic of being ignored…there has been nary an acknowledgment that these program directors even *received* my stuff. They say no news is good news, but was it too much to let me know that they were reviewing my materials? I just prayed that my packages weren't collecting dust underneath another fifty-five submissions, or that my e-mails weren't decaying away in someone's inbox.

I thought about the implications of getting that "amazing" job offer from a program director in Biloxi-Gulfport-Pascagoula,

Mississippi. Could I, a dyed-in-the-wool Jersey girl, survive in Middle America? That certainly didn't jive with my master 10-year reunion plan, but what had lately?

There were other things to consider. This move would mark the first time living on my own. Would I be able to handle a new job in a foreign environment while actually running a household? Then again, how much time could be spent maintaining a 500-square foot studio apartment, the most space I could probably afford? I'd work Monday-Friday, clean and do laundry on the weekends, and live off of wine, cereal and ramen noodles. It could work. Who knew, maybe I wasn't given the golden opportunity because I had more dues to pay, and this was my penance. Most A-List stars came from the humbling beginnings I just described; they didn't get their big break while commuting to auditions from Mommy and Daddy's sprawling Colonial tucked away in the suburbs.

Besides, I wouldn't be staying for *too* long. I'd be there for six months, tops. A bigger market, like Detroit (or Los Angeles!), would snatch me up in a second, and in a year's time, I'd be back in New York!

Another option I was exploring was the idea of resurrecting my old college radio show, *Girl in the Locker Room* and starting a weekly online radio show. I had a built in audience (the WSPS Internet stalkers) and enough contacts to book two guests per one-hour show to last me ten years, so why not? Let it become a huge success, and *then* let Dan come back and tell me I had no experience!

While I waited for answers, I'd also worked on marketing another entity: Katie's Kakes, the resurrected Kettle Black. I couldn't talk my friend out of the Kardashian-esque name, but it was growing on me. Another thing I couldn't sway Katie on was her choice of an interior decorator. When she told me that she wanted to enlist my mother's services, I was worried that my friend had fallen seriously ill. So many theories entered my mind. Did she have a walking concussion? Was this a sign of early onset dementia? Was she suffering from a stage four brain tumor? (She resisted all attempts to be driven to the emergency room.) In other words, who would want to pay money to hang out with Mom at her neurotic worst? But I let her win that debate; Katie wanted to have the place up and running in less than two months' time, and there was a lot of work to be done.

Katie paid me to help her design the logo, print business cards, format the menu and create the website. I'd publicized the grand opening event by hanging up flyers around town, taking out ads in the local newspaper, and posting about it on social media networks. Furthermore, I'd booked the mayor of Honey Crest to participate in the ribbon cutting ceremony.

But my biggest contribution was getting WSPS involved. As a favor to me, Tommy somehow convinced Dan to let him broadcast a special one-hour Saturday afternoon show live from Katie's Kakes (for free) while also finagling the marketing department to lend promotional support to the event (also for free). Apparently, he still felt bad about how things went down with Ruby. Why else would he be in supreme ass-kissing mode? (No complaints here!)

"How can I ever repay you, Carla? Look at everything you've done. You are so good at this!" Katie gushed last Thursday when I told her the news about WSPS.

"Maybe I missed my calling," I replied sarcastically.

"Maybe you did!"

For a split second, after that conversation, I thought about returning to school and getting a marketing degree. I had a knack for it, and it was definitely fun, but radio was my true love. The marketing/public relations world didn't give me the same rush that engulfed my body whenever we broke a huge sports story, or the awestruck sensation I felt whenever I met a legendary athlete, or the butterflies I felt whenever we did a remote broadcast from a huge event, like the World Series.

But I had to admit; when I approached the doors of Katie's Kakes, I felt the charge of excitement that the good parts of my job always brought. Everything we worked so hard on was about to come alive.

When I stepped inside the café, my jaw hit the floor in astonishment. Katie's Kakes was *stunning.* My mom had transformed the grungy coffee house into a modern yet comfortable masterpiece. She tossed the 30-year-old dark green shaggy carpet that adorned Kettle Black's floors and refinished the dark wood that was hiding underneath. The walls, once painted a light brown, were now a brilliant shade of burnt orange, accented by mirrors and abstract artwork of coffees and cakes. Gone were the tattered plaid couches, and in their place were sleek, golden olive green booths that outlined the perimeter of the seating area (the drapes that hung from the windows matched that translucent color). The booths were partnered with black wooden chairs and tables, and each tabletop was lit up by a small ceramic pumpkin lamp, in celebration of Halloween, which was a week away. In one back corner, a small platform stage had been constructed, which featured a keyboard and sound system for musical acts. I saw the WSPS engineer, Gus, fiddle with the equipment in the other back corner, where Tommy would be doing his show. I gave him a quick wave before turning to examine the large glass display case that was situated on the opposite side of the room. It was filled to the brim with Katie's various creations that sweetly fragranced the entire room.

I picked up a black leather-bound menu from the hostess station and flipped it open. I smiled as I read its contents, not only because it was beautifully designed (if I do say so myself) but because of what was being offered. Katie took Kettle Black's selections and ratcheted things up to the next fifty levels. While she still served all the traditional coffee house fare, she now offered zany desserts like banana cake topped with whipped peanut butter mousse frosting and bacon. Katie's Kakes also featured breakfast, the cornerstone being the incredible pancake assortments, like brown sugar oatmeal or blueberry sour cream (I think I gained five pounds by merely reading of these creations.)

"Carlaaaaa!" Katie sang, running around the counter to envelop me in a huge hug. Next to her, I felt very overdressed. I had on a purple sweater dress, black leggings, and peep toe pumps. My brown hair was blown out in big, bouncy curls, and I sported a face full of makeup. Meanwhile, Katie had on a black apron with an orange "Katie's Kakes" embroidered in sprawling calligraphy and dirty white sneakers. Her strawberry blonde hair was piled in a messy bun atop her head, and she had on not a lick of makeup. Despite her ragged appearance, her face glowed as if she had just left an all-day spa. "Do you like it?"

"This is amazing!" I exclaimed. "You don't know how proud I am of you." Truer words have never been spoken. I NEVER would have been able to pull off $1/16^{th}$ of what Katie did in such a short amount of time. I got stressed to the point of gray hairs producing a five hour radio show; I couldn't imagine what it felt like to oversee not only my show, but all the shows, and marketing, and accounting, and hiring, and sales...

"Thank you!" Katie squealed, breaking our embrace. "I know you think your mom is crazy—and she is, there is no denying that—but damn, she knows her stuff!"

"I know." I winced. "Just be prepared for her to act as if it's *her* grand opening. She's going to be bringing in a slew of potential clients today to show the place off."

"I don't care what she does or who she brings, as long as they are paying customers!" Katie roared. "Mama has a rent to worry about!" She jumped over the counter and ran into the kitchen. She fluttered back out holding a small plate. "Try this," Katie insisted. "It's a salt chocolate cake, infused with potato chips!"

I quickly grabbed the plate out of her hands. "You don't have to ask me twice. Those are my two favorite things!"

"I know!" Katie laughed. "Imagine if my old bosses saw what I'm serving? They would have a conniption! To them, offering flan was a walk on the wild side!"

"Yeah, and look at them now. They are rotting in white-collar jail next to Bernie Madoff's corpse," I quipped. Katie giggled and skipped back into the kitchen. I chuckled at her hyperness as I took a bite of the cake. I rolled my eyes back in ecstasy.

As I took another bite, I saw the WSPS promotions crew park the station's vehicle out front to draw attention from the passing traffic. Moments later, Tommy's black Mercedes pulled into the parking lot. I smiled as I watched Tommy pal around with the two promotions guys, who were busy constructing a tent under the October fall sun.

A few minutes later, I saw Tommy and the promotional staff walk towards the door. I hurriedly put down the plate and took a mirror out of my purse to make sure nothing was in my teeth.

"Hello, Daggs," he greeted, throwing off his shades. He leaned over to give me a kiss on the cheek. "This place smells and looks phenomenal."

"Hello. Thanks so much for coming, and yes, it's beautiful," I gushed, throwing the compact back in my bag. I gave him a quick hug and introduced myself to Ethan and Luis, who wore matching WSPS black polo shirts and barely looked old enough to drive.

"So promotions will be outside and inside," Tommy began. "Where will Dante and I broadcast from?"

I pointed to where the engineer had set everything up. "Ethan and Luis, you guys go there, and you and Dante will be next to the broadcast tab...Wait." I caught myself, realizing what

Tommy had said. "You and Dante? What do you mean?" I barely noticed the two boys scurrying away.

"Dan figured that, since Dante is from around here, we could do the show together," Tommy shrugged. "I didn't realize that Dante was also best friends with the owner! Small world!"

"Too small," I muttered. I tried to look at the (marginal) bright side. At least Dan hadn't thrown Ruby into the mix!

Tommy and I walked over to his section. Promotions quickly laid down WSPS key chains and t-shirts and other trinkets to give away to the "seagulls" (the nickname we give to the people that only come to our events for the free branded swag).

"Tommy, where are you going to sit?" Ethan asked in a cracked, barely post-pubescent voice.

"Right there," Tommy said, pointing to the right. I saw Ethan grab two stacks of headshots and Sharpie markers out of his blue duffle bag, and dutifully placed a set of each in their designated areas.

Curiously, I leaned over and picked up a photo from the left pile. Staring back at me, with his intense blue eyes and broad smile, was a close-up shot of Dante. On the bottom, it read "Dante Ezra" with the WSPS logo printed on either side. Had I not known what this was for, I would have thought it was an outtake from a GQ photo shoot.

"It's a sin how good looking that kid is," Tommy interrupted, peering over my shoulder.

I waved him off, placing the photograph back on top of the heap. "Ehhh, it's just a really good Photoshop job, that's all."

"Well, can they please Photoshop me to look like that?" Tommy laughed, pointing to his yellow polo shirt and khakis.

Right on cue, Dante walked in. He glanced in our direction, and without even bothering to say hello, walked towards the kitchen.

"He has the right idea," Tommy remarked. "Where can I get some food?"

"Follow me." I took Tommy to the kitchen, where I saw Dante and Katie having an animated discussion. When they noticed us, they stopped talking. Katie quickly put a smile on her face, while Dante looked visibly stressed.

"Sorry to interrupt, guys. Tommy wants to try something before the masses gobble it all up. Katie, what do you have?"

"I'll bring Tommy out front, and he can have anything he wants!" Katie replied brightly. She wiped her hand on her apron and extended it to Tommy. "Katie Lansford, nice to meet you. Thank you so much for everything."

"I can have anything, huh?" Tommy joked. "It's my pleasure! The place is great, and I'm happy to help." Tommy shook her hand, then turned to Dante and gave him a playful tap on the shoulder. "How are you doing, Dante? Ready for today?"

Dante cleared his throat. "Yes, I am, looking forward to it!"

"Let me get some grub and then we'll talk business. Katie, let's go, darling."

Katie giggled as she led Tommy to the storefront. Dante and I hung back, standing there in uneasy silence. I figured I would break the ice. "So how have you been? I haven't seen you since—"

"I think I'm going to grab something to eat too. I have a big day," Dante interrupted. "Excuse me."

I felt a pang of anxiety run through me as I watched him exit. What was that all about? Was he still upset about Stacy? His professional trajectory was on the up-and-up. He had nothing to feel bad about, especially being dumped by some average-looking, college dropout. He should trade places with me for a day. The kid wouldn't last an hour in my shoes!

I went back out front and saw a group of people already form a line. Beyond them, I saw Mom hold court with a group of silver-haired people, animatedly explaining her work. I decided to see what she had going on.

"My client originally wanted bright red walls, but I felt this shade added a little bit of warmth to the cozy atmosphere she wanted her customers to enjoy," I heard her explain.

"Hi Mom," I interrupted.

"Hi, baby!" she greeted. She took my hand and brought me to her group. "This is my daughter, Carla. She helped my client do the marketing and promotions for today's event. She did a *marvelous* job!"

I almost choked on my saliva. I knew she was using me to show off to her customers, but the compliment actually felt genuine. It was not too often I pleased her, and if I did, she hardly ever showed it.

"This is your daughter, Nancy?" one of the men said. "You two could pass for sisters!"

Mom beamed. "Thank you!"

"Nice to meet you," I said sweetly, shaking everyone's hand.

"Now let me bring you to the seating area," Mom smiled, nudging me with her eyes to scram. As they walked towards the back, she stayed behind to whisper in my ear: "Put on more blush on; you look pale. Is it your time of the month?" Before I could answer, she darted away to catch up with her group.

So much for being in her good graces. As I rummaged through my purse to locate my makeup bag, I noticed that Katie's Kakes had gotten significantly louder. Nearly every seat was taken, and the line was out the door. Katie's servers, all carried over from the Kettle Black regime, ran frantically behind the counter to keep up with the demand. Katie alternated between the kitchen and greeting customers at the door. She was in her glory.

I made my way to the bathroom, passing by Dante and Tommy, who were leaning up against the wall, each nursing a coffee. Tommy nodded in my direction, but Dante ignored me. His insolence continued to make me jittery.

The bathroom's warm décor mirrored the shop, except the lighting was stronger, which was much appreciated in my apparent makeup emergency. I located my makeup bag and took out my Mac blush. I studied my reflection. "What is she talking about?" I asked aloud. "My blush is fine." But just in case, I quickly swept another layer to my rosy cheeks. I heard the door creak open, and saw the reflection of a large woman waddle in. "Hello," a very pained-looking Andrea grunted. She was now almost eight months pregnant, and her stomach was stretched to non-human proportions. This was a girl who hated to leave her house whenever she had her period; the fact that she was fat, hormonal and stressed about her marital situation made her already-fiery personality all the more explosive.

"You look happy," I wryly observed.

"These babies think my bladder is a *fucking* trampoline," she complained as she shuffled past me. "I have to pee every five minutes!" She slammed the bathroom door shut.

"I'll wait for you."

"You are going to be waiting a while!" Andrea shouted.

"It's fine." As uncomfortable as Andrea looked on the outside, was how I felt on the inside. I hadn't figured out where I fit into today's event equation, and Dante's behavior only made it more confusing.

Nearly ten minutes later, Andrea emerged from the bathroom. "This is terrible," Andrea scowled, rubbing her lower back. She studied her reflection in the mirror as she washed her hands.

Despite her condition, she still looked dazzling. She had on a long, loose leopard print maternity dress and matching gold jewelry.

"You don't look as bad as you probably feel," I complimented.

"Thanks," she mumbled as she dried her hands. She looked at me and scrunched up her face. "Why do you have all that blush on? You look like a clown!"

"Are you kidding me? If it's not too little, it's too much. You people are going to give me a complex!

■ ■ ■

An hour later, the Mayor of Honey Crest, Dr. Victor Colombo, came by for the ribbon cutting ceremony. The entire café (including my mother and her group) filed outside the main entrance to watch Mayor Colombo, Katie, and her parents pose for photographs (Andrea and I stayed to the side, away from the crowd) Katie held a pair of giant ceremonial scissors up to the red ribbon, and the wattage of her grin could have lit up the Eastern Sea Board for weeks straight.

"Before we make this official, I just want to say a few words," Mayor Colombo announced. "On behalf of the town of Honey Crest, we want to wish Katie's Kakes and the Lansfords all the success in the world!"

"Here, here!" one of the observers shouted.

I felt myself get a little emotional as I watched Katie cut the red ribbon and heard the crowd erupt into huge applause.

Camera flashes fired off, and bursts of confetti showered down from the roof. The Lansfords hugged each other while Mayor Colombo dutifully shook hands with the towns' citizens.

"Do you have a tissue?" Andrea wailed, tears streaming down her face. She pulled me in for a big bear hug. "That was so beautiful!"

"Andrea…I can't…breathe," I choked.

I saw Katie make her way through the crowd. "Come with me," she ordered, grabbing my hand. "I want a picture of us with the mayor."

"I'm not taking a picture looking like this!" Andrea protested as we followed her.

"Only if I get to hold the silly scissors," I joked.

"But I need them to help cover up my fat belly!"

"We can all share!" Katie laughed.

We got to the entrance and saw Dante nervously pace around. "Let's hurry up and take this picture, guys. We go on the air in two minutes," he said sternly.

"Well excuuuuuuse me, Mr. Radio," Andrea snapped.

Amen, I wanted to add. Who did he think he was? We lined up in this order— Andrea, Katie, me and Dante. "Scissors please!" I jokingly ordered.

Dante dashed out of line and grabbed them from behind us. "Here," he said tersely, filing back in line next to Andrea.

I wasn't expecting the attitude, nor the heavy weight of the scissors. "Um, thanks," I mumbled as my shoulder dropped down. "You guys have to hold on to the handles with me, these are pretty heavy."

We each grabbed a section and posed for the pleasant photographer.

"Smile!" the older woman exclaimed.

I looked at Dante, who briefly glanced at me. He was not smiling, and his blue eyes were iced over.

I shook my head and took a deep breath to compose myself. I plastered a big smile on my face and looked into the camera. The photographer took a few shots. "What a lovely looking group!" she remarked before walking away.

"Doubtful," Andrea mumbled.

"Okay guys, gotta run," Dante said, gently touching Andrea's stomach.

"Me too, I got to get baking, we're running out of some product," Katie added. They both scurried inside.

"Dammitammit!" Andrea howled, stomping her right foot. "Come with me to the bathroom again." We made our way back inside, where it was almost too packed. Katie should have hoped the fire department didn't drive by and see.

"Pregnant lady coming through, move out of the way!" Andrea barked as we made our way through the crowd. "Move it, move it!" Miraculously, considering the sheer volume of people, the bathroom didn't have a line.

"Wait for me," Andrea pleaded.

I nodded as I took out my iPhone and checked my messages. I only had one:

> **Mom Cell: I see Dante is on the air with Tommy. Why isn't that you???? You should maybe consider the marketing thing. How much more time are you going to waste at that place?**

How was that for a motivational speech? I was tempted to forward it to my long-lost friend Xander, whom I hadn't seen in nearly a month, so he could add it to his collection of quotes. Disgusted, I threw my phone back in my bag and walked over to outside Andrea's stall.

"Andrea, have you talked to Dante?"

"Um, I'm a little busy right now!" she snapped.

"Good talk!" I walked back to the mirror and took out my hairspray to touch up my hair. A semi-familiar face entered the bathroom and stood at the mirror next to me. I couldn't exactly place where I knew the plump woman from.

"Carla D'Agostino?" she asked, smoothing out her frizzy, light brown hair.

"Yes?" I stopped spraying.

"It's Makalya Romano! Well, now my last name is Foster. We went to high school together!"

"Oh yeah, we had a bunch of classes together! How are you?" I smiled, but on the inside, I was stunned. This girl was my age? She looked as if she was pushing forty, easily.

"I'm good! I'm married, three kids. I'm a stay-at-home mom, but the house and my daughters keep me super busy. How about yourself?"

This was a sneak preview of what was to come at the reunion, and I did not like it one bit. How could I compete with that rundown? "Um, you know, I'm living," I nervously chuckled. "Things are good."

"You are at that sports station, right? The one that Dante Ezra is here with? My husband listens all the time and says he hears your name! I'm like 'I went to high school with that girl! Now I know TWO people on the radio!'"

"Yeah, yeah, that's me, I mean, us." I wanted to crawl under the sink and die.

"I remember you were best friends with Dante, and Katie Lansford, and Andrea Rocha. Wow, what a bitch she was!" she laughed. Her giant diamond sitting on her left hand caught the overhead light.

"Uh-huh." I nervously looked towards Andrea's stall.

"So...are you married?" Makalya asked.

I was spared from further embarrassment by Andrea emerging from the stall. "I am SO done with this place," Andrea proclaimed. "I want to go home."

"You remember Andrea Rocha, right?" I introduced innocently.

Makalya's eyes shot open in horror. I wanted to laugh; who was the fool now?

"Who are you?" Andrea questioned.

"We went to high school together. I'm Makalya Romano, now Foster."

"I don't remember you." Andrea brushed her off and made her way to the sink.

"It was a big school..." she trailed off. "But congratulations on your pregnancy! When are you due?"

"December," she sighed. Small talk was not Andrea's forte.

"Nice! That's when my middle child was born."

"Middle child?" Andrea repeated disbelievingly. "You've done this more than once?"

"I have three daughters," Makalya boasted proudly. "I am a professional baby maker. Any pregnancy issue you may have, ask away! I've been there, done that."

Professional baby maker?

"Oh yeah?" Andrea perked up. "What can I do to make these last weeks as comfortable as possible? I'm about to put a gun to my head."

"Are you going to be here for a while? Let's chat!" Makalya exclaimed.

"Okay!" Andrea chirped happily. The two walked out of the bathroom, completely forgetting the fact that I was standing there.

Incredible. This girl was just talking shit about Andrea, but like everyone did back in high school, bowed down when she graced them with her presence. For the first time, it dawned on me that Andrea was going to be a *mother* (paging Captain Obvious). I guess the fact was lost on me amidst her hormonal rantings and ongoing divorce proceedings. It was going to be weird seeing Andrea in that role.

I roamed out of the bathroom, deep in thought. The four of us were all going in separate directions; Andrea was a mom, Katie was a business owner, Dante was an emerging superstar, and I was …well, at least three of us were moving onward and upward. Despite our different lives, would we still be able to stay tight, or would my friends leave me in their dust? It was hard enough to keep our monthly brunch appointment as things stood now; what were we going to do when things *really* got busy?

I passed by the broadcast and saw Tommy and Dante bantering. Tommy threw me a quick wave, but as he'd done all day, Dante disregarded my company.

Apparently, the cracks in our Jade Meadow foundation were already forming.

13

Day 119

"We're going to switch gears for a minute and welcome a very special guest," Tommy Max announced. "We have Katie Lansford, the owner of Katie's Kakes in Honey Creek, New Jersey, here in the studio!"

"Hi, Tommy!" Katie greeted.

"We were broadcasting from the grand opening a few weeks back, and unfortunately, we ran out of time and didn't have a chance to get her on the show," Tommy continued. "But she's here today and brought us some amazing desserts. Katie, really, I've never put something in my mouth that tastes *this* good!"

"Oh really?" Katie giggled.

"Well, ok, maybe this is Top five," Tommy laughed.

Ruby rolled her eyes at the double innuendo.

Maybe they would have had more time if Tommy was doing the show solo, I thought bitterly.

I hadn't seen Dante since the grand opening. We didn't speak the entire rest of the day, but started lightly communicating a few days later via text:

> **Me: We haven't talked in awhile, and I'm not sure why. What is going on?**
>
> **Dante Ezra Cell: I'm okay. I just need my space. There's a lot going on.**

As you can see, things continued to be strained. I chalked it up to his still being upset about Stacy. In times of my personal distress, there were certain people I confided in more than others. For example, when Mark and I broke up I told my mother nothing; I gave Dante the summarized version of the story (since he was a boy and, at the end of the day, didn't really care); and I dissected, analyzed, debated and repeated every detail with Katie and Andrea. So for whatever reason, despite my vast expertise in the area, I was seemingly not someone he was comfortable talking about the breakup with; maybe he associated me with the night Stacy dumped him since I was the first outsider he saw, and my presence drummed up those horrible memories (signed, Carla D'Agostino, MD).

To boot, I absolutely hated confrontation, so I wasn't going to push the issue. And, admittedly, it was no secret that he hadn't been my favorite person lately. If he did come around, cool, but if not. . .fine.

Besides, I didn't have time to wallow in someone else's heartbreak, when I finally might be kissing mine goodbye! I met a *fantastic* guy on LoveAtFirstSite.com named Drew. I already had him pegged as my reunion savior. He's 32, from Queens, handsome (but Jewish; I'm not sure how my household would receive that one) and successful (he has his own insurance law firm). We'd been exchanging e-mails for the past couple weeks, and we made plans to finally meet in Manhattan, at Bamboo Sushi. I came to work dressed for the occasion—tight black pants, a sequenced gold tank top, and a beige blazer.

"Where are you going in that outfit, missy? Are you hooking tonight? Hee-hee-hee," Laney cackled when I walked in to work that morning.

Unfortunately, nothing was happening on the job front, but it was because of the upcoming holidays, I reasoned. Everyone was busy closing out the year, and probably wouldn't be thinking about new hires until January. Which was fine; I could get to know Drew for a couple months, have him fall in love with me, and then persuade him to uproot his business to where I'd be working, in Toledo, Ohio.

Tommy's voice broke my trance. "Katie, tell our listeners what you've brought in for us today."

As Katie rattled off her creations, my boss, Dan Durkin, appeared in the control room...with the most beautiful man I had ever seen. Dan first introduced the man to the studio engineer,

Gus, who quietly waved hello. Then they turned to me. "Carla, this is Miguel Martinez," Dan announced.

He didn't need any introduction. Miguel Martinez played left field for the New York Yankees, and I had been infatuated with him since the Bronx Bombers signed him as a free agent in 2003. He was a beautiful, 6-foot specimen of Cuban lean muscle, with the most amazing green eyes I'd ever seen. (I admit, I still had his poster hanging in my bedroom next to the other green-eyed Yankee hunk of my youth, Derek Jeter.)

But now that he was standing before me, I could honestly say that pictures did the man no justice. In person, he was a billion times more breathtaking. He had on crisp white sneakers, blue jeans, and a form-fitting black t-shirt that outlined his bulging muscles. I also noticed a platinum and diamond wedding band wrapped around his finger (such is my life). His bride of eight years only happened to be one of the most beautiful women in the world, Hollywood personal trainer Trisha Anderson, with whom he had three children.

It's okay, Carla. Who needed Miguel when I had LoveAtFirstSite Drew? I tried to convince myself. Yeah, right. I looked deep into Miguel's eyes. "Hi, I'm Carla D'Agostino. It's a pleasure to meet you. Great season this year!" I felt myself blush at how giddily I delivered the last line. *Way to play it cool, Carla.*

"Nice to meet you too, Carla! We came up a little short, but I'm confident we'll have a big year in 2017," he replied with a warm smile, his intense eyes locking in with mine.

I felt an electrical current traveling through every fiber of my being. I hoped my infatuation wasn't too obvious.

"I bumped into Miguel and his agent downstairs at Starbucks and invited them up," Dan explained, breaking our gaze. "Carla, can you call over to the Yankees and make sure it's okay that we have him on? I have Miguel's agent in my office; I don't want to leave him there alone."

"Of course," I cooed, immediately picking up the phone. Miguel did not follow Dan out of the room, and in the corner of my eye, I saw him reading the framed articles on the wall. I noticed Ruby studying Miguel through the glass with a look of sheer delight, an emotion that only showed whenever we had an athlete on the phone or in-studio.

I hung up with the Yankees' public relations department and turned to Miguel. I didn't realize he was standing directly behind me, and I accidentally bumped into his hard chest. "Sorry!" I shrieked, covering my face with both hands to hide my horror.

"It's okay!" Miguel assured, his famous smile spread widely across his face.

I was mortified over my klutziness, but I tried my best to brush it off. "They cleared the interview; all they ask is that you plug the Yankees' Thanksgiving food drive. They are e-mailing me talking points on it now."

Miguel continued to smile. "Sounds good."

I begrudgingly turned my attention to Katie's interview, which was wrapping up. "Tease that we're going to have Miguel

Martinez in-studio after the commercial break," I told Tommy in his ear. I saw Tommy's face light up. From his vantage point, he couldn't see Miguel standing behind me.

"Coming up, we have another treat for you. We have the one, the only, Miguel Martinez IN STUDIO to talk Yankees baseball. Carla, where the heck did you come up with him?"

I pushed the on-air button. "Miguel happened to be in our building, and was nice enough to stop by and say hello."

Ruby's smile immediately turned upside down upon hearing my voice hit the studio.

"Miguel truly is one of the good guys in baseball," Tommy remarked. "We'll have him coming on next. Katie, thank you so much for being here and bringing your delicious cakes. Check out her website, and make sure to get your rear ends into her bakery."

"Thanks for having me, and special thanks to your producer, Carla D'Agostino, for setting this all up. Carla's been one my best friends since childhood," Katie replied. I gave her a silent thumbs up for remembering to mention me. The irritated look on Ruby's face was priceless.

"No one's better than Carla," Tommy replied.

"And you did you say Miguel Martinez is here? Carla's been in love with him since high school. She must be freaking out right now!" Katie laughed.

My eyes shot open in embarrassment. I furiously mouthed to her "Are you kidding me?" I was afraid to turn around and look at Miguel; I could have sworn I heard him lightly laughing. I wanted to choke her with one of her eclairs. Ruby crossed her arms in amusement.

"Oh really?" Tommy asked. "Carla's never told me that. We'll have some fun then. We'll be back, right after this."

"Don't you dare," I whispered menacingly in Tommy's ear.

I took a deep breath and carefully turned back to Miguel, afraid of bumping into him again. "I'm sorry about that. My friend doesn't know what she's talking about," I insisted.

He laughed. "It's quite all right." I had noticed he took a couple steps back from where he'd been before.

Just then, the e-mail came in from the Yankees, and the laser printer quickly printed three copies. "Let me walk you to the studio," I said, grabbing the sheets of paper off the tray.

I opened the door and saw Katie balancing a couple of dark brown cake boxes while making small talk with Tommy. Ruby held a mirror up to her face while quickly applying lipstick. When she saw us walk in, Ruby smacked her lips together seductively and immediately stood up.

"It's a pleasure to see you again, Miguel. I'm sure you remember me from hosting spring training shows with M-L-B Network," Ruby sweetly greeted, deliberately ignoring me.

Miguel paused for a moment. "Of course, I remember!" he politely replied. "Nice to see you."

I smirked; all the media training in the world couldn't help disguise that fact that Miguel had no idea who Ruby was! I loved it.

"Miguel! It's been way too long, pal!" Tommy said, giving him a hug.

"It's great to see you too, Tommy!" Miguel replied.

"Miguel, this is Katie, the best dessert baker in the tri-state area, and my *former* best friend," I pointedly added.

"You are a dangerous person to know. Sweets are my downfall," Miguel chuckled.

"I'll leave some samples for you," Katie replied, blushing. "And I was totally kidding about the Carla thing. She doesn't have a crush just on you; she has a crush on the whole team."

"Katie!" I shrilled, my face turning a deeper shade of crimson.

"I mean, uh, she loves the whole team because she's such a big fan! She is such a diehard fan," she back peddled.

Ruby stared right at me with a look of discontentment. "That's our Carla, always keeping things professional." She started to get the hang of my name about a month ago. Better late than never, I guess.

Tommy loudly smacked his forehead.

"Yes, I always do," I too-sweetly replied.

Miguel let out a chuckle, clearly amused by the dynamics of our group. "No worries. It's all good."

"Okay," Katie giggled. I rolled my eyes. She never understood my crush, but I guess seeing Miguel in person drove the point home. Unfortunately, she'd lost her mind in the process at the expense of my reputation. It was at rare times like this that I resented her child-like enthusiasm.

"All right, we have to get back on the air in ten seconds. Party's over," I declared. "Here are your notes. See you all on the other side." I dropped the papers on the desk and rushed Katie out of the studio. Once back behind the glass, I noticed that Ruby slyly slid her chair closer to Miguel's.

"How did I do?" Katie asked as we walked back to the control room.

I looked at her in disbelief. "You were terrible!"

"Really?" Her face fell.

"Well, you *were* doing great until you dropped the anvil on my head!"

"I got so excited for you, I wasn't thinking clearly. I'm sorry," Katie said sincerely.

"Yeah yeah yeah." I gave Tommy the signal that we were back live.

"That Ruby really is a trip, by the way," Katie continued. "She barely said two words to me and refused to try anything because the desserts I brought in weren't her favorite kinds."

"How were you supposed to know what her favorites were?"

Katie grew fidgety. "Um, she said that was your job to find out."

I looked at her amazement. "You have to be kidding me."

"Nope."

"Well, I can't say I'm surprised," I rolled my eyes. "If it's humid outside, it's somehow my fault that she couldn't blow out her hair …for a *radio show*!"

"I don't know how you deal," Katie remarked.

"Well, for every hundred days of misery, sometimes you get one that is amazing…" I trailed off, gazing at Miguel through the glass.

Katie sighed, mirroring my dream-like expression.

"That's true. He's not my type, but there's no denying the man is lit."

I turned my attention to the show. Ruby wasn't her usual unbearable self and poured on the charm. If she were like this all the time, I could *start* to understand Dan's hire; but unless she was talking to Henrik Lundqvist or CC Sabathia or any other elite New York City athlete, she couldn't be bothered with anyone else. I couldn't wrap my head around her attitude. If she was that enamored with being around the players, why didn't she take her model looks and start an escort service?

Unfortunately, management still wasn't picking up on Ruby's split personality. As long as the ratings continued to hold steady, and the advertising checks kept rolling in, they turned a blind eye to everything else.

I shifted my focus from Ruby to Miguel, who was the consummate professional—charismatic, witty, and smooth. A move to the broadcast booth would be a natural transition once his playing days were over. (I could just see it in lights now: *Talking Baseball with Miguel Martinez and Carla D'Agostino.*)

After the segment was over, I rushed back into the studio. "You guys did such a great job talking about the food drive. The Yankees are going to absolutely love that spot!" I raved.

"Thank you," Miguel replied humbly. "Do you think I can get a copy of the interview?"

"Of course!" I answered brightly. "Give me your agent's e-mail address and I'll be glad to send him the MP3."

"Actually, would you mind e-mailing it directly to me?"

I was dumbfounded; athletes of his stature never gave out their personal information.

"Sure!" I exclaimed. "Come with me into the control room and I'll get your info." I saw the fire pouring out of Ruby's ears. I threw her a smug look and sauntered out of the room. Dan and Miguel's agent were standing by the doorway, waiting for us.

"One minute," Miguel motioned as we walked inside. I saw Katie packaging a cake box with a pretty orange bow.

"Hello, again," she giggled.

"Hello," Miguel laughed. "Is that for me?"

"Of course!" she exclaimed. "I hope you enjoy!"

"Awesome! I'm sure I will." He turned to me. "Do you have a piece of paper?"

"Here you go." I handed him a pen along with my show notebook. Katie raised an eyebrow as she watched him scribble his e-mail address.

"I'm going to give you my cell too, just in case you have any issues sending the file."

I froze. An e-mail address is one thing, but Miguel Martinez's *actual, personal* cell phone number?! "I don't anticipate any problems, but sure," I reassured him.

Miguel capped the pen and handed it back to me. "Just in case," he repeated. His hand lingered a second or two longer than it normally would. I wasn't sure if my mind was playing tricks on me, but I could have sworn his mossy green eyes were sparkling with a hint of mischief.

"You got it," I responded calmly, although I felt anything but. *Snap out of it,* I urged myself. *He's married to a beautiful blonde bombshell; like he would give that up to hook up with a short Italian girl with cellulite.*

"Thank you, Carla," he said in a hushed tone. He turned to Katie and grabbed the box. "Thank you for the treats!"

"Call me with any of your needs, er, cake needs," she caught herself.

When the door shut behind him, Katie and I locked hands and squealed as though we were eleven years old again, watching the newest *NSYNC video on MTV's *Total Request Live.* "I can't believe Miguel gave you his cell phone number!"

"I know!"

"Are you going to call him?"

The smile vanished from my face. "He's married! You didn't see his wedding band?"

"I must have not noticed it," Katie answered loudly.

"Well, it was there, so there is no reason for me to call him."

"Keep his number in case of an emergency." Katie mused.

"I won't *trash* his number; there's just no reason for me to dial it."

"Well, I'll tell you what. If he orders something from me, you can come on the delivery."

I smiled. "Deal."

"Okay, walk me out; I need to get back to the store."

"Okay, just one second." I turned towards my computer and pulled up Miguel's MP3 file. I dutifully emailed him from my work address, but made sure to include my cell phone number, "in case you have any problems opening it."

I walked Katie to the lobby. When I came back, the ominous sight of Ruby was waiting for me by the door. "Hey, Ruby," I casually welcomed.

"We need to talk," she answered, thrusting herself into the control room. She walked right over to my desk and eyed the notebook that was open to the page revealing Miguel's information.

"Did you send Miguel the interview?" Ruby demanded.

I slammed the notebook shut. "Um, yeah. Why?"

"Good. Just know that I don't need my producer to be distracted by fooling around with the athletes," Ruby remarked. "You wouldn't want me going to Dan with that information, right?"

I took a step closer to her. "What are you talking about? There's no information to go to Dan with. Our exchange was strictly business, plus he's *married*."

"If you think you're going to one-up me by getting the athletes on your side, you are mistaken."

That was the most ridiculous thing I had ever heard. "Aren't you just a little bit paranoid?" I blurted out.

"I've been in this business a lot longer than you. I know these things. Watch your step," she threatened. She gave me one last menacing look before slithering out of the room.

I looked back at Gus incredulously. "Did you just see that?"

He silently shrugged and turned his attention back to the show.

■ ■ ■

"Working at W-S-P-S must be the neatest job ever!" My LoveAtFirstSite.com date, Drew, exclaimed. There are two things wrong with that sentence: 1) WSPS is anything but "neat" and 2) I felt anything but "love at first sight" for him. It was more like "I should sue the website for false advertisement."

Looking at him was downright painful. I thought I was getting young Marlon Brando reincarnated but instead, I got Jonah Hill pre-weight loss. He had long, greasy, curly hair that had receded halfway up his head; a set of buck teeth that would have made Mr. Ed blush; and the waistline of a sumo wrestler.

Normally I would have called him out on lying and left, but I needed a few (free) drinks after the day's ordeal. Plus, I was dying to try Bamboo Sushi, a two-story upscale Japanese restaurant dubbed as one of New York City's best by Zagat. The lush décor and fresh selections were as fantastic as advertised, present company not included.

"It's pretty good, no complaints," I muttered, finishing up my second Kettle and club of the hour. (I obviously needed something much stronger than my usual merlot.)

"I was listening to the show today, did you get to meet Miguel Martinez?" Drew asked as he unsuccessfully tried to grab a piece of sushi with his chopsticks.

"Yes I did," I replied coolly, as Drew's chopsticks flew out of his right hand and onto the floor. He shrugged, and to my disgust, picked up the sushi with his bare hand. He messily dipped it into his soy sauce and brought it to his lips. The dark liquid dripped down his mouth and onto his pale blue sweater-vest.

"He is my favorite!" Drew exclaimed, mouth still full of fish. He rubbed his dirty hand on his chest. "And how is it working with Tommy and Ruby?"

I let out an exasperated sigh. Surely, my ticket to heaven was upgraded to first class after sticking this date out. "Everyone at the station is great. But I don't feel like talking about it. There's more to my life than W-S-P-S."

"Oh, sorry," Drew said, reaching down to get another piece of sushi. "It's just that I'm a huge fan, I listen all the time! Do you know any of the other hosts?"

I stared at him in repulsion. "I thought I said I didn't want to talk about W-S-P-S?"

He stuffed the fish into his mouth. "Sorry." He innocently chewed.

I'd had enough. I stretched my neck and desperately searched the vast premises to find our waiter so we could get the check.

I stopped my search when a familiar figure, sitting alone at the bar, caught my eye. He was staring attentively at his phone while lazily stirring his drink with a straw. Once I realized who it was, I almost hit the floor.

Miguel Martinez.

"Holy shit, it's Miguel!" I exclaimed, ducking my head.

"Miguel who? Where?" Drew shouted, getting out of his chair.

"Sit down!" I hissed. "It's Miguel Martinez. Lower your voice! I don't want to be obvious."

Drew immediately obeyed the order. "Okay, but where is he?" he whispered, leaning close to me. His bad sushi breath turned my stomach.

"At the bar," I choked.

Drew's eyes grew wide, still inches across from my face. "Do you think you can get me an autograph?" he gasped.

I would never, under any circumstance, ask an athlete for an autograph, especially out to dinner at one of New York City's best restaurants. But Drew just presented me with my out.

"Let me see," I sweetly replied, quickly sliding out of my bamboo-constructed chair.

"Really? Wow, Carla, you are the coolest girl ever!"

As I dashed to the bathroom, I glanced behind my shoulder to see what Miguel was doing. He was still sitting alone, playing with this phone. Oddly enough, no one seemed to notice or care that one of the city's biggest stars was in the house.

Once I freshened up, I casually made my way to the bar. As I walked closer, I noticed that Miguel had changed his clothes from before. He had on dark jeans with a white and gray button-down shirt. A shiny silver chain was hanging around his thick neck. He looked even more attractive than before, if that was even possible.

"Fancy seeing you here," I smiled, immediately regretting my choice of words.

Miguel's eyes lit up. "Twice in one day. How did I get so lucky?" He leaned in to give me a kiss on the cheek, a gesture that almost shot me up to the moon. "Have a seat! How was the rest of your day?"

"Great!" I exclaimed, forgetting all about the Ruby drama and my disaster date. I climbed on the black leather-bound barstool next to him. "How about yours?"

"Besides the fact that I wrecked my diet by eating all of your friend's desserts? Pretty good," Miguel laughed. "I seriously haven't had something so good in my entire life! I'll definitely spread the word to my friends, family, and teammates."

I put a hand over my chest; I was moved by his kindness. "That would mean so much. Thank you. Katie just started the business a month ago, so that kind of publicity would be huge!"

"Of course! Anything I can do to help, let me know," Miguel replied. "Would you like a drink?"

Miguel Martinez just offered to buy me a drink! I'm going to have an alcoholic beverage with Miguel Martinez!" the fifteen-year-old in me shrieked. "Sure! I'll have a Kettle One and club soda with a lemon and lime, please."

"Hey, that's my drink!" Miguel laughed. "I've never had it with both a lemon AND a lime, though. I'll try it." Miguel lifted up his left arm to get the attention of the bartender. I quietly gasped when I noticed the wedding band he was wearing earlier today was not around his finger. AND he was here, alone?

Very interesting...

After he had put our drink order in, he turned his attention back to me. "Thank you so much for e-mailing me the interview. I already sent it to my mom back home in Florida, she loved it."

"Aw, that's so cute," I gushed. "I was wondering why you wanted it. Most of the guys we have on don't request anything."

"Yea, she collects all my stuff. She's got big binders of all my magazine articles and newspaper clippings. She has hard drives full of my radio and TV appearances as well."

"Keeping track of all your stuff must be a full-time job for her," I commented.

"Ha! Something like that!" Miguel laughed. "We are super tight. I'm sure you are close to your mom, but when it comes to mothers and sons, there is no bigger bond."

"Ain't that the truth," I muttered.

The bartender placed the drinks in front of us. I noticed that the glasses were double in size from what I was being served earlier. That would mean these are drinks 3 and 4 for the evening, which was still young. I made a mental note to pace myself.

"Cheers, to new friends," Miguel said, looking deep into my eyes.

Friends? I gripped the glass tighter to prevent it from dropping. "To new friends," I repeated. We each took a big gulp out of our extra-large glasses, while managing to not break eye contact.

Miguel smacked his lips together in approval. "I like the lemon-lime thing. It dilutes the taste of the vodka even more."

"See that? You learn something new every day," I laughed.

"You're right," Miguel replied, taking another big sip. "So tell me, what's the story with your show? It seems like an interesting mix of personalities."

"You tell me," I answered, setting my drink down. "What do you think? And then I'll tell you if you are right or wrong."

"Okay," Miguel began. "Tommy is a cool dude; he's always been very fair to me throughout my career. He seems like a genuinely nice guy, but I can tell he's got a dirty old man side to him. Whenever I listen, he's always throwing in these little double entendres while making his points. It's pretty funny actually."

Miguel listens to the show? That means he had to know who I was prior to today. My heart started pounding a little faster. "That just about sums Tommy up," I nodded.

"You are the cute, eager producer who works harder than you probably have to in order to please your bosses, who are dicks. You are too old to be doing what are you doing, but too young to be taken seriously. What are you, twenty-four?"

"I wish," I frowned. "I'm twenty-seven. I'll be twenty-eight in January."

"You look young for your age. Shit, , to be twenty-seven again," Miguel sighed. "Shit, to be in my twenties again, period!" He bitterly threw back another big swig of his drink.

I smiled at his first sign of insecurity, although it didn't surprise me. Age was a very big deal to athletes; in their minds they could play their respective sport forever, but their bodies could only maintain that level of performance for so long before they had to give way to newer, younger, faster talent. Miguel was thirty-four, so while he had a few years left in the tank, he was on the wrong side of his career. "So you pretty much figured Tommy and me out. What about Ruby?"

"Ruby is just...fake," Miguel frankly stated.

My eyes widened at his candidness.

"I don't like to talk bad about anyone, but I just did not get a good vibe from her. She's very condescending and jealous of you."

"Jealous of *me*?" I repeated.

"She hates your guts! Come on, you know this," Miguel laughed. "You are younger, prettier, and have a much better personality. She's threatened."

"Well, she has nothing to worry about." I rolled my eyes. "My boss worships the ground she walks on. It's me he doesn't like."

"You are better than that place, Carla. You know how many sports broadcasters I have met in my lifetime? You'll be doing things in your career that Ruby can only dream of."

I couldn't believe that I was getting a pep talk from Miguel Martinez. For a minute, I forgot who he was; I felt as if I was bullshitting with a longtime friend. "Well…I'd like for those things to start happening soon."

"They will." Miguel held his empty glass up to the bartender, and he immediately made him another drink.

"So, who are you here with?" Miguel asked, changing subjects.

Ah, crap. I had totally forgotten about Drew! "Um..." I trailed off. Before I could explain, I saw my *Big Bang Theory*-reject date enter the bar area, frantically looking for me.

"It's a long story," I began, covering my face with my right arm.

"CARLA!" Drew shouted.

Miguel looked dumbfounded as he studied Drew. "He's with you?"

"Not really…" My voice trailed off.

Drew squeezed himself between Miguel and me. "What's taking you so long? Did you ask for my autograph? I have to get home and study for a case," he whined.

"No, I didn't get a chance to ask him yet," I nervously laughed. What was I supposed to do now? There was no way I was going to admit to being on a date with this Neanderthal. I had to come up with something, pronto. "Miguel, I want you to meet my lawyer, Drew. He is the best insurance lawyer in the tri-state area! We met here to discuss my case."

Before Miguel could introduce himself, Drew cut in. "Why are you saying I'm your lawyer? I'm your date!"

Miguel looked at me, dumbfounded. "Really?"

If looks could kill, Drew would have been six feet under the very restaurant. "You were my dinner date to discuss my case," I lied. "And you're right; you aren't my lawyer because...I haven't hired you yet! I was interviewing you." I grabbed my drink and fretfully sucked on my straw, not realizing until I got to the bottom that I inadvertently finished the rest of my vodka in one sitting.

"Whatever," Drew said, letting me off the hook. "I just want Miguel's autograph."

Miguel quickly grabbed a bar napkin while taking a pen out of his pocket. "Here you go, buddy," he said, scribbling his name.

"Oh wow, thanks!" Drew exclaimed, shaking his hand feverishly.

"Anytime." Miguel smiled.

Drew turned to me. "You know, there's only one other thing I need before I leave."

I exhaled loudly. "What's that?"

"Well, I paid the bill while you were gone. Do you have thirty dollars to cover your drinks?"

My mouth opened, but no sound came out. My vocal chords were paralyzed in astonishment.

Miguel looked more offended than I probably did. "You are seriously going to make her pay, bro?"

"Well, she ditched me tonight to hang out with you, so yes, she owes me money." Drew leaned in closer to Miguel. "Between you and me, she really wasn't a good date," he whispered.

"Um, I can hear you!" I yelled.

"Well, it's the truth!" Drew wailed.

"You're one to talk. You LIED on your profile and uploaded fake pictures!" I blurted out. *Nice job blowing your own cover, Carla.*

"You guys met online?" Miguel smirked.

"I didn't lie. I AM a lawyer!" Drew defended.

I took a deep breath to prevent my temper from spilling over. "Look, I'm sorry about the money, but I am not paying you. We met tonight under false pretenses; what goes around, comes around."

"Oh yeah? And what's your punishment for being such bad company?" Drew shot back.

"Don't worry, honey; my karma's already doomed," I retorted.

"Well…I hope you enjoy growing old alone with your twenty cats!" He turned to walk away, but something stopped him. "And go Yankees!" He cheered to Miguel. Then he mercifully stormed out of the restaurant.

I blinked back tears. First, Katie made a fool out of me, then Ruby tried to bully me, and now Drew was probably going to go home and curse me with some black voodoo magic. To top it off, most of this unfolded in front of one of my favorite human beings on the planet!

"He was…interesting," Miguel finally quipped.

"Extremely," I deadpanned. "I am so, so sorry for all of this. I should go." I grabbed my purse, but Miguel clutched my wrist.

"You aren't going anywhere!" he exclaimed. "I have a couple of friends meeting me here, and we will make sure your night turns around." He motioned to the bartender to bring another round of vodkas.

My head started spinning. Miguel wasn't scared off by any of this? He was asking me to hang out?

"Really?" I asked, astonished. "You don't think I'm a freak?"

"The people you choose to keep company with might be a little freakish, but you yourself are the furthest thing from a freak!" Miguel laughed. "I just can't understand why a beautiful woman like you would resort to online dating. I would think you'd have guys lining up around your block."

I arched my eyebrow. "Maybe you don't have me so figured out, after all."

■ ■ ■

A half hour later, Miguel's two childhood friends from Florida, Dennis and Sebastian, met us at the bar, and they were a *blast*! After downing a few more rounds of drinks and some sushi platters, we piled into Miguel's limo and club-hopped through the Meatpacking District. We received world-class VIP treatment wherever we went. What would Ruby Smith have to say about all of this?

Actually, what would *anyone* have to say about all of this? It was a night like this that made me actually happy to still be a woman-child. The Mommy Dearest from high school I bumped into at Katie's grand opening couldn't do this. She met her husband; she had her kids, and her life is over, all by the age of twenty-seven. *Bor-ing!*

"I bet you've never gone clubbing like this!" Miguel screamed in my ear as we danced to the techno.

"Nooooo," I giggled. I was very drunk at that point. I couldn't even tell you what club we were at; the pulsating strobe light blended everything together. I felt as if the music was carrying me to a place far from there.

"You're gorgeous," Miguel commented, holding me close. It felt incredible to be in his arms, and his saying things like that didn't help my transient state.

I slightly pulled away to look him in the eyes. "Really?" How could a creature so beautiful think the same of me?

"I want to kiss you so badly," he whispered. My body started to quake. I leaned into his ear to whisper the same to him, but something stopped me. It was the same something that had stopped me from going "all the way" with every guy leading up to Mark. As much as I wanted to make out with Miguel, I knew I couldn't. How could I hook up with him knowing he was married, with three young children?

"Aren't you married?" I asked.

"Carla, really?" Miguel said angrily, pulling away from me. "You know how to kill the mood."

I draped my arms around his neck and pulled him back close, desperate to recapture the moment. I again looked him in the eye. "If I didn't know you were married I would be all over you right now. But I saw you with your ring today."

"No ring now," he said, flashing his empty ring finger.

"I know, but…"

"What if I told you I was getting a divorce?"

I wanted to believe that in the worst way. But how could I? "I would say you were lying."

"I'm lying?" He snapped his fingers towards Dennis, who immediately broke his embrace with some supermodel-looking girl, and ran over to us.

"Dennis, am I getting a divorce?" Miguel shouted over the music. "Tell Carla what's going on."

"Yeah, it was just finalized on Wednesday," Dennis shrugged. "The news will hit the papers next week."

Miguel motioned for him to go back to his friend and looked at me smugly. "You see?" He hugged me close. "I wouldn't lie to you. I have to wear the ring until next week. Then I'm publicly a free man."

I still wasn't sold, but what superseded logic was the sensation I got from holding him. It was this crazy, magnetic, frantic feeling I'd never had with anyone before, not even Mark. As he lightly caressed my neck, my apprehension slowly faded away. I knew this was so wrong, but I didn't care. Miguel unlocked something inside of me that had been dormant for so long, and for the first time in my life, I just wanted to go with it.

Ever so slowly, he leaned in, and we started kissing. Slowly at first, but then it quickly grew deeper into the most amazing, wild, mind-blowing, passionate make-out session I've ever experienced.

And together, we floated away into the night.

14

Day 120

I gingerly opened my eyes and was greeted by the massive Empire State Building standing outside my window. I shot up in bed, realizing that I wasn't home. My head immediately started pounding, and the room started spinning. I looked to my right and saw Miguel Martinez sprawled out next to me, shirtless and passed out.

I froze. *What did I do last night?* I hurriedly lifted the comforter and breathed a sigh of relief as I noticed my clothes were still on. Then the details of last night started to flood back. The kisses, the passion, the intensity...the making out with a married man.

I shakily studied my surroundings. The whole left wall was one big window, offering an awesome view of New York City. The actual space was the most luxurious I've ever seen--Persian white carpet, metallic gold wallpaper, and a cathedral ceiling that twinkled with tiny built-in lights (a waste of electricity, considering the copious amount of natural sunlight pouring in). A trippy, acoustic-electronica song played softly through the surround-sound speakers. The plasma television screen propped up on the wall in front of us matched the length of the bed, roughly about half the size of a football field. My mother would be in her glory if she saw all this.

I winced at my last thought. Mom. I didn't check in with her last night. She was going to kill!!!!l me.

I noticed my iPhone screen projecting its light from the nightstand. I reached over to grab it. Sure enough, I had 23 missed calls and 15 text messages, mostly from Mom Cell. The others were from Katie and (surprisingly) Dante, warning me that my mother was "on the warpath."

I had two choices here. Since the damage had already been done, I could fall back asleep and deal with the fallout later, when my hangover subsided. That would buy me more time with Miguel, and perhaps more fun…

But then again, why delay the inevitable? I was wide awake anyway; I could call her, and then pass back out with a piece of mind. I threw the covers off of me and, iPhone in tow, climbed out of bed. I silently tip-toed out of the bedroom and roamed the long hallway. I didn't want to be caught snooping around, so I entered the first room whose door was open, figuring it had to be vacant. When I saw what I'd entered into, I gasped.

I felt as if I'd stepped inside the showroom of a high-end baby boutique— the room was painted a pale shade of blue, with wallpapered images of moons and stars trimming the walls. A rocking chair was situated by the bay window, overlooking the beautiful skyline. White, very expensive-looking baby furniture was assembled around the room, including a large crib against the far wall. Over the crib, in big fluffy letters, hung the name "Marco." I panicked. What if the baby was sleeping in there? I held my breath as I tiptoed over and delicately peered over the cage. Luckily, no signs of Marco; I guess Miguel's (ex?) wife and kids had gone away to their fifth home for the weekend.

Another attack of dizziness hit my equilibrium, and I clutched onto the crib to keep me upright. I wanted to curl in a ball on the fluffy yellow carpet and pass out but decided the rocking chair would be a little more comfortable. I sluggishly crawled over to the window. Once I settled in, I started to brace myself for the earsplitting voice that would soon be addressing me. I took a deep breath and hit "home" on my *speed dial.*

"Hello?" Mom answered in an unexpectedly hushed tone.

"Hi Mom," I said casually.

"CARLA KATHERINE D'AGOSTINO, WHERE HAVE YOU BEEN?" Mom erupted. There it was. I grimaced and pulled the phone away from my ear.

"I'm okay. I got a little drunk last night, and I slept at a friend's house." Hey, that wasn't a lie.

"WHOSE HOUSE?!"

"Andrea's," I quickly responded without thinking (because naturally, the person to get hammered with on a Friday night would be my eight-months-pregnant friend). But Andrea didn't call or text with a warning, so I figured she hadn't spoken to my mom.

"YOU ARE A LIAR! ANDREA IS AT THE HOSPITAL AND NONE OF YOUR FRIENDS KNOW WHERE YOU ARE!"

"Wait, why is Andrea at the hospital?" I cried.

"I DON'T KNOW, WHY DON'T YOU ASK HER YOURSELF SINCE YOU WERE WITH HER ALL NIGHT, YOU LIARRRRRR!"

Checkmate. "Okay, I wasn't at Andrea's house," I conceded.

"SO WHERE ARE YOU?"

"I'm in the city."

"ARE YOU AT A BOY'S HOUSE?"

I was too tired to argue. "Yes," I replied softly.

"WAIT UNTIL I TELL YOUR FATHER! YOU ARE DEAD, YOUNG LADY!"

This wasn't getting either of us anywhere. I rubbed my temple; her piercing voice was making my headache worse. "Look, nothing happened, all right? I'm safe; it's no big deal. End of story."

"NO BIG DEAL?" I heard my mother take a deep breath. "I thought you were dead," she continued in a dramatic tone. "Do I even know this person?"

"Kind of," I said, chuckling. Another non-lie. My mom isn't a baseball fan, but she is well versed as to who Miguel is; I remember begging her for weeks to let me hang his poster on my bedroom wall, despite its clashing with the color scheme. She finally conceded, but for months, complained every time she stepped in the room that the tape was ruining the paint.

"WHAT'S SO FUNNY?!" Her voice was back to a window-breaking pitch.

I sighed. "Nothing at all. Okay, I'm getting my things together and will be home soon."

"YOU'RE DEAD WHEN YOU GET HOME!" And she hung up.

Oh, how the tables have turned. A few hours ago I was being treated like New York royalty and ended up sleeping (literally) with one of People Magazine's *100 Most Beautiful People in the World*. Now I was in his son's nursery, intrusively sitting on the rocking chair Marco's mother (or nanny) used to lull him to sleep while getting reamed out by my mother for missing an arbitrary curfew. This might as well be *my* bedroom.

Speaking of babies, it hit me that I still had to get in touch with Andrea to find out what was going on. I hit her name stored under my phone's "favorites."

"Hello?" she groaned.

"Andrea! What's going on?"

"I started bleeding last night," she explained, sounding extremely exhausted and hoarse. "We're all okay, but the doctors want to monitor the situation, so I'm stuck in the hospital. The twins may come sooner than we thought."

"Okay, I'm in the city. I'll get there as soon as I can."

"Oh, so that's where you are! With everything going on, I forgot to give you the heads up about your mother looking for you. Who are you with?"

I rubbed my throbbing head. "It's a long story."

"You can't do that to me! It's not like I'm going anywhere."

I gave Andrea blow-by-blow details of what I could remember.

"It must be nice," Andrea puffed. "You're out gallivanting with the Prince of New York City, and I'm lying here waiting for my precious goods to be slaughtered."

I stifled a yawn. "Hopefully, you won't be pushing them out anytime soon."

We hung up. I gingerly rose up from the chair and snuck back into Miguel's bedroom. To my surprise, he was sitting up in bed with his arms crossed over his bare chest. His dark hair was tousled, and he had slight stubble sprinkled across his cheeks. He looked *extremely* sexy.

"Morning," he said cheerfully.

I seriously considered forgetting about whatever was going on in Honey Crest right then and jumping back into his bed.

"Morning," I repeated. I walked over to my side of the bed and picked up my purse, which was open on the floor.

He climbed over to me. "Where do you think you're going?" he smiled, wrapping his arms around me and drawing me into bed. My purse fell out of my hands and back onto the floor.

"I thought you snuck out on me," he pouted, lightly kissing my forehead.

I was mush in his arms. Andrea, what? Babies, who? "Nope, I just had to make a phone call."

"Is everything all right?"

I turned to face him. "My best friend is pregnant with twins and got rushed to the hospital last night because she was bleeding. I have to go see her."

"Oh." He frowned. "So you can't hang out?"

"No," I pouted. I honestly wanted to cry.

"All right then. Well, I'll walk you out," he shrugged, releasing me. He sprung out of bed and threw on a t-shirt that was slung over a chair. By the time I got up, he was already standing by the door, whistling to himself while waiting for me. I had to admit, his jarring change in attitude startled me. He walked me down the hallway, past baby Marco's room and past the living room where his friends and their dates were snoring away.

Miguel opened the front door. "If you need a ride back to your car, ask for Juan at the front desk. I would walk down with you, but, you know…"

I lowered my head in shame. "Yeah, I know."

He nervously glanced at my right fist, which was clenching my cell phone. "You didn't take any pictures or tell anyone what we did last night, did you?"

My minutes-ago conversation with Andrea flashed across my mind. "No pictures, and I don't remember enough of last night to recount what happened."

Miguel let out a sigh of relief. "Goooooood!" he exclaimed, clapping his hands. He pulled me in for a quick hug. "It was a fun night, though," he said quickly. "Take care." And with that, he released me and basically pushed me out the door.

I turned to look at him. "You… "

The door shut before I could finish my sentence.

"…too," I said slowly. I scratched my head. What had just happened there? My confusion quickly turned to anger as I walked to the elevator. Just like that, he throws me out, like a piece of trash? No promise to call? Did last night not mean ANYTHING to him?

Annoyed, I skipped going to the front desk and hailed my own taxi back to my car, which was in a parking garage by Bamboo Sushi.

My mother, after all these years, would get her wish— the Miguel Martinez poster was coming off my wall as soon as I got home.

■ ■ ■

Three Advil, a liter of bottled water, a doughy everything bagel with cream cheese, and two hours of aggravating New York City traffic later, I rushed through the entrance of Saint Brigid Hospital.

"Maternity wing?" I asked the receptionist.

"Fourth floor. Who are you here to see?"

"Andrea Deveroux. D-E-V-E-..."

She punched the letters on the keyboard. "I don't have an Andrea Deveroux on file."

"Andrea Rocha?" I suggested. She certainly wasted no time ridding herself of her married name!

"Room 402," she said a few seconds later, handing me a pass.

"Thanks," I mumbled.

The elevator was taking forever, so I ran up the emergency stairs and down the maternity wing's long, well-lit corridor.

Sir Walter Scott once famously said: *"Oh! What a tangled web we weave, when we first practice to deceive!"* I think the inspiration for his poetry came from the drama emitting from the people currently assembled in room 402.

There was Andrea, sitting up in bed, writhing in pain. There was Andrea's mother, an older looking version of her daughter, sitting in a chair next to the bed, clutching rosary beads while silently praying. There was Andrea's father, a rail-thin Brazilian man, who stood against the wall menacingly staring at Richard, Andrea's gay soon-to-be ex-husband, who was anxiously pacing around the room. Sitting on top of the windowsill, for reasons unbeknownst to me, was Xander, the man Andrea had fallen in love with. And finally, next to him was Dante, who immediately looked the other way when I entered the room. There were more storylines in this hospital than Shonda Rhimes would know what to do with.

I gave everyone a tentative wave and walked up to Andrea's bed.

"How are you feeling?" I said, gingerly wiping a piece of stray hair away from her makeup-less face.

"All things considering, I'm okay," she groaned, adjusting the pillow behind her head.

"Do you need anything?" I asked.

Andrea shook her head no while eying me up and down. "I like your outfit!" She briefly perked up. "Is that what you wore to the city last night, you dirty stay out?"

"Yup," I lightly laughed. Only Andrea would pay attention to my fashion choices while holed up in the hospital.

"So that's what you've been doing instead of coming to see me? Partying hardy?" Xander joked.

"I know, I've been bad," I agreed. "It's been a very busy time."

"Cut her some slack, will ya? Last night Carla hung out with *Miguel Martinez*," Andrea scoffed through her pain. From the corner of my eye, I saw Dante give me a questionable look. I had to act fast, considering a sports personality was in the room and could go public with my very top secret information.

"Andrea, please never mention that again. He'd kill me if..."

"I don't care if you are hanging out with the President. It's never too busy to get your fitness in," Xander interrupted.

"Shut up about her fitness! You are not her father!" Andrea snapped.

"So what's the latest?" I asked, hastily changing the subject.

"The bleeding stopped, and the babies are okay, but if their heartbeats drop again then they are going to do a C-section," Mrs. Rocha explained in her broken accent.

"But you're only a month away from your due date, so this isn't TOO bad, right?"

"Their lungs aren't fully developed yet, so they want me to hold out to 37 weeks. I'm at 35 now. I just hope...hope they are okay."

Mrs. Rocha started crying, which in turn made her daughter cry.

"I've just been under so much stress, with the divorce and everything," Andrea continued, blotting her eyes with a tissue. "And this is YOUR fault!" she screamed at Richard.

Richard shook his head. Mr. Rocha's facial expression grew angrier, and he clutched both of his hands in threatening fists.

"Carla, can I speak to you outside?" Dante suddenly asked.

"Sure," I answered, relieved to be taken out of this pressure cooker.

Dante and I exited the room, and he shut the door behind us.

"What the hell is Xander doing here?" I blurted out.

"She was working out with Xander when the bleeding started," Dante explained in a monotone voice. "He drove her to the hospital and wanted to stay to make sure she and the babies were okay."

I gave him a knowing look. "I see. And Richard?"

"Um, doesn't he kind of have to be here?"

"Do you *not* know the story?" I retorted, arching my eyebrow.

"Whatever," Dante muttered. "Speaking of illegitimate relationships, what were you doing with Miguel Martinez last night?"

A pang of annoyance hit my body. *Thanks, Andrea.* His tone was wrought with judgment, and who was New Jersey's resident womanizer to judge anyone in their dalliances?

"I'm not at liberty to say," I scoffed. In different times, Dante would have been the first call I would have made, not so much to deliver the nitty-gritty details, but because Miguel was his favorite New York Yankee and he would have gotten a kick out of my close proximity. But had Andrea not blabbed my business to the room, the story never would have left my lips--not to someone who had gone from blood brother to mild acquaintance.

We walked a little more in silence. He suddenly stopped and turned to me. "Carla, there's been something I've been meaning to talk to you about."

"What's up?" I chirped, sounding more confident than I felt because right then it finally hit me—these past few weeks of not talking had nothing to do with his breakup with Stacy.

His piercing blue eyes cut into me. "Is it true that you tried to get me fired?"

My mouth dropped open. "What are you talking about?" I shrilled.

"The night that I got drunk, is it true you told Dan that he should fire me?"

Oh no, he was NOT going there! I felt the anger that I'd been suppressing since September quickly rise up my body.

"Listen to what you just said, Dante," I countered. "'The night I got drunk.' Had I not dragged you out of your apartment and into the studio, your ass would have been *done.* And now you think I was trying to get you *fired*? Where do you even get off on accusing me of such lies?"

Dante smirked. "Right, so Dan just made it all up."

"Made what up?" I snapped.

"That you suggested he should hire someone more serious about the job, someone more like you."

"I didn't say that," I asserted.

Dante took a step closer to me. "You didn't? Why would Dan call me the next morning warning me to stay away from you?"

My Italian temper was about to pop off. "Oh, so *that's* what he called you up to say? He had nothing to say about your almost missing your show, but instead wanted to talk shit about *me*?"

"See, you did try to get me fired," Dante insisted.

"I did not try to get you fired!" I barked. "Dan called me freaking out that you weren't at the station yet. I had no idea where you were. He wanted me to come up with a solution, so I recommended myself."

"How convenient!" Dante threw his hands up in the air and started to walk away.

"Hey!" I ran around him, stopping him in his tracks. "There's a big difference between volunteering to fill in versus actually trying to push you out."

"Carla, you've been so bent out of shape since I started there. You saw a window of opportunity to get me out, and you tried to take it." Our noses were almost touching at this point.

"You tried to get YOURSELF out of there! You got fucking hammered the night of your show!"

"It's not the point, Carla. Besides, I would have found a way into New York."

"How?! You couldn't even stand up straight!"

"That's not the point," he repeated.

"Yes, it IS the point! You think life is one big party, and you have no sense of responsibility!"

"*I* don't have a sense of responsibility? I've been living on my own since I'm 18; meanwhile, you are 27 still living at home with your parents!"

"Living at home with my parents has nothing to do with this. At least I know how to maintain a job; you barely had a cup of coffee with W-S-P-S and you managed to almost fuck it up, as you've done with every other opportunity handed to you."

"Really? Enlighten me Carla; what else have I fucked up in my life?"

"Music. Sports. College. Shall I continue?"

"I don't think you want me to start comparing resumes, Carla," he warned.

By now we were engaged in a full-on screaming match. The hospital patrons had gathered near us to watch the free fireworks display.

Dante shook his head. "Look, I LOVE what I'm doing. Has it always been my dream? No. But I'm here now, and I'm doing a *damn* good job at it! Just because Dan doesn't think you are talented enough to do this is not my problem— "

I gasped, interrupting him mid-thought. "I can't believe you just— "

"...And because you are too thick-headed to see that, you let your insane jealousy ruin our friendship," Dante finished.

"No, what ruined this friendship is YOU. Dan has his head buried so far up your ass that you'd believe anything he says, instead of listening to someone who's known you for almost thirty years!"

"Dan has nothing to do with this. You showed your true colors since the day I took this job."

"And you now just showed yours." I gave him one last glare before turning to walk away. As I made my way to the elevator and out the hospital doors, I managed to keep myself numb. However, the second I stepped into my car, I took a very deep breath and starting quivering. I knew what was coming. When

I exhaled, the dam exploded. Everything from the past twenty-four hours came out in one big heap.

For the next half hour, I sat in the hospital parking lot, an inconsolable mess. People passing by probably thought I had just lost a loved one. But hadn't I?

■ ■ ■

It was almost three in the morning, and despite being physically and mentally drained, I couldn't sleep. I tossed and turned while replaying my conversation with Dante for the hundredth time.

Cutting into my thoughts was my cell phone vibrating on my nightstand. I lunged for it, hoping it wasn't more bad news.

Andrea.

"Are you okay?" My voice was shaky.

"I'm more than okay," Andrea said peacefully. "I'm here holding Nadia and Nico, and they can't wait to meet their Aunt Carla."

Without even thinking, I jumped out of bed. "I'll be right there."

15

Day 159

Miguel Martinez and I are lying in front of his fireplace, furiously kissing on the white carpet as if our lives depended on it. We're both still fully clothed, and I'm on top of him, grinding into his crotch.

"I want you so bad," he breaths. He immediately rips his shirt off, but before I can do the same, I notice that he is distracted by something outside.

"Will you look at that freakin' view? Wow,, I love being rich," he says, pointing out the window towards the twinkling New York City skyline. I climb down from him and hug my knees towards my chin, not sure what to do or say.

He jumps up and then reappears a few seconds with two glasses of wine. He hands me a glass as he finishes his in one big gulp. "To Ruby getting fired," he toasts, kissing me on the cheek.

My eyes light up. "She got fired?"

"I got her fired," he says, nuzzling my neck.

I rotate my shoulder, pushing him off. "What do you mean? I thought Dan-"

"Dan nothing. I don't like the way she was treating you. I love you, Carla, and it's the least I can do," he takes my wine glass away and drinks its contents in one shot. He throws the glass behind him and grabs my chin, sending chills down my spine. "I can't wait to make love to you," Miguel whispers.

"Me too. I'm just so nervous," I frown.

He holds me securely. "Oh, baby, what do you have to be nervous about?"

I hang my head in shame. "It's been so long, I don't know if I remember how to—"

"Oh, you will. You are so beautiful. I'll see to it that we make up for your lost time." He lowers the straps of my black dress, and slowly unzips my top. He never breaks eye contact as he continues to disrobe me. "Lie back," he orders lustily, caressing my neck with kisses.

I close my eyes, eager for what is coming next. I feel his fingers slip under my thong underwear, and he slowly pulls it down.

"Carla!" A female voice shouts.

I try to drown her out and focus on Miguel's movements, but he stops. He, along with everything in the living room, starts to fade to black.

"Carla!" The female voice repeats. It sounds so, so familiar.

"Not now Mom!" I shout. I try to will Miguel back into the picture, but he had already disappeared.

"It's Christmas morning, get up now!"

"What?" I fluttered my eyes open and saw my mother looming large above the bed.

"It's Christmas morning; it's time to open presents! Usually, you are the first one to wake everybody up."

"Oh yeah, uh, Merry Christmas," I grumbled, rubbing the sleep from my eyes. How did she get in here, anyway? I always kept my door locked to thwart off unwanted visitors, Nancy D'Agostino being number one on that dubious list.

Mom raised an eyebrow. "That was some dream you must have been having. You had a huge smile on your face and were hugging yourself. What was it about?"

I racked my brain. The last thing I remembered was... *oh shit!* I was hemming and hawing to Miguel about having sex (my insecurities are omnipresent, even in a parallel universe), and then, just when I was about to give in, my mother interrupting us.

I threw my comforter off, annoyed. Even in my subconscious she had to be a buzz kill.

"I was actually hugging you, Mom!" I laughed (and lied), throwing my arms around her. "I dreamt that you and Dad surprised me with a new car, with a big red bow wrapped around it. You know, like in those Lexus car commercials."

"I hate those commercials," she retorted, throwing me off of her. "We are running behind schedule, we have a lot of family to visit. Hurry up and get downstairs." She shot up from my bed and fluttered out of the room. Once the door shut behind her, I lunged towards the charging iPhone on my nightstand.

Call me weird, but I always leave my unattended phone face down on its screen. I revel in those couple of extra seconds of anticipation of what is awaiting me on the other side—a new job opportunity? Mark calling with a long-overdue apology? Or, in the case of these last 36 torturous days, a missed call, voice mail, text message or e-mail from #38 on the New York Yankees? But unfortunately, there were no Christmas miracles jumping out to greet me, just a few "Happy Holidays!" junk e-mails.

I sighed, tossing the phone on my mattress, and followed in its path, frowning at the ceiling. Why was I still holding on to the hope that Miguel was going to call after he unceremoniously kicked me out of his place? Besides, his "divorce" never hit the papers. After spending the night with me, he probably realized that the single life was for the birds and ran back home to his hot wife. It wouldn't be the first time another girl won out.

I winced as I thought about the scene unfolding at Casa Martinez right at this very moment... *Husband, wife, and kids are wearing matching red plaid pajamas and are sitting in a sea of endless presents under a massive Christmas tree. A fire is crackling in the stone fireplace. Trisha Martinez cradles baby Marco as she adoringly watches her two older children gleefully rip through the wrapping paper. Miguel tenderly puts a hand on his wife's shoulder and whispers, "How lucky are we to have such a beautiful family? I love you."*

"I love you too," Trisha smiles, feeling like the luckiest woman on the face of the earth.

They steal a kiss as the snow begins to fall lightly outside the window, completing the picture-perfect scene.

I glanced out the window and saw that it wasn't snowing. I think it was actually supposed to be in the 40s, which was warm for this time of year. But at the Martinez penthouse, a mere 20 miles away, it *would* be snowing; Mother Nature wouldn't want it any other way.

"CAR-LAAAAAAAAAAAA! WHAT ARE YOU DOING? COME DOWNSTAIRS!" Mom screamed, interrupting my runaway train of thoughts.

A part of me wanted to blow off my family and go back to sleep; it was not like anything from my grown up Christmas list would be under the tree. (I was not exactly sure what type of box you would use to package a man or a dream job.) But I was too tired to fight.

"Coming!"

■ ■ ■

Eight hours and 500 pounds of food later, I retreated back to my room. I escaped the day pretty unscathed; Mom was good and didn't say anything to make me feel bad about myself, and in general, the family got along. Christmas was, overall, a success.

I lay in bed and placed my laptop on my lap. I logged onto *Facebook*, and seconds later my eyes were assaulted with an onslaught of "had the best Christmas ever with my hubby!" and "Santa treated my kids very well this year!" -type status updates. Disgusted, I was about to sign off, but a chat notification stopped me.

> **Kevin Russo: Merry Christmas, Carla! How are you?**

Kevin Russo was an acquaintance from college; we had a bunch of classes together in our communications major and always got along well. After graduation, he got a producing job at NYS, the region's number one sports cable station, and we would randomly bump into each other at various games and events.

In other words, why would a minor character from my past reach out to me on Christmas?

> **Carla D'Agostino: Merry Christmas to you too! How is everything going?**

> **Kevin Russo: I've been better, but I'm ok. I have a really random question for you.**

Carla D'Agostino: Sure.

Kevin Russo: Well, I broke up with my girlfriend a couple of days ago. What timing, right? Anyway, I have tickets to this really cool event on New Year's Eve in the city. If you don't have plans, would you want to go?

There were various days on the calendar that were a single person's worst nightmare (the manufactured garbage of February 14th being the number one obvious) but personally, it was a certain day in December that slayed me...and believe it or not, it wasn't Christmas.

Don't get me wrong, the holiday season was almost disgustingly too romantic—the lights, the fresh snow, comfortable sweaters, cuddling by the fireplace, cutting down the tree...even the endless parade of parties and the insanity at the malls carried a certain romanticism. You got hit with pangs of loneliness at various times, but the distraction of all the commotion dulled the pain. However, after the pomp and circumstance were over, and all of the presents had been put away (or in my case, returned; why didn't *anybody* listen when I said I just wanted gift cards so I could buy my own stuff?!), we singles have one of the most daunting of obstacles to overcome...

New Year's Eve.

Isn't it such an overblown, amateur, DUMB holiday? Every establishment charges an obscene amount of money for crap food and entertainment, and you are forced to celebrate with untrained animals who haven't been out since *last* December 31st. But if you don't go out, you feel like a loser because "everyone goes out for New Year's Eve." Never mind gifts; all I wanted from Santa was the flu, so I'd have a built-in excuse to stay home.

Of course, I'd gladly spend New Year's Eve standing naked on a bed of hot coals in the fiery depths of hell if it meant bypassing the sheer agony of those *dreaded* twenty seconds that no person should ever have to endure…having no one to kiss for "The New Year's Kiss." For those lucky enough to have never experienced this phenomenon in their adult life, here is a first-hand account of how "The New Year's Kiss" looks from the sidelines:

> *"…Ten…Nine…Eight…!"*
>
> *I watch all the couples in the room clutch each other, joyfully chanting the countdown. I rub my temples to fight the oncoming stress headache.*
>
> *"…Seven…Six...Five…!"*
>
> *I gulp as they pucker their lips in great anticipation.*
>
> *"…Four…Three...Two…!"*
>
> *I hold my breath and close my eyes.*
>
> *"…One! Happy New Year!"*
>
> *My stomach drops as I feel everyone in the room (and in the Eastern Time Zone) embrace. I frantically start*

counting down to another ten seconds, since that's when the kisses would be over.

10987654321!

Breathing out a huge sigh of relief, I fling open my eyes. The ostentatious public displays of affection should mercifully be over…nope, wait a minute, there's a couple slobbering all over each other in the back corner, and there's another twosome humping against the bar. Come on people, it's 12:01, enough is enough!

I feel something tickle my face.

"Hap-py New Yearssss!" Katie slurs, drunkenly taunting me with a silver party blower.

That had been my New Year's Eve "celebration" for the past two years, and just when I thought it couldn't get worse, I get this out-of-the-blue invite from some dopey kid I went to college with. I was probably his last resort after he scoured his friends list and realized I was the last single girl on the planet.

I decided that, no matter what the event was, I would tell him no. I'd be perfectly happy ringing in the new year at home in my pajamas over a quart of wonton soup, far away from the crowds. Who knew, maybe this approach would work; instead of building up another year to be the "best one yet" I'd go into this one quietly and maybe see my vast expectations actually get realized.

Carla D'Agostino: I'm sorry to hear that. Thanks for thinking of me, although I'm still trying to figure out what I'm doing...

Kevin Russo: I figured as such, no pressure. It's just that I remember how much you loved Miguel Martinez back in college and the event is his annual charity New Year's ball.

Have I mentioned how much I love New Year's Eve?

Carla D'Agostino: How did you score those tickets?!

Kevin Russo: I have friends in high places, haha. The station has a table, and my boss asked me to go.

I had the grin of a Cheshire Cat as I merrily typed my final answer.

Carla D'Agostino: Well I don't want to make you look bad in front of your boss, lol...what time are we meeting?

■ ■ ■

"Why don't you ever take risks with your fashion?" Andrea huffed, rolling her eyes.

"I'm not wearing some weird fuchsia feather dress on New Year's Eve...or ever!" I shot back.

It was the next day, and before we did our annual Jade Meadow day-after-Christmas gift exchange with (what was left of) the crew, I had Andrea come with me to the mall. We were arguing in the middle of the busy Satriano dressing room as her five-week-old twins lay quietly in their double stroller. I was between two mini dresses—a black slit sleeve and a red one-shoulder with rhinestone accents. Meanwhile, Andrea was trying to convince me to try on samples from Lady Gaga's closet.

"Why did you invite me to help you shop if you aren't going to take any of my suggestions anyway? You are so difficult!" Andrea whined.

I ignored her as I went into the dressing room to try the dresses on for the third time. Both frocks were hot, and each would make it impossible for Miguel not to notice me. What's a girl to do?

When I emerged from behind the curtain, Andrea was reading a magazine while absentmindedly pushing the double-seated stroller back and forth.

"I don't know which to get," I pouted.

"Whatever," Andrea muttered. "Hey, did you know that in a baby's first year, its brain will double to become half its final size?" She looked up from the magazine, her face full of worry. "That's huge, isn't it? Are my babies going to have giant alien heads?"

I sighed. "No Andrea, your babies will be fine."

"Listen to this one," she continued. "The heaviest baby was born in Italy in 1995. He weighed 22 pounds, eight ounces. Can you imagine trying to push that thing out of you?"

"ANDREA! I don't have time for *Jeopardy: Baby Edition.* Pick a dress!"

She snapped to attention. "Well, you always wear black, so "be bold" and go with red," Andrea mocked.

"Kids, do you agree?" Nico was staring into space and couldn't care less, but Nadia actually looked in my direction and pointed towards the red dress. Andrea and I broke out into matching smiles. What a cool moment!

"Yayyyy!" I cheered, clapping the dresses together.

"She has Mommy's taste!" Andrea proudly boasted.

■ ■ ■

After I had blown all of my Christmas money on the $250 dress, matching accessories and sexy nude platform stilettos, we made our way to Downtown, where Katie was waiting for us.

"Merry Christmas!" Katie exclaimed, jumping out of her chair to hug us. After we had exchanged hellos, we settled into our seats— Andrea and Katie facing the door, me sitting opposite, and using the fourth chair to hold our purses and gifts.

I watched Andrea and Katie study their menus. When was the last time we were all together? It felt like ages.

Between Andrea's kids, Katie's shop and my, um, life, it had been difficult to get our schedules in sync for even our monthly brunches. I'm sure my rift with Dante didn't help our cause.

I shifted my gaze to study the festive seating area of Downtown. The rolling wood ceilings were draped with green garland and twinkling white lights. Each tabletop was decorated by a crafty, stemless wine glass centerpiece filled with fake snow and shiny ball ornaments, topped with a flickering tea light. The candles and the glow from above provided the only source of light in the dim restaurant.

Suddenly, a familiar wave of regret washed over me; I had not taken a single second to enjoy the season this year, for I was too wrapped up in my own malaise to even notice, or care. I hadn't helped Dad and Jimmy do any of the Christmas lights outside, a tradition of ours since childhood. To bypass the hysteria and synthetic cheer from the shops, I'd done all of my shopping online. I normally loved making batches of holiday cookies (to the chagrin of my mother, who despised a dirty kitchen only more than she hated sugary treats tempting her diet) or driving around town to look at all the decked-out houses while blasting Mariah Carey's "All I Want for Christmas is You". Come to think of it, I hadn't dusted off the *NSYNC "Home for Christmas" album, or even flipped on the radio to the 24/7 holiday music station. I was never going to get Christmas 2016 back, and that was sad.

Maybe that was my problem...I focused more on the things I didn't have than on what I did have, I thought as Andrea picked up an antsy Nico and lightly patted him on the back.

Look at yesterday morning; I had been so depressed about Miguel that I contemplated not going downstairs to my beautifully heated family room to open an embarrassment of presents with my mother, father, brother and soon-to-be sister-in-law. Meanwhile, the majority of the world was battling war, poverty, sickness, and death. I was one of the *lucky* ones!

The image of Tony Soprano popped into my head when he said to Dr. Melfi on *The Sopranos*: "You know my feelings: every day is a gift. It's just, does it have to be a pair of socks?"

I snickered. It was always one step forward, two steps back in this wacky head of mine.

"So what's new, guys?" I quipped, glancing over the menu. "I feel like it's been forever."

"I'm just happy the holidays are over," Katie sighed, rubbing her emerald eyes. "I'm so thankful that the shop has taken off so quickly, but it's been a lot of work, more than I anticipated."

"So are kids," Andrea huffed, still cradling Nico. "Thank God for my mother, or else I don't know how I could have handled all of this."

"Anything new with the divorce?"

"Not with the divorce, but I was waiting for the three of us to be together to tell you…" Andrea trailed off. "Xander and I are officially dating!"

"You are?" Katie and I squealed.

"The family court system is so screwed up, it could take over a year to get this done," Andrea sighed. "I could only hold out for so long! Besides, he's the BEST I've ever had; he's definitely worth living in sin for."

"Okay then, moving on," Katie laughed. "How about you, Carla, did you hear from Miguel?"

"No...but I will be seeing him on New Year's Eve," I happily replied.

"How does that work?"

"I got invited to his charity New Year's party by a friend of mine in the business. He broke up with his girlfriend, and he needed a date."

Katie's eyes widened. "Well forget about Miguel; who is this friend?" I was amused by her astonishment; she knew how much I hated dating and would only make time for someone I really, REALLY liked.

"It's not like that. He needs a favor, and I need answers. It was a win-win."

After the waitress had come by to take our drink orders, Katie broke out in a huge grin. "Guys, I have something to tell you. My life hasn't exactly been all work, no play lately..."

"Oh, I like the sound of that. Do tell!" Andrea exclaimed, placing a now-sleeping Nico back in the stroller.

"I have a boyfriend!" Katie shrieked.

I opened my mouth to speak, but I had no words. Katie had a boyfriend?!

"We met two months ago," she continued. "He was a regular customer of Kettle Black, but since I was always working in the back, we never met. Now that I'm out front, we started talking and…"

"You've had a boyfriend for two months and didn't tell us?" Andrea scoffed.

"No, he hasn't been my boyfriend for two months," Katie quickly answered. "He became my boyfriend on Christmas… *yesterday*! He gave me a custom-made Christmas ornament and had "Katie and Teddy, 12-25-16" engraved. That's how he asked me!"

We were all so engrossed in the conversation, that we didn't even notice the waitress bring our drinks. "So tell us about this Teddy," I smiled, taking a big sip of my merlot.

"Well, his name is Teddy Shay. He looks tough, but he's the sweetest person you will ever meet. He rides a motorcycle; he's got a half tattoo sleeve on each arm. He can drink me under the table…He's perfect!"

I thought of me bringing someone like that home to my mother. Yeah, that wouldn't go over so well, but if you Googled "Katie Lansford's ideal man," this was the first image that would come up.

"What does he do for a living?" Andrea asked.

"His family owns an Irish pub, and he helps run that. He's also a Honey Crest cop. He comes in with his co-workers all the time for the maple honey glazed donuts."

"So he's into perpetuating stereotypes," I cracked.

Katie laughed a lot harder than she normally would at my sarcasm. Her eyes were brimming with joy. My friend had it *bad.*

"You know how we stress out about guys and their bullshit?" she asked.

"Vaguely," I deadpanned.

"With him, it's so loving and comfortable and *easy*! When it's real, there's none of that nonsense; you fall into each other and just *be.* Me and Teddy hit it off and never looked back."

I felt my skin turn a bright shade of green as Katie fell into a trance again. To hear her wax poetic on the thrills of love was a sordid reminder that I'd never known what she was experiencing. With Mark, it was never "easy"; it was a constant tug-of-war of emotions. As for the rest of the men in my life? They never stuck around long enough to even entertain picking up the rope.

"I can't wait for you guys to meet him!" Katie finished.

"I just can't believe this is the first we are hearing about him," Andrea shot back, stirring her sparkling Pellegrino with a straw.

"Well, I didn't want to jinx anything, and you guys have your own, um, stuff going on…"

"Just because I'm going through a divorce and Carla's constantly miserable in love, doesn't mean we can't be happy for you," Andrea fired.

"Thanks for that," I mumbled.

"I don't think that at all…but you wanted to delete your *Facebook* because you couldn't bear seeing all of the engagement announcements, for crying out loud!" Katie retorted, pointing to me.

"But you are different. You're family. You don't want to end up like Dante, do you?" I added half-playfully.

"Yea, about that..." Katie started to say.

"About what?"

She motioned behind me. I turned around and drew my breath as I saw Dante walking towards our table. I hadn't seen him since our blowup at the hospital, and I wanted to keep it that way.

I swung back around to face my friends. "Why didn't you tell me he was coming?" I hissed.

"Carla, drop it. It's Christmas! We haven't been together in so long!" Katie pleaded.

I grabbed my purse, angry that they plotted to corner me like this. "I'm out of here."

"He got you in the grab bag, at least stick around to get your gift," Andrea suggested.

"Oh great, just what I want— a gift from him that was purchased with W-S-P-S money. No, thank you. How could you guys do this to me? You know I don't want to be in his company."

"We're sick of splitting our time between the two of you," Andrea complained. "Going through one divorce is enough; I don't feel like going through two!"

I rose up from my chair, placing a gift bag in front of Katie and two little boxes in front of Andrea for the babies. "Merry Christmas. I'm leaving."

Katie pushed the bag away. "Why are you being so selfish?"

Before I could reply, Dante appeared at our table. "Hey guys," Dante softly said, fully aware of the dynamics of our conversation. He turned to me. "Hi Carla," he added, holding out a small box. "Merry Christmas."

I gave him a dirty look, but he ignored it and extended his arms out to hug me. I was trapped; it was either give in or cause a scene. I lazily threw one arm around him. "Thank you," I answered nonchalantly, taking the package. "Merry Christmas. I was just leaving."

"I thought we were having dinner?" he asked, puzzled.

"You guys are. I'm out of here."

"Carla, sit," Katie pleaded.

I picked up my wine, chugged the remainder of it, and defiantly slammed the glass back on the table. "See you guys later."

I felt three pairs of eyes burn into my back as I exited the restaurant. The cold air didn't even faze me as I walked to the car. As I waited for my car to heat up, I studied the package Dante had given me. It was wrapped in a simple silver paper, topped with a white bow. Should I open it?

Just as I had my finger under the lip of the wrapping paper, I decided against it. I knew that inside the contents of the box had to be some sort of written apology. I was not going to accept it anyway, so why bother? I stuffed the gift in my glove compartment. One day, I was sure I'd get around to opening it. But I had more important things to worry about...

Like December 31st.

16

Day 166

The stirring of butterflies in my stomach woke me up at 4:30 a.m. Tonight was the confrontation I'd been waiting weeks for. But in order not to burn out, I needed to calm down.

I went to the gym with Andrea and ran on the treadmill for an hour. We relaxed in the locker room's sauna, and then I treated myself to a massage at the gym's spa. Afterward, I went home and drew myself a hot Jacuzzi bath and lit candles all around the bathroom.

Despite all of my efforts, my nerves were still shot.

"Where are you going tonight?" My Mom grilled as I headed out the door for my hair and makeup appointment at Mona Lisa Salon.

"I'm actually going to a work function," I lied. "It's a big charity gala with a lot of the area players." That was true; a lot of Miguel's teammates would be there.

"Where?"

"In New York." I braced myself for her reaction; she was so paranoid about the city.

"IN NEW YORK?! On New Year's Eve? Are you crazy? What if they try to blow it up?"

I rolled my eyes. "The security will be air-tight, Mom. Don't worry."

"Is Dante going?"

"No," I glared at her. "Why would he be going?"

"Because it's a work thing," Mom pointed out.

"Well, he might be," I recovered. "But he's been working every night this week. God forbid Mr. Superstar isn't on the air."

"Well, I'd feel more comfortable if Dante was going with you," Mom replied.

"Even if Dante was going, we wouldn't be going together."

"I think that's sad. You two used to be so close." Mom frowned.

"No, it isn't," I muttered.

"I still don't think you should be going to New York tonight."

"That's nice," I replied, trying my best to brush her words off my shoulder. I shot towards the door. "Bye!"

■ ■ ■

While Olga, my pleasant Spanish hairdresser, blow-dried my hair, I lazily skimmed through the latest edition of *This Week*, my favorite celebrity tabloid. Nothing really tickled my interest until I saw it right there, on Page 16: Miguel and his wife, running on the beach with big smiles plastered across their faces.

The caption read: *Major League stud Miguel Martinez works up a sweat with "Personal Trainer to the Stars," wife Trisha in Miami. Mixing business with pleasure seems to be working for this red hot couple!*

Even though this was probably a hidden-paparazzi candid shot, you would have thought it was an outtake from a professional workout video shoot. They looked impeccable. Trisha wore a white sports bra with matching yoga pants and sneakers. Her blonde hair was tied up in a messy bun; her product-less face looked fresh and youthful. Miguel had on black sneakers and black shorts, no shirt. I studied Miguel's tanned, chiseled chest, the same one I woke up to forty-two days ago...in THEIR bed.

I slapped the magazine on my lap. Divorce my ass! The magazine's slogan was "No Stone Left Unturned." They prided themselves on getting the exclusive celebrity dirt before any of the other outlets. If there was trouble in Martinez paradise, the caption wouldn't have been so rosy.

I felt an array of emotions—anger, because it confirmed that I had gotten duped that night; guilt, because I'd helped Trisha's husband deceive her and their children, and embarrassment, because I showed my naiveté to this "player" and he and his friends probably shared a hearty laugh at my expense. I had every intention to tell Olga to stop styling my hair, then cancel on Kevin, speed home, throw on my pajamas, and celebrate New Year's Eve in bed as I had originally planned.

"Olga?"

"Yes, dear?"

I bit my lip. My logical side urged me to continue with canceling my plans. However, this tiny corner of my brain, the hotbed of irrational thinking that almost always got me into trouble, started drowning out all of my other thoughts.

"*What do you think you are doing?!*" Irrationality roared. "*You are going if it's the last thing you do! Let him rue the day he was born!*"

"Yes, dear?" Olga repeated.

I gulped. Who would win?

"Never mind," I sighed quietly, picking the magazine back up.

■ ■ ■

"Carla, you look stunning!" Kevin gasped as we walked towards each other outside of The New York Club in the Financial District.

"Thanks," I blushed. "You don't look so bad yourself." While Kevin's ill-fitting gray suit did little to hide the imperfections of his soft frame, he looked adorable with his slicked back hair and gold pinky ring. We would be fine, as long as I made it known that nothing more would come from this evening.

As for me…too bad WSPS paid in peanuts, because if I had the money I'd have Olga move in with me so I could look like this every day. She styled my long, brown hair into a cascade of loose curls swept to the side in a romantic ponytail, and the smokey eye makeup she expertly applied heightened the look's drama. As for the dress, it was $250 well spent; it hugged my curves as if I'd had it personally made.

"Shall we go in?" he asked, holding out his arm.

I giggled and linked my arm with his. "We shall."

I started to shake with anticipation as we walked up the concrete steps. The doorman politely nodded to us and opened the grand wooden door. There was madness awaiting us on the other side. The marble entryway was jammed with wall-to-wall people, and the air was loud with excitement. We made our way to a very pretty young girl at the check-in table.

"Name?" she asked in a strong British accent, not bothering to look up from her clipboard. I never understood why these highbrow events always seem to employ such miserable souls. He handed her two tickets. "Kevin."

"Honey, I need a last name," the rude hostess responded, finally looking up. Her otherwise-stunning gray eyes were bloodshot; she was either already drunk or had just finished "powdering her nose" in the bathroom.

"Oh, right," Kevin laughed nervously. "Russo. And guest."

I smiled at "and guest." When was the last time I was on the right side of a plus one? It felt nice.

"Here is your place card. Coat check is on your left. Move the line, please."

After we had checked our coats, we tried to squeeze our way to the cocktail hour. However, there was major rubbernecking going on by the step and repeat, so we were stuck amid a sea of hungry photographers.

"Well, this sucks," Kevin muttered.

"A little bit," I puffed.

"I know you can't see, but I just want to let you know that Miguel is on the red carpet," Kevin reported.

I pursed my lips as I casually tried standing on the tips of my toes, but even then I was too short to see above the wall of people. The only indication that someone of stature was in our presence was the amount of glamorati bulbs firing off against the wall. Then suddenly, the crowd slightly parted, and I had a clear shot of the red carpet.

And I was going to be sick.

Zeus and Hera, aka Miguel and Trisha, were hamming it up for the cameras. Miguel was wearing a crisp, stylish tuxedo and his trademark million-dollar grin. Trisha's tanned, toned legs seemed to go on for days, and her presumably fake breasts perked up underneath her black couture dress. He had his left arm lovingly draped around her tiny waist, and she casually hung her right arm over his broad shoulder. Her other hand was on her hip, and I saw a diamond equivalent to the diameter of Mars perched on her finger. He whispered in her ear, and they shared a quick laugh.

"Are you jealous?" Kevin teased.

"Why the hell would I be jealous?" I snapped, probably a little too harshly.

"Whoa relax. I'm only kidding. You can put the claws away," Kevin uneasily chuckled.

"I know you are kidding," I blushed, slightly ashamed at how I jumped down his throat. Obviously, he didn't mean any ill will by his comment. I shifted my focus back to the Golden Couple. After a few moments, Miguel decided to end the photo op by grabbing his wife's hand, escorting her off the red carpet, and headed into the cocktail hour. The star-struck crowd started following suit, and we were allowed to move.

"Finally!" Kevin exclaimed. "I'm starving."

My stomach growled in agreement. In my excitement/dread/anger/sadness/anticipation, I had completely forgotten to eat anything but a bowl of Special K cereal for breakfast. (I should get overly emotional more often.)

Kevin quietly whistled as we entered the elegant ballroom. Various kinds of fancy food stations outlined the periphery. In its center, bartenders mixed drinks behind the vast circular bar, frantically trying to keep up with the high-profile patrons' demands.

"I can get used to this," Kevin quipped, picking a Kobe beef slider off a passing waiter's silver hors d'oeuvres tray.

"It's better than spending tonight at some dive bar with only cold chicken fingers to eat," I laughed.

We walked to the bar and got ourselves some drinks—Captain Morgan and Coke for Kevin, Kettle and club for me. Kevin and I reminisced about the good ol' college days, and we both agreed we'd give anything to go back to that simpler time. (I looked back at my time in college more fondly than high school. I was more confident, and it was a heck of a lot more fun.)

As we talked about our Intro to Broadcasting professor's ridiculously fake toupee falling off in class, my smile quickly faded as I noticed two familiar figures walking towards our section of the bar.

"Isn't that your boss with Ruby Smith?" Kevin whispered.

"Unfortunately," I muttered, trying to nonchalantly hide behind Kevin, but it was too late. They saw me and were heading right for us.

"Hi Carla," Dan said, giving me a casual peck on the cheek that felt all kinds of weird. "You're looking splendid."

"What are YOU doing here?" Ruby asked incredulously, crossing her arms.

"For the same reason you are here…" I trailed off for effect. "To ring in the New Year and support a good cause. Dan, Ruby, meet Kevin Russo. We went to college together, and he works as a producer for N-Y-S. He asked me to accompany him this evening."

"Nice to meet you both! Carla's said some wonderful things about you two and the station," Kevin replied. I smirked; he definitely knew how to play the brown-nosing game one must play in this smoke-and-mirrors business.

Dan and Ruby extended their hands, except Ruby didn't bother looking in Kevin's direction; she continued to gawk at my ensemble, which was rapidly making me feel uncomfortable.

"Um, is something wrong?" Normally I wouldn't even try to go there, but this was after-hours; I didn't have to put on a front as I was forced to do every Monday through Friday. Call this the beginning of my New Year's Resolution, "Thou shalt not take bullshit from horrendous co-workers."

"Nothing's wrong,"' she shrugged. "You usually dress like a slob when you come to work, so I'm a little taken aback seeing you look like a sophisticated woman."

Kevin gasped. Three months ago I would have too, but her rudeness occurred so frequently, nothing she said surprised me.

"It's a black tie affair, so unfortunately I had to put away the sweats," I chuckled.

"I wonder why," Ruby sneered.

"You wonder what?" I challenged.

Dan interrupted us. "Ruby, why don't we continue making our rounds?" He turned to me. "Be careful getting home."

"Remember to keep it professional," Ruby smirked before they walked away. I returned the smug look back.

"I hate her," I blurted out to Kevin once they were out of earshot.

"I can see why," Kevin replied, disbelief still across his face. "And I can't believe your boss lets her get away with talking to you like that."

"I hate him too!" I snapped.

"Could that be why?" He motioned across the room.

I followed Kevin's line of sight. In plain view, for the entire New York sports world to see, was Dan Durkin's hand glued to the taut backside of Ruby Smith. The thought of Dan and Ruby sleeping together crossed my mind more than once (thanks to Gwen's father), but I prayed it wasn't true. Female sportscasters have such a bad reputation for screwing their way to the top, and I wanted to believe that Dan—and even Ruby—conducted their business more honorably. But how else could you explain such a sleaze landing one of the premier jobs in all of sports radio? Now I knew why.

"Maybe I should start sleeping my way to the top," I joked, the tension from before melting away.

Kevin's eyes widened. "Hey now!"

"You know what I mean," I playfully shoved him.

■ ■ ■

Forty-five minutes later, the party shifted over to the main ballroom. With its Roman columns, intricate plasterwork, sky-high ceilings and breathtaking views, the space was quintessential New York City.

Kevin led me to a table near the dance floor. It had a stunning tree branch and tea light centerpiece, and neatly placed around its base was an assortment of New Year's Eve party favors—hats, tiaras, beads, foil horns and squawkers. Since we were the first to arrive, I made sure our seats faced the room so I could have a clear shot of Miguel. When I sat down, I opened the cover of the thick ad book lying on my plate.

> *Dear Friends,*
>
> *Thank you for your generous support. This year, The SportsArts Foundation raised five million dollars and helped keep sports and arts after-school programs in seventeen New York City area schools. SportsArts vows to continue our pledge to ensure that all of our children get the opportunity to express themselves positively and uniquely in a safe environment outside the classroom.*
>
> *We hope you have a happy, healthy and successful new year.*
>
> *Sincerely,*
> *The Martinez Family*

Beneath that soliloquy was a glossy studio portrait of the family in matching white t-shirts and jeans, barefoot.

What a crock of shit. I tossed the book onto the table and sighed.

"Still thinking about Ruby?" Kevin asked sympathetically.

"Yeah, something like that," I lied.

Before Kevin could respond, he stood up to greet a pleasant-looking older couple.

"Hello, Mr. Murillo!" Kevin exclaimed.

"Hello, Kevin!" The plump, grey-haired man replied equally as enthusiastically. "Who is this pretty young lady with you?"

"Mr. James Murillo, this is Carla D'Agostino, a good friend of mine from college. Carla produces the "Tommy Max and Ruby Smith Show" on W-S-P-S. Carla, Mr. Murillo is the program director of N-Y-S, and this is his wife, Justine."

I rose out of my seat and made sure to give them my most dazzling smile. I wanted to return the favor from before when Kevin handled my whack job co-workers with natural ease. "It's great to meet you both! And I like your first name; my father and brother are also James."

"The pleasure is all mine, Carla," Mr. Murillo replied. "Your father and brother must be men of good character. Kevin, you've done very well for yourself."

"Thanks," Kevin smiled. I bit my tongue. Normally, I would have jumped in to clear up our relationship status, but I just let the misunderstanding hang in the air. Kevin might not be a looker, but tonight showed me he was a definite keeper. I wondered how his relationship ended.

To my delight, Mr. Murillo sat next to me. Although I had zero desire to get involved in television, I still viewed this as a golden networking opportunity. Mr. Murillo was a powerful figure in the media world, and might know other radio station managers to connect me with—radio station managers who would hire me based on my skills behind the microphone, and not in the bedroom (not that I had much to lend in that department anyway).

"You must love working with Tommy Max," Mr. Murillo said. "He is a walking sports encyclopedia."

"He is definitely amazing," I agreed. "I've learned so much from him. Can you believe he does the entire five-hour show with not a single note in front of him? It's all in his head!"

"I can believe it!" Mr. Murillo chuckled. "I just don't know why Durkin paired him with that Ruby Smith; the show was good enough as it was."

The answer is on display tonight for all the world to see, I thought. "Ruby adds another dimension to the program," I answered diplomatically.

"You are on the payroll; you have to say that," Mr. Murillo laughed.

"True," I giggled, appreciating the older man's candor.

The rest of our table started arriving, and Kevin introduced me to the rest of the NYS hierarchy—the head director and his wife, the sales manager and his wife, and the general manager and his wife. Everyone was interesting, lovely and respectful, a far cry from my scum co-workers.

Suddenly, Miguel Martinez's voice boomed from the surround-sound speakers. My heart leaped out of my chest. "Can I have everybody's attention please?" Miguel announced from the podium. Once everyone quieted down, he continued. "I want to make this short and sweet since the worst thing about these dinners is the dragged out speeches." A few people in the room chuckled.

"Anyway, this is the third year we are having the SportsArts New Year's Eve gala. Some people still find it odd that I hold this event on the biggest party night of the year, but I like the idea of ringing in the next 365 days with the people who are most important to me—my loyal supporters, my teammates, family, friends, and of course, my beautiful wife."

That elicited some "awws" from the audience.

Oh, yeah? I thought bitterly. *Where was your beautiful wife six weeks ago?*

"None of this would have been possible without you all, and from the bottom of my heart, I thank you for being here tonight. So, if everyone could pick up their champagne glasses and join me in a toast..." He waited a few moments for everyone to rise out of their chairs.

"May this be the year all of our dreams come true!"

Well, it's not getting off to a good start, I glumly thought as I lifted my flute.

"Cheers!" The crowd erupted. I clicked my glass with the rest of the table.

"Salute a cent'anno," Mr. Murillo toasted to me.

"Cin cin," I laughed, thrown off by his Italian.

"Tu parli italiano?" Mr. Murillo asked as we sat back down.

"Only the necessary words," I smiled.

"That's a shame; it's really a beautiful language. Justine and I travel to Italy for three weeks every year."

After engrossing ourselves in a discussion about our Mother Land, he shifted the focus back to work. "So what's a pretty girl like you doing in radio? You should be working on television," Mr. Murillo complimented.

"I appreciate your saying that," I nervously giggled, "but I like the format of radio better."

"Why?"

"Television is so stringent; you have to follow the rundown to the exact second. In radio, you have a little bit more leeway, and because of that, I feel that the hosts can relax and showcase their personalities better than on TV. Plus, it doesn't hurt that you can get away wearing pajamas to work," I jokingly added.

"Fair enough," Mr. Murillo nodded. "What is your ultimate goal in radio?"

"Don't get me wrong, I love producing, but my dream has always been to be on the air. I can chew anyone's ear off about sports for hours, but as you know, it's hard to break into the number one market." I couldn't believe how effortlessly the words floated out. In five years, I never talked to Dan with this ease.

"Does your boss know this?"

"Um, sort of?" I grimaced.

As Mr. Murillo mulled over my answer, an overwhelming sense of determination seared through my body. Instead of waiting for Mr. Murillo to make or not make a move, why shouldn't I take matters into my own hands, and take a chance with this perfect stranger? Then maybe something good can come out of this horrific night.

"If you know of anybody hiring, by all means, please let me know," I smiled broadly.

Mr. Murrillo chuckled. "I'll tell you what," he said, opening his jacket pocket and taking out a business card. "We should talk sooner rather than later. Are you free to come by the station Monday morning at 8?"

"I am!" I was in complete disbelief over this reversal of fortune. A bigwig wants to rush-meet with *me*?

"Good. My address is on there. And be sure to bring your resume and demo tape."

I smiled and put the card in my silver clutch. Evidently, I couldn't have picked a better time to decide to grow a pair of balls! As I silently patted myself on the back, I looked up and noticed Miguel approaching our table…with Trisha. My optimism vanished.

Ohmygod…

Moving counterclockwise, they individually greeted the people sitting across from me. As I watched them work the crowd, I started to panic. *I don't know if I can do this.* There was still time for me to bolt to the bathroom. But how would that look to Kevin and Mr. Murillo?

Miguel and Trisha greeted Mr. and Mrs. Murillo with huge hugs; obviously, this wasn't the first time they had met. He still hadn't noticed me, despite my sitting right there. I started to quietly hyperventilate.

OHMYGOD…

"Miguel and Trisha, I'd like you to meet a couple of young, very talented producers," Mr. Murillo said, motioning to Kevin and me. His introductions were drowned out by the screaming in my head.

OHMYGOD OHMYGOD OHMYGOD…

Miguel locked those beautiful, mossy green eyes with mine. I flashbacked to That Night—gyrating to the club music, touching him, kissing him…is that what he was thinking about too?

"Nice to meet you, Carla," Miguel smiled politely.

Nice to meet you? The images in my mind quickly shattered. He wasn't thinking about That Night. He doesn't even remember who I am, or at least, he's pretending to not remember who I am.

"Nice to meet you too," I replied, feigning enthusiasm.

"Thanks for coming tonight!" Trisha said in a high-pitched squeaky voice, breaking our non-moment. She gave me a dead fish handshake.

Before I could respond, Miguel took his wife by the arm. "Come on, honey," he cooed, moving her to the next table of admirers.

I was frozen into silence by what had just transpired. Kevin lightly nudging me a few moments later brought me back to the room. "That was pretty cool, huh? You must be freaking out!"

"Yeah, I'm freaking out," I deadpanned.

I couldn't take being in here anymore. I needed to leave.

"Excuse me," I announced, grabbing my purse.

I briskly walked outside to the heated terrace that overlooked the Freedom Tower. A few patrons were outside smoking, but the filthy smell of the secondhand smoke didn't even faze me.

I leaned both hands on the iron rail and hung my head. What did I honestly expect out of tonight? I didn't even WANT Miguel to leave his wife at this point, so why did I seek out this unnecessary drama?

"Carla?" A concerned voice boomed.

I turned around and saw Kevin. "Are you okay?"

"Yea, I'm fine," I sighed. "I just needed some air."

Kevin walked over to me and leaned his back against the railing. "This holiday sucks," he stated. "I miss Heather so much."

"I'm sorry," I whispered, drawing him in for a quick hug. "Why did you guys break up?"

"She said she needed her space," Kevin shrugged.

I badly wanted to call out her excuse as obvious code for "cheating," but judging by the tears forming in his eyes, taking the tough love approach right now wouldn't be appropriate.

"She just got laid off from her pharmaceutical sales job, and was confused about what to do with the rest of her life," he continued. "Me included, I guess."

It was time to throw tact out the window. "But Kevin, losing your job shouldn't mean intentionally sabotage every other aspect of your life." I drew a breath, gearing up for my role.

"I know that, but she's cut herself off from the world. Her friends haven't heard from her. Her mother told me she stays locked in her room all day. She's freaking out, I'm freaking out. She won't take any of my calls. I don't know what else to do."

It was sad that Mark had conditioned me to think "I need my space to figure out my life" translated to "I need my space so you're not here to ask questions when a U-Haul pulls into my driveway and picks up me and my things to drive cross country to be with a girl that I have yet to meet in person," but such was my life. Kevin clearly was in a different boat—unless her mother was in on the hoax (as Mark's was), he was getting very promising first-hand information that the relationship wasn't dead.

"Have you gone to her house?"

Kevin scrunched his nose. "No. That would just cause a scene. I've called her plenty of times; she knows how to get to me. I'm not chasing her."

"Kevin!" I exclaimed, lightly slapping him across the head. "That's EXACTLY what you need to do."

"Why? So she could slam the door in my face?"

I sighed. How could men be so dumb? "She's not going to slam the door in your face," I assured him. "She's pulling this little "damsel in distress" game to light a fire under your ass, so you can go and save her."

"Why?"

"Plenty of reasons. Maybe she didn't feel that you were too comforting in her initial time of need, and wants you to step up your game. Maybe she wants you to show up at her door with an engagement ring. I wasn't in your relationship, I don't know the story. But she's pushing you away, to try and get *closer* to you."

It made perfect sense to me, but Kevin looked as if I had just finished explaining the principals of quantum physics.

"That's the dumbest thing I've ever heard," he finally replied.

"No dumber than you saying that you aren't going to chase the girl that you love," I shot back.

"I don't..." Kevin started to look worried. "Do you think she really wants to get engaged? We've only been dating for eleven months; that's way too soon."

"Why do guys have to take everything so literally?" I cried. "I was giving you an *example*!"

Kevin blushed. "Oh."

"Look, you just have to throw your pride to the side and find this girl. Where is she tonight?"

"Like, tonight-tonight?"

I rolled my eyes. "Yes, TONIGHT, right now. What is she doing?"

"When I talked to her mother this afternoon, she said Heather had planned on sleeping through the ball dropping," Kevin answered slowly. "Her parents had plans, but were nervous to leave her home alone."

"Where does she live?"

"Denwood, about 25 miles from here," he replied, visibly growing more excited with each passing word.

I pulled out my cell phone to check the time. 11:02 p.m.

"Perfect!" I clapped my hands. "Get in your car and go! There will be no traffic, but you have to leave now!"

"Okay!" he shouted. He started bolting towards the door but stopped in his tracks. "Dammit! I didn't take my car here, I took the train. I'm never going to make it."

I grabbed his hand and started pulling him inside. "C'mon, I'll give you a ride. I have my car."

We hurriedly bid the NYS contingency farewell. As we galloped out of the party, I saw Miguel and Trisha slow dancing. I made sure to toss them a mental middle finger (and for good measure, threw another one up for Ruby and Dan, wherever they were).

In a matter of minutes, we were in my car. We easily slid into the Holland Tunnel, and once we emerged, barreled down Interstate 78.

"I'm so sorry that I made you leave the party," Kevin said, punching his girlfriend's address into my GPS.

I waved him off. "Don't be sorry. These rubber chicken dinners suck."

"Very true," he laughed. "You seemed to have hit it off with my boss, though. Isn't he awesome?"

"Yeah, he is great!" I agreed. "He actually wants me to come in on Monday."

"Really?" Kevin said, surprised. "For what, an interview?"

"He didn't say," I shrugged, playing it cool. "I asked him if he knew of anybody hiring, and he actually agreed to help. I need to desperately get out of W-S-P-S, and I think you saw why."

"I did," Kevin laughed. "It seems like a lot of good came out of tonight."

"What's that?"

"You are on your way to getting a new job, AND I'm on my way to getting back with Heather."

"Not bad. I've had worse nights," I mused.

Kevin snapped his fingers. "Oh, and how could I forget about you meeting Miguel Martinez?"

"That's right," I replied wryly. "How could I forget?

As the GPS told us that we were getting closer to our destination, Kevin grew quiet and uncontrollably shook both his legs. For whatever reason, he was starting to make ME feel nervous. What if he got to the house and she wouldn't see him or worse, wasn't home? Maybe pushing him to come here was a bad idea...

We pulled up to the split-level home. Kevin took a deep breath and put his hand on the car door handle. Before he exited, he gasped.

"There she is!" he exclaimed.

"Where?!"

"In the upstairs window," Kevin whispered. "Be quiet and get down."

"Like she can hear us," I hissed. I cautiously peered over Kevin's hulking frame. Sitting on the ledge of a second story window was a very forlorn-looking girl, tilting her head against the glass, staring into the night sky.

It was a scene all too familiar. How many nights had I spent doing the exact same thing, dreaming about the object of my desire coming to my house to profess his undying love? The very big difference here was her Prince Charming actually had come to be by her side; I usually just pass out after these exercises.

I looked at the clock. 11:58 p.m.

"Kevin, you need to get out of the car now!" I ordered. "It's two minutes to midnight."

Kevin nodded, took a deep breath, and exited the car. I opened the passenger side window.

Heather was still staring into space but noticed a hulking figure walking towards her front door. She suddenly sprang to life and threw open her window.

"Kevin?" Her voice shrilled through the quiet, cold air. "Is that you?" She cupped both hands over her mouth in amazement.

"Heather, I love you so much," Kevin stated, choking up. "I can't spend another night without you. I need you."

"I'm coming downstairs!" Heather announced, slamming the window shut.

I glanced at my dashboard clock. 11:59.

"Hurry up," I quietly urged.

The door swung open, and a heavy-set girl wearing a robe and slippers ran through the door and jumped into the open arms of her resurrected love. "I can't believe you are here!" Heather happily cried out in the dense night sky.

They leaned in for a kiss. I glanced at the clock...just as it stroked midnight.

Just as it started snowing.

17

Day 168

Two days after New Year's Eve, my head was still spinning. Sure, I helped orchestrate my friend's happily ever after in the most romantic fashion *ever*, but while it felt great…it made my craving to have a love to call my own burn greater than ever before.

Maybe I should consider a career in television after all, but instead of sports, work as a producer and become the next Ryan Murphy. I could create a show filled with very pretty people and have my characters live out every single one of my unattainable fantasies. (However, with my luck, the network would probably push me to cast Trisha Martinez in her acting debut.)

But even in the throes of deep depression, I felt a small glimmer of excitement. Today was my big meeting with James

Murillo of NYS Network. This could FINALLY be the break I'd waited twenty-seven years for!

I put on another gem of a dress from Satriano's (aided by the help of Spanx, of course)—a black 3/4 length sleeve wrap dress, with a gold belt, black stockings, and black high heel pumps. I blew out my hair and applied a full face of makeup. Before I left my room, I double-checked my leather briefcase to make sure I included resumes and CD copies of the demo I taped with Dante.

I held my breath as I made my way downstairs, praying that my mother wouldn't be circling the waters. Thankfully, it was only my father sitting at the kitchen counter reading the newspaper. He looked up, shocked at my appearance. "Where are you going dressed up like that?"

"I have a sort-of interview in the city at eight."

"What's a "sort-of" interview?"

"I don't want to say," I responded cryptically. "I don't want to jinx it."

Dad nodded and took a sip of his coffee. "I understand. Good luck." He smiled and turned his attention back to the paper.

"Thanks!"

Why couldn't the encounters with my other parental figure be that easy? If that were Mom, she would have browbeaten me for answers, and when I wouldn't give them, she'd run upstairs in a tizzy to her home office and track my whereabouts on the computer, which was linked up to the GPS tracking device I'm convinced she secretly installed in my car. I mean, how else did she get her information? Russian spies?

■ ■ ■

NYS was located in the heart of Manhattan, a few miles away from WSPS in Lower Manhattan. Driving into Midtown was a bitch for us bridge and tunnel people, especially on the first day back to reality after a long holiday. But if you asked me, there was no "good time" to be entering the city via the Lincoln Tunnel. Cars burned gallons of precious non-renewable resources while they sat idly on the Helix at six in the morning, eleven at night, Thanksgiving, your sister's birthday, every Sunday, and Game Seven of whichever sport has Game Sevens because it doesn't matter, there would be traffic during all of them.

On this particular day, it took me two hours to get from Point A to Point B. In other words, it took an hour and twenty minutes more than it should have, which you can imagine did wonders for my stress level.

I parked my car in an overpriced garage and walked towards NYS' iconic building. The network's glass-encased, street level studio immediately came into view. I chuckled as I thought about the crazies that press themselves up against the windows during live shows; they were probably the same ones that called WSPS on a daily basis.

I walked into the grand lobby and gave my name to the receptionist. As I waited for her to grant me access to Mr. Murillo's office, I carefully studied the numerous Emmy awards in the trophy case. The prestigious equivalent in radio were the Marconi Radio Awards, given by the National Association of Broadcasters to the top stations and personalities in the country. Imagine the honor of being named the best in your field?

"Mr. Murillo will see you now," the receptionist said, interrupting my thoughts. "Go all the way up the stairs and make a right down the hall. He's the last door on the left." A loud buzz came from the direction of the door leading up to the staircase, and I let myself in.

I took my time getting to his office. It was like walking through a sports museum; photos of numerous New York athletes who had been at the NYS studios over the years adorned the beige walls—Joe Namath, Lawrence Taylor, Yogi Berra, Wayne Gretzky, Phil Rizzuto, Tom Seaver, Don Mattingly, Mariano Rivera, Patrick Ewing, Mike Piazza, Eli Manning...and so on and so forth. Never mind the Emmys; this was the ultimate collection.

As I approached the end of the hall, I noticed that Mr. Murillo's door was wide open. He was leaning back in his chair, casually listening to another man in the room. The person speaking sounded vaguely familiar, but I couldn't tell who it was from my vantage point.

Mr. Murillo's eyes lit up when he saw me. "Carla, come in!" He motioned.

"Hi, Mr. Murillo!" I stepped inside the immaculate office. When I saw the other person in the room, got goosebumps all over again.

"Carla, being a W-S-P-S employee, you must know Ron Benioff. Ron, this is Carla D'Agostino, one of the brightest young producers you have in your company."

Damn. I knew Mr. Murillo was connected, but this scenario never crossed my mind.

OSP Media Group was the parent company of WSPS and many other stations in the New York market. Ron Benioff was the general manager for OSP's entire cluster of New York stations. I knew he worked in my building, but I had never encountered him (and why would I). No sooner than I was filled with hope, self-doubt crept in. My direct boss didn't believe in my talents; wouldn't my boss's boss, one of the most powerful men in the radio industry, echo his sentiment?

I shook Mr. Benioff's hand. "We've worked in the same building for the past six years, but I've never had the pleasure to personally meet you."

Mr. Benioff nodded. "Nice meeting you as well."

His demeanor was very intimidating; you could tell he knew just how influential he was. His appearance did not match his body language, however. He was mostly bald, except for a ring of dark hair around the base of his head. He was wearing a brown sports jacket over his canary yellow shirt, which didn't hide the fact that he was slightly overweight.

"Sit down, Carla," Mr. Murillo ordered. "What would you like to drink? Espresso? Cappuccino?"

"Um, I'll take an espresso," I answered. Not that I needed anything to make me more jittery than I already was, but I didn't want to be rude.

Mr. Murillo leaned over to his phone and buzzed his secretary. "Arlene, when you get a chance, please make three short espressos."

"Yes, Mr. Murillo!" A perky voice answered.

Mr. Murillo leaned back in his chair. "Ronnie and I go way back. We graduated Fordham together and have surprisingly been close ever since."

"Why is that a surprise?"

"Because there is no such thing as friends in this business," Mr. Benioff replied pointedly.

Dante suddenly flashed in my head. "That's for sure."

"Carla is getting a crash course in the evils of our business by producing that blood-sucking Ruby Smith…"

Mr. Benioff threw his hands up in exasperation. "Again with Ruby Smith. Who cares?"

"…and that's not the only thing she's sucking," Mr. Murillo finished. "And you may not care, but your listeners do."

"They obviously don't care that much. Ratings have remained steady, and we've actually increased commercial revenue since we've brought her on," Mr. Benioff shot back.

"Is that all you care about, Ronnie?" Mr. Murillo chuckled.

"It's the *only* thing to care about," Mr. Benioff replied. "Durkin could have paired Tommy Max with a talking parrot, and as long as our bottom line didn't take a hit, I wouldn't know the difference."

Mr. Murillo grabbed a stray baseball from his desk and started flipping it in the air. "Durkin didn't have to do anything; he should have left well enough alone. Little Durkin made that hire, and that's going to come back to bite the entire station in the ass."

"That's not confirmed, Jimmy." Mr. Benioff replied sternly.

"It was paraded right in front of my face," Mr. Murillo chuckled.

Mr. Benioff shrugged. "If it's true, the ratings would be even higher. Consumer studies show all across the board how much the general public loves controversy."

I was very appreciative of this fly-on-the-wall experience... appreciative, and disgusted. As long as the numbers were there, Mr. Benioff had no regard for the quality and morality of his product. How unfair was that to the loyal employees and listeners of not only WSPS, but of all his stations?

An older woman rambled into the office, carrying a tray of three espressos, sugar packets, and a heaping pile of biscotti cookies. I watched her neatly place the items on Mr. Murillo's desk. As delicious as the cookies looked, I promised myself I would put my New Year's Resolution to work and resist.

"Thank you, Arlene," Mr. Murillo smiled. She nodded and walked out. Mr. Murillo's hand leaned underneath his desk and reappeared with a bottle of Sambuca. "How can you not have some Sambuca with your espresso?" he quipped as he poured a shot in all three cups.

"I agree, thank you," I replied as I grabbed my cup and took a sip. A little Sambuca wasn't going to hurt the waistline, right?

"Anyway, back to the subject at hand. Ronnie, I would steal this pretty girl from you to work for me, but she has no interest in television. She's wasting away producing Tommy and Ruby's show. What can you do for her?"

"What do you mean, what can I do for her? She already works for us."

"Yea but she wants to be behind the microphone."

Mr. Benioff furrowed his brow. "It's too early in the year to tell if we have the budget to hire—"

"Yeah, I get all that. Carla, do you have your demo tape?"

"Yes, I do!" I nervously chirped. I opened my briefcase, pulled the CD right out, and gave it to Mr. Murillo.

"Listen to me Ronnie," Mr. Murillo said as he removed the disk from its jewel case. "Give this girl a chance. She is better than the talking parrot and definitely better than Ruby."

I felt a wave of nausea as I watched Mr. Murillo load the CD into his computer. While his words were very flattering, they weren't based on any factual evidence. Never mind the fact that his ears hadn't heard the demo; he didn't know of my *existence* up until two days ago. How could this perfect stranger take such a huge gamble at my expense? What if it backfired? What if—

"Welcome back to "The Carla D'Agostino Show" on W-S-P-S, sports for the people, by the people," my own voice filled the air. **"Here to talk some Bronx Bomber baseball is W-S-P-S Yankees beat reporter, Dante Ezra…"**

I cringed hearing myself announce Dante's name.

"This guy is on our air now," Mr. Benioff remarked. "He's good."

"He's a star in the making," Mr. Murillo agreed. "Too bad they have him wasting away on the weekend overnights. Another fine decision by Durkin."

I swiped a biscotti (what's one cookie going to do?) and silently chewed off my frustration. While everyone seems to have varying opinions of Ruby, it's nice to know that Dante scores perfect tens across the board.

A few moments later, the audio drew to a close. **"Thank you, Dante Ezra, for joining us tonight. After the commercial break, we'll take your calls at 1-800-555-9777."**

"Excellent, Carla," Mr. Murillo complimented as he took the CD out of his computer.

I let out a breath I didn't realize I was holding. "Wow, thank you." One down, one to go. I turned to Mr. Benioff, who was wearing the most unyielding poker face.

"What do you think, Ronnie?" Mr. Murillo pressed, reading my thoughts.

"What did Durkin say when he listened to this?"

I gulped, "He thinks I'm too inexperienced."

Mr. Murillo shook his head in disapproval. "And what did you say to that?"

"Nothing."

Mr. Murillo frowned. *Shit! I said too much.*

"I'll put in a call to Durkin and see what we can adjust," Mr. Benioff shrugged. "But you know, I'm not a sports guy; I have Durkin in place to make those decisions..."

"...and you have friends like me that have a pulse on what sports fans actually want, and aren't afraid to tell you how it is," Mr. Murillo finished.

I slightly hung my head. After all this, my fate is still in Dan Durkin's hands?

In unison, as if there was an unspoken code signaling the end of a meeting, they stood up to hug each other in that quick, emotionless way heterosexual men tend to embrace. Mr. Benioff turned to me, nodded, and walked out.

"Good-bye," I spoke softly as he walked out.

Mr. Murillo sat back down, and I gave him a confused look.

"You know what your problem is, Carla?"

"Where do you want me to begin?"

"You light up every room you enter, but you can't get out of your own way. Stop listening to your head trash."

"Head trash?"

"Yes, the pile of junk between your ears that keeps telling you that you aren't worth it!"

My mouth slightly dropped at his candor.

"Don't be intimidated by Dan Durkin or anyone, Carla. When he told you "no," you should have kept scrapping away. It's not his job to chase after you."

I slightly nodded.

Mr. Murillo picked the baseball back up and resumed tossing. "There's a lot of synergy between W-S-P-S and N-Y-S, and without going into great detail, there's potential for even greater partnership opportunities. That's what we are working on now, and when it happens, I want the best people in place. Who knows," Mr. Murillo chuckled, flipping the baseball at me. "You might be working for me someday after all!"

I tossed it back, and a casual game of catch ensued. "Why are you helping me? I barely know you."

"I recognize talent when I see it, and the landscape of the industry is changing. It's not about hosting a radio show anymore; you need to be a brand. You're young, you're beautiful and extremely marketable. If our two worlds were to merge down the road, it would be in both of our interests to have everything in place from now."

"But you didn't even listen to my tape before presenting it to Mr. Benioff. How did you know it was going to be good?"

"I've been around a long time, Carla. I just knew."

"But Durkin doesn't see what you see," I protested. "If Mr. Benioff is going to leave the decision in his hands, nothing will happen."

Mr. Murillo caught my throw in midair and defiantly slammed the baseball on his desk. "Did it ever occur to you that you are in the position you are in because you lack any semblance of confidence? I have daughters in high school, and I would be very upset if they felt about themselves the way the way you felt about yourself. There's no reason for it."

"Yes, there is," I shot back. "No one has made me feel capable of doing anything great."

"It doesn't work like that. It needs to start within you. Once you believe in yourself, everything else will fall into place. Have some faith!"

I felt as if I was back in the gym working out with Xander and his corny motivational quotes, or hanging out with Katie over drinks, except Mr. Murillo's words packed more of a punch. My entire life, I had been my own worst enemy. I'd let outside influences stop me from flourishing into who I was meant to be. Who cares what they think, or what they do? Fuck 'em all!

"You may have been around a long time, but you are wrong," I finally said, teetering on the edge of tears.

Mr. Murillo crossed his arms over his chest. "How do you figure?"

"In order for me to start believing in myself, I needed to hear exactly what you just said. No one in this business has ever shown such an unwavering, honest conviction in me."

I grabbed my briefcase and stood up. "I get it now."

Mr. Murillo stood up gave me a hug, a much warmer embrace than he shared with Mr. Benioff. "Call me the second you hear something."

"Thank you," I smiled, brimming in my newfound poise.

■ ■ ■

My stomach was in knots during my entire shift. Every time the studio door opened, I jumped out of my skin. The waiting game would have been much more manageable if I had some sort of time table as to when Mr. Benioff was going to actually call Dan. Meetings in this industry could take days, weeks, even months to materialize, and I'm sure Mr. Benioff had more pressing matters to address.

Immediately after the show ended, the studio door flew open. "Carla, can you come into my office please?" Dan Durkin barked. He was gone by the time I could even answer.

Wow, that was fast.

I quietly sprinted towards his office. His door was cracked open. But before I could knock, I got hit with a pang of fear. How many times have I stood at this very threshold, thinking that I would finally be given the world, to only have it shattered?

"Have some faith!" Mr. Murillo's voiced encouraged.

I didn't even bother knocking; I boldly walked in. "Hey Dan, you wanted to see me?" I asked innocently.

"Sit," he replied shortly.

I obeyed and waited for what felt like years for him to stop fooling around on the computer. Despite the agonizing wait, there was a sense of calmness that washed over me; I just *knew* that things would come out in my favor this time.

Finally, he turned his attention to me. "Before I begin with what I'm proposing to you, I need to know something."

"Sure..." I trailed off.

"How the heck did you get in Ron Benioff's ear?" Dan asked, his voice filled with shock.

I let out a breath. "It's a long story, but I met James Murillo of N-Y-S at Miguel Martinez's New Year's Party..."

Dan cut me off. "Wait a minute...you were at the party?"

Say what? "Um, yeah, I talked to you, remember?"

"No."

"Yeah, by the bar...you were with Ruby." I shot him a knowing look.

"Oh yeah...you know, I'm still nursing a hangover from that night, I forgot that you were there," Dan chuckled nervously. He rubbed his eyes for effect, but I never wavered in my stare. Dan cleared his throat and regained his composure. "What does James Murillo have to do with getting you to Benioff?"

"Mr. Murillo and Mr. Benioff went to college together and have remained friends. Mr. Murillo introduced me to him this morning, and they both listened to my demo tape. Mr. Murillo loved it, and I'm assuming you want to talk to me about what Mr. Benioff thought."

"That's correct," Dan nodded.

"Right, so...." He wasn't taking the verbal cue, and kept on nodding! Was he on drugs?

I couldn't take it anymore. "Dan!" I snapped. "What did Mr. Benioff say?"

"Oh right," he answered, coming to. "Well, what I'm about to offer you is kind of a unique deal."

"Ok..." My chest started tightening up.

"Benioff thinks you are good. Not great, but good enough to deserve a shot..."

Backhanded compliment aside, I almost jumped out of my seat. *I'M GETTING A SHOT!*

"...but on a couple of conditions."

"Okay!" I chirped, not really caring what those conditions were.

"For starters, I would require you to continue producing Tommy and Ruby's show. You work well together, and I don't want to break up that core."

We work well together? What planet was he on? "I appreciate that you recognize that," I lied. "Balancing my hosting duties with my production responsibilities is a challenge I am certainly up for."

"I'm glad to hear that passion in your voice...because unfortunately, we don't have much in the budget to compensate you for the added workload."

Bullshit. "Okay...how much?"

"Five-hundred dollars."

"A show?"

"No, per pay period...a grand a month extra."

I just shook my head. I know I had no negotiating leg to stand on, but this was a slap in the face. WSPS took in MILLIONS, yet they couldn't properly afford to cover the scope of my work?

"Also, you will have a co-host," Dan continued.

I started to grow very uneasy. "Who?"

A small smile crept up on Dan's face. "Dante Ezra."

I couldn't move my mouth to speak. I was frozen in horror.

"I have to co-host with Dante?" I finally whispered.

"Carla, you just aren't ready to carry your own show," Dan sneered. "I think you can learn a lot from him."

"Learn from HIM?" I shouted a little too loudly. "I've worked in this environment for years. If anything, he could learn a thing or two from *me*!"

"It will be a good pairing," Dan assured.

I conceded. There was no use in fighting, and as shitty as this was, I didn't want cause a scene and have Dan reconsider altogether. I thanked him, accepted the offer, and graciously exited his office.

I spent the ride home in quiet disbelief. Since I was seven years old, all I ever wanted was to be a sports radio host on WSPS. My persistence and hard work were finally going to be rewarded thanks to my media guardian angel, Mr. Murillo. However, I never imagined that my call up to the major leagues would be wrought with backhanded compliments, a paltry salary and personal turmoil.

Maybe I should have told Dan no. As it was, I didn't have time for myself; what was I thinking by agreeing to add more to my plate? (Goodbye precious sleep and the gym regimen I never resumed.) And shouldn't my wallet be seeing a much bigger benefit from all the additional work? (See you later, condo overlooking the New York City skyline.) And what kind of mind-altering drugs were slipped in my water bottle when I gave Dan the green light to pair me with Dante? (Sanity, I never knew ya.) My former friend was all but dead to me, and now I had to face his resurrected ghost with thousands of people eavesdropping in.

And then there was Ruby. If Ruby was utterly intolerable before, she was going to be a downright beast now that I'm an official peer of hers.

I shook my head. *This wasn't how it was supposed to be. Not at all.*

18

"It's about time something good happened to this family!" Mom exclaimed.

"They should be paying you more," Dad, the staunch businessman, countered.

"My son is settled, now my daughter is on her way!"

"That stupid radio station makes so much money, and they couldn't pay you more?"

"Maybe I can finally have peace in my life!"

"I'm proud of you, but you should have demanded more."

About twenty minutes earlier, I came home and broke the news to my family. I was only half-paying attention to their (very predictable) reactions; I was too busy replaying the conversation with Dan in my head…

"What's your boss's number? I'll call him and straighten this out," Dad threatened.

"Oh stop it, James," Mom replied. "She's almost thirty years old; she can take care of herself."

Ding dong. Saved by the bell!

"Who could that be at this hour?" Mom asked.

"I'll get it," I offered, dashing towards the foyer.

Ding dong! Ding dong!

I opened the door and was hit in the face by a bunch of shiny helium balloons.

"What the hell…" I muttered as I pushed them to the side.

Standing at the door was the whole clan— Andrea and Xander, each carrying a bundled-up baby; Katie, holding a covered up something or other; and Vin Diesel's Irish twin brother, who I assumed was Katie's new boyfriend, Teddy. It was below freezing outside, but he was dressed like it was the dead of summer. He had on a short-sleeved gray t-shirt that showed off his broad shoulders and crazy body art, jeans and nothing covering his bald head. The bundle of pastel colored strings he was holding clashed with his macho man persona.

"Congratulations!" the girls shrieked in unison.

"How did you know?" I asked even though I knew the answer already.

"Dante told us the good news!" Katie chirped.

"I can't believe you wouldn't call us the second you heard," Andrea added.

"You've only been waiting for this opportunity your whole life!" Katie continued.

"You'll be on the air before the reunion..."

"...AND you have no choice but to make up with Dante!"

"Yes, it's all wonderful," I replied sarcastically. "It's freezing, come inside."

As everyone filed in, I introduced myself to Teddy. "Hi, I'm Carla, and why the hell are you not wearing a jacket right now?"

"It's not that bad," Teddy shrugged, handing me the balloons. "I'm Teddy."

"I figured. It's so nice to finally meet you. I've heard many great things."

"He's the best," Katie boasted, snuggling up against him. He tenderly kissed her forehead.

I quickly turned away. I was not in the mood to tolerate much, least of all romance.

"Hello, I'm Xander. Do you remember me, your long lost gym buddy?" Xander joked, giving me a hug.

"She won't be long-lost now. She's in the spotlight; she needs to get in shape!" Andrea laughed.

I sighed. "Let's go in the kitchen, I'll fill you all in."

My father had disappeared, but my mother was still sitting at the kitchen table, feverishly tapping away on her cell phone.

"Who are you texting?" I asked, tying the balloons to the back of her chair.

"I'm just spreading the good news," she replied happily, without looking up.

Everyone started sitting down around her. Teddy and Xander, being newbies to the situation, chose seats closest to my mom. Mom was in another world until Teddy caught her eye, and she stared at him with the same bewilderment one has when viewing gigantic zoo creatures.

Katie unveiled her latest creation, a poppy seed lemon cake. I gamely fetched some plates and utensils, sat down, and let out a big sigh.

Andrea and Katie exchanged worried looks. "I thought you would be happier," Katie commented as she cut her cake.

"Is this about Dante?" Andrea added.

Before I had a chance to answer, Mom chimed in. "Stop being a spoiled brat. You are never happy."

How quickly our dynamic can change. "You know you can leave," I snapped.

Mom rose out of her chair. "Do yourselves all a favor," she addressed my friends. "Don't have kids."

"It's kind of too late for that, Mrs. D'Agostino," Andrea laughed, rocking Nadia in her arms.

"Well, you're an IDIOT!" Mom sneered, and stormed out of the kitchen.

Teddy and Xander shared puzzled expressions.

"Welcome to my life." I shrugged. Katie stifled a laugh as she passed around the plates of cake, which Andrea and Xander (of course) refused.

"Ok, enough of this…what the hell is going on?" Andrea demanded.

"Although I'll be co-hosting with Dante"—my stomach did a flip-flop saying those words out loud—"I still have to produce Tommy and Ruby's show. My only day off will be Sunday. So it's a lot more work, not a lot more money, and a ton more bullshit."

"That sucks that you still have to deal with Ruby," Katie replied in between bites.

"I think the whole deal sucks," Andrea countered.

"My support system, ladies and gentlemen," I announced sarcastically to the men, stabbing the cake with my fork.

"At least you'll be on the radio, that's pretty awesome," Xander said.

"I agree. I listen to W-S-P-S all the time; it's going to be cool to know someone on there!" Teddy exclaimed, giving his plate to Katie for piece of cake number two.

"Can you get free Giants tickets?" Xander added.

I opened my mouth to answer, but Andrea cut me off. "When you finally get a boyfriend, how is having only one day off going to work?"

"I'll worry about it when the time comes, which will be never," I wryly answered.

"You don't have a boyfriend?" Teddy asked incredulously.

I glared at Katie. How did she not give her love the 4-1-1?

"Carla's hit a bit of a dry spell," Katie quickly responded. "But she'll be off the market soon."

I snickered. "Is that right, Nostradamus?"

"Everything is starting to fall into place for you. Today is only the beginning. Mark my words."

▪ ▪ ▪

About a half-hour later, everyone filtered out. My mother, hungry to gossip, came back downstairs to help clean up the kitchen. "Where did Katie find *that* guy?" she asked as she filed the dishes in the dishwasher.

"He's a cop in town. He seems nice," I replied while wiping down the table.

"He's scary looking through."

"Stop, he's fine."

"Carla, he's got a tattoo of a snake crawling out of a skull's eye socket covering his forearm. He's going to chase Katie's customers away!"

"Whatever, I'm not dating him."

"I don't even want to imagine!"

I dragged my feet over to the sink and draped the cloth over the drying rack. "I'm going to bed," I yawned.

"Ok honey," Mom said while she started the dishwasher. Spontaneously, she wrapped her arms tightly around me.

"You're…squishing…me," I breathed.

"I'm so proud of you," she whispered.

I smiled at the rare display of affection. "Thanks, Mom."

■ ■ ■

After the day I had, I expected to pass out the second my head hit the pillow. But ten minutes to midnight, I was still wide awake. Dante had the wherewithal to contact our friends, but didn't even bother to contact me? I should have been the *first* call he made, not only to congratulate me but to help come up with a game plan for our premiere show, debuting in four nights. That was what a responsible person would have done anyway. This poor sportsmanship was just another example of the conspiracy theory-believing *egomaniac* my former friend had become. That being said…should I be the bigger person and break the ice?

I sighed. "Fiiiiiine," I said out loud, throwing the crochet wool blanket knitted by Grandma Theresa off my body. I grabbed my iPhone and started pacing the room. "I hope I still have his number," I muttered as I browsed through my contacts. Knowing me, I had probably deleted his name off my phone in a fit of blackout rage. "Never mind, here it is. Shocking."

As the phone rang, I tried to figure out how to play the conversation. Should my tone be sweet? Confrontational? Non-committal?

On the fifth ring, he picked up. "Hello?" Dante answered wearily.

"Hello, Dante."

"Isn't it past your bedtime?"

"Well you know, I've had kind of a big day. The adrenaline hasn't worn off. Thank you for your congratulatory words, by the way. They meant so much to me. What were they again?"

"I bet you are excited."

"And I bet you are not."

"What do you mean? It will be an honor to share my show with a ray of sunshine like yourself."

"Our show," I corrected.

"Our show," Dante repeated.

"Look, we may not like each other very much, but I don't want our bad blood to spill out over the air."

"I concur."

"So we go in the studio, do our thing, and that's it."

"That's it," Dante repeated.

"There will be no carpooling to the station. We will not be hanging out off the air. If we do speak, it is to be about work only."

"Fine by me."

"Ok then."

"Anything else?"

I paused. "Yes—let's not fuck it up."

"I'll be fine," Dante huffed. "Concentrate on yourself."

"I can handle it. See you Friday night."

"See ya."

I climbed back into bed, feeling more uneasy than before. That call had done absolutely nothing to calm my fears. The universe has been giving me signs for years that I was treading the wrong path. Due to my inherent stubbornness, I refused to yield to the warnings and in turn, royally pissed off the gods. Tired of being ignored, Mother Nature decided to shake up my world in such a terrifying way that I had no choice but to take notice and finally break away from this dead-end life. How else could you explain this latest turn of events?

Well, I was now paying attention. This show was going to be an absolute, utter disaster. What had I gotten myself into?

19

Day 171

It figured that tonight was the night God had planned to call me up to be His indentured servant. At least He didn't bestow a long, drawn-out illness on me, for by the time my car rammed into the walls of the Holland Tunnel and burst into a fireball, a massive heart attack would have already taken my life.

My obituary will read:

> *Carla Catherine D'Agostino, 27, died on Friday, January 6, 2017, at New York Downtown Hospital. Carla was born and raised in Honey Crest, New Jersey, and spent the duration of her life living at her parents' home. Carla was a graduate of Honey Crest High School and obtained a degree in Broadcast Journalism at New Jersey University, managing to stay a virgin throughout that whole time (a Guinness world record). After finishing school in 2007, besides breaking the longest sexless streak in history, she*

started working as a producer at WSPS Sports Radio 950 AM New York. On the day she died, she was driving to the radio station to start her dream job, serving as a sports talk radio host. But it was not meant to be.

"My daughter died a loser!" An unnamed source wailed to the Honey Crest Express staff.

Carla is survived by her parents, Nancy and James D'Agostino, Sr.; her brother James D'Agostino, Jr. and his fiancé, Gwendolyn Carrington, and a large extended family. Carla had few good friends and passed away having no significant other.

The prospect of making my on-air debut was already giving me enough *agita*; not mapping out the first show with my co-host was putting me into a full-blown panic attack.

Every time there was a surprising score or a breaking story, my first impulse was to pick up my cell phone to contact Dante. But as quickly as the urge hit, it left. I'm the one who initially reached out to him; wasn't it *his* turn?

To his credit, our sweet-faced, newbie producer, Rusty, had been in constant contact with Dante and me all week. He earnestly kept us abreast of the guests he'd managed to book for our graveyard-shift show…compiled talking points…forwarded relevant articles…all the stuff that a good producer is supposed to do. I gamely "replied all" with my comments, with nary a word from Dante. Knowing him, he hasn't bothered to check his messages; he never was one for homework. Poor Rusty has *no* idea what he's in for.

Neither did I.

My nerves were shot for another reason—the massive amount of texts, e-mails, and social media messages I've received from family, friends, stalkers, and past and present work colleagues:

> *"Break a leg tonight, Carla!"* (and other such stereotypical clichés).
>
> *"This night must be so special for you! You've wanted to do this since you were a little girl and you're finally doing it!"* (Thanks for the reminder, people.)
>
> *"Wow...really? Don't mess this up!"* (Why even bother messaging me?)
>
> *"Why couldn't they put you on earlier? These shows are going to mess up my sleep schedule."* (Guess who?)

Don't get me wrong, I was appreciative of everyone taking such an interest in my career (authentic or otherwise), but I didn't need the pressure of knowing everyone's ears were listening.

One person who surprisingly didn't chime in with her two cents was Ruby Smith. I thought she was going to make my life more miserable than she already did, but this week was nothing out of the standard, obnoxious ordinary.

Surprisingly, I pulled into the parking garage with my life still intact. With trembling hands and jelly knees, I gathered my items and headed to the studio.

I walked into the lifeless hallway. None of the lights were on, and there was none of the hustle and bustle of a normal workday. In the newsroom and studio, however, you would have thought it was twelve in the afternoon. All the flat-screen TV's were blaring ESPN, NFL Network and the ends of various college basketball games. Pizza boxes and two-liter bottles of soda were strewn everywhere, while a couple of bored-looking interns played on the computer.

"Hi, I'm Carla! I'm the new overnight co-host!" I chirped. They didn't seem impressed, even when I walked to each of them and shook their hands.

"Why are you here so early?" one boy asked.

"Dante doesn't usually get here until about a half hour before," the other one added.

"Well, I'm not Dante," I snapped.

The kids shrugged, and turn their attention back to their monitors.

Annoyed, I walked into the control room to greet Rusty.

"Hey, girl! You ready for tonight?" Rusty greeted me with a big hug.

"I am...I just hope my co-host is," I replied. "I haven't heard from him all week."

"Reeeeeeally?" The color left Rusty's face.

"That's Dante," I chuckled.

"Well, I've been talking to him. I'm sure he's ready," Rusty tried to assure me.

"Are you sure?" I retorted.

"I- I don't, I don't know," Rusty stammered.

I softened my tone. "Well that's why I'm here early, I'm hoping he comes in soon so we can go over a few things."

Rusty arched his eyebrow. "Well, Dante usually comes in— "

"I know when he usually comes in," I interrupted, getting snippy again. "But I'm hoping he takes the time out of his *terribly* busy schedule to come in early for the sake of the show."

Rusty shrugged and uneasily walked out of the control room. I silently screamed as I followed suit.

I settled at an empty cubicle in the newsroom and arranged the notes and articles I'd collected during the week around the desk. I started jotting down points I wanted to bring up, while every so often checking the time and the door.

Finally, at about a quarter to two, as I started to clean up my workstation, the White Knight of Sports Radio galloped into the newsroom. The once-listless interns sprang up to attention.

"Dante, my man!" one exclaimed, slapping Dante five.

"What's up, my dude?" the other added, following suit.

"Oh, you know how it is...another night, another show," Dante boasted.

"Yeah, dog!" Rusty suddenly appeared behind him, giving him a quick slap on the shoulder and shaking his hand. "You ready to do this?"

"Always, bro!" Dante replied.

I snarled at this pathetic display of "bro-hood" unfolding in front of me. It was usually easy for me to be one of the boys (sometimes easier than being one of the girls), but how was I going to be able to immerse myself with this (idiotic) fraternity?

"Where is she?" Dante muttered to Rusty.

I didn't give Rusty the time to answer. "I'm right here," I stated, rising out of my chair.

Dante slapped his hands together and meandered towards me. His minions leaned their chins on top of their cubicles, waiting with bated breath to hear what their Master would say next. "Doing your homework, I see." Dante laughed, motioning towards the pile of papers I was cradling in my arms.

"One of us has to."

"I don't need any of that crap. It's all up here," Dante replied, tapping his index finger on his forehead.

"Let's hope. I don't want to spend half the show bailing you out."

"Don't worry about me, young Carla. So how do you want to start the show?"

I motioned my head towards the large digital clock. "You want to have this conversation NOW, ten minutes to air?"

"When did you want to discuss it, on Tuesday when we had no idea what would be going on?" Dante pointed out.

"Well, no, but it would have been nice to be in communication throughout the week to talk about different things," I replied.

"You have a phone, Carla. You could have used it to call me."

"Well, you have working internet, Dante. You could have e-mailed me...BACK! Unless, did you forget to pay your bill?"

"Whatever," Dante rolled his eyes. "Let's just have a good show. I'm a fly-by-the-seat-of-my-pants guy anyway, you know that. Just follow my lead." Before I could answer, he walked towards the studio doors.

"Follow YOUR lead?" I muttered, shuffling behind him.

Wearing a big smile, Dante held open the door and ushered me inside the studio, which was outfitted with three posts that each contained a microphone, headphones, console and an outdated computer. Dante plopped down in front of the center mic, where the main host usually sits. Not bothering to argue seating arrangements, and not wanting to occupy the same chair Ruby did during her show (since it surely had the *malocchio* on it), I settled in on Dante's left. I quietly arranged my show notes while doing my best to ignore him.

"Two minutes until show time, guys," Rusty's voice boomed on the studio speakers.

Dante yawned, breezily placed the headphones over his ears, and threw his feet up on the desk.

Meanwhile, I was anything but casual. My heart was beating so fast, I was surprised it didn't leap out of my chest and hit Dante in the face. My shaky hands picked up the headphones as if they were made from fragile glass. I gulped. This was the last act before the start of a new chapter of my life! I took a deep breath, and...

"Stop being so dramatic and just put them on," Dante quipped.

"What?!" I exclaimed, accidentally dropping the headphones on the desk.

"I know you. *'This all becomes real once I put these on. All my wishes are about to come true. Pinch me, I must be dreaming!'*" Dante screeched in a high pitched voice, flailing his hands in the air.

I picked the headphones up and threw them on my head. "Shut up. I don't sound like that."

"One minute!" Rusty yelled in our ears. I winced, and leaned over to my volume knob and turned down the sound.

"Yeah you do," Dante laughed. "Who knows you better than me?"

"Not anymore."

Dante frowned.

"Thirty seconds!"

"Don't give me that look. What did you expect to happen when you attacked my character and accused me of such blatant lies?"

"There is no doubt in my mind you tried to get me fired." Dante chuckled smugly.

Our horns were officially locked. "I did NOT try to get you fired!"

"Ten seconds!"

"Yes you did, Carla," Dante replied calmly. "But for the sake of the show, I have chosen to put it behind me. Why can't you do the same? It might make you a lot less bitter in life."

"Five, four, three..."

"I am NOT bitter!" I shrieked.

"I don't understand why you just can't forgive and forget," Dante persisted.

"Because I'm not a saint, nor do I have DEMENTIA!"

"And we're on!"

I froze. I felt as though I was just sucked into a tornado vortex. Here we were, at the start of our first show, and I was a sweaty, panting, raving lunatic with no thought except that I wanted to murder my co-host. What riled me up more was that Dante looked to be the textbook definition of cool, calm and collected.

"This is W-S-P-S and you are listening to Dante Ezra in the overnight," he began. "Now, we have a crap load to get to, but first, we have to meet our new friend to the program, although she is definitely no stranger to the W-S-P-S family. She serves as the *esteemed* producer for "The Tommy Max and Ruby Smith Show," and she'll also be co-hosting the weekend shows with me. I know we're going to have *a lot* of fun together. Ladies and gentlemen, Carla D'Agostino!"

"Thank you for that warm introduction, Dante. But can you say 'crap load' on the air?" I teased.

"We're on in the middle of the night. Who do you think is listening?"

"Well for starters, the entire town of Honey Crest, New Jersey," I replied sweetly. I moved the microphone closer to my lips. "What Dante failed to mention, folks, is that we're childhood friends who grew up not only in the same town but on the same street!"

"Where you still live," Dante made sure to point out with a smile.

"And where you still visit on a daily basis for your mother to do your laundry, feed you and give you a bath," I shot back.

"Hey, you can't go wrong with Mama's home cooking," Dante recovered.

"So if you hear us fighting like brother and sister, it's because, in a *former* life, we were," I finished.

Dante scowled. I, on the other hand, was all smiles. The panic from a few minutes before had been washed away by a supreme adrenaline rush.

"Anyway, we will do our best to make Bear country, and the rest of the metropolitan area, proud," Dante replied.

"So Dante, what do we have on tap for tonight? And keep it to non-alcoholic items, please."

"Always. This is a dry show."

"Not as far as one of us is concerned," I cracked.

We continued to trade barbs while we transitioned the show to full-on sports talk. About fifteen minutes later, we stopped for a quick commercial break.

Dante's intense blue eyes connected with mine. "Are you having fun?"

"I am having a freakin' BLAST!" I laughed. "Are you having fun?"

"Oh yeah, I always love getting verbally abused in front of thousands of people."

I shook him off. "Oh stop, it's all in good fun."

Rusty burst into the control room. "The phone lines are lighting up, people are loving you two!"

"Why?" Dante sniffed.

My ears perked to attention. "Already?" Historically, the graveyard shift shows posted the lowest ratings for the station, for obvious reasons. When I produced the overnights, I used to have to practically pay my guy friends to call in to fill up the time.

"Wait a second..." I narrowed my eyes. "Do all these people happen to be from a certain small town in New Jersey?"

"The calls are coming from all over."

Dante and I looked at each other, wide-eyed.

"I don't know, but whatever you guys are doing, keep it up!" Rusty bellowed, running out of the room.

I turned to Dante and shrugged. "I guess people like the verbal abuse."

"Who knows Carla, with all the guys clamoring to speak to you, maybe you can actually score a date," Dante taunted.

I ripped a piece of paper from my notepad, crumpled it up into a ball, and threw it at him. He tried dodging it, but it hit him square in the face. We both laughed, and put our headphones back on for Round 2.

■ ■ ■

I skipped to my car after the show. I was rejuvenated! Born again! Untouchable! Take that, Honey Crest High School Class of 2007! The phones had not stopped ringing all night, with most of the callers paying us (well, me) some sort of acknowledgment:

> Smith from Connecticut: *"I wish I had a woman around who can tolerate sports. Carla, can you speak to my wife? She always gives me a hard time about my football Sundays."*

> Anthony from Staten Island: *"She's a fireball, Dante. Are you sure you can handle her?"*
>
> John from Hoboken: *"How do you think the Jets will rebuild their defense this off season? But not you Dante, I want to hear from the girl."*

After we wrapped, a part of me wanted to give Dante a huge hug in celebration, but I knew I couldn't – the boundaries I firmly set wouldn't allow that. Yet, the energy from our friendship's death helped morph this weird dynamic that listeners apparently were into, which at this point in my life, was my only concern.

I was feeling like Supergirl...until I pulled out of the parking garage and noticed the sun's early rays peeking through the plum sky. It was a little after six in the morning, and reality hit that I hadn't slept in almost 24 hours. I knew there would mercifully be no traffic at this time, but still, it would be a looooooong ride home.

Forty minutes later, I dragged my heels inside my house. I couldn't keep my eyes open at this point, and all I wanted to do was hit my bed with a vengeance...so imagine how annoyed I was to find my entire family, including Gwen, sitting at the kitchen table that was set with our finest china and glassware.

"Breakfast!" Mom announced the obvious.

"C'mon," I groaned, but my protests went ignored.

"You did such a great job, I couldn't wait to celebrate," Mom boasted, pulling my arms towards the table.

"Why couldn't you wait?" I grumbled.

"Jimmy made his brown sugar and walnut pancakes, Dad made scrambled eggs and bacon, and Gwen brought these delicious bagels!" Mom grabbed a sesame seed bagel from the heaping pile that sat in a glass bowl, and started to generously spread cream cheese on its halves. "I know I'm going to hate myself because of the carbs, but who cares? It's my baby's celebration!" She finished fixing the bagel and grabbed a glass pitcher. "Orange juice?"

"Mom, I appreciate all this," I said, watching my father place a plate of sizzling bacon on the table that admittedly smelled delicious. "But I want to go to bed. I've done two shows and haven't slept in-"

"You can have a little breakfast," Mom insisted. "Gwen woke up early on her Saturday morning to come here, the least you could do is be appreciative."

I glanced at Gwen, who mouthed "sorry" to me.

"Mom, Gwen doesn't care-"

"Eat," Mom ordered, dumping a large spoonful of eggs on my plate.

I was too shot to fight with her. "Pass me the bacon," I mumbled.

"Of course, honey." Mom replied sweetly, as if our exchange ten seconds ago never happened. "So tell us, how was it to be on the radio?"

"How do you think it was? It was great," I said through a mouthful of food.

"Did you and Dante get along?"

"I don't know, you tell me. Did it sound like we did?"

"No," Jimmy chimed in.

Gwen stifled a laugh with her napkin. "Jimmy!" She slapped my brother playfully on his abdomen and turned to me. "Don't listen to him; he wasn't even up for the show."

I gave him a tired smile. "Off the air, we tolerated each other the best we could. But on the air..."

"Yeah?" Mom probed.

"Jimmy was right, we didn't really get along, but for whatever reason, it worked."

"Harry and the Leatherneck made millions by yelling at each other every day for twenty years," Dad pointed out.

"Well then, keep fighting!" Mom roared. "You don't need friends. Maybe then I can finally retire!"

Comments continued to fly by, but I was too out of it to fully grasp what they were. Finally, I was excused.

"Carla, you have such heavy bags under your eyes! You must go to bed," Mom ordered.

"You're just noticing this now?" I chuckled.

"Yes. Go upstairs. Now."

I nodded "thank you" to everyone and practically crawled to my bedroom. It was good to know that no matter how much fame and fortune I might reach in my career, I could always come home and be reminded that all I really am in life is Nancy D'Agostino's little girl...and now apparently, her future meal ticket.

20

Day 279

"W-S-P-S, what would you like to talk about?...What?...Did you just ask me what color underwear I'm wearing? Are you serious?"

Click.

Despite my weekend shows being an added burden to my schedule, they were an island vacation compared to what I endured Monday through Friday. (It didn't hurt that I also happened to love the gig.) The life of a radio producer was ninety-five percent aggravation, five percent satisfaction, and zero percent glory. All day long your phone was ringing with weirdos, and while you were dealing with them, you needed to have one eye on the show and one eye monitoring the wire for any breaking stories. In the middle of this chaos, you had to nurture the delicate egos of your radio hosts by keeping them well-informed and comfortable at all times. (In my case, that included making sure the thermostat in the studio read seventy-two degrees at all times, and fetching lukewarm water with lemon at the top of every hour. Guess who that was for.)

And my mother wanted to know why I'm too exhausted to go to the gym after work; she wouldn't last here half a day!

"W-S-P-S, what would you like to talk about?...Yankees winning streak, great. What is your name?"

As I was typing up the caller's information, I heard the control room door swing open. I cradled the receiver between my neck and shoulder as I turned around to see who it was. I almost dropped the phone when I saw my boss Dan "The Man" Durkin wearing on ominous look.

"Come to my office, please," Dan barked.

"Now?" I mouthed.

"As soon as you hang up," he ordered and walked out of the room.

I turned my attention back to the caller. "Okay, Chris, I'm going to put you on hold for just a few moments, okay? Thanks for calling!"

Doing my best Spiderman impression, I slowly scaled the hallway leading to Dan's office. Even though Dante and I were doing very well with our show, I continued to have this nightmare scenario in the back of my mind—Dan popping up out of nowhere to pull the rug from under my feet. Was this it?

When I entered Dan's office, I saw my answer sitting on the puffy, black leather couch: Dante Ezra, my former friend, current foe, and co-host ... looking as confused and concerned as I was.

Oh geez. If perennially cool-as-a-cucumber Dante was worried about this meeting, what the hell was I supposed to feel like? My chest tightened as I plopped down next to Dante. We looked at each other, and our eyes exchanged an unspoken "Uh oh…"

Well, this was it, my nightmare come true. The one thing that got me out of bed in the morning was about to be taken away. Overall, it had been a good run; I had no regrets. I didn't think the beginning would meet the end so quickly, but I had to agree with whoever complained to Dan--our show was too much fire, and not enough substance. In the days, weeks, and years to come, I would analyze every word from my on-air stint and extract the lessons. They would serve me well in my next endeavor, perhaps as host of the local mental ward's closed-circuited radio station.

Dan cleared his throat. "I'm sure you wondering why you're both in here today."

"A little bit, yeah," Dante answered softly.

"Well, we're shuffling things around, and effective immediately, Jackie Grimes and Eddie Moore are no longer hosting the mid-morning show..."

I felt Dante fidget in his seat. I held my breath and clenched my eyes, bracing myself for the other end of that sentence —

"And we'd like to move you two into that time slot."

"Pahhhhh." My eyes shot open as the air loudly left my mouth.

Dante sprung up from his seat and peered over Dan's desk. "What do you mean?"

"I mean what I mean...what do you mean?" Dan scrunched up his face in confusion. "You two are being moved to the mid-day slot."

Dan turned to me. "Carla, this means you are no longer producing Tommy and Ruby."

A wash of numbness came over my body. All I could do was blink back at him.

"Oh..." Dante trailed off, sitting back down. From the corner of my eye, I could see Dante turn to look at me, but I couldn't move; I was literally paralyzed.

"We need both of your undivided attention to bring this time period's ratings from out of the gutter," Dan continued. "I cannot stress enough how big your roles are. You will now be the lead-in for the country's biggest sports radio show. Do you think you can handle it?"

Dante burst out laughing. "Is that even a question?"

Dan turned to me. "What about you, Carla?"

"Uh huh," I barely managed to muster.

"Great." Dan smiled, clapping his hands. "Things are going to be moving pretty quickly over the next twenty-four hours. We have to get contracts together for your agents to review, and marketing needs to meet with you over headshots, bios, that sort of thing."

Dan's office suddenly transformed into the Graviton. "What about today's show?"

"Rusty is on his way in to take over your duties for the rest of the afternoon, and we'll have the new producer in place tomorrow. Rusty will continue working with the both of you. Any more questions?"

"Nope!" Dante replied brightly.

I started to get feeling back in my limbs, and raised my hand. "I do."

"Yes?"

"Why?"

"Why what?"

"Why all THIS?" I exclaimed, extending both my arms out. "I mean...this is...like...*unbelievable*!"

"We believe that a special show like yours deserves better than to air in obscurity. You are both young, unique, and extremely talented, and we believe that's going to resonate with our next generation of listeners and..." He trailed off. "Wow, that's a good quote for the press release," he muttered to himself. He turned to his computer and typed out his words.

My eyes bugged out of their sockets. I'd waited YEARS for Dan to use words like "talented" to describe me. To hear the words finally come from his mouth was a redeeming moment, one I was still hard-pressed to believe was actually happening.

Dante and I both rose from the couch. "Thank you, Dan," Dante said, extending his hand. "We won't let you down."

"You better not," Dan laughed.

"You don't know how much I appreciate this," I gushed.

Dan took my hand. "You've come a long way, Carla."

"Thank you," I smiled, although I did not agree. I'd been this way all along; it was my fault that I never made him realize. But now was not the time to look back on past failures. (I mean, I didn't have all day.)

"Ok, so call your agents, and do whatever you have to do. Meet back here in an hour."

Dante and I quietly filed out of his office. As we walked down the hallway, I felt Dante grab my arm and pull me into the copy room.

"Ow!" I protested, tugging my arm out of his grasp.

"Carla, do you understand what just happened in there?" Dante gasped.

"Actually, no," I laughed. "I don't even know what's going on right now."

Dante leaned his head up against the wall. "Wow…" he whistled, dragging his body down and ending up sitting on the floor.

"You're telling me." I settled next to him, drawing my knees towards my chest.

"And I thought this was going to be a short-lived gig," Dante sighed. "I guess I can kiss my music career goodbye."

"What career?" I sniffed.

"Funny. You didn't have much of a career either until two minutes ago."

"You're wrong; I've always had a career. I've just never had a life up until now, or at least a life to be proud of…" Just then, the details started to hit me. I excitedly turned to Dante. "I don't have to produce Ruby anymore!" I shrieked, shaking his shoulders as I jumped up. "I don't have to deal with that demanding, evil, ANNOYING, crazy bitch ever again!" I gleefully announced, pacing around the room.

Dante snickered as he bent his knee and rested his forearm on it. "Tell us how you really feel," he quipped.

"You have no idea what that woman puts me through. I felt trapped in a torture chamber six hours a day. It was INSANE!"

I clasped my hands together and raised them to the ceiling in victory. "I'm finally free. I'M FREE!"

I kneeled down next to Dante. "Not only am I free," I hurriedly continued, grabbing his leg. "But I have weekends again. I'm getting a raise! I'M ACTUALLY GETTING A RAISE! I haven't had a raise in YEARS!"

"So this is what you are happy about? Nothing else?" Dante questioned.

"Of course, I'm happy about the other stuff!"

"Maybe that's a good thing—," Dante started to say

"It's just that right now," I interrupted him. "I may be a tad happier knowing that the black cloud that has followed me since birth is finally gone."

"Yeah, but now I feel like the trapped one," Dante sighed.

"Why?!" I screeched.

"I don't want to be doing this forever! I mean, it's fun and all, but I was born to be under the lights, performing on the big stage."

"But you are on a stage," I calmly explained, despite the panic rising through my body. "It's just a different kind. And you could still do music."

"Yeah, I don't know," Dante frowned. "I don't think I can do this. Would you be mad?"

"WHAT?" I shot up. "I'd KILL you! Without you, there's no show! Dan wouldn't dare put me on by myself!"

Dante's blue eyes were filled with worry. His face turned a deep shade of red.

"Do you really not want to do this?" I cried.

Dante dramatically stood up. "I love fucking with you," he cracked.

I slapped him on the shoulder. "I hate you!"

"Repeat what you said about the show," he said in between big, boisterous laughs. "That without me...what?"

I playfully kicked the back of his knee as we walked out of the copy room.

■ ■ ■

The rest of the afternoon was a firestorm of activity. I had to call my brand-new agent (a family friend my father insisted I use when I started the weekend shows) and get him in touch with the WSPS Legal Department. Dante and I met with Marketing to go over the whole promotion plan for the show and ourselves.

"We need to book you for professional headshots, and you need to submit bios by the end of the week," WSPS' fast-talking marketing director, Brenda, ordered in her heavy Brooklyn accent. "We are going to set each of you up on all the major social media sites, and it's up to you to keep it constantly updated. Each week we're going to tape a video blog with you for the website, and you are required to submit a written one as well, on deadline. Got it?"

"Done!" I chirped.

"Why?" Dante complained.

Brenda rolled her eyes. "You need to connect with your listeners around the clock. It's a different world for you now."

As Brenda continued to ramble off our new tasks, I studied my reflection in her office mirror. My makeup-less face looked tired and bloated; months of stress and total neglect had definitely taken their toll. There was no way in hell I was doing a photo shoot looking like this! *If I'm going to be front and center, I need to get serious about making some changes*, I vowed. I promised myself to give Xander a call the second I got to my car.

From there, we went back to Dan's office to meet with Legal and our agents, who rushed into the city. An hour later, I had an official contract hot off the press, ready for me to sign. Dan wasn't kidding when he said things would move quickly!

As I went through each page and initialed the bottom, I encountered the number of my new salary. I bit the bottom of my lip to prevent myself from freaking out. I looked at Dante, who clearly was on the same page of the packet; he was ready to rocket out of his seat. We smiled at each other, and gleefully initialed the bottom of *that* page. What's up new car…new wardrobe… new life! (Who was I kidding? My parents were going to make me sock all of that in savings.)

As soon as our names were on the dotted line, Legal and our agents booked it. Dan held us for a few more minutes to talk over some things, then finally, we were done. My head was swimming with new information and things to do, but on the top of that list was catching up on what I'd missed today in the world of sports. I did have a show tomorrow to prep for, after all!

As Dante and I bid Dan goodbye, the door swung open. "What the hell?" Dan choked as Ruby Smith barreled in.

"Why wasn't I informed of this change?" she barked, pushing Dante and me out of the way and stood nose-to-nose with our boss.

"It all came down last— "

"You don't think I'm owed some sort of explanation? What kind of Mickey Mouse organization are you running?"

"Ruby, calm down. It's not like that."

"I DON'T DESERVE SOME SORT OF SAY?" she shouted.

Dante's mouth dropped in horror. He had a taste of Ruby months before, in this very office, when he first got hired. However, he hadn't been treated to a showcase featuring her in all her glory…until now.

I leaned over and whispered in his ear. "Rookie," I snickered.

"Ruby, please, let me explain— "

"Not that Carla did any sort of special job anyway," Ruby continued, ignoring him. "But to yank her in the middle of the show ruins my flow. It is unprofessional."

"I understand, but I had to— "

"What did she screw up?" Ruby sneered. "It must have been a doozy for you to act in such an irrational manner."

"She didn't," Dan proclaimed, his forehead full of perspiration. "I promoted her."

Ruby gasped. "You…what?"

"I promoted her," Dan repeated. "And Dante. Meet your new lead-in show!"

Ruby turned around. I pursed my lips together and gave her a short wave. Dante shifted uneasily in his place. "You promoted…*them*?" Ruby said, aghast.

"I meant to tell you later— "

"ARE YOU OUT OF YOUR DAMN MIND?"

"Ruby—"

"I know a THOUSAND people better suited for the position than these two," Ruby sneered.

"Corporate wanted them," Dan shrugged.

Ah, the truth comes out. Thanks for the vote of confidence, Boss! Dante cleared his throat, upon feeling the knife spear through his back from his "buddy."

"My agent is *definitely* going to hear about this," Ruby threatened.

Dan hung his head in shame. She grunted as she ran out of the room, slamming the door behind her. An uneasy silence filled the air.

"That was Ruby's way of saying she's going to miss me," I cracked.

▪ ▪ ▪

The second I got in my car, I called Xander to get back on his personal training calendar. *"Cowabunga, dude!"* was his reaction. How did Andrea wind up with such a cornball?

After we had hung up, it took all my might not to dial home. In the whirlwind of the day, I hadn't had a chance to call my family to announce my promotion, but since I'd come this far, I decided to break the news to them in person.

As I came out of the Jersey side of the Holland Tunnel, my phone rang. It was Mom. I had no choice but to pick up, unless I wanted to hear my phone ring continuously for the next thirty minutes. "Hi Mom," I said casually.

"WHY DIDN'T YOU TELL ME YOU GOT PROMOTED?"

"Huh?" I gasped.

"I JUST GOT A GOOGLE ALERT ON MY PHONE THAT THE STATION PROMOTED YOU AND DANTE."

Ugh, she was so loud. "I wanted to tell you in person. I didn't know it would be online already. What does it say?"

"D'AGOSTINO, EZRA NAMED— "

"SAY IT, DON'T SCREAM IT!"

"Fine," Mom sighed, clearing her throat: *"D'Agostino, Ezra named new mid-day hosts for W-S-P-S Sports Radio 950 AM.*

"W-S-P-S, the nation's number one sports radio station, today announced the promotion of Carla D'Agostino and Dante Ezra to the weekday mid-day slot, effective immediately.

"D'Agostino and Ezra have co-hosted the weekend overnight show since the start of the year. Additionally, D'Agostino served as producer for The Tommy Max and Ruby Smith Show, *the country's number one syndicated radio sports talk program. Overall, she has been an employee of W-S-P-S for five years. Ezra has been with the station since last summer.*

"'It became rapidly apparent that a special show like Carla and Dante's deserved a marquee spot in our lineup," said Dan Durkin, founder and program director of

W-S-P-S. "The chemistry of this duo transcends the airwaves. Their fiery passion and vast sports knowledge will resonate with our current listeners, and their exuberant youth will help introduce the esteemed W-S-P-S brand to the next generation of New York sports fans."

"D'Agostino and Ezra, both from Honey Crest, New Jersey, will be the new lead-in team for Smith and Max.

"'I started my career at W-S-P-S, and have been very fortunate to work in a place that nurtures talent and encourages growth while learning from the best in the business,'" said D'Agostino. "'It has been a privilege producing The Tommy Max and Ruby Smith Show, and we are honored to be passing the baton to them each afternoon.'"

"'This whole experience has been very humbling,'" added Ezra. "'For Carla and me to be representing the station in such a big way, and to have a spot in W-S-P-S lore, is an absolute dream come true.'"

Bullshit 101, ladies and gentlemen.

■ ■ ■

The next morning, I woke up with a renewed sense of purpose. Instead of throwing on a sweat suit and wrapping my curly hair in a messy bun, I actually took the time to get ready; I wanted to look as good as I felt.

But of course, I had to deal with some level of self-inflicted drama. (Why can't *anything* ever be easy in my life?) The last thing I needed to do was to pluck some stray hairs from my eyebrows, but I couldn't find the tweezers in my jumbled-up mess of a purse. Now I was frantically searching my bedroom, with only five minutes to spare.

"Could it be in here?" I muttered to myself, rummaging through each disorganized drawer of my desk. I opened the top drawer and hunted through a bunch of dried up pens, stray envelopes, and loose CDs. Towards the back, I found a crumpled up ball of paper with my handwriting scribbled all over it. Curiously, I opened it up.

"Aw!" I exclaimed when I realized what it was. It was the blueprint of my "grand ten-year reunion plan," one that was supposed to hatch in roughly two months.

Abandoning my tweezers search, I sat on my bed to read my words from ten months before. It's not that I forgot what I wrote, but over the course of the past few months I've misplaced a lot more than just beauty supplies:

> I will walk through the Honey Crest High School gymnasium doors an amazing, accomplished woman. I will have a handsome, successful lawyer on my arm, who had just recently proposed with a 2 karat, platinum Tiffany Novo ring. I'll have a rock-hard, size 4 body. I'll have my own sports-talk show on WSPS. My 500+ former classmates will rush to congratulate me on all my achievements (and when I'm not looking, most will enviously talk behind my back). My fiancé, my best friends, and I will merrily drink and dance the night away. At the end of the night, my man and I will retire to our brand new waterfront condo overlooking the New York City skyline, and make passionate love until the sun comes up.

As things stood, one item definitely, surprisingly had come true (WSPS). One could come close to being true if I stuck to what Xander told me (body). One could come true, but not right now (condo). And one was so far from ever coming true, I might as well scratch it off this list (love).

Without even thinking twice about it, I tore the paper up and threw it in the garbage. So what if I was batting .250 in this game? I was damn proud of my one hit. The rest would fall into place, at the proper time. I was no longer going to sweat it.

See what a little success can do for the soul?

21

Day 313
Knock, knock, knock!

“It’s too carly,” I moaned, throwing a pillow over my head.

KNOCK, KNOCK, KNOCK!

“Stoppp!” I pleaded.

POUND, POUND, POUND!

I knew it was never going to stop. I begrudgingly peeled myself off the most fluffy, comfortable bed in the universe to get the door.

“CARLAAAAAAAAAA!”

"Yeah, yeah, yeah, I'm coming." I yawned, rubbing my eyes. I unlocked the deadbolt, and there before me stood my aggravating human alarm clock.

"Our wedding day is here!" Mom cheerfully announced, pushing past me. She started twirling around the room like a ballerina and stopped at the window to throw open the blinds.

I shielded my face against the glaring sun. "*Our* wedding day?"

"It is the most beautiful day for the most beautiful of weddings!" She walked up to me and hit the back of my head. "Now wake up. Your hair appointment is in an hour!"

I stretched my arms to the ceiling as I watched Mom skip out of the room, slamming the door behind her. Today was my brother's wedding day, and she was already off to a flying start in setting the new bar for "annoying".

With my eyes now adjusted to the sunlight, I strolled over to the window. I studied the gorgeous, manicured lawn of the 24-acre compound, home to a legit castle big enough to host both families for the weekend. (I was sure our side could have easily made the hour drive, but Mom insisted everyone be together: "What if somebody gets in a car accident and dies on the way up here? It'll ruin the wedding!") For once, I didn't find fault with her paranoia—I felt like royalty staying there. The building was over 100 years old, with big fireplaces in every room, stained glass windows, and intricate wood detailing (not to mention cloud mattresses).

I took a quick shower and put on the snug, white cashmere robe Gwen gave as bridesmaid gifts. As I casually hummed an original off-key tune, I neatly laid the pale yellow bridesmaid dress and silver accessories on my bed. Before I headed over to Gwen's bridal suite for hair and makeup, I checked my phone and—UM, WHAT?

Miguel Martinez Cell: Hey! Long time no talk, how is everything?

I tightly clenched the phone and frantically searched the room—in closets, outside my window, and under my bed. Were there hidden cameras in here? Was I being *Punk'd*? There was no way in hell this was real.

Once I verified I was alone, I knelt on the bed and looked at my phone again. There it was, an actual text message, sent by "Miguel Martinez Cell" at 11:39 p.m.:

Miguel Martinez Cell: Hey! Long time no talk, how is everything?

"You have got to be kidding me," I said to no one. In the weeks after our hook-up, being with him again was the only thing on my mind. The fantasy of our reunion is what woke me up every morning, carried me through each day, and when the call never came, tortured me to sleep every night. But the cruel disaster of New Years' Eve snapped me back to reality, and Miguel was banished from my heart forever. Even the breaking news of his divorce weeks ago (while on the air with Dante; wasn't *that* an interesting day!) didn't stir my emotions.

Or so I thought.

As I walked down the opulent hallway towards Gwen's room, I started to question every aspect of the text. *He didn't address it to "Carla," so maybe he meant to send it to someone else? And if he actually did mean to send it to me…then why? Why today, and not yesterday, or last week, or last month? What are his intentions? What did he expect me to respond with? How should I respond? Should I play dumb and pretend to not know who it is?*

My head was throbbing by the time I knocked on Gwen's door.

"Howdy, Carla!" Dalila, one of Gwen's Southern Belle older sisters, warmly welcomed me. "Come on in!"

I dragged my feet inside. "Do you have any Advil?" I pleaded, not caring that I was asking a favor from a relative stranger.

"Let me fetch some for ya," Dalila replied, dashing away.

Gwen's fancy bridal suite was converted into a full-service salon. A couple of the girls were getting their hair curled while a few more were getting makeup applied. Normally, I'd be very excited about the prospect of getting made over by a team of beauty professionals, but right then I was extremely distracted…

He texted me at 11:39…was that a booty call? Or was he just bored? How could he be bored, though, he's in the middle of the baseball season? He was just finishing up his game; did he notice someone in the stands who looked like me?

Then, I puffed out my chest. *Maybe he recently came across the mid-day show and decided to reach out.*

"Um, hello? Earth to bridesmaid!" A rude, smoky woman's voice yelled. I turned to my right and saw one of the hairdressers snapping her fingers in my direction. "Come on, sit in the chair," the older women ordered, cracking her gum. "There's a lot of yous, and we're already behind schedule!"

I nodded and quietly followed her to a stool.

"I'm Dolores," she introduced, draping a black salon cape over my shoulders. "What do you want today? The bride said yous are free to pick whatever."

I exited out of Miguel's text to pull up a photo of Carrie Underwood sporting the hairstyle I wanted—a romantic, side-swept, half-updo.

"Oh, so pretty," Dolores cracked her gum. "That girl is such a doll."

As Dolores got to work curling my hair, Dalila appeared with two Advil and glass of water.

"Thank you!" I exclaimed, shoving the pills in my mouth.

"The wine got ya last night at the rehearsal dinner, huh?" Dalila commented sympathetically.

"Something like that," I muttered. "But I'll be okay."

"Your tiny body can't handle the alcohol!"

"I guess not," I shifted in my seat uncomfortably. What tiny body? My blood, sweat and tears in the gym only yielded a four pound weight loss thus far, much to the chagrin of Xander (*"You want results? THEN EAT LIKE IT!")* But Dalila wasn't the only person to blindingly compliment my so-called slimness; friends, family (not Mom) and people at work all remarked about my "new look". What they didn't know was that their positive reinforcement actually set me back, because whenever the Fat Girl trapped inside me heard these compliments, she overruled all my other senses and urged me to eat more since "I'd earned it." If these praises continued throughout the day, I'll be up a stone or two by tomorrow morning.

However, what the Fat Girl didn't understand was that the compliments were less about my phantom weight loss and more about the confidence I'd inherited with the mid-day show being a smashing success. My "glow" wasn't because I was staying away from complex carbohydrates (plus, I was not) or grinding through 7 a.m. personal training sessions, six days a week; it was because I was finally getting to do something I genuinely loved, and that went a long way. I could feel the joy oozing from my pores, and maybe that was why I hadn't put such a premium on my weight loss as I had in the past…I didn't need anything else. I was perfectly content, right here.

Or at least I was up until a half hour ago when Miguel flipped my zen thinking on its head.

Dalila was still standing over me. I peered at her through the top of my eyes, silently begging her to leave me alone. But instead, she pulled up a folding chair and sat right in front of me. *C'mon, man!*

"I hate to admit this, but since I turned 30, it's gotten much harder to keep my figure. I've gained five pounds since Christmas, and I'm still unable to lose the weight! How did you do it?"

I sighed. Since she wasn't picking up on my nonverbal cues, I had no choice but to humor her. But what do you say to someone who never had to worry about her weight until her third decade...*"Karma's a bitch"*? (And let's be honest, she still didn't have to worry. I mean, it was *five pounds*; there was no need to ring the alarm and open a Lane Bryant credit card account.)

"Lots of sacrifice, discipline, and patience," I lied.

"I think that's my problem; I've never had to diet or work out before, and now that I have to start, I'm finding that I have zero willpower."

If my hair wasn't currently entangled with a 300 degree piece of metal, I would have excused myself out of his conversation. Instead, I diverted myself by pulling up Miguel's text message, and reading it for the umpteenth time.

Dalila finally got it and rose from her chair. "Well, I'll see you later. Your hair is looking fantastic!"

"Thanks!" I replied distractedly, my eyes glued to the screen.

As soon as Dalila's shadow disappeared, another one, unfortunately, took its place. I looked up to see my mother's panic-stricken face looming over me. And was she…crying?

"Already you're starting with the waterworks? The wedding isn't for another four hours, get a grip."

Mom ignored me and leaned close to my ear. "We have a problem, and you need to keep calm when I tell you what I'm about to tell you."

"Sure, I'll just follow your lead," I quipped.

"Gwen wants to back out of the wedding."

"SHE WANTS TO BACK OUT OF THE WEDDING?!"

"SHHHHHHHH!" Mom exclaimed.

"Honey, don't move otherwise you are going to burn the both of us," Dolores scolded.

I ignored her. "What happened? What are we going to do?"

"When you're done, come to my room. And please, don't tell anyone." And with that, she darted away.

"Close your eyes, I'm going to spray you," Dolores ordered.

As the pungent hairspray whizzed around me, my thoughts switched from Miguel to Jimmy. *What the hell changed from last night until now? They looked so in love at the rehearsal dinner…Hell, they*

ALWAYS look so in love. What caused her to get cold feet? How could she do this to my little brother?

"Oh honey, you look so beautiful," Dolores swooned. She handed me a jumbo hand mirror to show me her work.

"It's gorgeous," I remarked. But who knew if I was going to be able to show the masterpiece off?

I thanked Dolores, and casually exited the room. Once I hit the hallway, I bolted towards my mother's hotel room. As I waited for Mom to open the door, I heard her voice piercing through the walls. "HOW STUPID COULD YOU BE? LIFE ISN'T *THE HANGOVER*, YOU KNOW!"

So much for flying under the radar; bodies buried six feet under in Australia could have heard her voice. "SOMEONE LET ME IN!" I pounded the door.

The door flew open, and there stood my annoyed father. Close behind him was my hyperventilating mother, and sitting dejectedly on their bed was Jimmy. "Your mother's nuts," Dad announced by way of greeting.

"Tell me something I don't know," I replied, pushing past him. "Mom, it sounds like somebody's getting murdered in here. Keep it down."

"WELL SOMEONE IS ABOUT TO BE...YOUR FATHER!"

"Why?"

"IT'S HIS FAULT THAT MY SON WON'T BE ABLE TO GET MARRIED TODAY!"

"Why?"

"BECAUSE YOUR FATHER WANTED TO BE COOL AND TOOK ALL THE GUYS TO A STRIP CLUB AFTER THE REHEARSAL DINNER LAST NIGHT!"

"Don't make it sound like it was just me," Dad countered. "All the other men, including Gwen's father, went too."

"WELL, YOU WERE THE RINGLEADER! I DON'T CARE WHAT ANYONE ELSE DOES; YOU PIGS SHOULD HAVE LEFT MY SON OUT OF IT!"

"Okay, so Gwen found out the guys went out, and she's a little upset? She'll get over it; it's not a big deal."

"OH, YOU THINK IT'S NOT A BIG DEAL, HUH? IT'S NOT A BIG DEAL? IT'S...NOT...A...BIG...DEAL!?" Mom repeated, growing louder with each line (if that's humanly possible). "I'LL TELL YOU WHAT THE BIG DEAL IS! SOMEONE WAS STUPID ENOUGH TO TAKE A PICTURE OF JIMMY GETTING A LAP DANCE AND TEXTED IT TO GWEN'S BEST FRIEND. NOW SHE WANTS NOTHING TO DO WITH MY SON!"

"Yea, that's a pretty big deal," I agreed.

"Carla, tell her to stop screaming, please," Dad sighed.

"Well, you *are* an idiot," I shot back. "All you men are idiots. Besides, Jimmy doesn't even like those places. And a strip club, up *here*? We're in the friggin' woods! Who was dancing on him, Mama June?"

"I DON'T CARE WHO WAS DANCING. ALL I KNOW IS THAT YOUR FATHER IS GOING TO DIE!"

"How was I supposed to know this was going to happen? It's not my fault Jimmy and Gwen have dumb friends!"

"AND HE'S GOT AN EVEN DUMBER FATHER!"

I sighed. "And I think we can all agree Jimmy is the dumbest, and the person who sent the picture is 1A."

"HE NEVER WOULD HAVE BEEN IN THIS SITUATION IF IT WEREN'T FOR YOUR FATHER!"

"Would you stop? This is nobody's fault!" Dad exclaimed. "If anything, it's Gwen's fault; she's the one that's overreacting. This is just what guys do."

Maybe I was in the predicament I was with men because I'd been raised in part by this "Boy's Club" bravado. What was even more annoying was even in the throes of the biggest self-inflicted blunder in Jimmy's history, my parents still refused to let him be accountable for his actions.

Mom, not taking lightly to my father's last comment either, took off her high heel shoes and heaved one at him. "THIS IS

WHAT GUYS DO? WE'LL SEE HOW THAT ARGUMENT HOLDS UP IN DIVORCE COURT!"

Dad ducked as another shoe flew over his head.

"IF THIS WEDDING DOES NOT HAPPEN, I AM CALLING MY LAWYER FIRST THING MONDAY MORNING!"

"Look, this isn't getting us anywhere," I snapped. "Where is Gwen? I know she'll listen to me, I'll talk to her."

"Her mother is the only one who knows what's going on, and she can't find her," Jimmy replied glumly.

"WHAT DIFFERENCE ARE YOU GOING TO MAKE?" You-know-who added.

"Let me handle this," I raced out of the room, to the tune of my mother's continuous, blood-curdling screams.

■ ■ ■

I checked the entire compound twice (still wearing my slippers and bathrobe, mind you) before I found the runaway bride, wearing an identical outfit, hidden in a rose garden.

Gwen was lying face-down on a granite bench, and her body violently shook as she audibly sobbed into her arms. I took a seat at the base of her head and, in her hysteria, she didn't even notice that she had company. It was only after I started to stroke her thick, blonde hair that she flinched to attention.

"What do you want?" she mumbled miserably, the whites of her eyes matching the color of the roses.

I skipped the pleasantries and got right to the point. "I know what he did was stupid, but you are not walking out on my little brother on his wedding day. Besides, my hair looks too good to have it go to waste."

"You're not funny," Gwen retorted, burying her head back into her hands.

"C'mon Gwen, he didn't mean it. For whatever reason, this is what guys like to do before they get married. I'd prefer a deep tissue massage and a good night's sleep, but to each their own."

Gwen shot back up and adjusted her body to sit Indian-style next to me. "I explicitly told him, NO STRIPPERS for his bachelor party! And the night before our wedding, he's not only at a go-go bar, he's gettin' intimate with the dancers!"

"Intimate? He didn't have sex with them, Gwen. He just got a lap dance. It's harmless," I lied. The more I talked, the angrier I got with the men in my family. How could they have done this to this sweet girl, on what was supposed to be the happiest day of her life?

I took a deep breath to stop myself from spiraling out of control. I couldn't let her see me upset; the sole purpose of the conversation was to get her ass down that aisle. We could commiserate on men being horny buffoons another day.

Gwen stuffed her hand into her pocket, pulled out her cell phone, and stuck the device in my face. "You consider THIS harmless?"

I gasped at the image before me. Jimmy was sitting on a velvet sofa while a G-string clad brunette sat on his lap. My little brother's hands held her Size Z boobs in place as he buried his face between them. Worst of all, there was a very noticeable bulge coming out of his pants.

"GET THAT AWAY FROM ME!" I shrieked, covering my eyes.

"Now do you see what I'm talkin' about!" Gwen cried. "I know he's your brother, but you can't defend that!"

"I can't," I agreed.

"So how do you expect me to marry him?"

I had to think quickly, something I've become markedly better at since I started spending more time on the air. "Jimmy was petrified to propose to you. He had no idea what to say, when to ask. But I told him to just go with the moment, and everything would be okay. And I'm telling you the same thing—despite this little bump in the road, everything is going to be fine."

"But what if Jimmy is going to make a habit out of going to these places? What if we get married and he turns around and sleeps with someone else?"

I was out of things to say—I would have these same fears, thanks to years of being lied to and cheated on, strippers or no strippers. Then again, I never had a guy put a ring on my finger and promise to spend the rest of his life with me. That had to stand for something, right? "Jimmy's not really a partier. You know that. I can guarantee you that he will never step foot in another place like that again," I finally said.

Gwen looked at me with a blank stare, and I continued grasping at straws.

"And...there are 250 people that spent a lot of money to come up here for the weekend, and you don't want them all pissed at you for wasting their time."

"Like I care about anyone else right now," Gwen snipped. "If they saw this photo, they'd understand."

"True..." I trailed off. "But then you wouldn't get to open all of your amazing gifts, or go on your honeymoon to Turks and Caicos, or wear your custom Vera Wang dress!"

"I don't care about that stuff," Gwen repeated.

"Well...if you don't get married today, then you won't be able to live in the dream home Jimmy built for you! And think of all the bullshit you had to deal with while decorating with Mom; that's time you're never going to get back!"

"So? They could sell the house," Gwen sobbed. "I don't want to live with a man who behaves like this."

Okay, now she was really starting to make my blood boil. Doesn't this stupid, idiotic girl know how lucky she is? I flew off the bench and stood over her. "Are you even mad that he went out, or is this an excuse so you can back out of the wedding?"

She rose up to meet me, nose-to-nose. "Have you lost your mind? Of course, that's not the case!"

"Then why are you so willing to start over from scratch?" I challenged. "You honestly think there's better out there? You think you're going to find someone that's never going to make a mistake, or get you angry?"

"No…" Gwen sniffled.

"Believe me, Gwen; I've searched high and low, and that "perfect man" doesn't exist! But hey, if you want to trade the closest thing to "perfect" for a string of bad dates, awkward kisses, crazy quirks and a lifetime of misery and loneliness, then be my guest. But I'm warning you, it's not fun."

Gwen chewed on that for a bit. I crossed my arms and searched her face for an answer.

I guess the prospect of living like me did the trick because it made Gwen snap out of it and envelope me in a huge hug. "Thank you for talking me off the ledge," Gwen whispered.

"You and I both know Jimmy loves you more than life itself, and that he would never intentionally hurt you."

"I know."

"Are you sure?"

She pulled away from me, her tears all but evaporated. "Yes. Let's get married!"

■ ■ ■

The ceremony started on time without a hitch.

After Jimmy had gotten engaged, I dreaded the prospect of walking down this very aisle. One of the many reoccurring nightmares I had involved the congregation jeering at Jimmy's "old maid" sister while throwing lemons in my direction as I made my way to the altar. But today's trip felt anything but bittersweet—I had a hot piece of arm candy to escort me (Austin, Gwen's totally hot-yet-married cousin…such was my life) and I stood a little taller knowing my heroics saved the day (and I was a proud big sister too, yeah, yeah, yeah).

As I got to the end of the aisle, Jimmy (who looked so handsome in his black tuxedo) gave me an enthusiastic thumbs up. I glanced over at my parents, who were sitting in the front row. Dad looked like 140 pounds had been lifted off his shoulders (as in, the approximate weight of my mother). Speaking of, I couldn't tell if she was at a wedding or a funeral.

When Gwen and her father appeared at the top of the castle's stone stairway, audible gasps filled the air. She marched towards her groom wearing a stunning, satin ball gown, embellished with intricate embroidery, beads, and crystals. Peeking from underneath the full-length skirt was a pair of chic yellow cowboy boots, an ode to her Texan roots (thankfully she didn't make the bridesmaids pay homage). Her best accessory, besides the extravagant bouquet of yellow roses she was clutching, was her dazzling smile.

Jimmy wiped a tear from his eye as he shook hands with Mr. Carrington, and again before pulling back Gwen's veil. The soon-to-be Mr. and Mrs. D'Agostino lovingly joined hands and locked eyes. They looked completely smitten, and it was hard to fathom that only a few hours ago, this union had been in serious turmoil.

When the energy died down, and the pastor kicked off the service, my mind immediately wandered to where it had been this morning—Miguel. *What would our reunion be like? Would it be riddled with awkwardness? Or would I be able to jump right back in? Should I confront him about New Years? Psh, after New Year's he's lucky if I even* do *reach out to him…*

The Q&A session continued to swirl around in my head until I heard my cue to snap back to reality: "I now pronounce you husband and wife. You may kiss the bride."

Released from my thoughts, I grabbed my bouquet and sprinted behind the giddy newlyweds.

■ ■ ■

After the wedding party had taken endless amounts of photos around the compound, we joined the rest of the flock in the lower terrace for the cocktail hour. This hour of goodness was what heaven had to be like—miles of tables full of first-class seafood, prime cut steaks, greasy hors d'oeuvres and top shelf liquor... calorie-free, of course. As I plucked my 3rd pig in a blanket off the waiter's sterling silver tray, I heard two familiar voices calling my name. "Finally, we found you!" Andrea said, kissing me on the cheek.

"You look like such a princess!" Katie gushed, kissing me on the cheek.

I popped the cocktail in my mouth. "More like a damsel in distress."

"Why what happened?" Katie asked.

I pulled my cell phone out of my silver clutch and retrieved Miguel's text. "Read."

Both of their jaws dropped to the floor.

"My reaction exactly. I have no idea what to do."

"Well I do—just ignore him!" Andrea exclaimed.

"What he did to you was wrong. He doesn't deserve a response after all this time, especially after that New Year's party," Katie added.

"Besides, I thought you were over him."

"I was…um, I am." I threw my hands up in the air exasperatedly. "I don't know, I mean, what's one date?"

"It's more than just one date!" Andrea exclaimed. "You're both high profile people, him especially. It's only going to end in disaster."

"Carla, I don't know too much about your business, but if you get caught with an athlete, can't you lose your job?" Katie added.

"It's worked for most of the girls on E-S-P-N," I shrugged.

"But if you got fired for something like this, it's going to affect Dante as well. And that's not fair to him."

I rolled my eyes. "Dante is untouchable. If I actually did get fired, Dan would just pair him with someone else."

"Waaaaaait a second," Andrea took a step back. "You'd be willing to lose your job over some fly-by-night baseball player?"

"Who said that? I'm just telling it how it is when it comes to Dante."

"By even hinting towards that hypothetical, it means that there would be a chance you'd get canned."

"I didn't say that!"

"You didn't deny it either."

"Because there is nothing to deny!"

"STOP!" Katie snapped. "We all know—even you Carla—that getting back in touch with Miguel is a bad idea. Now let's just forget about this and enjoy the night."

"Easy for you to say; you both have dates here," I muttered.

■ ■ ■

Between eating, drinking, and mingling, I managed to shelve my thoughts about Miguel for a few hours and had a decent time. But the reprieve didn't last long. After the Venetian hour, all 250 guests were ushered outside to a large balcony and treated to a fireworks show, an ode to the Fourth of July night Jimmy and Gwen got engaged.

As the brilliant array of colors filled the night sky, I reminisced about our family vacations in Wildwood every summer. Every Friday was the "Summer Fireworks Extravaganza" and the four of us would settle on Wildwood's amazingly wide beach to watch. I remembered studying the sea of couples surrounding us, who were either holding hands, or snuggling, or full-on making out. (Looking back, some of those couples might have been doing more than making out.) Even at my young age, it wasn't lost on me just how romantic the setting was. I couldn't wait to get older, so *I* could do that with someone. Well, I was older now...yet I was still waiting.

And I refused to wait anymore.

I pushed my way through the crowd and went inside. I made a beeline for my table, sat down and grabbed my cell phone. I understood where Andrea and Katie were coming from, and I appreciated their wanting to protect me. I hadn't had these butterfly feelings in such a long time; didn't I owe it to myself to at least find out what he wanted? I opened Miguel's text message and started typing away.

Me: Hey stranger! Everything is good with me, how is everything with you?

I placed the phone down and tapped my fingers on the table. I looked around the empty dining room and counted to ten. I checked my phone—nothing. Counted to ten again—still nothing.

I was an idiot. I should have responded the second I received the text that morning. He probably forgot all about—

My phone lit up.

Miguel Martinez Cell: Everything is great. I heard you on the radio not long ago. Congratulations on the show, you deserve it!

Beaming, I immediately wrote back.

Me: Thank you! It's been going great. The Yankees are having an incredible season so far, so you're definitely making my job easier :)

As soon I hit *send*…

Miguel Martinez Cell: Thank you, it has. We should go out to celebrate. What are you doing Wednesday night?

My heart dropped to the floor.

Me: Nothing so far! What did you have in mind?

I knew I was breaking every dating rule in the book by making myself so available, but WHO CARED?

Miguel Martinez Cell: Let's do dinner. I know of this great new Italian spot downtown. We have a day game Wednesday, and we're off on Thursday, so we can really enjoy ourselves ;)

It's SO ON!

Me: Sounds perfect! What time?

Miguel Martinez Cell: Let's say 7 o'clock. The place is called Gufo.

Me: Great, I'll see you then!

Miguel Martinez Cell: Ok gorgeous. See you soon.

At that point, I heard the door open, and everyone started to file back in.

I gave the crowd a sly smile. While the fireworks show ended for them...they were only just beginning for me.

22

Day 317

Four long, agonizing days later, Wednesday mercifully arrived. After spending the past few days (ok, *months*) shrouded in a blanket of hair-pulling angst, that morning I emerged from my cocoon a rejuvenated butterfly—and the world smiled back. The sun was shinin', the birds were chirpin'; I could have skipped all the way to work (or better yet, skipped it in general).

Actually, I'd probably be doing our listeners a favor if I called in sick; I just could not focus. When we took calls about the Yankees, the mere mention of the team launched another one of my frenzied Miguel fantasies, rendering me useless throughout the rest of the conversation.

"Earth to Carla!" Dante had to say more than once.

After the show, I hopped a cab to a swanky spa for an afternoon of luxurious pampering. So what if the cost almost equaled a week's worth of salary? I had to look my absolute best and, more importantly, *relax* my jittery anticipation. At first, it actually worked; I managed to float away from my thoughts for a couple hours.

Then...lunch happened.

After I had settled in with a gourmet meal of lemon-sage chicken with scallions and pine nut rice, I rebelled against the place's no-electronic-devices-allowed policy and checked the score of the Yankees' matinee game. To my dismay, they were losing to the lowly Minnesota Twins 3-2 in the top of the seventh inning. Miguel had not registered a hit in three tries, putting his modest 13-game hitting streak in jeopardy.

To you and me, losing one1 game out of 162 wouldn't be that big a deal. But to a fierce competitor like Miguel, it's the difference between life and death. Worse, a defeat would not put him in the optimal dinner-date mood.

A worrisome thought flashed in my mind: *What if he cancels?* Suddenly, the $45 chicken dish tasted like sawdust. My uneasiness continued to swirl up until the last stroke of the makeup artist's brush. The second he announced his work of art was complete, I bypassed checking his effort (and all manners) and whizzed to the locker room. My heart sank as I read the headline:

Yankees Fall to Twins, 4-3; Martinez Hitting Streak Snapped, Registers Two Errors

Of *course,* Miguel would have his worst game of the season today; why would my luck have it any other way?

Despite the box score, there was no cancellation message. Since dinner reservations were in an hour, I took that as a safe sign and got dressed. I put on a brown, one-shoulder, ruched silhouette dress with gold sandals and matching accessories. Thanks to all of the spa treatments, I glowed from head-to-toe— but felt the complete opposite.

Fifteen minutes later, I was in the back seat of a taxi, praying for my life. I appreciated that the driver took to heart my words "Move it!", but this was ridiculous; he was practically driving on the sidewalk! "Can you please slow down?" I demanded.

"You told me you were in a rush, now you want me to slow down?" he snapped in a heavy Middle Eastern accent.

I wanted to knock the white turban off his head. "Okay, but you almost hit that group of Asian tourists back there!"

"Sit back and be quiet, please. I'm the driver."

"UGH!" I grunted, crossing my arms. See, this was why I didn't do public transportation.

Moments later, we pulled up to the WSPS parking garage with our lives still intact.

"Can you wait here? I'll be right back, I just need to throw my bags in the car."

"Hurry up!"

The damn elevator was taking centuries, so I awkwardly sprinted upstairs in my three-inch heels, threw my stuff in the car, and did a swift about-face. However, halfway down I must have put too much thrust on my engines because I completely lost balance.

"AHHHH!" I screamed as I slid down the concrete steps on my back, landing on my butt at the bottom. My eyes immediately went to my right ankle, which was already starting to balloon. I looked up helplessly across the parking lot to the cab driver, who was glaring at me through the open window.

"What are you doing? Get up!" he shouted.

With the help of the railing, I gingerly tried standing upright. The second I put a pound of pressure on my ankle, it buckled.

"I...I can't!" I cried. "It hurts!"

He muttered what I assumed to be expletives in his native language, and barreled out of the car. "Let's go," he ordered, pulling my arm out of its socket.

"OW! Stop, you're hurting me!"

"Make up your mind. What hurts, your arm or your leg?"

"Both... *now*!"

The cab driver rolled his eyes and crouched down at my feet. "Let me see."

I glared at him. "What do you know about twisted ankles?"

"Please be quiet, for five seconds. I beg you," he demanded as he gently pressed on my ankle.

"I can't believe this is happening," I whined, ignoring his wishes. "I have a really big date in, like, ten minutes and— "

Crrrrrrrrrrack!

"WHAT THE HELL ARE YOU DOING?"

"I popped your ankle back in place. Stand up now."

I glared at him as I attempted to slowly walk. There was still so much pain, but at least I wasn't toppling over myself.

"How did you do that?" I breathed.

"I'm a magician," he deadpanned.

"Well is there any way your powers can shrink my ankle back to normal?"

"No. You have big ankles anyway; no one will notice the difference."

"I'm going to pretend I didn't hear that. Thank you, um—"

"Mohammed."

"Nice to meet you, Mohammed. My name is—"

"I don't care what your name is. Get in my car, please. And no talking; you give me a headache."

I scanned my body to make sure I didn't have any other bumps or bruises. Once I declared myself okay, I limped towards the car and climbed in the front.

"What are you doing, get in the back!" Mohammad ordered.

"I need your mirror! I have to make sure my hair is okay."

Mohammad grumbled more Arabic and put the car in drive.

Luckily, my hair was fine, but I think it was the only part of me that went untouched. I leaned my aching head against the headrest and closed my eyes. I was already so spent…and the night hadn't even started yet!

"Where do you need to go?" Mohammad demanded.

"Gufo Restaurant in Little Italy."

"Do you have the address?"

"Actually, no," I replied, twisting my body to grab my purse from the back. "Let me look it up."

"Why doesn't that surprise me? Don't even bother."

As Mohammad set up his GPS, I noticed I had one new notification. A text from Miguel!

> **Miguel Martinez Cell: Hey Carla, can we do a rain check? Bad game today, really not up for going out tonight.**

I KNEW IT! But even though I had predicted it, it didn't make me any less angry. I mean, are you serious? You're going to text me—not even call me, TEXT ME—and cancel SECONDS before our date, all because you lost one, stupid, little game? And so what if you couldn't manage a hit off of a borderline minor league pitcher; does that give you an excuse to lose all decency and class? It was a thirteen-game hitting streak; it wasn't like you were in Joe DiMaggio territory.

I glared at my ornery cab driver. To hell with his rules; I had to give Miguel a piece of my mind.

"Mohammad, I'm sorry, but I have to make a phone call."

Without taking his eyes off the road, he put his index finger to his lips. "What did I say? Shhhhhhhhhhhh!"

"I will give you double the tip. Please, let me make this call!"

Mohammad angrily shook his head. Taking that as a yes, I hit "*send*."

"Hello?" Miguel answered glumly on the fourth ring.

"Heyyyy," I too-sweetly purred. "What's going on?"

"Baby, I'm not in the mood to be out in public. It was a really ugly game."

"I know. But you still have to eat."

"Yeah, but on nights like this, I'm better off being alone in my apartment, watching game tape, and ordering in."

Then we'll hang out there, I smirked. I didn't say anything and waited for his invitation.

"Hello?" he asked.

Guess not. "That's not a healthy approach, Miguel. You need to get away for a couple hours and clear your head."

"I'm never away from it; that's the problem. People don't care you're out to dinner, or at your kid's school play, or at your ex-wife's grandmother's funeral. They just want a picture, an autograph, or an opportunity to tell you what a piece of shit you are. It's a lot for one person to handle, and I'm in no mood to deal with it tonight!"

With the lovely exception of his divorce proclamation (it sounded so much better coming from him than from the press), all I heard was *"blah, blah, blah!"* I had to bite my tongue from replying with, *"Quit being such a cry baby. You make more money than half the population of New York City put together; suck it up!"* If I learned anything from dealing with Ruby, it was how to tame the animal with gentle strokes.

"If anyone understands the tremendous pressure athletes are under in this town, it's me. I wouldn't be able to help the psyche of my distressed callers if I didn't— "

"Yeah, you help by riling everybody up," Miguel bitterly finished.

He *did* have a point. "But if fans didn't have us as a sounding board, you'd have triple the amount of people bothering you."

"I guess. Okay baby, I'm going to go. I'll talk to you soon, okay?"

"WAIT!" Despite better judgment, I wasn't ready to throw in the towel. "I'll tell you what. I'm already on my way to the restaurant. I'll talk to the owner and make sure our table is in a private area where nobody can bother us."

"Um, I'm boys with the owner. He already knows to do that."

"Soooo...what's the problem?"

"The problem is the walk to and from the restaurant."

"You're freaking out over a few steps?" *If anyone should be, it's me*, I thought as I rubbed my increasingly throbbing ankle. "What if...what if I walk in with you? Maybe people will see that you're busy and leave you alone!"

"Just what I need, pictures of me in Page Six out on the town after a bad loss."

"You think I want to be caught on a date with *you*?" I blurted. "I could lose my job!"

"So see? It's a bad idea for both of us."

I shook my head. My girlfriends were right; I never should have given Miguel a second chance. Look where it's left me—defeated (again) and (even more) crippled.

Wait...crippled.

"Miguel, what if I told you I had a great way to get in the good graces of any potential haters *and* the press?"

■ ■ ■

Nearly an hour later, Mohammad made his umpteenth trip around Mulberry Street.

"How much longer?" he growled.

"Oh, what do you care?" I snapped. "I'm running up the meter."

"I care because I'm getting dizzy! We go around and around because of you!"

"I'll *triple* your tip, all right?! Just keep driving around the block until I tell you to stop."

Mohammad was right—this was ridiculous. When Miguel agreed to my plan, obviously I was elated, but as time dragged on I wished I had just kept my big mouth shut. Was a dinner with Miguel Martinez really worth all of this pain (literally)? It was not like I could ever be in a relationship with this man. His high maintenance alone would put me in the grave before our first month anniversary!

So why am I here, getting abused by some crabby cabbie while racking up hundreds of dollars in taxi fare? Is this my one last gasp at perfecting my reunion story?

My phone rang. Miguel. I briefly thought about declining the call, but I'd come this far; I owed all parts of myself to see this through.

"Hello?"

"Hi, baby. I'll be there in two minutes."

"Assume positions," I said slyly.

"My thoughts exactly," Miguel cooed. "See you soon."

I turned to Mohammad. "Well, this is goodbye. You can drop me off at the corner of Mulberry, and I'll take it from there."

"*Wah, wah*!" Mohammad pretended to cry, then got serious. "Fifty-seven dollars, please. Plus triple tip."

"It's criminal what this city charges." I handed him the money as I stepped out of the car. "Thank you for everything."

"I hope to never see you again." He bowed his head and sped off.

In the too-far distance, I saw the neon sign for Gufo. I winced and started gimping away on the deserted sidewalk.

Paranoid weirdo, I thought as I got closer to the restaurant. *There's not a soul around here.*

"EXCUSE ME!" A man rushed by me, almost knocking me over. Three other guys followed him.

"CAN'T YOU JERKS SEE I'M DISABLED?!" I screamed after them.

I took a few more excruciating steps and noticed the posse had stopped in front of Gufo. Why would they be going in there? It's not like they were dressed up; they were wearing jeans and...Yankees jackets.

"NO! How the hell do they know?" I said aloud.

Suddenly, a black, tinted-out Escalade pulled up in front of the restaurant. The collector trolls took out their baseballs and Sharpies while licking their lips in anticipation. Meanwhile, nosy neighbors crawled out of the woodwork to investigate the hoopla.

Way to travel incognito, Miguel. Miraculously, I finally made it to the restaurant, and I nonchalantly waved behind the crowd to the Arnold Schwarzenegger-lookalike driver. Right on cue, he jumped out of the car to open Miguel's door. The horde swarmed around him as he attempted to exit.

Just as we discussed, I fell to the ground, which wasn't much of stretch at this point.

"OW!" I dramatically shrieked, putting my Italian pipes to good use. Twenty heads turned and collectively gasped as they saw me writhing on the pavement.

"Everyone stay back!" Arnold Schwarzenegger ordered, creating a path for Miguel to escape.

Miguel rushed over to me. "Are you okay?"

One look at him and all my pain floated away. He had on a baby blue button-down shirt and jeans, which nicely complimented his dark tan. His green eyes were filled with genuine concern.

"I think I twisted my ankle," I replied faintly, not so much from the pain, but from the scent of his sensual cologne.

"Okay, hold onto me and I'll pick you up."

I wrapped my arms around his thick neck and immediately felt an electric current.

"You girls and your high heels." He smiled, his face only inches away. "No one should wear shoes that high; you can really hurt yourself."

"Thanks for the advice, Doctor Scholl."

"Okay ready? One, two, three!"

The gallery erupted into boisterous applause and camera flashes as Miguel lifted me up.

"You're a hero, Martinez!" one whistled.

"Thank you!" he nodded as he whisked me inside.

After we had crossed the threshold into the restaurant's vestibule, we burst out laughing.

"That'll be on *TMZ* in a couple hours," he half-joked as he gently let me down.

"At least it will be for something positive," I giggled, steadying myself with my good leg.

"It's okay, it's worth it now that I'm here with you," Miguel smiled, his eyes glowing just as they had that night back in November.

Just as I was about to collapse again (this time from sheer ecstasy), we were interrupted by a short, middle-aged Italian man standing at the main door of the restaurant.

"Miguel!" he greeted, wrapping him in a tight hug.

"Massimo! Meet my friend, Carla. Carla, this is the best Italian cook in all of New York City."

"Piacere di conoscerti," I smiled.

"Oh, you speak-a Italian? I like-a her Miguel, she's a keeper. Italian girls are the best!"

"I agree," Miguel replied, giving me a lustful look. I felt myself turn red.

"Come to my restaurant!" Massimo motioned to us. "It's a-small, but very nice and romantic. I have a nice-a table set up in the corner!"

Gufo is Italian for "owl," and even the most ignorant of people would figure that out by going there. There were owls everywhere—incorporated in the hand-painted mural, sitting on the shelves, hanging from the ceiling. A theme like that had a dangerous potential to be perceived as corny, but in true Italian fashion, the décor was artful and refined.

"My mother loves-a the owl," Massimo explained. "I name the restaurant for her."

As I continued to study the dimly-lit room, I noticed two pairs of terrifyingly familiar owl eyes staring at me. *What the hell?* I rubbed my eyes and looked again, just to be sure.

Dan and Dante. Dan, as in my boss and the person who was responsible for all of the hiring...and all of the firing. And Dante, as in my current co-host and, more importantly in this situation, former best-friend who was privy to the fact that Miguel and I had previously hooked up.

In other words, I was seriously screwed. Of all the restaurants in this city, they had to be here, tonight of all nights? WHY?!

I had no time to ponder the thought. I had to launch in damage control mode... *Rapidamente*! I cleared my throat. "Excuse me, gentleman, I have to go say hello to a couple of work colleagues who are sitting over there."

"Who?" Miguel shrilled.

"My boss and co-host." I tightly smiled.

"You work-a with Dante? Oh, what a beautiful man; he has the voice of an angel!" Massimo exclaimed.

Too bad he's not up there singing with them, I wryly thought.

I wobbled over to Dan and Dante's table. Their eyes were still unblinking.

"Hi, guys!" I laughed nervously.

Dan cut right to the punch. "Carla, what are you doing here with Miguel Martinez?"

I attempted to make light of the situation. "Oh my God, I am so embarrassed; I was walking down the street and *clumsy me* fell and twisted my ankle. Miguel happened to pull up at that time, and brought me in here."

The men simultaneously looked down at my feet.

"Which ankle is it?" Dan asked.

"I don't know, I can't tell," Dante replied dryly.

"It's the right one," I grimaced.

Dante's eyes continued to beam into me while Dan resumed his questioning. "Well, who are you supposed to meet then?" Dan asked.

"I wasn't supposed to be here at all, actually. I was going to meet some friends down the street—"

Dante raised an eyebrow.

"Not those friends. Other friends."

He narrowed his eyes at me. "You're dressed up like that to meet up with a few friends?"

"We weren't exactly going out for brownie sundaes at TGI Friday's in Honey Crest Plaza, you know," I shot back.

"Carla, are you on a date with Miguel Martinez?" Dan scowled.

"What do you think?" Dante muttered.

"Noooo!" I nervously laughed. "Besides, I think I can ask the same about you and Dante. You two sure are looking cozy! Like, get a room, guys!"

"It's business," Dante snipped, completely disregarding my poor attempt at humor.

My heart stopped. Amidst the chaos, it hadn't occurred to me what else their little meeting here could be ruining. "Well, isn't your business is my business? What's going on?"

"This has nothing to do with W-S-P-S."

"Right," I huffed.

"Hello, Dan," I heard a familiar sexy voice purr behind me. My body went stiff.

Dan's demeanor immediately changed from stern boss to star struck little boy. "Good to see you, man! Rough game today, I'm sorry."

"Ah, what are you going to do?" Miguel shrugged. "We'll get 'em next time."

"Yeah you will! Allow me to introduce you to Dante Ezra. He co-hosts the mid-morning show with Carla."

Miguel extended his hand. "Nice to meet you, Dante, I'm a big fan of the show. You two are awesome together."

"Thanks," Dante glowered.

I wanted to shake him. *Really Dante? The biggest sports star in the city just gave your sports show a ringing endorsement; the least you can do is show some appreciation!*

"Anyway, I see you've picked a wounded bird off the street," Dan continued. "You're Superman!"

"Thank you, but not exactly..." Miguel chuckled. "I was coming in here to eat dinner, and I saw her lying on the ground. I scooped her up and brought her in here to collect her bearings."

"What a guy!" Dan hollered.

"Your timing is impeccable," Dante drolled.

"At least it was right for *something* today. Good thing I found her before work tomorrow, right?" Miguel quipped, patting Dante on the back.

"Is it though?" he retorted.

At this point, I wanted to grab a fork from a nearby table and stab Dante in the eye. "See Miguel, that's the reason we're so good on the air…it's because we honestly can't stand each other off it!"

"I see," he chuckled.

"So who are you meeting here, some other dudes from the team?" Dan asked brightly.

"No, I was coming in alone."

"Really?" Dante smirked.

"Well, it's hard for a newly single guy to fend for himself; I can barely fry an egg! I've sadly become the adopted son of many restaurants around the city."

"Well, why don't you sit with us?" Dan's eyes twinkled.

My eyes darted to Dante, and we shared a bewildered look, for completely different reasons. *Um, what?*

"Really? I don't want to intrude."

"Don't be ridiculous. Pull up a chair!"

No Dan, YOU are the ridiculous one! This was NOT happening right now.

Miguel waved to Massimo. "Massimo, please set us up over here."

"Us?' I thought she was meeting friends," Dante sneered.

"I was," I answered glumly. "But I guess I can stay for a little." I helplessly watched Massimo and his team transform the table from terrible twosome to fearsome foursome. Miguel had always been part of my answer for, *If you were having a dinner party, what three guests would you invite?* but not like this!

■ ■ ■

Four entrees, two bottles of homemade wine and one ruined date later, I officially wanted to kill myself.

"She refused to understand that when I come home from a game, I want to be left in peace," Miguel complained.

"I feel you, bro," Dan agreed sympathetically.

"I'd walk through the door, and she'd attack me like an eager puppy. 'The air conditioning isn't working; can you fix it?' 'Your daughter lost her Barbie doll; can you help her find it?'..."

"...it's like, SHUT UP!"

"Exactly! It's not like we can't afford to get the air conditioner fixed by a professional, call him up! And while you're at it, have the live-in nanny I'm paying thousands for find the stupid toys. Why do you have to bother me for after a shitty game?"

"So annoying!"

Dan, what the hell do you know? You've never been married, I crossly thought as I shifted pieces of veal Milanese around my plate. Dante and I had stopped contributing to the conversation hours before, but I'm *pretty* sure nobody noticed. What more could we do besides politely eat our food and observe their banter with glazed-over eyes?

"Your ex-wife sounds like a pimple on my ass, but you know what? No disrespect, but she's smoking hot," Dan inappropriately professed.

I buried my face in my hands.

Instead of getting him by the collar and throwing him across the room, Miguel agreed. "Why do you think it was so hard to leave her? There isn't a more beautiful girl in the world."

I slapped my hands down on my lap. *Well, isn't that special?* Just as I was locating the nearest exit, Massimo appeared balancing a large tray.

"Four espresso and my-a special tiramisu," he announced as he placed the items on our table.

"Massimo, you didn't have to do that!" Miguel exclaimed.

"I was actually just leaving," I added.

"You can't-a go anywhere yet, Carla! I made this just for your table," Massimo ordered. "Buon appetito."

"Thanks," I mumbled as he walked away.

As Dan and Miguel continued to chat, Dante leaned over to whisper in my ear. "Where are you going?"

"I told you, I was supposed to meet some friends," I whispered back.

"You think I believe that for a second?"

"Believe it, buddy. If this were a real date, you think I'd tolerate sitting with you and Dan, of all people?" To prevent myself from completely unleashing my fury, I shoved a forkful of (divine) cake in my mouth.

"What are you doing after dinner?" Dan asked Miguel (just in case there was any confusion).

Miguel quickly glanced at me, his first acknowledgment since we sat down. "I was actually going to go home and watch some game tape from today. You?"

"Oh, that sounds like fun…" Dan disappointingly trailed off. "I guess I'm just going to call it a night too."

"I'll have my driver drop everyone off," Miguel offered.

Finally, the light at the end of the tunnel…I can ditch these losers and go home!

After we polished off the rest of the desserts and Miguel paid the bill, we piled into his Escalade—the men in the back, and me in the front (Dante cut me in line, thus preventing me from sitting next to Miguel. Not that it mattered at this point.)

"This was fun, man! We should do it again sometime," Dan exclaimed.

"Definitely! It's not every day I can hang out with the media in this light. It's refreshing."

"Let me get your number, and we'll hook up soon."

I wondered how I was going to manage the drive home, being that my eyes were now permanently glued in the rolled position.

In what seemed like centuries but in reality was only a few minutes, we mercifully pulled up to the WSPS parking garage.

"I'm on the first level," Dan announced, jumping out of the car. He extended his hand to Miguel. "Catch you later man!"

"Anytime!"

And then, there were three. We drove up to the second level in uncomfortable silence.

"Carla, let me help you!" Miguel exclaimed when the car came to a stop.

"No, I will!" Dante shot back.

The both sprung out of the car and appeared before me at the same time. Gee, how did I get so lucky?

"I can help myself," I insisted.

Miguel swooped in past Dante and wrapped his arms around my waist. "I got you, babe," he said, hoisting me out of my seat. Funny, I didn't get the same rush as when he cradled me before.

"My car is over there," I pouted, pointing my keyless entry remote towards the white Mazda.

"I told you I was going to get her!" Dante exclaimed, sprinting after us. Miguel ignored him as he gently placed me in the driver's seat. I shoved off my heels and immediately felt some comfort, the first positive emotion I'd felt in hours.

"Better?"

"Now I am," I genuinely smiled.

My bliss was sadly short-lived as Dante shoved Miguel out of the way. "Are you okay to drive?"

"Dude, she's fine. Relax," Miguel laughed defensively.

"She can't drive barefoot!"

"Nothing I haven't done before!" It may not be the smartest way to drive, but I've done a lot of things that haven't been too bright, agreeing to this evening being one of them.

"Be careful. If you need a ride to the station tomorrow, let me know," Dante continued.

I glared at him. "I'd rather walk." My expression stayed stone cold as I turned to Miguel. "Thank you for dinner."

"Bye, beautiful."

I stuck my key in the ignition, and watched Miguel saunter back to his car while Dante dragged himself to his.

"What a disaster," I said aloud, putting the car in drive. Just as I pulled out of the garage, my phone rang. Miguel.

"Hey, sexy, so sorry this night turned out the way it did."

"Yeah, it definitely wasn't one of my better dates," I admitted. "But we were stuck."

"It was an awkward situation. Your boss kinda latched onto me."

"Really, he annoyed you?" I laughed. "You two seemed to hit it off pretty well. I felt like I was intruding."

"Well, I couldn't be a dick to the guy..." Miguel slowly trailed off. "But now that I've done dinner with him like that, I am guaranteed good press from you guys at least until the next homestand."

"Uh-huh." I cringed at his words. Must every word, every move be calculated to help boost his image? *You can start by not going 0-4 in a game, buddy.*

"Well…do you want to come by my place?"

"Um…" For once, my angel and devil were deadlocked in agreement: *Get the hell out while you can.* I mean, what's next; go to his apartment and see my mother babysitting his kids? But how can I bow out gracefully?

"What's with the hesitation?" Miguel chuckled.

I heard my call waiting beep through. Dante. I quickly hit *decline*. "There is no hesitation; I had another call coming in."

"Okay, well, you seem on the fence. Are you coming over or what?"

I couldn't believe how forceful he was being! "Thank you for the offer, and believe me I would love to, it's just that it's late, and I'm in a lot of pain. I really need to go home."

"I can take away the pain for you," Miguel purred seductively.

Dante beeped through again, and again I brushed him off.

"I have no doubt in my mind that you can, but I'd rather come over on a day where I'm in peak form."

Beep. I was growing increasingly flustered.

"Hold on," I growled, and clicked over.

"Dante, unless you got in a very bad car accident and need my help, I'm hanging up on you."

"Are you on the phone with Miguel?"

"WHY DO YOU EVEN CARE?"

"Because I do. Are you?"

"YES! Ok? Yes, I was supposed to be on a date with him. You people ruined it, are you happy now?"

"So what? You are making plans for a night cap?"

"Dante, we may have a show together, but in case you haven't realized this, we don't have a personal relationship anymore. Leave me alone!"

"I think you are making a huge mistake."

"That's nice, but I didn't ask your opinion. I'm hanging up now, and please don't dare call me back. Good-bye."

I heard Dante sigh as I clicked over to Miguel.

"Sorry, Dante had car trouble," I lied.

"He seems to have other trouble too. I think he's sweet on you."

"The only thing Dante is sweet on is himself. His panties were in a bunch because for once, he wasn't the center of attention."

"Whatever. I'm still waiting for an answer."

"I told you, I don't think I can." I was *so* over this conversation.

"Carla, tonight took a lot of effort, between your boss, and your ankle…I didn't even want to go out in the first place! I usually don't put this kind of work in."

I started feeling nauseous. "And what is that supposed to mean?"

"It means that I deserve to be handsomely compensated."

"Are you kidding me right now?" I laughed.

Beep. What doesn't Dante understand? But I was too heated with Miguel to care at this point. "Miguel…if anyone deserves to be handsomely compensated, it's me."

"What do you mean?"

"The lies, everything that happened tonight, New Year's Eve..."

"What happened New Year's Eve?"

"What? You don't know?"

"I have no idea what you are talking about. Which year?"

He's such a *LIAR*! "At your New Year's party THIS year, the way you ignored me."

"Ignored you? Baby, if I had seen you there, I would have been all over you!"

"Yea, that would have been a good look with YOUR WIFE hanging all over you!"

"Well, we are divorced now. Does that count?"

"No, that doesn't count! Miguel…sleeping with you is just not worth it."

"Carla, do you know who I am? Countless girls around the city would die for the opportunity I'm presenting you right now."

"Let them have you. I have to go."

"Your loss."

"No Miguel…*your* loss."

I hung up the phone feeling surprisingly okay. It would have been cool walking into the reunion knowing I bedded Miguel Martinez… but it's even cooler knowing that I turned down the chance.

I noticed that Dante left me a voicemail. I debated deleting it, but I figured I'd listen to what he had to say.

"Hi, Carla. You'll probably be sneaking out of Trump Tower when you get this message, but I just wanted to thank you for helping me make the biggest decision of my life to-night. I got an offer from a record company tonight, and tomorrow I will be handing in my resignation at W-S-P-S."

23

Day 321

The next morning, I waited by the radio station entrance like an angry pit bull for Dante to arrive. True to form, he strolled in fifteen minutes before show time, dark sunglasses adorning his face.

"What the hell was that voicemail you left me?" I demanded before he could even step foot inside.

Dante brushed past me and rambled his way down to Dan's office. I helplessly followed behind.

"Dante, what about the show?"

He said nothing and continued walking.

"You just signed a deal here. You can't go back on that!"

Dante stopped in front of Dan's closed door, threw off the sunglasses, and urgently knocked. A few steps later I caught up with him. I grabbed his shoulder and forcefully turned him around.

"DANTE! You have to talk to me!" I gasped at his appearance. His normally alive blue eyes were sunken in and puffy. His hair was disheveled. And was he wearing the same outfit I saw him in last night? "Look at you, you're a mess!" I said in my best Nancy D'Agostino voice. "If this deal was such a home run, you wouldn't be walking around looking like some strung-out crack addict."

"Carla, leave me alone," Dante warned.

"I'm not letting you do this," I replied defiantly.

The door swung open. "Dante, come in!" Dan greeted warmly. "Carla, fun night."

Yea, what a hoot. I pushed Dante out of the way and stormed into Dan's office.

"What are you doing?" Dante demanded.

"Dan, I know what Dante is here to do…and I forbid it."

"Well Carla, it's not exactly your call…" Dan began.

"What are you, some kind of masochist?" I snapped. "Why would you orchestrate having Dante, your friggin' butt buddy over here, leave the station when our show has gotten the best ratings EVER in that timeslot?"

"Butt buddy?" Dan asked, confused.

"Carla, stop, you're getting out of control..." Dante cautioned.

"He doesn't care about YOU," I continued. "He wants you to get famous in music so he can be your date to concerts and the awards shows. He'll pester the musicians for autographs like he does the athletes!"

"What's wrong with getting autographs?" Dan questioned.

"I didn't think you would be this upset," Dante remarked.

"I'm...I'm not upset you are leaving," I stammered, caught off guard. "I'm worried about the show!"

"I can't worry about that. Onward and upward."

"Of course, you can't. You never did."

Dan stepped in between us and held out his arms. "Both of you, just stop."

I attempted to calm my nerves by taking a deep breath. "What's going to happen to the show, Dan?"

"I don't...I don't know. I need to figure out a plan."

"You don't even have a PLAN?" I shrieked.

"This all came down last minute. I didn't think my friend from Sony would fall in love with Dante so quickly…not that I blame him," Dan backtracked and beamed at Dante, who remained emotionless.

I was about to bust, but instead, I decided to ask the million dollar question: "Am I still going to be on the air?"

Dan furrowed his brow and paused before answering. "I'll tell you what. You and Dante do the show today like normal. Take tomorrow off, and on Monday we'll make an announcement about everything."

I felt tears sting my eyes, not over what Dan said, but what was between the lines. I was toast. Done. Finito. I thought he finally turned a corner and saw the light when he gave us the show. But now I realized it was all bullshit. Dan still viewed me as a marginal hack whom he was forced to put on-air thanks to some bullying from his bosses. Here was his chance to evoke revenge…as a matter of fact, that was probably the motivating factor in helping Dante get a record deal, behind obtaining rare memorabilia and backstage passes. I'd probably get demoted to producing, or just be let go altogether. And here I thought I'd be walking into the reunion tomorrow night in good shape. Instead, I'm the worst shape of my life.

I turned my head towards the door so no one could see the ripe drops about to shower down my face. "Okay," I whispered, and rushed out the door.

I don't know how I managed to get through the show, but I did. Not once did I look over at Dante, and I'm sure it was the same story on the other side. After we wrapped, we silently exited the studio, and I left WSPS for possibly the last time.

■ ■ ■

"Dante's wanted to do music his whole life, can you blame him?" Andrea asked.

"*Yes.* He signed a two-year contract; he has a commitment here!" I whined.

"And he wants a life out of there! God forbid someone ever held you back from doing anything you wanted."

I gave Andrea the middle finger. "That's not the point. If Dante leaves, I'm out of a job. He doesn't know if he's going to have success in music. He could potentially be screwing both of us over!"

"Guys, which cake design do you like best?" Katie interrupted, flashing us two intricate sketches.

"The second one," I grumbled.

"Well, I like the first one," Andrea countered.

"You would. It's oversized and extremely tacky."

She stuck out her tongue at me.

Andrea and I reported to Katie's house to help her with last-minute reunion details. Needless to say, I didn't want to be here. I had more important things to do, like stare at my bedroom ceiling and fret about the life of my radio career.

"Carla, you are going to do the slideshow. And Andrea, you are going to make the "*Hits of 2000's*" playlist!" Katie happily ordered.

Of course, I got hit with the harder task. I enviously watched Andrea lean against Katie's wood headboard, pop in some ear buds, and casually browse her laptop.

Katie plopped next to me at her desk. "Okay, so in alphabetical order, you are going to alternate each person's "then" photo with their "now!" The first part is done for you; Teddy scanned everyone's senior year photo from our yearbook, and they are on his external drive in a folder titled *Senior Year Photos...*"

"Yes, Charlotte York," I interjected.

"And for each person's "now" slide, I need you to go on *Facebook* and pull a recent photo."

We had 532 people in our graduating class; I'd probably be done with this by the time our 30-year reunion rolled around. "What if they don't have *Facebook*?"

"Then don't include them in the slideshow! Also, underneath the "new," include new last names, or fiancés, or their kids' names..."

"What about jobs? Some of us don't have any of those things you mentioned," I retorted.

"Sure, you can put jobs," Katie replied sweetly.

I opened the yearbook and started searching the computer in alphabetical order.

"Beth Aaron," I muttered to myself. I typed her name in *Facebook*, and she came up as "Beth Aaron Jones." Married, no kids. I saved her wedding photo to the external drive.

"William Ackler," I continued. His default was his wedding photo. Obviously married. Right click, save.

"Sophia Amorrosi." Except now she went by "Sophia Amorrosi-Marzella." Well, isn't that a mouthful?

"Dawn Apizzi." Here we go, not married! I clicked on her information page to verify.

"Engaged to Chris Ecklestein." Shit.

And down the list I went. It took me an hour to get through everyone. Out of all the souls that made up Honey Crest High School's Class of 2007, a mere five people were not on the social networking site. (With all this technology, why did we need a stupid reunion anyway? Couldn't Katie just have designated a time for everyone to log onto their computers and video chat from the comfort of their pajamas?) I didn't even bother calculating the percentage of married verses single since I didn't want to bum myself out even more.

"My playlist is soooo retro!" Andrea laughed. "Check it out. "Say It Right" by Nelly Furtado; "Stronger" by Kanye West; "Because of You" by Ne-Yo; "Snow Patrol" by Chasing Cars; the entire FutureSex/LoveSounds album by Justin Timberlake…" She looked up from her laptop, concerned. "Is it bad that I still listen to these songs?"

"Don't forget the timeless classics by Dante's Inferno!" Katie added. They both laughed.

"What song should I use for the slideshow?" I asked, stone-faced.

"You have the pictures done already?" Katie gasped.

"All but five were on *Facebook*."

"Who don't you have?" Andrea asked.

"Mary Cochman, Joe Damon, Nicole Davis, Tiana Neese and Lionel Roberts," I rattled off.

"I don't even know who those people are," Andrea sniffed. "I never paid attention to the genetically-challenged."

I plopped down next to my bitchy friend to study her playlist for ideas. I settled on "Home" by Daughtry, and got to work.

In a few hours' time, I was done. Katie and Andrea watched it once through.

"This is amazing!" Katie complimented.

"My babies are waaaaay cuter than everyone else's," Andrea beamed.

"We all are doing pretty well for ourselves," Katie commented. I stayed silent.

"Carla, you have a smokin' hot radio show AND you were featured on *TMZ* this morning. You are doing fine," Katie insisted.

Oh yes, *TMZ*. And *Page Six*. And the corner front page of the *New York Daily News*. Miguel was right in the attention he would garner...and I was right in that it would all be positive:

"Miguel Martinez: Gotham's Newest Superhero"

By Robin Stevens, Page Six Correspondent

Drape a cape over those pinstripes! Yankees super-slugger Miguel Martinez has proven to be clutch both on and off the diamond.

As these exclusive pictures show, Martinez saved W-S-P-S Sports Radio 960 AM mouthpiece, Carla D'Agostino, from nearly bleeding to death on the streets of Little Italy.

"Miguel's limo pulled up in front of Gufo [one of the city's hottest new eateries], and a swell of people surrounded the vehicle," dished a source. "The girl's whimpers were overshadowed by our cheers."

"When Miguel stepped out of the car, he noticed Carla writhing on the ground in pain. He separated the boisterous crowd—much like Moses parting the water in the Bible—and rushed to her side."

"She must have taken a huge fall because she was beaten up pretty badly," added another source. "If Miguel didn't come to her rescue, she could have died right there on the sidewalk!"

Miguel hoisted the brown-haired beauty on his back and carried her into Gufo to collect her bearings. But in an interesting twist, neither Martinez nor D'Agostino exited the restaurant for hours.

"Carla was so thankful for Miguel's heroics, that she invited him to chow down with [W-S-P-S honcho] Dan Durkin and [D'Agostino's co-host, radio heartthrob] Dante Ezra, whom she was meeting for dinner," a restaurant patron snitched.

"The four of them feasted on rich Italian fare, homemade wine and [Gufo owner Massimo Marzella's] famous cannolis, all on the house. They had a marvelous time filled with tons of laughs."

Will the W-S-P-S starlet continue to show her appreciation for the newly-single slugger, who just finalized his divorce from bombshell beauty Trisha Jefferson?

"Miguel is just playing the field and isn't interested in dating right now," a Martinez insider confides.

In my freshman year of college, I took "Intro to Journalism". My professor drilled "ethics" and "fact checking" into our skulls. Evidentially, they didn't teach that anymore.

"It might have been cool to see myself in the paper for like two seconds, but that thrill is *long* gone," I sighed. "Everyone is going to ask me about the show tomorrow night, and I have to pretend like everything is okay."

Andrea and Katie frowned.

For the first time in a long time, I was about to become a runaway train of pity. The only way to slam on the brakes was to be alone through the night and the weekend...including the reunion. I slapped the laptop screen shut and rose from my seat. "I'll burn you a copy of the slideshow and leave it in your mailbox. I'm going home."

"You don't have to do that, just bring it with you tomorrow night."

I stuffed the laptop into its carrying case. "I'm not going tomorrow night."

"Carla, you HAVE to come," Andrea demanded.

"I don't have to do anything I don't want to."

"Carla, I've been working my ass off to make this an amazing event. I'll take it as a slap in the face if you don't come," Katie snapped.

"The thought of facing everyone tomorrow night with my future hanging in the balance is making me sick, and it's been making me sick ever since you sent out those save-the-dates."

"So, what? It's my fault now?"

"No. This has nothing to do with you."

"Do you think I wanted to stay up to listen to you and Dante during the overnight shows? Of course not, but I wanted to support my friends because that's what a good person does. I expect the same respect out of you."

"Because I don't feel like waxing poetic on Mrs. James' 7th period Home Ec class with my classmates, it makes me disrespectful?"

"No, but I'm starting to think Dante raised some valid points with you."

My rage started to boil over the surface. "Oh, did he?"

"Guys, stop…" Andrea hushed.

"I'm stopping," I hissed.

Andrea bowed her head in defeat, and Katie looked out the window, tears quietly streaming down her cheek. I said nothing and left the room.

24

Day 322

Thank God I made my executive decision about the reunion because I barely slept a wink. My back felt so stiff, I might as well have been lying on an airport tarmac instead of my normally comfortable bed (not to mention my ankle was still creaky). If I wasn't tossing and turning, or thinking nightmarish thoughts, I was checking my phone to see if my rapidly-growing list of frenemies tried contacting me. However, my phone was crickets.

My lowest point of the night came when I decided to do some reminiscing. I sifted through the piles of clothes that had accumulated on my closet floor over the past couple hectic months, and located my high school photo albums.

I started with senior prom. I cringed at Katie's pale green frock with embroidered flowers; I shook my head at Andrea's slinky black dress that had cutouts around her waist and a long slit up the center; I frowned when I saw Dante in his tux, singing on stage with his band; and I slammed the book shut when saw myself in my deep pink ball gown. I grabbed the next photo album—senior prom weekend—and continued to overdose on bittersweet nostalgia. As the sun started peeking through my window, I finally dozed off for a couple hours.

I bummed around in my room the whole morning and early afternoon. Last night, I told my parents in passing that I was off, but I didn't dare divulge details of my latest work and personal drama. Instead, I chalked my random day off to the reunion—I was helping Katie set up, and Dante was getting his band ready. But it was already 1 p.m. In a couple of hours, my cover would be blown once my parents got home, and I'd have no choice but to fess up.

My body started to get the shakes, so I threw on my robe and shuffled downstairs to make some brunch. Usually, depression is a great precursor for weight loss (Lord knows I need it...I'm up three pounds this week!), but I wanted nothing more than to be face-down in a stack of fresh blueberry pancakes, warm butter, and a sea of maple syrup.

My flapjack dreams flopped at the sight of my mother sprawled on the couch. *Oh man, what is she doing home?* In her presence, I couldn't indulge in my craving; I had to settle for an egg white omelet. Worse, my cover had been blown, and I now had to quickly put together a story.

Except…Mom didn't notice I was there. And as I walked closer, I saw that she was…crying?

"What's wrong, Mom?" I shrilled. Panic swept through my body. Did something happen to Dad? Jimmy? Grandma Teresa? Or did the station make their announcement that I was out of a job, and it hit her Google Alerts?

"Oh Carla, I'm sorry you had to see me like this," she cried, shielding her face.

"Is everything okay?"

"Yeah, I just get down sometimes, since…since…"

"Since what?"

"Since I lost my son!" Mom wailed.

I rubbed my temples. I knew she's been in a slight depression ever since the wedding, but I hadn't seen her like this. "Mom, you didn't lose Jimmy," I said through rolled eyes.

She waved me off. "Oh, yes I did. He barely stops by to see me, yet goes to Gwen's parents every weekend for dinner. It's always like that…you become closer to the girl's family, and the boy's side is forgotten about."

"There are always exceptions," I said pointedly. "Look at *Everybody Loves Raymond*."

"I know you wish you were married and out of the house, but enjoy your youth while you still can," Mom sniffled. "Believe it or not, one day you are going to get married, have kids...and then see them get married and LEAVE YOU!"

Through her dramatics, she had a point. Here I was in the prime of my life without the burden of any real responsibilities. Yet instead of enjoying it, I was miserable.

Instead of being ashamed of my situation, I should consider it a blessing that I was bestowed extra time to sow my oats, figure myself out, and follow my heart's desires. Who cares if I don't have a job on Monday? I've accomplished just as much as my peers have, just in a non-textbook way. I still get to call my own shots, which is the biggest success of all.

And what better way to celebrate my freedom tonight, at the reunion?

"Thanks, Mom," I said, hugging her.

"For what?" she asked.

"For helping me see how lucky I am."

My mother smiled through her tears. "I love you, baby. By the way, how is your ankle?"

"I love you too mom. And it's perfect."

■ ■ ■

I dusted off Britney Spears' *In the Zone* album (my favorite album from my high school years) and placed it in my stereo, a motion I haven't done in years. Who would have thought that the CD would become obsolete in less than a decade?

"Showdown" blasted from my speakers. I laughed as I remembered putting on my old prom dress to this very song ten years earlier. I sang off-key to the lyrics and danced around my room: "*Here comes the showdown/What goes around comes around/And the crowds are waiting.*" Britney was the epitome of fun, sexiness, and independence. Then she got married, had a couple kids, and things went downhill for a while. See where selling your soul for a "textbook life" can potentially land you?

Battling Britney for my attention was the New York Yankees game playing on my television screen. The random flashes of Miguel still gave me butterflies, but it was the dreadful, bad kind I wanted nothing to do with. Loser.

When the clock struck seven, I stepped into my junior prom dress—a deep purple, strapless, A-line gown. It had a sweetheart neckline, a fitted bodice, an asymmetrical waist, rhinestone accents and a laced up back. My hair cascaded down my back in soft, loose curls and my makeup was perfectly applied, thanks to Olga & Co. fitting me in for a last-minute appointment at Mona Lisa Salon. If I had to get ready with a rugrat wrapped around my leg that never would have happened!

I studied myself closely in the mirror. Ten years later, I didn't look all that different, and my face still had a smooth, youthful appearance.

I checked my cell phone. It was now ten after seven, and I imagined the gym quickly filling up with bodies. I shut off my TV and stereo, grabbed my silver clutch, and raced to Honey Crest High School.

■ ■ ■

My heart pounded as I walked through the familiar concrete maze that lead up to the gymnasium. With each step, a million different memories flooded my mind.

When I entered the old, rundown gym, I gasped. Katie had turned the space into an elegant masterpiece. Brown and gold balloons completely covered the scruffy hardwood floor. Dramatic yellow and purple uplighting decorated the plain brick walls. A huge disco ball, covered with twinkling lights, hung from the high ceiling. The room's usual musty scent was masked by the sweet smell of flowers that decorated the center of each round, gold cloth-covered table.

On stage was Dante's Inferno, and Dante's singing filled the air. My slideshow looped silently behind them on a jumbo projection screen. As much as I couldn't stand the sight of him (and cringed at the sound of the very voice that had effectively ruined my career), his stage presence still grabbed me. I closed my eyes to take in his lyrics:

> *"She hides behind abstract dreams,*
> *Nothing she says is what it seems.*
> *When it gets too real,*
> *She runs away,*
> *so she can't feel,*
> *And he's left behind, again."*

"Thank you," he said as he finished the song to thunderous applause. He and his bandmates exited the stage, and the DJ immediately threw on some Timbaland song.

I went by the open bar set up in the back of the gym to locate my girlfriends, specifically Katie. Neither of them had any idea I had decided to come after all. But before I could move, somebody tapped my shoulder. I turned around to see a tall, balding man with glasses hover over me.

"Carla D'Agostino! I love your show!"

I jogged my memory to figure out who this guy was, but I came up blank. Before I could answer, I was swarmed by my former classmates while multiple camera flashes attacked my eyes.

"Can we take a picture?"

"Can I have your autograph?"

"How is your ankle?! I saw what happened in the paper!"

"You look so pretty on those billboards!"

This was the moment I had wished for, to be the belle of the ball. I humbly accepted my classmates' adoration, graciously answered everyone's questions, and happily posed for pictures.

"Carla!" A familiar voice rose over the crowd. I saw a very concerned Katie pushing everyone out of the way to get to me.

I broke away from my fan club. "Katie!" I shrieked, engulfing her in a huge hug. "I'm so sorry about yesterday— "

"What are you doing here?" she demanded.

That was not the reaction I was expecting. "Would you rather me go home?"

"We need to talk." She gripped my arm and led me into the girl's bathroom, which still had the same stench of disgusting stale cigarettes it had ten years ago.

"Katie, what is going on?"

"Hold on." I watched her pick up her pale green dress past her ankles and swiftly looked under each stall.

"What the hell are you doing?" I chuckled.

"I had to make sure we were alone," Katie breathed.

"Why? Do you plan on killing me or seducing me?"

"I don't know how to tell you this…" Katie said in near tears.

Now I started to grow worried. "What?"

Katie took a deep breath. "Mark Falcone is here."

I had done such a good job purging myself from that horrific name that at first her words did not compute. "My Mark Falcone?" I repeated, confused.

"YOUR Mark Falcone."

I felt like a thousand knives were stabbing me up and down my body. Instinctively, my right hand gripped the sink to hold myself steady. Katie and everything else around us started to fade away.

"Are you okay?" Katie worriedly asked.

I grabbed the other side of the sink with my free hand and faced the mirror. My expression was one of confusion, anger, and fear. I had never seen my face contorted like this.

I slowly turned to Katie. "He didn't even go to this school," I roar.

"Remember Mary Cochman, one of the people you couldn't find on *Facebook*? You couldn't find her because she now goes by Mare Cox, she is an infomercial model, and that is who Mark left you for. They are now married with a kid."

I couldn't even begin to process the information Katie had thrown at me.

"How do you know this?" I asked, feeling faint.

"I was at the bar, and she came up to get a drink. I had no idea who she was, and after we had started talking, he appeared next to her."

"You SAW him?! He TALKED to you?! YOU TALKED BACK?!"

"He acted as if he didn't know who I was. Carla, I appreciate your wanting to surprise me, but I sure wish you had called so I could have warned—"

"I'll be right back," I interrupted, and ran out of the bathroom.

25

I rushed into the dark, vacant trophy room and sat down on the windowsill. Unfortunately, this room was no stranger to many of these moments in my heartbreak history. It was here where I'd flipped out to Katie and Andrea for two hours over John Vargas's not giving me the time of day at the freshman formal... and where I got dumped by Nick Voss at our sophomore pep rally for "not putting out"... and where I saw my crush, Al Monroe, walk into the basketball state championship game holding hands with some underclassman senior year.

In other words...ten years later, my story was exactly the same.

Of all the reunion scenarios I had conjured up the past year, this wasn't even a blip on my radar. Mark Falcone was dead to me; he ran off with some virtual hooker, and it might as well have been to Mars because I sure as hell wasn't going to chase him. His actions still hurt me to this day, but I never mourned the loss of *him.* What was there to be upset over? He was a boy playing in a man's clothing.

But now he had risen, and I had a front-row seat to the story of his afterlife—that is, if I wanted to watch.

Did I?

Dizzy, I pushed myself off the windowsill and started walking towards the gym so I could say goodbye to Katie. I had no interest in learning about his life after me. I'd had my little fun being the resident celebrity here; now as far as I was concerned, there was nothing left for me and the night was over.

The gym door swung open, startling me. When I looked up at the culprit, my face probably reflected those who saw Christ floating in the sky three days after he was nailed to the cross—because stumbling towards me was my first love and his wife. They were laughing wildly, clearly drunk, and had no idea they had company.

Mark stopped laughing and nudged his wife.

"Carlaaaa, hi! It's been soooo long! " "Mare Cox" slurred, throwing her arms around me.

I didn't respond. I just stared at Mark with a look that could break rock, and he guiltily looked away.

Time (or karma) had not been kind to him. The California sun (and who knows what else?) had aged Mark to look more on the wrong side of 40 than 20. Deep wrinkles were etched into his forehead, and even in the limited lighting coming from the security bulbs outside, I could see his light brown hair was peppered with gray. The goatee he sported did little to conceal the wear and tear on his skin. It actually made it worse.

I had spent many nights immediately after our breakup wondering if I was going to get a chance to get closure on the situation. However, as time passed, so did my yearning for a tidy ending. A breakup of this magnitude didn't deserve to be packaged in a neat red bow; it just needed to be buried six feet under.

But here it was, the face-off. What was I supposed to do now?

I shifted my gaze to Mare. To use my sensitive friend Andrea's words, Mare was the definition of "genetically-challenged" back in the day. Her mousey brown hair was always a greasy mess she wore bottlenose glasses to match; and she enjoyed the cafeteria lunch buffet a little too much, to put it mildly.

But I'm guessing she robbed a bank, ordered "the works" from Heidi Montag's plastic surgeon, and had her entire anatomy orifice nipped, tucked, sucked, and contoured. Her hair was now a brilliant shade of blonde. D-cups sat perkily on her chest, and her legs looked like two toothpicks coming out of her jean jumpsuit (did she *read* the invitation noting "formal attire"?) She was a Barbie Doll wannabe...that is if Barbie worked as a day-shift stripper at the Bada Bing.

Mare stumbled around the room before running over to the trophy case. To my shock, horror, and utter amusement, she channeled Miley Cyrus and started humping the display.

"I can't wait to do this all night, Mark, uh-huh!" she grunted.

Classy.

Mark walked over to me. "I think about you every day," Mark whispered. (Or at least, I think that's what he said. It was hard to hear anything over his wife's guttural moans.)

I snapped my neck towards him. "Don't you even dare."

"I miss you so much," he continued.

I looked away and saw his wife simulate oral sex on a trophy she grabbed off a shelf.

"You got everything you deserved," I sneered, and left Mark to tame his wife, who was now pretending to get penetrated from behind by the trophy while fondling her plastic boobs.

I decided to not even go back into the gym; I just wanted to go home...NOW. I'd explain everything to my girlfriends tomorrow.

By the time I closed my car door, my emotions had bubbled to the surface, and I became a hysterical crying mess. Seeing Mark was the straw that broke the camel's back; this week had been too much to take. I rested my head on the steering wheel and bawled in agony for what seemed like hours.

After the initial tears had subsided, I opened my glove compartment to grab some tissues. As I rummaged through the mess of receipts, tampons, and PBA cards, I noticed a small box wrapped in silver paper. What the hell was this?

I tore off the paper to reveal a little jewelry box. I opened it, and inside was a pretty flat silver heart covered with tiny diamonds. I flipped the pendant over to the other side... and my world stopped.

Inside the heart was a picture of Dante and me from when we were kids, both with huge, toothless grins on our faces, holding each other tightly. We couldn't have been more than seven years old.

Where did this come....ohhhhh. Dante had gotten me in the Christmas grab bag, that's where it came from. I had been so pissed that my friends framed me that day, that I completely disregarded his gift!

Guilt then washed over me. This was such a beautiful, thoughtful gesture, and I never even said thank you. He probably thought I threw it away.

I noticed that there was a small folded piece of paper taped to the inside of the box. I carefully removed it, and revealed a letter written in Dante's chicken scratch handwriting:

> *Carla,*
>
> *You don't know how much it has been killing me to not have you in my life. This may not be the best time to tell you this, but I need to finally come clean with the*

truth...for as long as I could remember, I have been in love with you.

I loved you in kindergarten, even when I teased you about having cooties; I loved you in fifth grade, when you went through your awkward puberty phase; I loved you every time you announced my name at all of my games; I loved you when we were with other people, even though it killed me; and I loved you throughout our big blowout fight last month at the hospital.

This is why I got on your case about Miguel and every other guy you have gotten twisted up over; I may not be perfect, but those guys are far from it. I'm tired of watching both of us float through life as lost souls, especially since I feel that our souls should be journeying through life as one.

As for the W-S-P-S job, I took it to be closer to you. I also wanted to prove that I was serious about providing a future for you. I know I almost messed it up, but I was so drunk the night you had to come rescue me because you seemed to be slipping further and further away from me, and that wasn't my intention.

Please take the time to think this over. Even if you don't return my feelings for you, I hope you can find it in your heart to forgive all of the hurtful things I said, and that we can resume being the best of friends again.

Love,
Dante

A large lump formed in my throat. The waterworks threatened to open up for Round 2.

Dante was in love with me? How? He knew every nuance of my personality, every story, all my secrets...and there was nothing attractive about most of that. Meanwhile, he was gorgeous, talented, and all-around amazing. He could have any girl he wanted; what possessed him to want *me*?

As I settled with this groundbreaking news, visions of what could be danced around my head—getting lost in his eyes for hours, holding hands, his lips over mine, melting bodies, making love...all with someone I could unequivocally trust with my life.

I gasped at the vividness of these fantasies. I needed them all to happen, *now*.

I cleaned up my face and shot out of my car. I had to talk to him.

■ ■ ■

"Excuse me!" I shouted over the crowd as I frantically started to look for Dante.

I bumped into Andrea, who was proudly wearing her black senior prom dress, and Xander on the dance floor. "There you are!" Andrea exclaimed. "Katie said you were here. I hope you didn't bump into—"

"Where is Dante?" I demanded.

"I don't know. Why?"

"Did you know that he is in love with me?"

Andrea gasped. "He finally told you?"

"YOU KNEW!?" I shrieked.

"It was the worst-kept secret for years. We all knew," Andrea replied. "Why do you think we kept pressing you to make up with him? The past six months have been killing the poor guy."

I shook my head and continued towards the stage, ignoring Andrea's calls to me. I pushed my way closer to the stage and spotted him helping his band mates pack up their equipment.

I made a beeline to him.

"We need to talk," I ordered sternly.

"We do?" he replied, his blue eyes looking down at the ground.

"You love me?" I spit out.

He jumped back, looking startled. He grabbed my arm and walked me to a quiet corner. "Who told you that?"

"You did!" I exclaimed, shoving the letter in his face.

"You just read this now?"

"YES!"

"You are the most impatient person I know. How did you wait six months before opening it?"

"Does it really matter?" I asked. "I need to know what the hell is going on."

"The letter said it all for me, Carla. It's up to you to talk."

"You've been nothing but an asshole to me lately," I started.

"You haven't been so nice yourself," Dante retorted.

"Touché," I agreed. "How could you keep this a secret from me for all this time?"

"I don't know..." Dante trailed off. "I was too scared to settle down and I didn't want to hurt you by jumping the gun. But the older I got, I realized it wouldn't be settling."

"What would it be?"

"It would be exactly how the first 28 years of our lives were, except we'd hang out more, and there'd be a lot more sex," Dante reasoned with a laugh. "That's definitely not scary."

I felt a chill travel down my spine as I met his eyes. "I like that," I smiled, but then it quickly faded when I had another thought. "But what about my mother? You know when you date me, you date her, right?"

"I can handle Nancy," Dante laughed.

I was going to launch into all the reasons why God himself couldn't handle "Nancy," but I had a more urgent question. "What about the show?"

"If we're together, and we really try to make it work, I'll stay."

My heart leaped out of my chest, for more reasons than one. "You will?"

"As long as we keep work and life separate. I still want to go to war with you on the air."

"Well, your opinions are wrong 95% of the time, so that won't be an issue," I joked.

Dante gently put his hands around my shoulders. "I want to make you happy, Carla. Whatever it takes."

"Wow," I started shaking. This was all too much for me to process.

"Are we really going to do this?" he asked hopefully.

"I…I…" I had no idea what to say, but the flurry of butterflies (the good kind) told me all I needed to know.

Thankfully, the DJ's booming voice interrupted me saying something stupid. "Okay, Class of 2007, your ten year reunion is coming to a close. Grab your significant other and bring him or her out here for one last moment like this." A familiar guitar melody started playing behind his words— "A Moment Like This" by Kelly Clarkson.

I laughed at the DJ's play on words. "I liked what he did there."

"You would, you cornball," Dante laughed "Do you want to dance?"

"I would love to."

He grabbed my hand, led me out to the dance floor, and found an open hole between Andrea and Xander, and Katie and Teddy. He held me very close, and the electrical current flowing between us almost made me hit the ground. I caught Andrea and Katie's expressions, and they both stared with ear-to-ear grins.

"So Carla," Dante said, pulling away slightly to lock eyes with me. "You still haven't given me an answer."

"What was the question again?" I answered playfully.

He smirked.

"Instead of answering, I think I'd rather show you." And with that, I leaned in and kissed him squarely on the lips. He was shocked by my move at first, but quickly responded (very incredibly, may I add).

As we kissed, I couldn't help but think there were *so* many things off about this scene. For starters, I was making out with my best friend. The physical act itself wasn't weird, but the emotions it gave me were—I had never felt this warm sensation that was currently engulfing my body with anybody else. Another thing that I found surreal was that, for the first time, I knew I was kissing someone who cared for me as much as I cared for him. Usually, the scales were tipped to just my side. To top it all off, it was to a sappy Kelly Clarkson song. Kelly songs are there for me in times of suffering and pain, not in beautiful, pure, unconditional love…

Speaking of pain—think of the misery I could have avoided if this scenario played out years earlier! However, if I had a husband, 2.5 kids, and a dog surrounded by a white picket fence like everyone else here, I would have been pissed at all I would have missed out on. Myself.

"Get a room, you guys," Andrea joked.

We broke apart and laughed, and extended our arms to include her and Xander.

"What about me?" Katie mock protested, and she and Teddy joined our little circle, as we all closed out the song, together.

"Some people wait a lifetime for a moment like this!" We sang along as the song faded out. Dante leaned in to kiss me again, and it shot me to the moon. I don't think I'll *ever* be coming down.

"That just about wraps it up here," the DJ announced. We all started enthusiastically clapping.

"Goodnight, Honey Crest High School. We'll see you in ten years!"

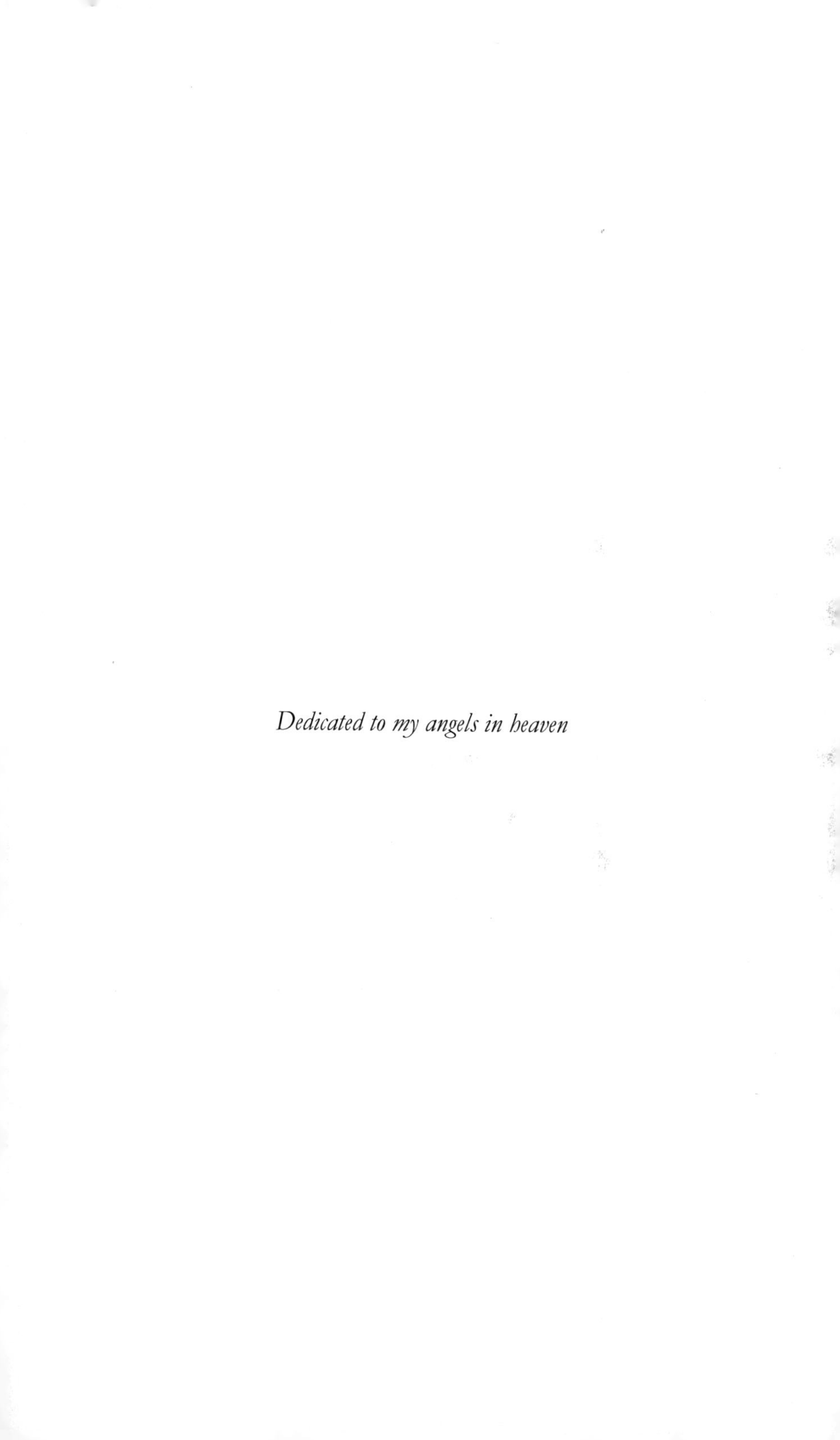

Dedicated to my angels in heaven

ACKNOWLEDGMENTS

I need to start off by saying that I still cannot believe I wrote and published a freakin' BOOK! This definitely isn't the first time I've taken a chance in my professional life, but nothing prior can compete with how scary yet exhilarating this all is!

I want to thank my editor, Linda Chasdan, for legitimizing my writing and believing in this story. Noelle Alix and Angela Martin, thank you for the introduction! Mickey Andreko, you are a proofreading all-star. Your eagle eyes are much appreciated!

I want to give a shout out to the folks at CreateSpace for giving authors a platform to be heard. Your guidance throughout the whole publishing process was stellar.

To the creative geniuses at Damonza.com, thank you for designing the prettiest, most iconic book cover I have ever seen. Eva Lesko Natiello, thank you for the referral!

Although most of my inner circle didn't even know "Ten Years Later" was in the works, it never would have gotten done without some truly remarkable people by my side. I have the best family, friends and staff in the world, and I am so appreciative of their unconditional love and support in everything I do.

The biggest thanks has to go out to YOU, the reader of this book. I am deeply humbled that you took the time to visit this little world I created. I hope we meet again!

Lisa Marie Latino is CEO and executive producer of Long Shot Productions, a full-service media production company based in Fairfield, New Jersey.

Latino's career has produced numerous commercial, corporate, and entertainment programs that have taken her throughout the United States as well as Europe. In 2014, Latino co-launched Hip New Jersey (HipNewJersey.com), a lifestyle program featuring the latest trends around the Garden State.

Latino has appeared on a wide variety of local television, network cable, and radio shows, including TLC's "Cake Boss" and works in-season for the New York Giants Radio Network. She has also served as an adjunct broadcasting professor at Seton Hall University. Latino graduated from Montclair State University in 2006 with a degree in broadcasting and speech communication.

She currently lives in New Jersey.

Made in the USA
Middletown, DE
26 April 2019